WILDEST DREAMS

L.J. Shen is a *New York Times*, *USA Today*, *Wall Street Journal*, *Washington Post*, and #1 Amazon Kindle Store bestselling author of contemporary romance books. She writes angsty books, unredeemable antiheroes who are in Elon Musk's tax bracket, and sassy heroines who bring them to their knees (for more reasons than one). HEAs and groveling are guaranteed. She lives in Florida with her husband, three sons, and a disturbingly active imagination.

Website: authorljshen.com
Facebook: authorljshen
Instagram: @authorljshen
Twitter: @lj_shen
TikTok: @authorljshen
Pinterest: @authorljshen

Also by L.J. Shen

Forbidden Love Series
Truly Madly Deeply

Sinners of Saint Series
Vicious
Ruckus
Scandalous
Bane

WILDEST DREAMS

L.J. SHEN

HODDER &
STOUGHTON

First published in Great Britain in 2025 by Hodder & Stoughton Limited
An Hachette UK company

The authorised representative in the EEA is Hachette Ireland, 8 Castlecourt Centre, Dublin 15, D15 XTP3, Ireland (email: info@hbgi.ie)

1

Copyright © L.J. Shen 2025

The right of L.J. Shen to be identified as the Author of the Work has been asserted by her in accordance with the Copyright, Designs and Patents Act 1988.

Internal design © Sourcebooks 2025
Internal art © Madmire 2025

All rights reserved. No part of this publication may be reproduced, stored in a retrieval system, or transmitted, in any form or by any means without the prior written permission of the publisher, nor be otherwise circulated in any form of binding or cover other than that in which it is published and without a similar condition being imposed on the subsequent purchaser.

All characters in this publication are fictitious and any resemblance to real persons, living or dead, is purely coincidental.

A CIP catalogue record for this title is available from the British Library

Paperback ISBN 978 1 399 74341 9
ebook ISBN 978 1 399 74342 6

Typeset in Adobe Caslon Pro

Printed and bound in Great Britain by Clays Ltd, Elcograf S.p.A.

Hodder & Stoughton policy is to use papers that are natural, renewable and recyclable products and made from wood grown in sustainable forests. The logging and manufacturing processes are expected to conform to the environmental regulations of the country of origin.

Hodder & Stoughton Limited
Carmelite House
50 Victoria Embankment
London EC4Y 0DZ

PLAYLIST

"Spiracle"—Flower Face

"Recomposed By Max Richter: Vivaldi, The Four Seasons"—Max Richter (*My Brilliant Friend*)

"Washing Machine Heart"—Mitski

"Soaked"—Shy Smith

"The Tortured Poets Department"—Taylor Swift

"Wildest Dreams"—Taylor Swift

"I Like the Way You Kiss Me"—Artemas

"Crazy Girls"—TOOPOOR

"Lilith"—Adeline Troutman

"Bulletproof"—La Roux

"I'm Not in Love"—10cc

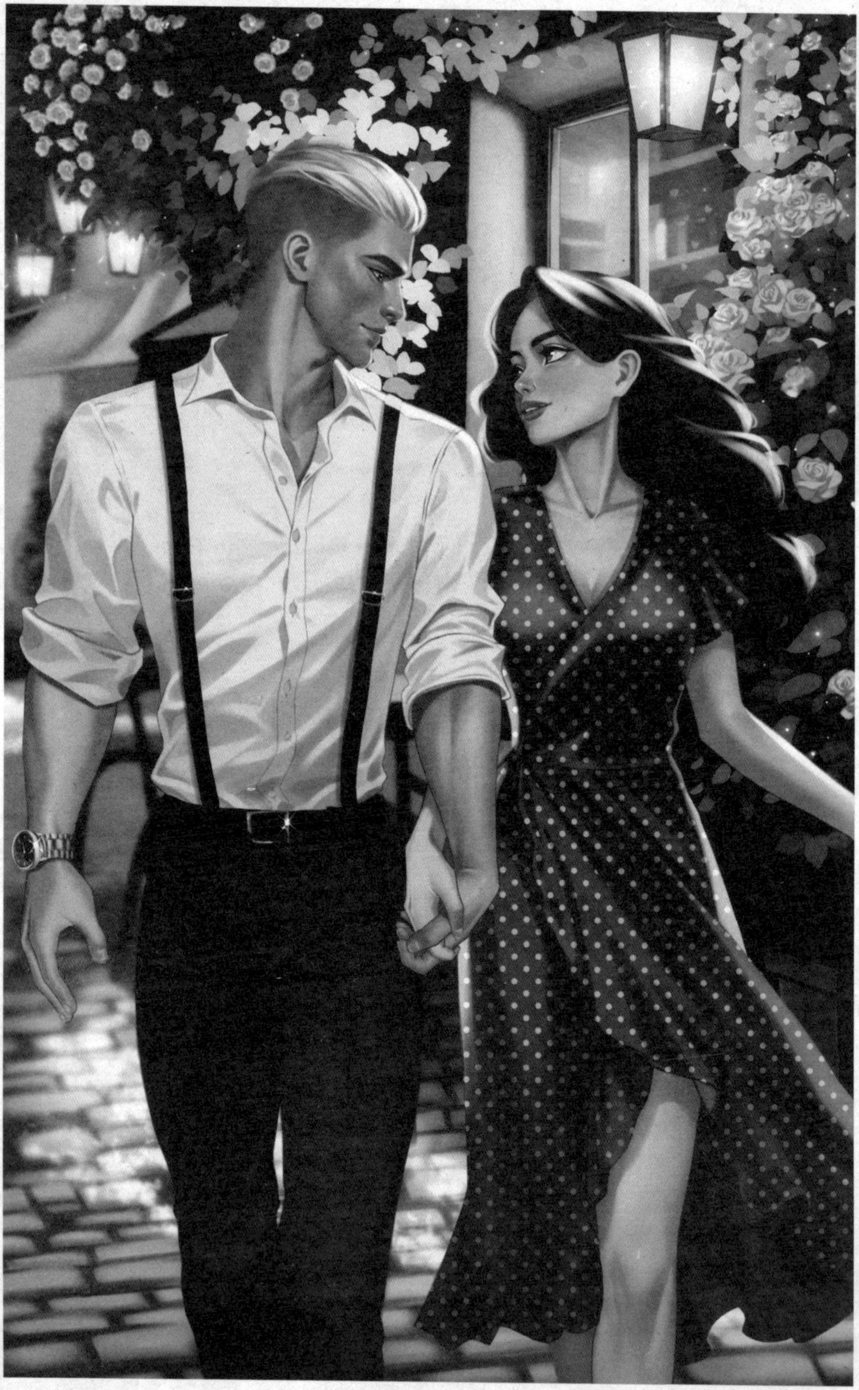

CHAPTER ONE
DYLAN

There were worse ways to be greeted in your own home than by catching your mother spread-eagle, plastered against the glass backyard door, getting mauled by her fiancé. But I couldn't think of any of them as I stood at the entrance tightening my fist around the door handle, fighting—and losing—a war against my gag reflex.

"Yes, Marty! Yes. Right there, *dio mio*—don't stop." Her muffled cries, blurred by his palm as he tried to make sure they wouldn't wake the toddler upstairs, trickled into my brain, burning themselves into my core memory.

My knee-jerk reaction was to scream, "MY EYES, MY EYES!" à la Phoebe Buffay and charge out of the house, town, state, and planet with my arms flailing in the air. Unfortunately, I couldn't do that. First, because my three-year-old was asleep upstairs and I wasn't going to leave her behind. Second, because at the age of twenty-six, I still lived with my mama, albeit in the gorgeous mini mansion my brother had built for her. She had more right to this house than I did.

Third? *Get it, Mama. Props to you for living your best life.*

Throwing up a little in my mouth, I shut the door with a soft click and flung myself back into my red 1999 GMC Jimmy, giving them their privacy. I slammed the ancient driver's door behind me. In retaliation, it tore off its hinges, collapsing onto the muddy ground with an angry thud.

Closing my eyes, I choked the steering wheel, inhaling deeply.

Everything is okay. More than okay. Great, really. You have a roof over your head. A steady job. A kid you worship...

My phone danced inside the flimsy front pocket of my diner uniform. The outfit consisted of a pale pink minidress short enough to moonlight as a napkin and a checked apron with an array of indistinguishable stains, from tomato sauce to coffee, vomit, and grease.

What can I say? It was a life of luxurious extravagance, but someone had to live it.

My eyes tapered to the image of my best friend Cal's face on my screen. It was a photo of her with her head tossed back, laughing carelessly, my brother's demonic face buried in her neck as he kissed her, with the Eiffel Tower as their backdrop. I chose this as her contact picture to remind myself of the one and only flaw in her otherwise sunny character: she was screwing Lucifer's doppelgänger, a.k.a. my overbearing, controlling older brother.

I mean, they *were* married. And hella cute together. Maybe I was just annoyed because everyone around me was paired up, cocooned in their own loved-up universes. My only boyfriends in the past four years had been battery-operated and made of silicone.

I glided my finger across the screen but didn't speak. I was afraid I'd throw up if I opened my mouth.

"Dyl," Cal laughed breathlessly on the other end of the line. Row growled in the background in that grizzly-bear way he always used whenever he was kissing her.

I wasn't jealous Cal was living her happily ever after. She'd earned it through taming my half-civilized sibling.

"You won't believe who we just ran into in Cannes!" she shrieked.

Closing my eyes again, I talked myself out of a spontaneous mental breakdown.

Ed Sheeran? Taylor Swift? King Charles? *God?*

Their life was full of celebrity parties and Pinterest-worthy vacations and food too picture-perfect to eat.

It wasn't Cal's fault I'd just finished a twelve-hour shift at my dead-end job in Dahlia's Diner. It wasn't Cal's fault I was a single mom. It wasn't Cal's fault I was still living with my mother. It wasn't her fault my life felt like the middle section of a painstakingly boring book, the pages stuck together, a never-ending chain of to-do lists and chores.

"Dylan? You there?" Cal moaned after a few seconds of silence.

Unfortunately.

I thought I heard Row grunt the words "stand still and just take it." Seriously, who'd I kill in my previous life to deserve tonight?

The wind shrieked and swirled in a violent dance, slipping into the car like a thief, burrowing into my bones.

"*Row*," Cal chided, "I'm trying to eat here."

"So am I."

Oh god. Would Child Protective Services intervene for a twenty-six-year-old?

"I just caught Mama and Marty boning each other against the backyard door," I blurted out.

This is why you're bussing tables and not keeping government secrets, Dylan.

"Holy shit," Cal—or Dot, because of the cluster of freckles on her nose and cheeks, proof God had sprinkled her with magic dust—said. "I mean, go Zeta. She deserves some action, but also…sorry for your loss." Cal snort-laughed. "You know, of appetite, libido, et cetera."

"It gets worse." I mustered a smile, mainly so she could hear it in my voice. "They're also going to leave a mark, and you know I'm the one who cleans the windows around here."

Jokes aside, my mom had endured a terrible marriage with my father. When he passed away six years ago, I never thought she'd take a chance on love again. I was glad one of us had. Hell knew I wasn't touching another man, *ever*, with a ten-foot pole.

"Are you ready for a sibling?" Cal teased. From the silence echoing around her, I gathered Row was done trying to molest his wife and was actually paying attention to the conversation.

"Thanks. I already vomited in my mouth."

"I'd say you might be pregnant, but I've met nuns who get more action than you." Cal laughed. "Didn't she know you were coming?"

"I was supposed to do a double shift, but it was a slow night, so Dahlia sent me home early."

"Where are you now?" Cal asked.

"Seeking refuge in the comfort of Jimmy." I reached to wipe a thick layer of dust from the dashboard. "But the driver's door just fell off, so I'm not even cozy and warm."

"This is definitely not your day," my bestie said sympathetically. "I'm sending cake." Pause. "And a charger for your Magic Wand, because I know you keep losing yours."

Row gagged in protest in the background. Good. I'd had to see and hear him defiling my childhood best friend on a monthly basis ever since they got together. The least I could do was inflict my own damage back.

"Chargers have legs," I protested, forcing out a laugh that felt metallic and rusty in my throat. "There's no other explanation as to why they keep disappearing. So are you in Cannes now?"

Row and Cal split their time between New York and London. Row had Michelin-starred restaurants in both cities, but they liked to travel all over.

"Yup. We're going back to London tomorrow morning, probably for a good stretch of time. Row is opening a new restaurant in Edinburgh. He'd like me and Serafina close by."

Serafina was my niece. She'd just turned two and had her mom's huge blue eyes, her dad's wild onyx curls, and the neighboring opera singer's lungs. The girl could scream her way to a catastrophic earthquake.

"Dylan..." Cal hesitated. "I have an idea."

She and Row always had ideas. All of them revolved around

trying to fix my fucked-up life. Not that I blamed them. My existence *was* the kind of pitiful that demanded intervention.

"No," I sighed, using the bases of my palms to rub my eye sockets. "All I have left is my pride."

"You sure you still have that?" Row drawled sarcastically.

"Ha-ha. Fuck you."

"No thanks, Dyl. And for the record, your standards have plummeted in the past few years. Incest is not a cute kink."

"Shuddup, shuddup, shuddup." I kicked my gas pedal, wanting to kill someone.

"We're going to need someone to house-sit our New York apartment," Cal plunged on, ignoring our antics. "Why don't you do it? You've always wanted to live in New York."

Yes, but that was *before*.

Before I realized I'd never go to college.

Before I got knocked up and had a kid at twenty-three.

Before the baby daddy left me publicly for the town's crooked mayor, with whom he had an affair.

"Dude, what are you talking about? I can't afford life in New York." I barked out a laugh.

"What's to afford?" Row butted into the conversation, his voice dark, gruff, and perpetually sneering. "We're going to hire someone anyway. You won't pay rent, because you'll live in our apartment. Groceries are taken care of—they'll arrive at your door twice a week. You just need to clean up the fridge and the pantry. Utilities are also included. I'll throw in some admin work for you and put you on the company's payro—"

"No." A panicky squeak wrestled its way out of my throat. "I don't want to be another nepo hire of yours."

Ambrose "Row" Casablancas loathed most people, so when he stumbled across someone he didn't completely hate, he tended to hire them on the spot. That was how he'd ended up working with his childhood friend, Rhyland, for half a decade before they parted ways. It was why he became good friends with his business partner, Tate. Why he let Mama work for him as a "social media influencer" for the crazy sum of $250K a year, even though he didn't have any Instagram, TikTok, Facebook, or X accounts.

"I don't know how to break it to you, Dyl, but your life circumstances don't allow you to have this kind of ego," Row quipped dispassionately. "Take the job."

Cal gasped, and I heard her swat him. "Row, what an asshole."

"Promise I'll get to say that later tonight, and I'll buy her a new car to go with the apartment," Row murmured.

Yup. I am never recovering from this conversation.

"I don't want your New York apartment," I ground out. "I wouldn't be able to afford childcare, and I'm not working an imaginary job and living a kept woman's life at twenty-six." I was no sugar baby. I was carving my own path in life, even if I was doing a messy job of it.

"You're being stubborn and unreasonable," Row accused.

"You're being cocky and rude."

Row snorted. "That can't be news."

"Your love is suffocating me," I said.

"Your attitude is exasperating us all," he shot back.

"Please," Cal interjected. "Just…think about it, okay? You can apply for jobs there. Maybe something in marketing?" she suggested brightly, and I heard my brother kissing his way along her skin again, making my stomach roil with a mixture of anger, annoyance, and exasperation. "We'll figure out childcare for Grav. There are plenty of options. You need to get out of there, Dylan," Cal said softly. "Your job there is done. Your mom no longer needs you. She's engaged, for crying out loud. Time to take care of yourself."

Easier said than done. I didn't know how to do that. I'd never taken care of just myself. I'd always devoted my life to someone, be it Mama or Gravity.

"No." I bit down on my lower lip, calculating in my head how much it'd cost to fix Jimmy's damn door. "Now, if you'll excuse me, it's been over ten minutes. They should be done by now. I must retire to my fainting couch."

"If you're referring to the sofa in the conservatory...don't. Row and I christened it last time we stayed over."

"*Cal*," I barked out.

"Also, the entire kitchen, guest room, and every shower in the house," Row informed me lazily. "Really, stay away from the whole fucking house if the idea of people porking on its surfaces annoys you."

I hung up on them and screamed into the ether for two minutes straight.

By the time I got home, Mama and Marty were no longer reenacting *Fifty Shades of Grey Hair* in the living room. Thank the Lord for small mercies. The place was dark and quiet, save for the humming of the fridge. I filled myself a cup of water, rinsed the dishes in the sink, and took the stairs up to Gravity's room. It was precious, with flowery pastel wallpaper, a toddler bed Marty had assembled himself and painted in her favorite shade of purple, and white shelves laden with Grav's favorite books. It was a messy room, with science kits and LEGO strewn across the shaggy carpet and her little desk, coloring books and traceable letters everywhere. I put my everything into Gravity. I wanted her to know she could be anything she wanted.

I strode over to her bed, my heart clogging my throat. Every shift I finished, every tip I pocketed, I always thought of her. She elevated my mundane, dull, unsatisfying existence to a higher purpose.

Gravity was the thing that kept me anchored. The steady ground beneath my feet.

Staring down at my beautiful girl, I tucked a tight hickory curl behind her ear. Even her ear shells were perfect. A laugh bubbled in the pit of my stomach, twisting up before I swallowed it down. When Gravity was born, she looked like an angry old man. Now, she was breathtaking—and the exact copy of her runaway father.

The same sooty, curled lashes framed the most striking pair of eyes: green-yellow irises bracketed by dark blue circles. I ran the tip of my finger over the slope of her elegant, upturned nose, watching as her cherry-red lips twitched in a tiny smile. What was she dreaming about? What would she be when she grew up? In my dreams—the few I allowed myself to have these days—I imagined kicking down door after door for her, helping her reach every height and goal her heart desired.

Could I really give her all that here, in the small town of Staindrop, Maine? The same Staindrop that had one school, one daycare, zero prospects, and barely any residents? Even the new mall and flashy hotel they built a couple years ago hadn't made the quaint beach town any more habitable than it was.

What if Grav ended up like me, stuck in a place she wasn't happy in, settling for what was present instead of what was possible?

Leaning down, I dropped a feathery kiss on her cheek, barely breathing so as not to wake her up.

Sleep tight, my sweet girl, my heart sang. *Mommy loves you.*

It was ridiculous, but the final straw that broke my back was when I shoved my panties down twenty minutes later to pee for the first time in eight hours. I was sitting on the toilet staring down at my frumpy cotton panties and I realized I didn't own a pair in any color other than beige. And that I had no real lingerie. No fun clothes anymore. No heels I could wear out. No friends to go out *with*.

My cheap, tattered underwear was a perfect metaphor of my entire life. Pale, insignificant, an afterthought—something uninspiring and sad and practical.

With a pang, I realized I wanted...well, *more*.

Life wasn't black and white. Either dazzling Cannes fantasy escapades or dowdy, never-ending diner shifts and household chores. I didn't *have* to live the life my luck arranged for me.

The last time I made an error of judgment, it was in the form of a broken condom while propped against the arm of the couch, cheek pressed into the top of a cushion. It had resulted in my daughter. Even though I loved Gravity more than life itself and would never change the outcome of that so-called mistake, the trajectory of my life had changed completely because of it. I'd become a coward, too afraid of making mistakes.

But *this* was a mistake. This town. This job. This aimless life.

I deserved more, and so did Grav. I could always come back here. But something wild and rebellious and newly alive in me told me I wouldn't. That once I broke free, I wouldn't stop running. I felt like I'd just woken up from a years-long coma. Like I'd just come up for air after sitting at the bottom of a muddy pool.

I hastily grabbed my phone from the edge of the sink and called Cal before I even flushed.

"Dot?"

"Please tell me you're accepting our offer."

"I'm accepting your offer."

"Attagirl."

CHAPTER TWO
DYLAN

"Shit, shit, *fuck*, shit." I banged my forehead against the steering wheel, my ponytail falling apart to match the rest of my life.

In the rearview mirror, I watched as Grav's mouth hung open, her eyes as big and wide as the moon. She was buckled into her car seat, hugging Mr. Mushroom, her chubby penis-looking pink stuffie. She was hopelessly attached to the thing. A gift from Cal to me that had somehow ended up being my toddler's transition object.

"Mommy!" she chided with a gasp. "Grandma will be mad when she hears."

"I'll let you drink Mommy's soda if you don't tell her." I bribed her with a can of Coke.

"Okay!"

Our fresh start in New York had started off with a broken-down vehicle that couldn't even roll to Row's Fifth Avenue building and a line of twenty cars honking and yelling at me.

I fumbled with my keys, trying to fire the engine. I was literally ten feet away from the gates of Row's parking garage when Jimmy decided to plotz.

"Wake up, wake up, wake up." I jacked the handbrake up, then down, then up again. Rage suffocated me. *This damn car.*

When I bought Jimmy two years ago, proud of myself for not accepting Row's charity in the form of a superior secondhand

Silverado, it already had a hundred thousand miles on it and corroded doors that tended to dance in the wind whenever I went over forty miles per hour. But it was five hundred dollars below book, and I couldn't resist the bargain. It left me money for Grav's swimming lessons as well as the monthly book subscription her preschool teacher had recommended. I was now seeing the error of my ways.

I tried to turn the ignition again. Nada. Jimmy was deader than Armie Hammer's career.

Another loud blare of honks thundered between my ears. Road ragers shook their fists out their windows, roaring profanity and trying to cut through the other lane.

"Get this old piece of junk outta the road, asshole."

"Learn how to drive stick, rice turd."

"D'you see the ass on that lady? She could ride my stick any day of the week."

My face flooded with heat. Why me? I wished life would send me fewer lessons and more money.

I slipped out of the car, craning my neck as I observed the line of pissed-off drivers behind me to try to gauge who looked the least psychopathic and could be persuaded to help me push my car toward the parking gate.

"Mommy, I wanna get out," Gravity moaned, her pink Skechers kicking the passenger seat in front of her.

"In a minute, honey."

"I'm boooored."

More honking. More profanity. Fifth Avenue was a four-lane street, aggressively stacked with midrise buildings on one side and Central Park on the other. One lane was for buses, and one was jammed with trucks. That left two lanes, and I was currently blocking one of them.

"I need help getting my car to this gate." I flailed my arms in the building's general direction. I was sweating and itching under my navy-blue sweatshirt and my baggy mom jeans. My hair was a mess. If I were a crier, I'd cry.

"Sounds like a you problem." The driver right behind me spat phlegm through his window.

Welp, I'm not in Maine anymore, that's for sure.

"Unless you wanna pay for it." The driver gave me an appreciative once-over.

"Sure." I jutted out a hip, smiling at him sweetly. "Do you accept knees to the nuts and sucker punches?"

"Bitch," he muttered, rolling his window up on me.

"Mommy!" Gravity shrieked louder. "I wanna get out. Out. Out. Out."

"Just a sec, sweetie."

"I want soda!"

Shakily, I pulled my phone out of my back pocket. I couldn't call Mama or Row—I was desperate to do this on my own. Desperate not to be this needy, flailing, train wreck of a woman who failed at everything she touched.

I called the insurance company instead, my whole body breaking out in hives.

This was a mistake. I should never have come here. Seriously, what was I thinking? I couldn't even manage my life while I lived with my mother in my hometown; New York City was twenty sizes too big for me.

I was pacing back and forth behind my trunk, waiting for a representative to answer my call, when Jimmy's back door flew open. It took me a second to register what was happening. Grav had had enough after the eight-hour road trip, unbuckled her seat by herself, and was now sliding out, falling flat on her ass on the busy road and rolling into the next lane.

"Jesus!" I shrieked hysterically, dropping my phone to the ground.

My daughter rose up on wobbly knees, a frightened expression stamped on her face. She stumbled straight into the moving cars, looking for me through a haunted, terrorized gaze. Seeing my entire life flash before my eyes in the moments my legs carried me toward her, I desperately resisted the urge to pounce on her and scare her straight into the rush-hour traffic.

Suddenly—and seemingly out of nowhere—a tall, broad, thunder of a human scooped Gravity up with one hand, tucked her under their armpit like she was a football, and zipped to the sidewalk to safety.

I dropped to my knees and coughed out all the air trapped in my lungs.

She could have died. She almost did. Because of my stupid lack of attention.

Blinking away the tears, I stumbled toward the figure holding my child. More specifically, the man suspending her by the ankles, gently shaking her body as if she were a newly torn piñata. "Where's the candy?" His deep, dark drawl rumbled. No baby talk for *him*. "I know you have some. Don't play."

"I don't!" Gravity giggled, trying to kick the air, arms flailing. "I ate it all on the way here."

Snitch.

"I suppose I'll just have to eat *you* then."

Another fit of giggles. "Nooo, Uncle Rhyrand. Mommy won't let you! She woves me!"

My heart finally slowed. I wiped my clammy hands on my sweatshirt, feigning nonchalance as I joined them on the sidewalk.

Them being my daughter and Rhyland Coltridge.

Rhyland Coltridge being my brother's best friend.

A man-whore.

A cocky bastard who knew he was God's best creation to date.

A debauched, selfish piece of work clad in a Prada suit.

Too bad that piece of work was a *masterpiece*.

Rhyland put the "fun" in "dysfunctional." He was a menace who got a free pass for all his faults through his striking exterior. His princely features included six feet and four inches of bronze, taut, flawlessly muscled body, gold-spun hair the color of an endless wheat field, and eyes as green and bright as the shiniest emeralds. Everything about him, from his cruelly sharp jawline, cartoonishly high cheekbones, and full lips to his straight nose, screamed perfection.

And we *hated* each other.

Actually, *he* couldn't muster enough shits to have any kind of strong feelings about me or anyone else. It was one of the reasons I detested him. He was living, breathing proof that you could live with no heart inside your chest.

"Hello, Rhyland." I strode toward him, putting my fake bravado on like it was a fancy hat.

"Hello, fuckup," he parried tonelessly, hoisting my child onto his arm and leveling me with an acutely bored glance. He wore a coin pendant on a plain black chain on his neck. Still. He'd been carrying that shit around since we were practically teens. I would ask what it meant, but I'd never really cared.

"Watch your mouth in front of my child," I warned him coolly.

"Mommy said 'fuck' in the car," Gravity provided cheerfully, giggling.

Traitor.

"It's called wishful thinking, kid." Rhyland flashed a predatory canine smile that made my bones freeze a little.

He wasn't pretty-boy sexy. He was half-Viking, half-Hozier sexy.

The honking intensified into one long blare that just kept on going. We both ignored it.

Rhyland gave me a withering look. "Pull yourself together, Casablancas. Your kid could've died." He sneered. "While you're at it, take her back. I'm not a babysitter."

That was all it took for me to officially and finally lose it.

Not the eight-hour drive, punctuated by ten pee-pee stops, sponsored by Starbucks caffeine and suspiciously cold gas-station hot dogs.

Not the fact that Jimmy had died on me ten feet from the parking garage.

Not that I was broke, jobless, single, and raising a kid, even though half the time I felt like I was still one myself.

And not even the realization he was going to be my neighbor, because Row and Cal's apartment was a floor below Rhyland's place. They'd planned it that way so they could always be close.

That.

"It'll be a cold day in hell when I start taking parenting tips from *you*." I snatched Grav into my arms, feeling my vocal cords tearing with a scream. "She was strapped in. It's not my fault she's smart enough to figure out how to unbuckle. We had a terrible journey here. My car died. It's blocking traffic. The insurance company didn't answer. I haven't slept in three days. I don't even have the money to fix this car—"

"I take it you're Row's latest charity case and will be living in his apartment," Rhyland interrupted brusquely, twisting his wrist to glance at his watch. He looked eager to move on with his day. Like he had something better to do than grab a first-row seat to my breakdown.

God, I hated him. So much it hurt.

"I'm not anyone's charity."

"Don't knock it before you try it. Becoming a stripper named Charity might be the answer to all your financial problems."

"You're a pig," I snarled.

He winked. "Oink, oink." And then, because apparently setting each other on fire was only on my agenda, not his, he added, "Come on. Let's get that car out of people's way."

"I don't want your help."

"What a coincidence. I don't want *to* help." He flashed another devilish grin, rolling his dress shirt up to reveal veiny, muscular forearms. "Unfortunately, you're my best friend's baby sister, and I have some level of decorum not to leave you and your child to get stabbed by a cab driver."

He yanked open the driver's door and slipped inside, twisting the key in its hub. "Lights are working, so it's not the battery. Probably the spark plugs. How old is this thing?"

"Not as old as you." What was I, five? Who talked like this?

Pulling his phone out of his pocket, he frowned, ignoring me. "I have a meeting in a few minutes, but I'll go into the auto shop later and get it fixed. Meanwhile, I'll push it into the garage."

"Uh, okay."

"Better take your suitcases out first. The garage elevator is small and takes forever."

I hated that he was helping me. Hated that I was frazzled enough to accept said help. And I hated that I looked like a mess when all this was unfolding.

Rhyland got out, hurled all six of my suitcases and duffel bags onto the sidewalk, and stopped a well-built Amazon delivery guy, convincing him to clear out the lane so he could push my car into the building's parking lot. They both pushed the trunk, rolling it into the underground garage. I perched Gravity on top of a suitcase, her legs straddling the handle, and deposited her iPad, clad in a butterfly-shaped case, into her hands. I put her kitty-eared headphones on her ears. Her face lit up at the sight of *Caitie's Classroom*. Then I went and retrieved my broken phone from the road.

With a mixture of humiliation and mortification, I watched Rhyland and the delivery man work. When the car was safely tucked inside the garage, Rhyland reappeared through the lobby. He looked significantly less put-together, one silky strand of his sandy hair loosening from his man bun and falling across his eye. His cheekbones were marred pink. I almost felt bad as he approached us. I opened my mouth to thank him.

"Is there a reason why the child is holding a penis?" He flicked his gaze to Gravity, who was hugging Mr. Mushroom on the suitcase while she watched her show intently.

The child. He talked about her as if she were a problem in need of fixing.

"It's not a penis. It's Mr. Mushroom," I corrected haughtily.

He gave me a flat look punctuated with a half-moon smirk that threatened to light my panties aflame.

Despite my aversion to him now, I'd always had a thing for Rhyland Coltridge.

A happy-to-get-on-all-fours-for-you-at-a-moment's-notice kind of thing.

Which obviously didn't help matters.

"It's a long story, okay?" I picked my daughter up again, cradling her head in the crook of my neck. "Anyway, thanks for the help. You can go back to being New York's favorite *fuckboy*." I mouthed the last word voicelessly so Grav wouldn't hear, shooing him away with my hand.

"Are you shaming me for being a sex worker?" He arched a thick eyebrow, one shade darker than his hair.

"No. I'm shaming you for being a douchebag."

"Why? History dictates it's your favorite taste in men." He chuckled brusquely.

1–10 to the home team.

My ex, Tucker, was definitely a walking, talking condom advertisement.

"You know, Rhyland." I parked my hip over a tall suitcase, mustering every acting skill in my body to appear self-composed and nonchalant. "There aren't enough synonyms in the English language to describe how much I hate you."

This didn't contradict my desire for him. I also desired three Valiums and an entire mango key lime cheesecake and still knew they had the power to destroy me.

"Flattered." He put a hand to his chest, bowing down with flourish. "I don't think there's a word for how I feel for you, but it's somewhere between disdain and total boredom."

"Indifferent," I offered charitably.

He snapped his fingers and pointed at me. "See? And everyone thinks you're just a pretty face. Dylan Casablancas, a walking dictionary, ladies and gents."

"All I took from this is that you think I'm pretty, and while I agree, you don't stand a chance. I'm done dating losers."

"That's a bit of a pickle, sweetheart."

"Why?"

"I doubt anyone who isn't a loser would have you."

Just when I thought I was going to assault my brother's best friend in my first hour in Manhattan, we were interrupted by a real-life cowboy. He was ambling toward us, accompanied by another suited man, waving a hand at us.

"Howdy, Coltridge."

The man looked as out of place in New York as a Disney princess in a BDSM club, with his Western hat and embellished shirt, cowboy boots, and worn-out denim. He gulped in the scene of us—the suitcases, Gravity, me, and Rhyland—his wide-set mouth breaking into a delighted grin. He looked to be in his early sixties and in excellent shape. A thick gold ring sparkled on his wedding finger.

"Marshall," Rhyland greeted back with an easy smile, but I noticed he cleared his throat. "You're early."

"The early bird catches the worm." The man winked, stopping a few feet from us and thumbing his longhorn buckle. "Well, ain't that a sight? Rhyland Coltridge, I had no idea you were a taken man. With a kid, no less. That definitely gives you brownie points in my book."

What?

I opened my mouth to clarify that he wouldn't find any love lost between Rhyland and me, not even if he used a microscope, when I heard the latter chuckle good-naturedly.

"Never judge a book by its cover, Bruce."

To my horror, what followed was Rhyland's arm wrapping around my shoulder. I froze into a statue, my eyes taking over my entire face. What in the name of Taylor Swift was going on here?

"And who do we have here?" Bruce fussed over Gravity, who dangled her feet from the suitcase, hugging Mr. Mushroom. Thankfully, she was squeezing the stuffie hard enough that it was indistinguishable.

"That's Gravity." Rhyland ignored the way I slapped his touch away, smoothly removing his arm from my shoulder and picking my daughter up, holding her close to his chest. He grinned down at her. Gravity's eyes were still obliviously glued to the screen. "A.k.a. the light of my life."

"You must be living in the Dark Ages then," I muttered under my breath, folding my arms over my chest.

Rhyland shot me a murderous look.

"Bruce Marshall." The man offered me his hand with a warm smile. "Pleasure to meet you, ma'am. And you are?"

"Not a ma'am." I untangled my arms to take his hand in mine. "And also not Mrs. Coltridge, *thank God*."

Bruce Marshall's smile evaporated, and Rhyland inserted himself between us, barking out a laugh. "She means not *yet*," he clarified. "But as you can tell, we can't wait to get married."

Bruce's gaze dropped to my bare fingers. "I ain't seeing no ring."

What was Rhyland doing? More importantly, *why* was he doing it?

Rhyland gave him a leisurely clap on the back. "Don't spoil all my surprises, Brucey boy. She asked for something different than I gave her. She's a hard woman to please."

"No," I drawled. "You just suck in bed."

Bruce's eyes ping-ponged from my daughter back to me. I saw his judgment there and then. Even though I knew there was nothing wrong with having a child out of wedlock—especially as *I* was the one to be dumped—I still found myself feeling naked and vulnerable.

"Gravity's not mine," Rhyland hurried to explain, grabbing her from me. "Although she feels like mine in every way that matters."

What a load of baloney. Rhyland couldn't stand children and, in fact, always tried to be on the other side of the room when Gravity and Serafina were around. Even Gravity gave him a "do I know you, sir?" glare.

Bruce turned to cast his warm, approving glance on Rhyland, nodding slowly. "Didn't peg you for the kind of man who'd take on extra responsibilities if he doesn't have to."

"Well, there's a lot you still don't know about me and my character," Rhyland responded enigmatically. Asshole had not only thrown me under the bus, but he was also making sure to drive back and forth a few times, leaving skid marks on my body. Why was he lying through his teeth?

"You're doing the right thing, son." Bruce clapped Rhyland's shoulder. "I respect a good family man. Am one myself. Don't know if you've read the *Forbes* article about me, but seventy-three percent of my staff attend the same Sunday service as I do. Birds of a feather flock together, hey?"

Rhyland smiled brightly, and just like that, I understood his game.

I bit down my lower lip to stop myself from laughing. Rhyland put the "heat" in "heathen." The man was such a sinner I was pretty sure he'd burst into flames if he ever got less than three miles away from a church. His day job was literally dating and screwing women for money. And he did that with gusto. I'd estimate he'd slept with more women than were registered to vote in this district. And as exhibited right here and right now, he had no qualms about lying, deceiving, and cheating his way into achieving his goals.

"Absolutely right, sir. There is no bigger fan of monogamy and children than me," Rhyland clucked, his voice honeyed menace.

"All righty." Bruce rubbed his hands together. "I'll go get myself comfortable in that fancy coffee shop you recommended and have me one of them uppity pastry thingies, and you help your lil miss get her suitcases upstairs and join me. No rush, yeah? Family first."

"I'll try to rip myself away from them." Rhyland sighed exaggeratedly. "But it'll be hard."

"I can always throw you out the window to speed things up," I suggested cheerfully.

Rhyland elbowed me.

Bruce and his aide wobbled their way down the road to a trendy coffee shop. As soon as they'd disappeared behind the door, Rhyland shoved Gravity back into my hands as if she were made out of radioactive explosives.

"We need to talk." He hoisted the duffel bags onto his shoulders, herding the rest of my suitcases toward the main entrance of the building.

It was a prewar mid-rise with stunning white arches and columns. The lobby had gray-veined checkered black-and-white limestone, and the unmanned front desk and mailboxes were made of sleek, black-painted wood. The elevators were old-school, a black wrought iron cage surrounding the wooden doors. The place had a European quality to it, and for the first time since I'd started this journey, I got giddy.

"Please." I massaged my temples. "No more talking."

"Mommy has a headache," Gravity murmured sweetly, adjusting her iPad so it perched on my chest.

Mommy also really needed to pee. And eat. And savor three mimosas.

"Mommy needs to do Uncle Rhyland a big, big favor." Rhyland's wolfish glare pinned me with deliberate foul intent, his raspy voice running down my spine like sweet summer rain. Our eyes met, and like a lit match, they sparked the entire lobby on fire. "And she'd better make the right choice for a change."

CHAPTER THREE
RHYLAND

"Fuck that," Dylan mouthed noiselessly over Gravity's head, enunciating each vowel between those luscious lips of hers.

"There's my delicate flower." I smirked mockingly, trying to swallow down the cue ball of hysteria wedged in my throat.

Bruce Marshall thought my best friend's baby sister and I were together. It didn't take a genius to see he'd gotten a hard-on at the idea. Me. A family man. Accounted for. The first sign of interest from him so far. Which meant the charade must continue. I couldn't blow this chance.

"I'm not pretending to be your fiancée, Rhyland," Dylan clarified.

"Just…" I massaged my temples. "Listen before you slam the idea, okay?"

She already has a good-for-nothing ex. There is nothing you can offer her in exchange for this favor.

The elevator arrived, and I pushed open the rusty gates, hurling the suitcases and duffel bags inside before holding the door open for Dylan and her daughter. Dylan stepped inside, still staring at me like I was crazy. In her defense, I *had* just propositioned her with something that only made sense in low-budget rom-coms.

I'd spent my entire adolescence actively avoiding this girl, only to get a phone call yesterday from Row that his baby sister was moving into the building. He asked me to watch over her, probably because he wasn't aware of how closely I'd watched *her* while growing up.

Oh, watching Dylan wasn't a punishment by any stretch of the imagination. It was listening to her that made me want to hurl myself directly onto the tracks of a moving freight train.

And now I wanted her to pretend to not only like me but actually convince people she'd willingly tie her future to mine.

The elevator doors slid shut. I pushed my hair out of my face.

"Look, I'm sure you have a lot of questions."

"Nope." Dylan popped open her purse, took out a piece of gum, and threw it into her mouth without offering me any. The scent of lime and cherry filled the small space. "None at all. Because I'm not going along with this nonsense."

"But—"

"This is not a Hallmark movie, and you are not Nicholas Galitzine."

"Slow your roll here." I raised my palms in surrender. "I think we can agree both me and Nicholas Galitzine are far too good for straight-to-cable mov—"

"The answer is no."

Okay. Tough crowd. I *had* done something to cause her to hate me, but that was fucking eons ago. What was with the elephant memory? I couldn't remember what I'd had for breakfast this morning.

Oh, wait. Yes, I do. The blond from my hot yoga class.

"Here's the thing." I licked my lips. "Bruce is a potential investor for my start-up app, App-date. If I secure his investment, it'll allow me a monstrous budget, a mouthwatering one-off paycheck, not to mention connections. Marshall is a very powerful guy. You might know him from *Shark Tank*? The last season?" I glanced at her hopefully.

She pretended to look over her shoulder. "Oh, you're talking to me? I thought you were talking to a boomer who actually *does* watch broadcast stations."

I inwardly groaned. Dylan was trouble in every way imaginable. A lethal combination of heart-achingly gorgeous—the kind of beautiful that seeps into your system like fine whiskey, making your bones liquid and your common sense sparse—whip-smart, sarcastic, stubborn, and emotional to a fault. She had no filters, no inhibitions, and no fucks to give when it came to what people thought about her.

Even as a kid, everything made her cry. Injured animals. People who took lunch alone in the cafeteria. Super Bowl ads. She felt everything, all at once, in vivid color. I, by contrast, felt nothing at all. Ever. By choice. We were like oil and water. Black and white. Hot dogs and real meat. You get the drill.

"Listen—" I started.

The elevator pinged, and the doors slid sideways. I grabbed the suitcases and followed her like a bellboy. She stopped in the middle of the hallway, staring at me expectantly. I realized she'd never been here before. Not in Row's apartment and probably not in New York. Save for a few London trips to visit her brother and Cal, Dylan hadn't really seen the world.

"It's this one." I jerked my chin toward the right door.

She stuck her chin up proudly, and we both ignored the crimson staining her cheeks.

Dylan opened the door and coughed in disbelief. Yeah, the place was pretty neat. Gravity squealed in excitement.

"Wow! Big windows!" She wormed her way out of her mother's embrace. The little girl dumped her headphones on the floor and darted to the hallway to explore.

I wheeled all the luggage inside, staring at Dylan pointedly.

Her forehead creased in annoyance. "Oh. Sorry." Her frown smoothed out, and she grabbed the Target purse from her shoulder, rummaging through it and slapping a five-dollar bill into my hand. "Thank you, sir. Have a nice day."

She fucking *tipped* me.

That just happened.

I lied. I wasn't indifferent to her.

I wanted to *kill* her.

Slowly. Methodically. Over the course of a few days.

We were engaged in a silent, hostile stare down. She waited for me to retreat. I wasn't going to—not before I squared that fucking circle. I knew Bruce Marshall was holding back on the deal because his wife thought I was a sleazeball player who would turn the app into Ashley Madison 2.0. She wasn't wrong. I *was* a sleazeball. Damn proud of it too. A womanizer, a slut, a sex addict. You name it.

But I now had a chance to pretend to be an outstanding member of polite society as opposed to one of the pillars of its demise. And to become disgustingly rich as a result. Dylan was the entire package: a young mother with a chubby-cheeked child.

"Wouldn't you like to be temporarily engaged to a man in finance—who is six foot five, with blue eyes?" I coaxed.

She peered behind my shoulder nonchalantly. "Sure. Where is he?"

Exasperating.

"It's me." I stubbed my thumb into my chest.

She snorted. "You're six three on a good day, dude. Besides, I know that song. You don't work in finance."

"I'm about to, if you don't fuck shit up for me."

"You're also not a trust-fund baby," she maintained.

It was so my luck to need a favor from the one straight woman who was immune to my charms.

"You're going to need someone to help you with that piece-of-junk car, changing a light bulb, getting shit done here," I pointed out, handing her the blinds remote when she began to walk aimlessly around the patio doors, trying to figure out how to open them. "I mean, let's admit it, Dyl. You're a mess."

"I can get by on my ow—"

"Can you though?" I slammed my teeth together. "Row and Cal aren't going to be here most of the time. Your mom is all the way in

Maine. You have no friends around. No relatives. Look at your first hour here, for fuck's sake." I gestured to the door. "What would've happened if I wasn't there to save Grav? To push your car into the garage? Carry your luggage? Admit it. We need each other right now, and we can help each other. A mutually *beneficial* arrangement."

"I can do this alone," she insisted, eyes glittering with brazen determination.

I knew she was in over her head, and I was going to capitalize on that shit till the cows came home. There was no low deep enough for me not to stoop. People were a means to an end. And her means could put an end to my sticky financial situation.

"No, you can't," I snapped irritably, glancing at my watch. Bruce Marshall appreciated punctuality, and I appreciated the four hundred million dollars he was willing to give me as an advance if we signed the contract. "You don't even know where the AC unit is, how to fix the heater, or what to do when the Wi-Fi gets spotty. I'm offering you a goddamn get-out-of-jail card to prove to your family you can survive in New York, Casablancas. Take the damn thing and run with it."

"Row's gonna lose his shit if he thinks we're dating." She was walking around, opening cabinets, familiarizing herself with the place.

Now we were getting somewhere. She was actually considering it.

"Not that he has any reason to," I pointed out.

She gave me a face. "With all due respect, Rhyland—and let me assure you, I have none for you—you are more damaged than Cal's hair when she went through that phase changing its color every week. *And* you've never had a steady girlfriend. *And* you are a literal, *biblical* man-whore. *And* the only feelings you are capable of are horniness and annoyance. So frankly, I can totally understand why he wouldn't be happy to see us as a couple."

Talk about a humbling experience. Engaging with Dylan

Casablancas did so much mental damage I was surprised she wasn't hired as a torture tool at Guantanamo Bay.

"We'll tell our friends the truth," I assured her, my come-hither smile on full display. "He knows I want to charm Marshall into working with me, and everyone will be happy I'm helping you settle in. He knows I'll never break bro code."

She rolled her eyes at that before gnawing on her lower lip in contemplation. In the background, I heard Gravity screaming at a high pitch, ping-ponging from room to room in the hallway. God help me, I detested kids. Even this one got on my nerves, and she was, by all definitions, cute and well-behaved.

"I'm not doing this for free." Dylan parked a hand on her waist. "Especially if we have to be seen at events and pretend to tolerate each other."

I snorted out a laugh. She stared at me blankly.

Oh. She was serious. She wanted me to pay her for...what, exactly? I didn't even know if Bruce would need more than this half-assed meeting on the street to believe we were together. Then again, knowing the anal-retentive bastard, it was on-brand for him to make me jump through hoops, and I'd end up parading her around like a prize horse. This deal was far from over, and I was bound to see him a few more times at least before it was signed.

"Name your price." Whatever it was, chances were I couldn't fucking pay it. I was Armani without the money. Dressed to the nines with zero in my bank account.

Her eyes widened in amazement. She didn't think I'd bite. That made two of us. But I needed this temporary arrangement. Besides, if things went my way, it would last for less than a month before Bruce would sign the damn contract and bring our fake engagement to an abrupt end.

"Uh..." She looked around, unsure. Dylan had no fucking clue what to charge, because the only work she'd ever done was bussing tables at a diner in our small town. "Like...two thousand dollars a week?"

"Deal."

"Wait, no. Ten thousand a week!" she blurted out breathlessly.

I tapered my eyes. "Now you're just making numbers up."

She hitched one shoulder. "Julia Roberts charged three thousand in *Pretty Woman*, and I think it was less than a week. That was in 1990. Just think about the inflation."

"Julia Roberts offered a hell of a lot more than holding hands and looking pretty," I ground out.

"So am I, though." Dylan licked her lips nervously, fingers twisting together. "Sex is going to be the only upside to this deal."

"What'd you say?" I yawned to pop my ears. I must've been hallucinating. I really needed to tamp down that not-so-casual coke habit.

"I said, sex is on the table."

Silence.

"Or anywhere else you'd like to have it, to be honest. I'm not picky."

My.

Jaw.

Was.

On.

The.

Goddamn.

Floor.

"I'm sorry." I swallowed back saliva—and possibly my fucking tongue with it. "My grasp on the English language has loosened in the past five seconds. Do you mean to tell me you want to, uh, *fuck*?"

She stared me square in the eye, calm if a little flushed. "I mean, the relationship will be fake, but the orgasms had better be real. If I have to put up with you, I want to at least have a little fun. We're both grown-ups. I haven't had any action in a while. You're deplorable but undeniably hot. And I mean, you can't be *that* bad in bed, with all the experience you've amassed…"

This woman was lethal to my ego.

"As long as it's with full consent…" She pretended to examine her busted-up nails, and I wondered if, now that I was apparently going to pay her fucking $10K to breathe in my sphere, she'd invest in some mani-pedis. I wanted her to. And I wasn't even fucking sure why.

"You don't have to have sex with me to get the money," I stated the goddamn obvious. I always knew I gave fuckboy vibes, but creeper? That was a new one.

"I know you're not asking. I'm *offering*, if it wasn't clear." Another eye roll—Dylan's signature "I don't give a shit" tic whenever she definitely gave a shit. "I mean, come on. You are a sex worker. Don't be a prude."

"First of all, I'm not being a prude. I'm checking for signs of a head injury." But the truth was she had me rattled there for a second. The idea of burying myself between those long, lean legs had me undone. "Second, there's no shame in sex work, and mine happens to be done by the book. With an ironclad contract. Third, I've been retired for three months now."

All in preparation for launching myself fully into App-date. Which meant there was even more on the line here.

"Fourth…"

There was a fourth—something about her offering her body for money and how I'd rather just pay her not to do any stupid shit—but I forgot what it was. Honestly, the fact that I was even speaking English right now was a miracle in itself. Dylan Casablancas, the hottest woman in the Americas and probably any other continent, had offered me sex for pay.

"Fuck it, Dylan. My mind draws a blank. Just…promise me, if you ever need money that bad, come to me, and I'll give it to you. No strings attached."

The word "strings" made me think about bondage, and my dick was so hard at this point all it needed was its own pant and shoe to qualify as a third leg.

"It's not about the money. I have some savings." She nibbled on the dead skin around her thumb, and for a reason I did not want to look into, I didn't find it as gross as I normally would. "It's not something I'd have offered *anyone*. I wouldn't mind if there's sex included in the deal since I'm practically regrowing my hymen over here, and there is no way I'd ever catch feelings for someone as appalling as you."

"Why, thank you." I breathed slowly through my nose. "Always love meeting new fans."

"Hey, at least I find you physically attractive."

"And personally repulsive."

She jerked one shoulder up.

"Do you want your brother to kill me?" I inquired. That'd definitely happen if we slept together.

"It'll be a nice bonus," she admitted evenly, "but there's no reason why he should find out."

I ran my tongue over my teeth. I couldn't think straight with ninety percent of my blood in my dick. "Ten K a week is fine. Do we have a deal?"

"You're going to need to build some things around here." Dylan glanced at the room. "Grav's toddler bed, some bookshelves, stuff like that."

"That's not gonna be an issue." My father was a handyman—building shit was no biggie for me. "What else?"

The child popped her head in from the hallway, grinning. "Mommy, can I make a fort with the pillows?"

"Uh…yes, honey," Dylan said distractedly. I'd wager she'd let Gravity cook meth in there, she was so eager to get back to the conversation. She flushed even redder under her deep Italian tan and thick obsidian hair, wrenching her gaze back to me. "If this includes sex, I have some hard limits," she whispered.

This was the part where I needed to tell her that sex would not be included. I wasn't going to take advantage of my best friend's baby sister. Shit, I wasn't going to take advantage of *anyone* like that. It was wrong.

But...was it really?

She suggested it. I'd have said yes to her number anyway, and maybe she knew that.

Row is going to cut you into ribbons and slow-cook you in your own bone broth if you take liberties, asshole.

Tell her there'll be no hookups. Tell her the deal only includes the regular rom-com shit. Be a Nicholas Galitzine, not a goddamn...I don't know, King Joffrey.

"Let's hear your limits."

Dammit, asshole, what did we just talk about?

It was her turn to look scandalized. She wasn't expecting me to be game. Hey, negotiating putting my dick in Dylan Casablancas wasn't on my year's bingo card either. But it was all in theory anyway.

"No hurting me." She erected a finger for every rule, counting them with her hand and starting with her thumb. "No audience, you always have to use a condom—I am *never* getting pregnant again—and we'll have to be exclusive."

I nodded. This was easy enough. Even though I was a big fan of pussy, I didn't care for the complication of variety. If there was one thing I'd learned in my former gig as a gigolo, it was that a pussy was a pussy.

The irony wasn't lost on me. I'd made a career of fake-dating people, and now I had to pay for someone to fake-date me.

Karma, you filthy little animal.

"Sounds like a plan," I said. "We have a deal."

"Wait—I'm not done."

I pinched the bridge of my nose, drawing in a breath. "Of course you're not."

"I might need babysitting."

"Look, I'm the first one to agree you're a mess, but I think you should be fine. Just google shit if you run into big words."

"For Gravity, you tool bag."

"Oh, I don't do kids."

"You just saved Gravity from sure death."

"I imagined she was a squirrel," I quipped. "Seriously. My *la vida* is a little too *loca* to throw kids in the mix. No way."

"Well, I'll need someone to help me with her while I look for work. Seeing as you're the only non-stranger here, I only trust you." She gave me a slow once-over. "*Kinda*. No offense."

"None taken. I wouldn't trust me. Which is why I beg you to reconsider the last item on your request list. Plus, why the hell would you need a job if I'm paying you ten K to breathe?"

"You can sign the contract with Bruce tomorrow morning, and then what?" She lifted a brow. "I wouldn't be able to provide for my kid. No. I need to find steady work. Gravity trusts you. Babysitting duties must be included. At least twice a week."

I drew in a sharp breath, rolling my tongue along the inner walls of my cheeks. I hoped the kid liked McDonald's and vegging in front of the TV. "Fuck. Fine."

"Try not to curse in front of her." Dylan made a face.

"I have some asks too," I informed her.

"Go ahead." She nodded.

Meanwhile, in the kitchen, Gravity busted open a bag of chips and was wolfing them down between fits of giggles.

"One, you will be my fake date as many times as I need within the time constraints. You will be prim and proper, and you will look at me adoringly. You will not blow our cover and won't tell *anyone* about that time a balloon got stuck in my braces in eighth grade and everybody thought it was a condom."

She gave me a frustrated look. "Rhyland, it *was* a condom."

"It was a beige-colored balloon, Dylan."

It was a condom. I'd wanted to see how far I could blow it up before it exploded. But this could never worm its way into the four-page piece about me in *Forbes*, if and when I signed the deal with

Bruce. Either way, Dylan had an unsavory habit of telling the story every time we were in the same room, because she knew how much I detested it.

"That includes work travels in and outside the States," I added.

"As long as you give me enough time in advance and Grav can come, I'm okay with that."

"And…" I stopped. Bit my tongue until warm, thick blood filled my mouth. Still, I couldn't stop the words from falling.

From completely passive and apathetic, I'd just become animated and on fire. For the first time in eight years, Dylan and I were in the same room, completely alone, allowed to finally take out our claws and teeth and be ourselves without worrying about offending Row and Cal.

"And?" She arched an eyebrow, waiting for the other shoe to drop.

We'd always shared this wild attraction, me and her. Since she was eighteen.

The air became thick and charged between us. I stepped toward her. She didn't retreat, though I detected a glint of fear in her dark, upturned eyes. I leaned into her personal space, a breath away from the shell of her ear. No need for her daughter to accidentally hear the depraved man in their apartment.

"No condoms, Casablancas. We exchange clear medical sheets, you get on the pill, and you've got yourself a deal."

The pill wouldn't be necessary, I knew, but I didn't want to delve into that. Not now. Not ever. She couldn't know. Couldn't learn the level of fuckery that was my life.

"*Whoa*. Do you always do it without a condom?" She looked grossed out.

"Nope. Never."

"Why skip it with me?"

"Because I want to. That should be reason enough."

It was misogynistic. It was dark, twisted, and screwed up. And yet my cock was already throbbing, achingly excited at the prospect of doing filthy, wicked things to my best friend's baby sister.

A shudder ripped through her entire body. I watched as her silky skin pebbled into a trillion goose bumps. And that was before I'd even touched her.

"If it's too much, forget—" I started, already regretting everything I'd said.

"Deal," she said in a rush, sounding like she'd just run a marathon. "It's a deal."

CHAPTER FOUR
RHYLAND

I wish I could say I was able to concentrate on some (or any) of what Bruce Marshall blabbed about in our meeting, but the truth was I was too busy shifting in my seat to adjust my six-foot hard-on. All I could think about was Dylan and the million implications of what we'd just agreed to.

Who'd brought up sex first? She had, I was sure of it. My mind hadn't even gone there. And not for lack of attraction to her. She was forbidden, completely off-limits, which begged the question: What were we doing?

I couldn't screw my best friend's little sister. There were limits in this world. Sure, I never adhered to any of them, but this one I actually cared about. Row was more than a buddy. He was my ride or die. He'd given me a job and taken me for a spin all over the world in our early twenties. This was insanity. I wasn't going to cash in on Dylan's offer.

Not initiating sex with her was one thing. I could do that, even if it shaved off a few years of my life and a good amount of my sanity. But if she threw herself at me? I was only human—and a terribly immoral one at that.

Maybe we should cancel the whole thing.

As if he were privy to my inner turmoil, Bruce lounged back in the velvet recliner in the trendy coffee shop, sipping his black coffee, which he'd asked his aide to fetch from "the shittiest, dirtiest diner you can find on this block, no fancy-schmancy stuff."

"About that pretty lil miss of yours…"

I snapped back to attention.

The meeting had been a disaster. Everything I'd planned for it—the spreadsheets, market overview, presentation, layout, audience research, sales pitch, app mock-up—had evaporated in a fog of sweet, aching desire as soon as I stumbled out of Dylan's apartment.

"That dog don't hunt, I'm thinkin'." Bruce stroked his stubbled chin, chewing on the tip of a stir stick. "Why would you hide someone like that from the world? None of our mutual friends ever mentioned her, and I sniffed around about ya."

"Love that you are so committed to the canine analogies." My tone was clipped. I decided to go for some version of the truth. The fewer lies I had to remember, the better. "She just moved here from the small town we grew up in," I supplied. "It's new, but it's real. We're as serious as a heart attack."

"How new?"

"A few months, but we've known each other forever. She's *the one*." It took everything in me not to hold my fucking nose as I said it. "When you know, you know."

In reality, I wouldn't marry Dylan if she were the last woman on earth. She was, among other things, a rebellious, stubborn, foul-mouthed, sharp-witted troublemaker. A twenty-six-year-old Swiftie, she was sex on legs and as manageable as an F5 tornado. Even if I were crazy enough to contemplate marriage, she'd be at the bottom of the list, right after Catherine the Great and that woman who boiled a bunny in that eighties movie.

Didn't mean I wasn't still thinking about fucking some sense into her, as though I didn't also need a re-up. But Bruce looked so fucking pleased, his stern scowl finally relaxing into a smirk of approval, his brow smoothed out of wrinkles for a change.

"I'm searching for another ring for her now," I heard myself say. "Something perfect, just like her."

Really now, asshole? But the truth was, to strike a deal with Bruce Marshall, I was willing to drag Dylan down the aisle kicking and screaming. This was my shot at becoming a billionaire. Not a millionaire—a *billionaire*. I had a once-in-a-lifetime idea and a lot of background knowledge. I just needed the connections, engineers, and seed money. This deal was so much more than just money. It was prestige. It was validation. It was *everything*.

"You do that now, son." He rapped the table between us, standing up. "That's a good idea right there."

He was glowing with pride. This was good. Fantastic, even. Now all we needed was to sign the dotted line.

Instead of doing that, though, Bruce slapped his thigh and clucked his tongue. "Welp, I definitely want to hear more about that little app of yours."

"More?" I blinked, confused. "I thought this meeting was it?"

"Yeah, I didn't become a billionaire handing over huge amounts of money to people I don't know." He shook his head. "We don't have to rush into this so fast. We're a family company and like to get to know our partners and their families. Let's take this one step at a time and see if we all get along. My wife will definitely want to chat with your lil miss, and I like to spend a weekend or two with people I consider accepting into my professional circle." A weekend or two? Was he freaking kidding me?

Clearing my throat, I asked, "Do you have a timeline of how long it usually takes you to make a decision?"

"A month." He shrugged. "Sometimes two. All depends on how fast we get to know each other and you send me all the info I need on your app. It's not just about creating relationships. I have to make sure this idea of yours is legit."

Fuck my life.

That meant a good number of 10k-a-week salaries to keep the hellion downstairs happy.

Looked like I was going to put an engagement ring on Dylan Casablancas's finger after all.

CHAPTER FIVE
DYLAN

DYLAN, 18, RHYLAND, 22

> *Roses are red*
> *Violets are purple blue*
> *Your beauty is too much to take*
> *Please let me be your favorite mistake*

I tossed another one of Tucker Reid's desperate poems into the trash, yawning into my arm. My high-school bully turned besotted stalker was no Lord Byron. In fact, most of his weekly poems had more cheese in them than a baked ziti, to the point that I was beginning to develop lactose intolerance. If this was all Staindrop had to offer in terms of eligible men, I was inclined to become a nun. I wasn't losing my virginity to *that*.

Row stuck his head through the gap between my bedroom door and the doorframe, a cigarette hanging from the corner of his lips. "Dyl?"

Whirling around on my squeaky desk chair, I kicked the trash can under my desk. "What's up?"

"Are you going to the graduation party in the moorlands tonight?" he murmured around the cigarette. "Rhy and I wanna crack open a few beers, but I figured I'd ask you first in case you need a ride."

Something melted in my chest like butter on a hot pan. "Sitting this one out."

There was no reason for me to go to the graduation party, really. Everyone was going to get drunk and celebrate moving away to college, while I was staying here.

It wasn't that I didn't have the grades to go to college. My GPA was 4.3, my extracurriculars were stellar, and I had letters of recommendation from everyone who'd ever met me. I *loved* studying. It wasn't that. It was just...I needed to stay. For *Row*.

Row had been the one to take care of our mother all these years, and now that he was off to study abroad, someone had to hold the fort. It was time for me to pay my dues. To make sure Dad wasn't hurting her.

"You sure?" Row's dark eyebrows knit into a scowl. "I don't mind not drinking. It's no skin off my back."

"Positive." I picked up a book from my desk, leafing through it. My eyeballs stung with unshed tears, but I didn't let them loose. I was going to be brave, just like Row had been.

Brave when my dad beat him whenever he was drunk, which was every day.

Brave when, after nights of taking abuse from Dad, he smiled at me across the breakfast table in the mornings, passed me the cereal box, gave me lunch money, and pretended he wasn't dead inside.

Row didn't know I was aware of the abuse Dad inflicted on him and Mama. I didn't know why I was lucky enough to escape his wrath. But it didn't matter.

It was my turn to watch over our parents, make sure Dad didn't kill Mama, and I was ready.

My brother drummed his fingers over the back of my door, stalling. "I invited some friends over. Rhy, Piper, and Chrissie. That okay?"

"Sure," I said brightly. "Of course."

It wasn't out of the ordinary for my brother to hang out with pretty, interested girls from home when he vacationed here from Le Cordon Bleu, but I knew he'd never have any of them. He was hopelessly in love with my best friend, Cal.

"Dyl…" Row halted.

"Hmm?"

"Why aren't you going to college?"

The question impaled my stomach like a rusty knife. I inhaled through my nose. My shoulders tensed. "Honestly? I don't want to accumulate student debt to get a BA in bullshit. I'll figure things out at my own pace. Decide what I want to do."

"It's not because of me, right?" Row asked after a beat.

It is, and I won't ever let you drop out of culinary school. You've already sacrificed too much.

I snorted. "No, Row. The world doesn't revolve around you."

The next few hours slogged by. My parents weren't home: Dad was at work, and Mama was visiting Uncle Antonio in New Jersey. I retired from my desk to my bed, texting with Cal and skimming a book. I wasn't even sure what I was reading. There was a murder, a cabin, and a good amount of cheating between two couples. Downstairs, I could hear girlish giggles and screeching and beer bottles popping open. Row and Rhyland were talking in their deep, authoritative voices. My ears tuned out everything other than Rhy's voice, though. The husky, deep burr of the last guy I should be attracted to.

My stomach rumbled, announcing it was empty.

I sighed and put the book on my chest, glancing at the clock on my nightstand.

Just grab something quick. You can't avoid him forever.

Checking my phone to procrastinate, I noticed a few text messages.

> Cal: We should go to the graduation hangout. I'm leaving tomorrow for New York.

As much as I was happy for her, I was depressed for myself. Cal was my only ray of light in the otherwise gloomy Staindrop.

> Tucker: Want me 2 pick u up 4 the party?
> Tucker: I rlly like u.
> Tucker: You're eyes look like 2 graceful beetles. Shiny and black.
> Tucker: Your so beautiful dylan. Idk how I never noticed it before.

Flinging my legs over the bed, I padded downstairs. The lights were turned off in the kitchen, the house mostly dark in the dusky evening. I glanced past the backyard doors and caught Row and his two lady friends sitting around a bonfire, drinking beer. I noticed Row had stuck to water. Probably didn't trust me not to change my mind about the party.

This is why you're doing this for him.

He's always taken care of you. He's loyal to a fault.

The toilet in the house flushed noisily, followed by the sound of a faucet running. I grabbed a bowl from the overhead cabinet and poured some pretzels into it. I dumped a few grapes and baby carrots into the mix, my stomach brushing the kitchen counter. I was about to turn around and go upstairs when two hands bracketed me from either side, fingers splayed across the countertop. I immediately recognized those fingers. Tan, long, and rough from manual work. He worked in construction every summer when he was off from college.

I sucked in a breath. *Rhyland.*

An erection ground between my ass cheeks through our clothes. A hot, humid mouth came crashing down over the shell of my ear. The faint fumes of beer and the bitter bite of weed skulked into my nostrils.

Was he drunk? Stoned?

Knowing Rhyland, he was both.

Ropes of exhilaration twisted around every nerve ending in my body like ivy while my mind ran in a hundred different directions. This was shocking. Rhyland had never touched me before. Never indicated he liked me this way. Other than the lingering looks between us. The steadfast, agonizing tension that clawed my neck every time I caught him glaring at me silently, squeezing hard until I was out of breath.

We'd have entire conversations with our gazes alone, and still we'd barely talk. We scarcely acknowledged each other's existence. All I had to go by was his gawking and that look on his face like he wanted to tell me something. But he never did.

I needed to stop this. Now. Row wouldn't approve. And I never did things he didn't approve of.

My mouth dropped, and I tried to push a rejection out, but then he snaked a hand up my waist, cupping the underside of my breast, brushing my puckered nipple through my flimsy white shirt with possessiveness, and I leaned into him, pathetic little sobs of passion ripping from my mouth. His thumb drew circles around my nipple, making my breast feel heavy and full in his palm.

"Finally," he groaned into my neck, grinding his cock up and down the slit of my ass, the girth pushing between my cheeks. "I thought I'd never get you alone."

He doesn't know it's you. He thinks you're someone else.

Piper, most likely. We both had long black hair, olive skin, and long legs.

I grunted a refusal, but it came out as a desperate whimper. Of its own accord, my back arched, and my ass searched for more of his length. Honeyed warmth gathered under my navel. I was still a virgin and hadn't even seen a penis up close. The furthest I'd gone was heavy petting. But now I wanted more. I wanted *everything*.

"How about we reenact all the dirty texts you've been sending me?" Rhyland growled into my skin, straight teeth sinking to the delicate flesh of my collarbone.

Before I could protest, he kicked my legs apart and sank his knee between my thighs, his muscular thigh pressuring my empty center, making it throb deliciously as it begged for more.

"Now what should I do to yo—"

Before he finished his sentence, his palm halted on the golden necklace. A gift from my mother. It had a distinct thin cross. I'd worn it since I was fourteen. Rhyland grunted, grabbing my shoulder and spinning me around at the speed of light. His jaw went slack, his gold-speckled eyes igniting into flames.

"Jesus fucking Christ, Dylan, what the hell are you doing?"

"What am *I* doing?" My gaze snapped up to his, confused and defenseless and emotional, and *fuck*, Rhyland was hooking up with Piper. It shouldn't have hurt like this. It shouldn't have hurt at all. Why him? I could've liked anyone else and easily dated them. "Not assaulting my best friend's sister, that's w-what." I snatched my pretzel bowl with a haughty huff to prove I was down here for food, not to get molested by a rando.

"Why didn't you stop me?" he spluttered, blocking my way to the stairs.

"I froze. I had no idea what was happening," I lied. The truth was too humiliating to contemplate.

"Don't bullshit me, Dylan. You're not the kind of girl who freezes."

"Yeah? What kind of girl am I, then?"

"The type to wedgie the devil to start a fight." He crowded me back against the kitchen counter.

This was more than we'd spoken the entire year. The entire decade, to be honest.

"Are you victim-blaming right now?" My brows pinched into a *V*. "This gives strong 'but she was wearing revealing clothes' vibes."

His eyes flared in horror. I had him there.

I didn't feel even a little guilty for lying. My lust-filled gut swam with warm liquid, and I felt empty, my skin tingly, begging to be touched. My chest rose and fell with my erratic breaths. I wasn't wearing a bra. He glanced down at my tits, then back up at me.

"This was a mistake," he conceded, sounding serious and regretful for the first time in, well, ever. "I'd never—"

"Yeah. Me either. Gross."

His throat worked as he swallowed. He didn't make a move. Neither did I. There it was again—that look. Like he was holding back from saying something.

"What?" I rolled my eyes to stop them from watering.

"Nothing." His voice was strained. "I'm sorry."

"That you were born? Yeah, so am I." I plastered the bowl to my chest, sidestepping him to go upstairs.

He moved in the same direction, trying to give me space. I stepped to the other side. He did the same. I growled in frustration.

"Get out of my way," I said. I had to go upstairs and flick the bean before I exploded.

"Trying to."

"Well, just stand still, and I'll go around you," I snapped.

I didn't mean to be this harsh, this awful, to him, but my ego had taken a huge blow, and I was trying to salvage whatever was left of it. Rhyland's ego didn't need stroking; it needed its own freaking zip code. He'd gained notoriety for being the hottest player in town. And he went to a good college. He'd survive.

Rhyland stood stiffly, his jaw so tense I thought it was going to snap out of his mouth. I sidestepped him with a headshake.

"Enjoy Piper," I spat out, taking the stairs up.

He snatched the hem of my shirt, pulling me to him. The pretzels flew into the air, landing on the floor. My chest slammed against his. He grabbed my hips, sneering down at me, disgusted with himself.

"Fine. I lied. I do want you."

"Join the line, loser," I huffed, determined not to thaw under his touch.

"I want you like I've never wanted anything in my fucking life." His voice was thick and dark. "I know I'm a pig, but I can't stop fantasizing about fucking you."

"Show me," I dared him, my voice barely trembling.

He clasped my jaw and tilted me against the wall as his lips collided with mine. A strangled gasp escaped me, and he swallowed it whole, opening his mouth. Our tongues touched, electricity zinging between them, and my eyes rolled over in their sockets, fluttering shut as fireworks exploded against my eyelids.

My whole universe shrank to this moment—to the sensation of his lips on mine, the stroke of his tongue, the way his hand fastened itself around my waist when he held me. His lips were firm, smooth, perfect. He tasted of debauchery, of decadent sin. I wanted more of it. I threaded my fingers through his hair, the sound of my heartbeat drowning out the moans and gasps we exchanged between us. All my blood rushed to my clit, to the tips of my nipples, to my toes as they curled over the cheap plywood. For the first time, I understood the term "*falling* in love." This was what it felt like: plunging into something dark and delicious and unknown. Gravity abandoned me. My knees buckled. Our kiss deepened, becoming faster, more desperate, urgent to steal more, more, *more* before we got caught. His hands tightened around me like a belt. My hands fluttered all over him like a butterfly. And I already missed him. Missed *this*. Most of all, I missed the part of my heart he'd taken from me the moment his lips touched mine. I knew, with depressing certainty, I was never getting it back.

That I would compare every other boy to him, and every other boy would fall short, because that was just what they'd be: a boy.

Rhyland was a man.

"What the fuck?" a feminine voice shrilly demanded.

A bucket of ice water doused the flame between us. Rhyland

pulled away, righting me against the wall, wiping his swollen lips with the back of his arm.

Piper was standing at the backyard door holding empty beer bottles by their necks between her fingers, wearing a white tee and a pair of black leggings, just like me. *Figures.* It was all the reminder I needed that Rhyland hadn't meant to kiss me. He'd meant to kiss her.

"Rhy?" Piper demanded, her saucer-size eyeballs shifting between us frantically. "What's going on?"

"You can't tell Row." Rhyland's flat voice was eerily scary. It held a threat, a promise of something bad. I liked that he cared more about Row than about salvaging whatever they had together, even if it made me a bad person.

"Are you hooking up with his baby sister?" Piper's eyes pooled with tears, and I felt bad for her—and for me—that we'd caught the attention of a mythical creature as lovely and devastating as Rhyland.

"Would you keep it the fuck down?" Rhyland snarled gruffly, grabbing her by the arm and walking her over, away from me. His eyes frantically searched for Row outside. "It was a mistake."

"A mistake?" Piper and I asked in unison.

I snorted. "I've met actual cereal boxes more decisive than you. Pick a lane, my guy."

"Dylan." He turned to me sternly. "Can we have some privacy?"

Sure can, in your own house. Truth was I wanted to pull myself together after what had happened. "Looks like you two wanna kill each other." I shrugged. "I wish you both success."

I took the stairs up and rounded the first corner of the stairway, staying close by. I hoped they'd stay in the kitchen.

"I've been waiting for our hookup for ages," Piper whined.

The knowledge they hadn't been together yet shouldn't have filled me with relief, but oh, it did.

"I feel bad for her," Rhyland explained, as cool as a cucumber and just as phallic.

I felt myself dwindling into something small enough to fit inside a pocket, becoming smaller still when he added, "I thought she was you."

Piper snorted. "I'm hotter."

"Okay, Pipe, no need to kid yourself." He chuckled.

I blushed. Rhyland was a party animal, a fun guy, but he could sometimes be cruel.

"Anyway, it's sad, you know, that she's staying here. Taking on a waiting job. She's not a dumb kid, just impulsive and overly emotional."

"She's not your problem," Piper all but mewed.

"Let's not get carried away here. I was just copping a feel, not filling in her college application." He laughed.

Bile coated the back of my throat.

"Mistake or not, you have to keep your mouth shut about this, Pipe," Rhyland warned. "Row can't find out, and history isn't kind to people who fuck me over."

"Okay, okay," she huffed, flustered. "I won't say a word."

"Good girl," he said in that derogatory way. "You keep my secret, and I'll keep yours."

"What secret?"

"That pink coke bag that disappeared from Allison's locker senior year?"

"So...are we off?" Piper asked finally.

Girl, he just blackmailed you. Have some self-respect.

"We're off," Rhyland confirmed. "This was a bad idea anyway."

"Yeah," she said unconvincingly. "Totally."

The conversation seemed to be over, with the sound of beer bottles clinking, dishes being washed, and trash bags being filled. My blood simmered with rage as I perched on the stair on the second floor, my heart in my throat.

He felt bad for me.

My life was *sad* to him.

In one careless moment, he'd shattered years of pining and teasing and daydreaming about the what-ifs. I'd always burned for Rhyland Coltridge. Now all I wanted was to burn him down.

But I was Dylan Casablancas. Fun. Witty. Creative. Unhinged.

And Dylan Casablancas *never* cried.

So I did the only thing I could do to ensure Rhyland knew I was over our so-called misunderstanding. I went to my room, put on my most sexy, cute getup, did my makeup, curled my hair, spritzed on a small pond of Libre by YSL, and took the stairs down two at a time, barreling through the backyard doors. I looked like a million bucks and felt like fifty cents, but I kept my smile intact as Rhyland, Row, and their girlfriends all hung their stunned, awestruck gazes on me. Rhyland's expression darkened into something feral when he gulped at the sight of me.

"You gonna let your sister go out of the house like that?" he growled at Row.

Row shot him a puzzled look. "Yeah," he said slowly. "I don't own her. Wrong era, asshat."

"She looks like fucking prey," Rhyland countered, scowling at my brother.

"How she dresses is none of my business," Row maintained. "And you know I make a lot of her shit my business, so let it go."

"Sorry, Rhyland." I patted his shoulder with a sweet smile. Something dangerous rippled up and down my spine. "I know you want me, but I'm too much for you to handle. Not gonna happen. Take the L. Row?" I snapped my fingers.

"Yeah?"

"Drive me to the moorlands. I'm going to that party."

And I was going to fuck Tucker Reid and his bad poetry and his dubious intentions and my entire freaking future, all at once.

After all, I was Dylan.

Impulsive.

Overly emotional.

And a very sore loser.

CHAPTER SIX
DYLAN

The next day, after a morning walk, finger-painting, sensory play, and cookie baking, Grav decided she'd had enough of our quality time and retired to her new room to flip through her books.

I heated up some water in a MacKenzie-Childs check tea kettle I got for no other reason than the fact that I saw it in a Nara Smith video and wanted to feel wholesome and belligerently perfect. I didn't even like tea—I was a coffee girlie through and through. Three shots, at minimum, before I started my day. But I felt like reinventing myself now that I was in the big city.

As I waited for the water to boil, I leaned a hip against the kitchen island and stared out the floor-to-ceiling windows. The apartment overlooked Central Park, and even though the park was just one small slice of lush, heavenly green in a concrete jungle, it very much felt like living in a tree house.

The water came to a boil, and I rummaged through the cabinets for tea bags, delighted to find some of the Italian staples Row and I grew up on. Caffè d'orzo, amaretti cookies in a colorful vintage tin, and grissini. A private grin tugged at my lips. My brother and I may have been born in the U.S., but we were hopelessly Italian: passionate, opinionated, and deathly protective of our family. I was grabbing my phone from the counter to call him when Kieran's name flashed on the screen. I swiped to the right.

"Hey, handsome."

"Hello, gorgeous," he purred back in his deep, alluring tenor. "Changed your mind about marrying me yet?"

"Nope, but please keep trying. My self-control has always been wanting." I grabbed a mug and the caffè d'orzo and fixed myself a cup, pinning the phone between my ear and my shoulder. Fuck tea. I was still Dylan Casablancas. "Whatcha doing?"

"Just finished physical therapy and about to hit the shower." He groaned, and I imagined him naked, draped across the exam table, a tiny towel protecting his modesty. "The therapist twisted my legs like I was made out of playdough," he complained. "I'm never recovering from this injury. How 'bout you?"

Lazily stirring, listening to the teaspoon clink against the delicate mug, I blew a lock of hair from my face. "Settling in at Row and Cal's apartment. Manhattan is, um, a lot." My laugh was self-deprecating.

"Once you get used to the big city, you fall in love with the anonymity of it."

But Kieran wouldn't know. Inconspicuousness was something he'd never experience again in this lifetime. He was one of the biggest soccer players in the universe. A striker for Ashburn FC, known for his lethal penalty strikes and merciless dribbling that often had defenders stumbling over their own feet trying to chase him, he was, without a doubt, the fear of every goalkeeper in the Premier League and the one legendary player every kid in Europe and South America had a poster of on their wall.

"I'll take your word for it." I clucked my tongue, reaching for the remote on the kitchen island and turning on the TV. I flipped through shows on the streaming service, settling on *Grey's Anatomy*. Something about complicated medical conditions and drama always soothed my soul.

An ad appeared before the episode started, and I sighed. I couldn't believe my multimillionaire brother didn't pay extra to avoid these. Just as well, as the ad was for a Tom Ford perfume and featured soccer player Marcello Sarratore. He was lying on a golden dune in the middle of the desert, sweat gliding down his sculpted, bronze six-pack. Groomed black curls graced the expanse of his mammoth chest, along with prominent stubble covering those knife-sharp cheekbones. Sarratore looked like a real-life gladiator, all bronze and bigger than life.

I swallowed hard. "Is Marcello Sarratore taken?" I blurted out.

Wow. I really needed some vitamin D. And I'm not talking sunlight.

Kieran yawned. "Dunno. I've never met the guy. He plays for Inter Milan."

"You both play in the Champions League, though," I challenged. Since Kieran and I became friends a few years ago, I'd made a point to learn about soccer.

"We've never crossed paths. He only transferred to Milan two seasons ago, after staying faithful to his shitty hometown team, which was at the bottom of Serie A," he explained absentmindedly. "Trust me, if we had, I'd have passed the ball right between his legs on my way to their goalkeeper."

As left defender, Marcello Sarratore had recently won the World Cup with Italy.

"Besides, he's the only soccer player in the world who is actually openly out." I heard the snap of a waistband slapping taut skin as he put his clothes on. "So I'm afraid you're out of luck there."

"Marcello Sarratore is *gay*?" I moaned. "Figures. All the good ones are."

Kieran was deep in the closet. In fact, our friendship had started because last time he came to visit our hometown of Staindrop, he'd pretended to hit on me, telling everyone who was willing to listen that he wanted me as his wife.

He'd been up-front about what he was doing. He'd never led me on. But he'd pursued me relentlessly, wanting me as his beard to get rid of those pesky tabloid columnists and the persistent paparazzi.

He'd offered me his kingdom, all the wealth and power he'd achieved. Gravity and I would be his family, he'd said. I could even take a lover on the side. All he wanted was for the entire world to stop asking him when he'd find a girlfriend and settle down.

I never, *ever* criticized or questioned Kieran's decision to be in the closet. I wasn't the one about to be on the receiving end of the blowback if he came out. But I couldn't help but wonder: If the macho Marcello Sarratore didn't give two shits, why did he?

Kieran must've read my mind, because he explained, "He can get away with it because he's a six-foot-five left-wing defender, built like a tank, and he screams toxic masculinity. I can't. I'm *nimble* and *pretty. Sports Illustrated*'s words, not mine."

I could practically envision him rolling his eyes on the other end.

"Don't worry. I'll come out eventually. After I retire. I'll have my moment in the sun."

I opened my mouth to protest, then closed it. It really wasn't any of my business. But it hurt to know a dear friend of mine, whom I adored with all my heart, didn't get to experience love and sex and first dates and sordid texting and uncontrollable butterflies.

Neither do you, you hypocrite.

Kieran was afraid to take a chance, but so was I.

"Enough about that," Kieran grunted. "Tell me all about your past few days."

"Hmm. Let's see. My car died for the millionth time, Grav is mad at me for taking her away from her granny and Marty, and, oh, apparently Rhyland Coltridge and I are in some kind of a fake engagement deal."

"Impossible," Kieran said confidently. "I've already asked for your hand in fake marriage, and you declined. I'm richer, handsomer, and you actually tolerate me. Why would you say yes to his proposal?"

"First of all, to deflate that continent-size ego of yours…" I snorted, eyes fixed on the TV. "Second, because he needs to impress a traditional cowboy business investor, and I need a helping hand here and some money while I figure out my next steps." I sipped my drink. "Speaking of, I *do* recognize a pattern here. Why do I get so many fake marriage proposals, never real ones?"

"What does it matter? You're not ready for a relationship," Kieran observed matter-of-factly.

"Would you be? Tucker ruined men for me."

"You need some closure with him," Kieran said.

"Ha." I shook my head. "I'd have to find him first."

There was a beat of silence on the other end of the line before Kieran said, "I'm not sure how I feel about all this. Rhyland is a man-whore."

"Sure is. But this is strictly business. You know I don't catch feelings."

Whenever I got butterflies in my stomach, I called pest control, the exterminator being the memory of being Tucker Reid's girlfriend. The cheating, the fighting, the secrets, the letdowns. He reminded me of my late father, a volatile, toxic man who was only good at two things: failing and blaming others for the outcome of his actions.

It was surprisingly easy to turn your back on love when the only love you'd ever experienced was ugly and scarred.

"And the dick?" Kieran asked bluntly. "Will you be catching it?"

"Catching, stroking, licking…" I ran the tip of my finger over the rim of my cup, my head swimming with daydreams. "Why not? We're both single and emotionally damaged enough not to get attached. No drawbacks."

"What about Row?" Kieran asked. He and my brother had become fast friends since Row moved to London about three years ago, though they'd started out as sworn enemies.

"Row is not the boss of me."

"Don't do anything stupid," Kieran warned.

But therein lay the problem. I'd spent the past four years trying so hard not to make mistakes, not to do anything foolish after accidentally tangling my destiny with Tucker's, that I hardly did anything *at all*. Maybe moving to New York marked the beginning of a new me. Or, more likely, the *old* me. The me who took chances. The me who was bold and curious and creative and fun. The me who'd learned Latin one summer because it seemed interesting, played every sport at school for the fun of it, and kissed strangers in theme parks just so she could pocket the memory and win a bet.

Well, maybe not that last part.

The doorbell rang, along with the phone app, to signal someone was outside.

"Look, I gotta go." I pushed off the kitchen island. "Someone's coming."

"That someone better not be you," Kieran tutted. "Last time you came, it ended in an unwanted pregnancy, a runaway groom, and a small-town scandal."

"You're being a prude."

"No. I'm being a bitter old hag," Kieran corrected primly. "If I'm not getting some, neither should you. We need to start a Hot Sexless People club. We'll be the founding members. We'll have bingo nights—"

"We're abstinent, not eighty."

"Fuck that, Dyl. You and I both know bingo is a badass activity, and once you sit down for it, it's the bomb."

The doorbell rang again. I didn't remember ordering a stage-five clinger.

"I gotta go."

"Okay. Remember. No catching feelings."

I hung up on the ridiculous man, shaking my head as I made my way to the door.

Me. Catching feelings. For Rhyland Coltridge.

Hell would become a ski resort first.

CHAPTER SEVEN
DYLAN

On the other side of the door was an Amazon delivery man holding a box—probably full of the new toys and books I'd ordered for Grav. Rhyland stood beside him, messing with his phone and looking like corruption in a sage-green suit.

"Sorry, I didn't order this." I pasted on an apologetic smile.

"Didn't order what?" The delivery guy tilted his head sideways.

"A package of red flags." I gestured toward my upstairs neighbor.

Rhyland barked out a laugh, clearly delighted to be the bane of my existence. He tucked his phone into his pocket and strolled inside—not before plucking the package from the clearly bemused delivery man and slamming the door shut with his foot. I followed him, narrowing my eyes at the nape of his neck in the hope he'd catch fire.

"Actually, I have something to give you too," Rhyland announced, placing the Amazon box on the island.

"Not interested in your chlamydia, but thanks."

"Lies." His nonchalant grin stretched wider, revealing perfect white teeth. "You can't wait for me to give you chlamydia and any other STIs I picked up along the way." He shoved his hand into his front pocket, producing the key to Jimmy and tossing it into my hands. "In other news, your car's driving like it's brand-new."

"Was it the spark plug?" I didn't even know what a spark plug was, to be honest. I just wanted to participate in a grown-up conversation about something that wasn't unicorns, fluffy animals, or *Cocomelon*.

"Among other things." The bastard took a sip of my drink without asking, scowling at the mug. "That's some weak-ass coffee. Anyway, I also changed the brakes, the oil filter, the alternator, the battery, and the water pumps."

I blinked in shock. "Did you keep anything at all? The Little Trees air freshener on my rearview mirror?"

"Changed that one too." He glided like a swan over water toward the fridge, flinging it open and peering inside. "No offense, but it smelled like the underside of toenails after you cut them."

"You're depraved," I announced with a scowl.

He shrugged. "And you're still interested."

"Did you do this all by yourself?" I dangled the key in my hand.

"Yup."

That seemed excessive for someone who wasn't a mechanic. "And are you sure you knew what you were doing?"

He sucked in his teeth. "Guess we'll find out."

"That's reassuring."

"I believe the words you're looking for are 'thank you.'"

Regrettably, he looked like he belonged in a Ralph Lauren catalog. The only thing he was missing was a horse and the Hamptons as his backdrop. He wore a chunky gold watch, slim green chinos, and beige sneakers. His man bun was haphazardly tied, the silky strands of pale and dark blond locks begging to be smoothed back.

Grav chose that moment to careen from the hallway, fisting three Barbies by their hair. She football-tackled Rhyland's legs, slamming into them in a hug. "Uncle Rhyrand!"

His spine snapped straight and he grimaced, physically repulsed. My hackles went up.

"Now, now." He patted Gravity's head as if she were a Yorkshire terrier, untying her from his legs. "Ever heard of the term 'personal space,' kiddo?"

Oh God. What a jackass.

My sweet bundle of joy peered up at him innocently, her chubby arms still encircling his knees. "No. What's that?"

"It's when someone is a soulless ghoul, so they act like a donkey in front of literal toddlers." I hurried toward them, scooping Grav up and hugging her close to my chest before she got her first rejection. What kind of animal was this rude to a *child*?

Rhyland appeared undaunted by the daggers of hate I threw his way with my eyes, flipping his brown leather briefcase open. I didn't even know why he had the damn thing. He was a boyfriend for hire, not a lawyer.

"Hey, kid, I got you something."

"Oh, I love somethings!" She clapped excitedly. "What is it?"

He produced a stuffie of a white sheep with a pink tutu, face, and ears. Grav wiggled out of my hands, rushing toward the stuffie and hugging it to her chest.

"Aw, I love it!"

"Does that mean you're going to get rid of Mr. Mushroom?" he enquired.

"No!" she said cheerfully. "I love Mr. Mushroom."

"I'm sure Mommy does too."

I swatted his shoulder, grateful for the chance to touch him. No doubt I needed to stock up on good vibrators and some Jade West books to spice up my life. I mean, I propositioned the man within my first twenty minutes in New York. After he humiliated me when I was eighteen.

"And there's something else." Rhyland reached for his briefcase again, producing a small puzzle. "It's a twenty-piece puzzle of your face. Do you like it?"

"Yes!" Grav pumped the air with her fist.

"Good. Go do it somewhere else and give Mommy and Uncle Rhyland some privacy," he said flatly, tossing the puzzle at her, again as if she were playing fetch.

I tried to tame my visceral reaction to how cold and offhanded he was with my daughter, despite buying her gifts. He *had* just fixed my car. Grav ran back to her room with the puzzle, and I forced myself to turn to him with a tight smile.

"Thank you for her gifts."

He threw a dismissive hand between us. "I needed her out of our hair for the next few minutes."

"Do you always keep photos of other people's children lying around in case you need to make a puzzle out of them?"

"I got it off your Instagram." Rhyland gave me an amused, unbothered look. "And if it makes you feel any better, my online assistant made it into a puzzle, not me."

"Online because people can't stand you in person?" I batted my eyelashes.

"Online because I tend to fuck any woman I spend more than a couple hours a week with."

Gross. We were going to kill each other. It was only a matter of time.

"What do you want?" I snarled.

"We need to look legit. Marshall wants to spend time together, *get to know me.*" He made quotation marks with his fingers before splaying his hands on the breakfast nook between us, and I noticed, despite his impeccable suit, that his hands were rough and tanned, worn out from physical work. "We both know what happens once people start getting to know the real me."

"You're insufferable." I nodded. Finally, something we could agree on.

"Yeah, but you aren't. So I figured I'll bring you along to make me look good. You'll need to work hard at appearing unappalled by me. Friend me on social media. Like my shit. Post pictures of me. Maybe gush a little at my thirst traps."

"You post thirst traps?" I scrunched my nose.

"What were you expecting?" He motioned toward his perfect

body. "In-depth articles about post-Bronze Age colonialization in Greece?"

"And this needs to happen today?" Not that my schedule was packed with anything other than watching *Grey's Anatomy* and pretending to look for a job.

"Yeah," he confirmed. "And make it convincing."

I rolled my eyes. "I could strangle someone right now."

"Hey, don't kill the messenger."

"Well, don't stand so fucking close, then."

His laugh, casual and careless, crawled beneath my skin. My stomach bottomed out. This must be how eagles felt when they dove sharply from the sky to snatch their prey. Kieran was right: on paper, he was probably more handsome than Rhyland. Still, I'd always had this irrational, unabashed attraction to the forbidden. To my brother's best friend. Sylvia Plath had it right. We do desire the things that end up destroying us.

"Get ready to be smothered with eggplant and droplet emojis." I snatched my coffee cup from the kitchen island, placing it in the sink. "I'll play along, but I'll be the most unhinged teammate you've ever had."

"Remember, your paycheck depends on it," he hedged me. "I'm the kind of man who's fun to fuck and dangerous to fuck over. Remember that."

"I agreed to this deal on the basis it was carte blanche. I ain't changing my colors for you."

"It's just social media. Relax."

"I *am* relaxed," I countered, yelling.

He shook his head, amused. "You need to touch more grass."

"And you need to stop smoking it."

"I actually stopped three months ago, back when I retired," he said brightly.

I wondered if the two were connected. If he used pot to numb whatever he felt about selling his time and his charm and his body to complete strangers. Then I pushed the thought to the periphery of my mind, reminding myself I wasn't supposed to care, especially when he definitely didn't.

"You need to start looking the part of an engaged woman." Rhyland continued with his checklist.

"Oh?" I waltzed over to the wine room—because I had a wine room now, see—taking out a random merlot and pouring myself a glass without offering him any. It was five o'clock somewhere. Maybe even in New York. I hadn't checked, since I was unemployed and living with a toddler. "What does an engaged woman look like? Should I start wearing modest dresses and a fancy hat and only touch people when I wear my velvet gloves? Be your little trophy wife?"

"You're not a trophy wife, sweetheart. More like a punishment fiancée." He smirked.

"I promise I'll live up to the title."

"Just a heads-up—this is not the best way to go about it if you want to ride my dick."

"I said sex was on the table. I didn't say I'd make any special effort to have it," I clarified.

Rhyland paused, his eyes zeroing in on something behind me. I whipped my head around to find the oval dining table. Was he imagining… *Of course* he was. The horndog.

"My eyes are up here." I snapped my fingers in front of his face.

"Yes, I know." He rolled his tongue over his upper teeth. "They've been fucking me with greedy looks since I walked in here."

Carnage. There was going to be carnage if he didn't walk out of here in the next two minutes.

"Thanks for the task, the car, and the nausea-inducing conversation. Anything else keeping you here?" I asked.

"Yeah." He reached for the third time into the briefcase, yanking out a small box and flinging it into my hands. "Open it."

I did, feeling my nose creasing into a disapproving scowl. It was a navy-blue box, and I immediately knew what was nestled inside it. My heart rattled in my chest. The last time I was given an engagement ring, I ended up throwing it into the ocean. I'd considered pawning it for all of five seconds before deciding I didn't want anyone's love story to be tainted by the shitty piece of jewelry that represented the death of my own fairy tale.

The box opened with a crisp click, and in front of me was cushioned the most beautiful engagement ring I'd ever seen in my entire life—movies, pictures, and reality combined.

It wasn't just any ring, though. It was *the* ring that had caught my eye and snatched my soul in a magazine when I was fourteen. I'd cut it out of the *Vogue* issue and hung it on my Big Fairy-Tale Wedding pinboard. I still had that pinboard somewhere in the attic, laden with clippings of the perfect wedding dress, the perfect bouquet, the perfect flower arrangement...

The only thing you forgot to envision was the perfect groom, and we all know how that turned out.

I clamped my mouth shut to prevent myself from gasping. Mom always said coincidences were a sign from the universe.

"W-what made you go for this one?" My voice was gauzy, bodiless in the space between us.

"I remembered the engagement ring Tucker gave you." Rhyland's voice skimmed over my skin like the briefest touch of rough knuckles. Goose bumps erupted everywhere. "Then I remembered Tucker was a first-class moron, so I figured the safest route was to go with the opposite of everything he chose for you. Instead of a cushion, I went for an oval shape. I got you a thin band instead of a thick one. A Harry Winston instead of Costco."

I wagged my finger at him. "I take digs against Costco personally. It's my favorite brand in everything. I'd happily be Mrs. Kirkland, given the choice."

"You love it, don't you?" His voice dropped seductively, fluttering in my stomach like a delicate bird, and every cell in my brain revolted, reminding me I didn't do butterflies or crushes or men.

I drew in a deep breath, a reminder that this was a fluke. Rhyland didn't know this was my dream ring. I cleared my throat. "I still need to see if it fits."

"It fits," Rhyland reassured me.

"How do you know?"

"Because I've spent half my fucking lifetime studying every curve and measurement of your body."

Our stares struck like a match over red phosphorus. For a second, I had this crazy thought that maybe he harbored this great, agonizing love for me, the same way Row had been secretly in love with Cal. But Rhyland's mouth twisted into a sour smile.

"Oh, sweetheart." He shook his head as if I were a lost cause. "Nothing wholesome and sweet like that. I wanted to fuck you is all. I want to fuck most things that move. I'm no Prince Charming. The only scenario in which I'd have a redeeming bone in my body is if I got in a car accident and my body melted into someone else's."

A shock of heat slapped at my cheeks, making them burn from the inside. The urge to throw the ring in his face and release a chain of Italian swear words was strong.

But no. I wasn't going to give him the satisfaction.

A teasing smile puckered my lips. "If that's all, you can leave now."

He slung his briefcase over his shoulder and made his way to the door. He stopped a couple feet from it. "Oh." He snapped his fingers, pointing at me. "By the way, I'll pass on the bumping uglies offer. Flattered but no longer interested."

"I'll try to move on from the disappointment," I bit out sarcastically, sliding onto a stool at the kitchen island.

Stupid, stupid, stupid.

"Also, the ring is a rental, so don't get attached."

"I pity the woman dumb enough to form an attachment to anything you gave her."

The door closed on a soft final click.

I turned off *Grey's Anatomy* and burst through the master-bedroom door, smothering my face in a pillow and yelling into it in frustration. Rhyland underestimated me. So did the rest of my family. Well, they had another thing coming.

I was going to make it in New York.

Not just for me. For Gravity too.

CHAPTER EIGHT
RHYLAND

"You, my friend, are fucked. And not in the way that makes you want a cigarette and a stiff drink afterward." Tate Blackthorn—billionaire pseudo mobster, corporate shark, and a royal pain in the ass—sat across from me at the Grand Regent's rooftop bar. He tossed my business plan across the low concrete table between us, sitting back and taking a drag of his cigar.

He wore a black button-down shirt to match his black button-down heart. Nothing could pierce through that fucker's chest, I was sure—not even a 5.56 mm bullet. A sculpted arm was slung over the low, upholstered leather couch, his hand toying with the hem of the minidress of the woman he'd brought with him: a barely legal Norwegian supermodel who'd just made her Victoria's Secret debut. He didn't look like the CEO of GS Properties, the largest real-estate company in America and Europe combined; he looked like David Gandy trying to sell a megayacht.

"Why? What's wrong with it?" I demanded, thumbing through the pages. I'd written the business plan myself. The first time I'd put my business management degree to use since I graduated.

"Nothing. I'd give it a B-plus, and I've never graded a business plan higher than a C." His aloof, frigid eyes found mine across the thick smoke of his cigar. "But it's useless. Bruce Marshall won't work with you. Asshat acts as if he's running a mom-and-pop shop in bumfuck Montana, not a company as big as Google." The amusement in his voice told me he considered any emotion or moral beyond greed and power a weakness and that he'd found Bruce's. "He notoriously doesn't get into business with young, unattached people. Worst small-dick symptom I've ever encountered."

"That must be an exaggeration," I insisted, ignoring the way his fingers trailed between the woman's thighs beneath her dress. He remained completely stoic, as though he were popping a clam, not (possibly) a cherry, with his fingers.

"It's not." Smoke skulked out of Tate's mouth. "The Caufield family once shorted one of his companies to strong-arm him into business. I was the one to handle the nitty-gritty details of it. It dove sixty-three percent on one stock market after he refused to sell them dead-ass lots in the swamps of Florida. Marshall didn't even flinch when he took a four-billion-dollar hit."

"Maybe he just hates you," I offered. "You *are* uniquely unlovable."

"It was a good deal for everyone involved," Tate said stoically, withdrawing his hand from between the woman's thighs just as she began to pant, the sadist. "Then he found out I'm thrice divorced."

"*Thrice?* Je-sus, man. You're in your early thirties."

"When you know, you know."

"You obviously *didn't* know since none of the marriages lasted." I tucked my business plan back inside my briefcase. But the truth was I couldn't picture Tate committing to anything as altruistic as marriage. There was probably a bigger picture to all this. "Anyway, Marshall doesn't know how single I am."

"He'll figure it out once he invites you and your wife over for dinner and you show up with a half-deflated sex doll," Tate assured me, reaching for his whiskey and knocking it back in one go.

"He thinks Dylan Casablancas is my fiancée."

Tate choked on his whiskey, coughing into his fist. "He *what?*"

"Long story." I took a pull of my beer. "He walked in on what he thought was a lovers' quarrel but was actually Dylan trying to stab me for helping her with her prehistoric car."

"I forgot the little train wreck moved to New York," he snarled. "That's exactly what this city needs. More wannabes."

The words "train wreck" and "wannabe" made me want to punch his facial organs into the back of his head, and I found myself clenching and unclenching my fist. Dylan was a lot of things I didn't like, but she was the realest person I knew.

"She actually agreed to help me by pretending to be my fiancée for a little while."

"Row's gonna love that," Tate muttered sarcastically into the fresh glass of whiskey that had been placed directly where the empty one was seconds ago. There was a little note with the waitress's number underneath the tumbler, crumpled and damp. "What does she get out of the arrangement?"

My dick, if she has her way.

"I'm paying her week to week while she job-hunts."

"In what currency are you paying her, exactly? Potatoes?" He stroked his fingers under his chin, reaching for the woman's number and tossing it into the blue fire that danced on the table between us. The model giggled, but he wasn't acknowledging her presence anymore. "You're broke as hell."

"Well, if you give me a loan—"

"I only give loans to people who can pay them back." Tate sliced into my speech. "And I have no confidence you'll seal the deal with Marshall. At any rate, I charge a forty-two percent monthly interest rate."

"Christ, Tatum. That's a fucking loan shark's rate."

He stared at me, steadfast.

Huh. Guess he dabbled in that too.

Tate was as nocturnal as a viper and twice as venomous, a cold-blooded creature best suited to dark places. I'd yet to find one redeemable quality about him, save for the fact that he was (probably) mortal and would eventually relieve this earth of his toxic existence. I'd found myself friends with him on account of him being one, a corporate genius who saw any event or catastrophe as a fiscal opportunity, and two, well-connected to anyone worth knowing. I needed that right now. I was not the kind of rich he, Row, or Kieran were. I didn't have a special talent like them. I didn't know how to cook, play ball, or spin shit into gold. All I had was my looks and my charm, and at thirty, I knew I was fast approaching the day my bulging biceps and piercing green-blue eyes would no longer open doors or smash ceilings for me. I needed my app to launch and for it to do well, *fast*.

I'd made good money from being a gigolo. *Great* money. My penthouse was a gift from a former client, paid up front and in cash. But up until three months ago, I'd never made one good financial decision. I'd burned through money like it was fucking s'mores. Fast cars, designer clothes, and private charters. So once I decided to retire abruptly after a client tried to cop a feel—no, not cop a feel: sexually *assault* me—my funds began to dwindle at stunning speed.

This app was a last-ditch effort before I sized down, sold the condo, and admitted defeat.

"Admitted defeat" meaning going back to selling my time, my body, my charm, my fucking *being*. I didn't want to do that. But I couldn't afford not to.

I just really wanted to be more than a pretty face and a stunning dick.

"Are you going through some sort of brain aneurysm?" Tate swirled the amber liquid in his tumbler stoically. "Because if you think I'm driving you to the hospital, you've got another thing coming. I have a ten o'clock conference with Hong Kong."

"No." I shook my head, disoriented. What the fuck was I thinking, agreeing to pay Dylan $10K a week? Tate was right. I didn't have that kind of money. Though for a reason beyond my grasp, I wanted her to think I did. "I'm fine."

"Bet you won't be in the next five minutes," Tate sneered, standing up and glancing over my shoulder.

I whipped my head back to see what had caught his attention. Row slid past the bouncers of the trendy bar, wearing a ball cap and a biker jacket. He shouldered through a sea of socialites and finance bros in suits.

"Oh, this should be good." Tate buttoned his shirt. "I love blood sport. I'll watch from the bar while getting head. Come, Branka."

"It's Brina."

He ignored her. "Hey, whatever you do?" He squeezed my shoulder on his way out. "Make sure this deal with Marshall happens. You're working on an app. He all but owns the fucking App Store. He's formulaic as shit, but whatever he does works. His PR, engineers, creative team—everything is top-notch. Don't let this opportunity slip by."

I wasn't going to fuck it up.

My entire future was on the line.

Telling Row about my fake engagement to his sister was relatively pain-free. Relatively, because I got to keep my internal organs, but with a warning that he was going to skin and shave me into pastrami slices if I ever touched her.

"This is not a figure of speech," my best friend insinuated slowly and menacingly, his mouth moving over the rim of his White Russian. His tone, like his expression, his demeanor, his *existence*, was wry and monotonous. "I know where you live, and I'm very trigger-happy when it comes to my sister. The last thing she needs is another emotionally stunted fuckboy who breaks her heart. If you as much as touch her pinkie, yours gets chopped off. Understand?"

This was probably not the right time to inform him that said sister wanted to fuck me for money. Or that I was tempted to take her up on the offer. My dick was *constantly* hard. When I fixed her car. When I took business meetings. When I was working on the app. When I went to the gym. Even when I watched the presidential debate. Which, let's admit, was less sexy than a shit-soaked mop.

"You think I'd ever do you this dirty?" I slid the coin pendant of my neck chain—the one I never took off—from side to side.

"I think you earn your bread making women feel special and good, and Dylan is in a vulnerable position," Row countered, upturned brown eyes, just like his sister's, zinging threateningly. "And I think she can't handle another heartbreak after what happened with Tucker."

"It's going to be strictly professional. I just need this deal with Bruce Marshall. And he still lives in the Middle Ages or something." According to a quick Google search, Marshall and his wife had five children, ten grandchildren, and an entire orphanage they were sponsoring.

Row jerked his chin in a nod. "I know. That's why I invited him over to the launch of my spice brand in two weeks. He'll be here in New York. It'll give you the chance to play a loved-up *asexual* couple with my sister."

My jaw goddamn near hit the floor. "Wait—you knew about our arrangement before you walked in here?"

"Dylan told Cal." He shrugged.

Of course she did. Dylan's mouth ran faster than Usain Bolt. I should've known.

"She also mentioned you were already pissing her off, so maybe I shouldn't worry so much," Row noted.

I sniffed, willing my hardened jaw to relax. "Liaising with your sister is like herding cats."

"Leave any pussy analogy out of this conversation. I'm agitated as it is," he chided me.

I got out of there before Row had the chance to change his mind about the arrangement and slipped into my custom black

McLaren—a splurge I'd made two years ago. A gift to myself after working for four months with a filthy-rich client. She'd needed a fake boyfriend to parade after a nasty divorce that ended with an out-of-wedlock child by her maid and multiple lawsuits.

The engine purred to life, and I closed my eyes, thumping the back of my head against the cool leather. My phone vibrated in the central console, dancing to its own rhythm. I opened my eyes, frowning at the screen.

Mom.

Well, that was an overstatement. I hadn't spoken to the woman since last Christmas, and not for my lack of trying. I'd hoped to spend last Easter with my parents but found out through Facebook they were in Iceland on a northern lights tour.

Picking up the phone, I stared at it calmly. "What kind of favor do you need from me now, *Mother*?"

But I didn't answer the call.

Instead, I killed it by pressing the red icon and floored it back to my apartment.

CHAPTER NINE
RHYLAND

@DylanCasablancas2000! just followed you on Instagram.

@DylanCasablancas2000! commented: hello 911? I'd like to report a murder.💀

@DylanCasablancas2000! commented: OF MY OVARIES.

@DylanCasablancas2000! commented: you 💦 my butt when you get home 2nite

@DylanCasablancas2000! posted a new picture.

I clicked on the notification, quickly following her back and clicking on her latest post. It was a picture of her grinning, including a close-up on the mammoth engagement ring, clutching a tall man's arm. You couldn't see his face because he was taller, but she stared up at him with pure, unadulterated adoration.

For a reason I was definitely not going to explore, the image made my blood boil to the point it seared through my veins and gave me third-degree burns. I picked up my phone and called her. She didn't answer—out of spite, no doubt. I opened our text box. The last message from her was two years ago, a generic, Row said he'll pick you from the airport at nine, to which I'd responded with an equally hostile thumbs-up reaction.

I blew out air, still sitting in my car in the underground parking lot.

> Rhyland: Who the fuck are you hugging in that picture?
> Because it sure as hell ain't me.

Her reply was immediate—further proof she hadn't answered my call simply to rile me up.

> Dylan: A friend.
> Rhyland: You don't have any friends here.
> Dylan: I made one today.

Like hell she had.

> Rhyland: Where? When?
> Dylan: At Target.
> Rhyland: He works there?
> Dylan: Yes.
> Rhyland: Not anymore he doesn't. I'll see to it that he gets fired immediately.

What the fuck was wrong with me? Why was I jealous? No—not jealous, just protective of the Bruce Marshall deal. I really didn't need her to screw it all up with a meaningless fling. What if Bruce found out she was seeing someone else? What if that asshole posted a picture of himself with Dylan and Bruce somehow saw it?

> Dylan: I doubt you can get him fired.
> Rhyland: Oh yeah?
> Dylan: Yeah.
> Rhyland: Why?
> Dylan: He is a mannequin.

I stared at the text. Blinked. Went back to the picture she'd posted. Examined it more closely. Sure enough, there was an inch of exposed skin poking through the man's sleeve, and you could see his complexion was gray. I chuckled, shaking my head.

> Dylan: I had to get creative. And Grav wanted frilly socks.
> Rhyland: Those IG comments are deranged.
> Rhyland: I asked for soft launch, not soft porn.
> Dylan: Is anal considered soft porn? Idk.

I pressed my lips together, suppressing a smile. We really needed to stop talking about sex. Especially in light of her brother wanting to make a BLT sandwich out of me for simply playing pretend with her. It was hard though. Dylan was funny. Imaginative. *Real*. It was why I'd kept my distance from her up until now.

> Rhyland: We need to keep it PG-13. Remember, Bruce is a person of faith.
> Dylan: So am I.
> Dylan: I firmly believe people who want to get their butt fucked should. It's no one else's business.

CHAPTER TEN
RHYLAND

Three days had passed since Dylan propositioned me for anal in front of my forty thousand followers.

Three days since I last spoke to her or Bruce Marshall.

I'd refrained from following up with Marshall on Tate's advice, not wanting to seem desperate, knowing I'd see him soon at Row's event in New York. But something was gnawing at me. I wanted to do more to push this deal into completion. But I also didn't want to appear as panicky as I really was.

I spent my day going to the gym, grocery shopping, and sweet-talking a few potential investors. I then made the mistake of checking my bank account and regretted the decision immediately. I was fast approaching being in the red, and I still had to pay Dylan an unfathomable amount of money. By the time I returned to the apartment building, it was ten at night.

I ended up hitting the fifth-floor button on my way up to my penthouse.

It was Dylan's first week in New York. The least I could do was make sure she'd survived it.

I rang the doorbell. No answer. I glanced at my Patek Philippe, frowning. Ten at night. She must be home. She didn't have a babysitter, and I imagined it was way past the child's bedtime.

Had something happened to her?

If so, it's not your goddamn responsibility. You already saved her once, the metaphorical devil on my shoulder said.

She's your best friend's baby sister. If the chick is dead, Row will be a major pain in the ass. Already he's irrepressibly grumpy, the angel on my shoulder countered.

Making an executive decision, I pulled out the extra key Row had given me and turned it inside its hole. I pushed the door open, peering into the apartment. It was quiet and dark, save for the bluish hue of electronic screens. Maybe Dylan had just called it a night early. But I wasn't going to leave before confirming she and that annoying mini version of her were okay.

Stepping inside, I closed the door and sauntered past the living room and kitchen. I stopped in the hallway, filling the doorframe to the nursery. Her daughter was curled up in a too-small cot, her stubby, Pillsbury-boy arms encircling that damn pink penis. She seemed perfectly fine.

I advanced farther down to the master bedroom. Pushed the door open. The bed was empty, still made, the linen pressed under the mattress like in a hotel. I listened to the hum of the AC, the traffic blaring from downstairs, and detected the gentle noise of water swishing. My throat bobbed with a swallow. She was taking a bath.

Good. Now you know. Turn around. Walk away.

But something stopped me. What if she'd drowned? Got injured? Fallen when she got out of the bath?

I stepped to the ajar en-suite door, feeling very much like the creeper I apparently was. A tiny sigh echoed in the bathroom. It had a floor-to-ceiling view of Manhattan, one of those reflective-finish windows that gave the glass a one-way mirror effect. She could watch the entire stretch of Fifth Avenue without it watching her back.

I caught a glimpse of her, and my pulse kick-flipped right down my pants, making my cock throb.

Dylan had her naked back to me, everything from her spine

down covered by a sheet of bubbles. Her hair was caught in a white claw clip. She was staring out the window—not down at the busy, lively street full of people but up at the sky. Her chin was propped on the back of her hands, and in that moment in time, she was that beautiful girl I left behind in Staindrop.

The most beautiful girl in the world.

Wild but soft. Brave but lost. Imperfect but whole.

"Oh, look," she said, our eyes locking through my reflection in the window. "It's my wallet."

Her words were harsh and sarcastic, but there was something tired and defeated about her demeanor. Something that made me step inside without being invited and lean a shoulder against the wall.

"You shouldn't have let yourself in," she said, her voice void of anger, and I remembered Dylan had never really had her privacy. She'd always lived under other people's roofs, never spreading those beautiful, black-tipped wings of hers.

"That is no way to greet your fiancé," I tutted.

"I forfeit, smart-ass. I feel too much like shit to engage in this battle of wits." Her gaze rolled back to that invisible spot in the sky. To the liquid darkness and the stars that spun inside it like silver freckles.

"What's going on?" I asked.

"I've spent the past few days obsessively looking for a job and putting Grav in front of the TV," she explained. "She didn't do anything fun. And she misses her granny and Marty. I feel like the worst mom in the world."

"In the *world*?" I snorted, pushing off the wall, striding toward the foot of the clawed bath and taking a seat on the edge of it. I reached down to touch the water, watching the suds disperse as they met my skin. "Bitch, please. You're not even top twenty thousand worst mothers in the state. What about that asshole woman from Westchester who killed her kid and called 911 after a month?"

No comment. More star-watching. It was the first time I'd seen the seductive, feisty Dylan Casablancas being contemplative and vulnerable.

Finally, she opened her mouth. "I have a job interview tomorrow at eleven. I need you to babysit Grav."

Shit. I knew it was coming, but I'd pushed it to the back of my mind.

I worked my jaw back and forth. "I'm not good with ki—"

"We have an agreement." She cut me off, whipping her head around to look at me. "And I know you won't let me down, since you need me on your arm for Row's spice-brand event."

She had me there, and she knew it.

Dylan soldiered on. "I would also appreciate it if you could build her toddler bed. It's in a box in the guest room. And you'll need to do my groceries. I canceled Row's auto-deliveries, because they're full of ingredients I don't use. I've been so caught up with job hunting I don't even have milk."

This Bruce Marshall plan had better work, or I was basically paying $10K a week to be Dylan's servant.

"Whatever," I said. "What's the job?"

If Dylan felt self-conscious about talking to me while stark naked under those damn persistent bubbles, she didn't let on. "A marketing intern position at Beaufort. I'm not sure it's enough to keep us afloat once our arrangement expires, but I have to start somewhere." She turned her head back to the sky.

I didn't want to sound like a bigger asshole than I already was, but I couldn't think of one damn reason why a twenty-six-year-old woman who'd poured diner coffee her whole life would be called in for an interview at one of the world's largest fashion brands, second only to Chanel.

It wasn't that Dylan wasn't great—it was just that you couldn't see all those things through her résumé.

"I'll be there," I confirmed. "Is there anything in the sky I should know about? A UFO? A crashing plane? The apocalypse?"

Please say the apocalypse. That way, I won't have to babysit tomorrow.

Her reply came somber and off guard. "You know…ever since I gave birth, I've stopped dreaming," she croaked out, her eyes still stuck on the sky. "I spend my days either working or with Gravity. And I love her. I truly do. But being a single mother is the loneliest existence one can have. Between taking care of her, meeting her needs, working, tidying up, making food, and doing the dishes, I barely have time to think. It's so exhausting that by the time my head hits the pillow, I'm too tired to dream. And I miss my dreams. So every night, before I go to bed, I always look at the stars and dream in my head while I'm wide awake."

Well, fuck. Now I felt bad.

"What do you dream about?" I murmured around the figurative foot I'd shoved into my mouth.

She parked her chin on her curled fists. "Lazy weekends on the beach. Traveling. Dancing with friends. Going back to school."

I couldn't help but notice she hadn't mentioned a relationship.

I nodded. "Wild dreams, huh?"

"The wildest."

Silence stretched between us. She was still looking at the stars when she asked, "Is that all? The water's getting cold."

"Yup. See you tomorrow, Cosmos." I saw my way out.

She didn't respond to her new nickname. The one I made up on the spot.

She wanted her dream to last a little longer before she went to sleep.

CHAPTER ELEVEN
RHYLAND

Whoever said kids didn't come with a manual had obviously never met Dylan Casablancas.

The woman had printed out a sixty-five-page manifesto annotating food allergies, preapproved activities, a schedule, a menu, and some kind of sorting system for her playdough. She then spent twenty minutes running through the manual with me to ensure I understood everything. Then she left me in a cloud of her perfume and anxiety, standing next to her almost four-year-old.

The child and I stared at each other reluctantly. She seemed just as unhappy as I was with the arrangement.

"So...do you wanna watch *South Park* or something while I build your bed?" I rubbed the back of my neck.

"Mommy says no TV," she murmured, her big, dark blue eyes clinging to my face.

Riiight. Page fourteen, section B of the manual. How could I forget?

I grabbed said manual from the dining table and flipped through it, the child still openly gaping at me. There was a list of child-friendly activities Dylan had put together.

She was a mess, but I had to give it to her: she was an involved, loving, deeply caring parent.

"Uh, let's see. Do you want to do some coloring?"

"No."

"Puzzles?"

"Nope."

"Arts and crafts? Letter tracing? Dress-up? Foil presents? Bake some cookies?"

"No, no, no, and no." She shook her head violently.

I tossed the manual back on the table, exasperated. "Then what do you want to do?"

She pointed to the hallway.

"Get out of my sight?" I asked hopefully.

"Help build bed," she huffed, folding her arms.

"You can't," I said. "It's dangerous."

"Don't care." She blew a raspberry at me. Her mother's daughter, no doubt.

"Yeah, me either, actually, but social norms, et cetera."

I didn't want this kid to end up in the hospital. Mainly because *I* didn't want to end up in one, and Dylan would murder me and then resurrect me just to kill me again in a different, more brutal way if we did. My eyes strayed from the kid to the dining table, where there were a bunch of crayons, and I had an idea.

"I'll need someone to decorate the frame, I guess, if you're up to that."

She just stared at me as if I were talking to her in Amharic. I'd never spoken this much to a three-year-old before. "What do you mean?"

"I need you to make the bed pretty with your crayons," I explained in simpler terms.

"Oh! Yes! I can do that."

We got to work.

———

One of the very few perks of being the son of a carpenter/handyman who rarely showed up to work and instead sent his son to do his assignments for him was that I was *very* good with my hands. Especially with wood. All puns intended, naturally. I could build almost anything from scratch in no time. In college, in between my construction work during the summers, I'd make a buck assembling furniture from IKEA.

The child and I were done within forty minutes. She drew rainbows and clouds and unicorns on the frame while I put it together. She also didn't shut up for one second and wrestled me into a conversation about ice cream flavors and fluffy animals. I grunted every few sentences to show her I was still there but refused to engage in the conversation.

After that, we went downstairs with Dylan's grocery list. The child tried to convince me to buy her chocolate, but it wasn't in the manual, so I refused. She started crying and screaming. By the time we'd returned upstairs and unloaded the groceries, I was flustered, frustrated, and done with my day. How did parents manage not to become alcoholics? That was a case for the FBI.

"Uncle Rhyrand." The child tugged at my pants, looking up at me. "I'm hungry. Can we eat?"

Dammit. I'd forgotten to give her a snack. It was in the manual, but so were a hundred fucking other things.

"Sure. Just let me..." I grabbed the manual, leafing through it. No way was raising children this precise.

When my eyes landed on Gravity's preapproved meals, my entire soul left my body. *Chicken breast, organic wheat quesadilla, spaghetti and meatballs, broccoli casserole...* All those things required cooking from scratch. Most of my meals were Trader Joe's prepacked dinners or pussy. There was no way I was whipping up any of these home-cooked dishes.

I looked around, fists planted at my sides. "Well, shit."

"You said bad word." The child's eyes widened. "You give me five dollars." Her palm was open and outstretched in a nanosecond.

The apple really didn't fall far from the tree.

I rummaged in my wallet with a grunt. "I don't have any cash on me."

"That's not my problem."

Christ. What kind of demon did Dylan make?

"Do you accept Zelle or Venmo?"

"What?"

"Nothing." I pushed my wallet back into my back pocket. "Tell you what, I'll treat you to a Happy Meal, and you'll forgive my potty word."

"What potty word?"

Did she have memory issues? "Shit."

She giggled, bringing her small hand to her mouth. "You owe me five more dollars."

God dammit. Outwitted by a toddler. I was taking this to my grave. Of course, said grave was fast approaching, as spending time with this kid would likely lead to a heart attack.

I opened my mouth to reprimand her for tricking me, but she beat me to it. "Now I get Happy Meal *and* milkshake."

Kids truly were the best advertisements for contraception.

CHAPTER TWELVE
DYLAN

"Oh, I love your outfit! It's gorgeous," I gasped breathlessly, palms sweaty, cheeks flushed, delirious with the need to impress.

The subject of my admiration glanced at her colleague, who sat by her side, the two exchanging the sly look of Siamese cats that were about to swallow a canary whole.

I was the canary. I knew that before I even sat down for the interview. But I truly thought kindness had the power to change the trajectory of one's day. Not in this case, clearly.

"Ew." Cute Outfit, who was only a few years older than me, twisted her contoured nose. "How adorable that you think I'd take that as a compliment."

What?

"My name is Stassia, and this here is Tara."

Her colleague, whose hair held the same blond hue of champagne, pouted at my printed CV.

"So what made you think you could work at Beaufort, Miss Casablancas?"

"Well, I—"

"Is it really true that you've worked at a *diner* your whole life?" Tara burst out before I could answer the first question, a snide giggle tugging at her lips.

My gaze skidded between them uncertainly. Panic flared,

pressing against my rib cage. This wasn't an interview. This was a bored mean-girl setup. A way for them to pass the time during lunch break. And I'd walked right into it.

"I, uh, I think on my feet…"

"See, that's gonna be an issue, because we're looking for someone who can think with their *brain*." Stassia tapped her temple with a shellacked fingernail.

I curled my own beat-up, short fingernails into my palms, hiding them. I wished I could hide myself. "It's a turn of phrase," I said flatly.

"How lovely you know those, considering you didn't even go to college." Tara's put-on sugary tone was faker than her lips.

The next ten minutes were extremely painful. I pushed myself through the interview, determined not to stand up and leave halfway through. My heart sank lower, like an abandoned ship, drowning deeper with each cutting word and patronizing joke.

This was the only interview I'd been invited to after sending more than three hundred applications. I'd thrown a wide net too, applying for positions in marketing, sales, and administration. This was beyond bad. It was catastrophic. How was I supposed to pay for my life once my deal with Rhyland was over?

And yet I didn't stand up and walk away. Didn't give them the pleasure of seeing me break. I sat through the whole thing, even tossing a few quips their way myself.

"Well, this was fun." Tara and Stassia stood up in unison, smoothing down their preppy dresses with seamless choreography. "Don't call us—we'll call you."

"Doubt it," I murmured under my breath, inwardly furious with myself for thinking I'd stood a chance at getting this job.

They obviously heard me, because they exchanged amused looks, pressing their hands to their mouths and giggling as they turned their backs on me.

I stumbled out of the gorgeous building to the Manhattan sun and the pulse of the city—cars, tourists, businesspeople, food carts—beating against my skin.

I couldn't breathe.

I'd never had a panic attack before, so I couldn't tell if I was having one now. I just knew the world was spinning out of focus, blurring at the edges, like a photo being devoured by fire.

Snap out of it. You can't afford to be weak. You have Gravity to think about.

I grabbed my phone and texted Rhyland. I didn't want to call. I knew there was a good chance I'd burst into tears if I heard another human voice.

> Dylan: Is Grav okay?
> Rhyland: She is fine. I, however, want to fling myself out the window. She talks constantly. About the dumbest shit. Extorted me twice before noon. Threw three public tantrums. Chased after a dog instead of vice versa. I'm 99.5% sure I got all my cardio for the week running after her.

A smile tugged at my lips. Maybe having him as a neighbor wasn't the worst thing to happen to me.

> Dylan: Welcome to toddlerhood.
> Rhyland: Forget welcome. When am I seeing the farewell sign?
> Dylan: So...this is probably not the right time to ask you this. I just got out of the job interview, but I need a little time to clear my head. Can you stay for another hour?
> Rhyland: $%^^$#@@#%&&
> Rhyland: Everything okay?
> Dylan: Yeah. I just need a second to collect my thoughts.

> Rhyland: Do you need a dick pic to brighten up your day? Just because we can't hook up doesn't mean I'm not charitable.
> Dylan: Drop dead.
> Rhyland: It was worth a try.
> Rhyland: Stay safe.
> Dylan: What do you care?
> Rhyland: If something happens to you, I won't survive taking care of this kid until a family member comes to pick it up.

Did he just refer to my daughter as "it"? All the same, I knew I couldn't face my child right now without her seeing the defeat and utter desperation on my face.

In the end, I didn't take an hour. I took three.

Walking aimlessly through the city. Weaving in and out of crowds. Disappearing in the mass of human bodies. New York made me feel anonymous and small, and for a fraction of time, I wasn't Dylan—single mom, waitress, the second, problem child of Zeta Casablancas—I was just another face. Storiless and enigmatic. Someone who wasn't invited to an interview across town just to get humiliated. Someone who maybe had her shit together. Someone who could've had a degree and a job and maybe even a boyfriend.

At around three thirty, I called Kieran. He answered with his usual greeting of, "Have you changed your mind about marrying me?"

"Kieran..."

He ignored me. "My agent just told me he's fixing me up with a *Hollyoaks* actress who was a contestant on *The Weakest Link* for charity and got kicked out in the first round for thinking

Australia had a border with Slovakia and Switzerland. Should I kill myself?"

I sighed, slumping against a building. *"Kieran."*

"That's a yes."

I said nothing.

"Oh shit, you're quiet. You're never quiet." His tone changed. "I know what this means. Who am I killing?"

I told him about the interview. About my aimless wandering. About how I now knew my place was not in an office doing marketing or an admin job. I wouldn't be able to handle it. The fakeness. The politics. Spending my entire day in an air-conditioned box just to keep the capitalistic blaze burning.

"I feel so bad for Grav," I groaned. "She has a clueless mom and a father she's never met because he's too much of an asshole to care about her." The words rushed out of me. "She's never going to have anyone to fall back on if I don't pull myself together."

Thick silence came from the other end of the line before Kieran spoke. "You need a drink."

"No shit," I scoffed.

"No, like, you need to restart your brain. You are obviously going through a small panic attack."

"I knew it," I cried out. "My skin is breaking out in hives. What do I do, Kieran? I'm five seconds from taking you up on your fake-marriage offer I'm so stressed."

"First of all, thank you," he said sarcastically. "Second, there's a bar not far from your new building. The Alchemist. They make the best cocktails. Listen to me carefully now, Dyl. I want you to go there, order yourself the Roku Koori Negroni with a piece of carrot cake, meditate for a few minutes, and think about what you want to do with your life. *Nothing* is off the table. Don't be practical. Be passionate. Even if you think it's too late. Even if you think it's too hard. Then call me and let me know what it is, okay?"

"Okay," I panted. "Okay."

CHAPTER THIRTEEN
DYLAN

I arrived at the Alchemist ten minutes later. It was a trendy bar two blocks down from my apartment. I felt bad for leaving Rhyland with Grav all day. At the same time, I knew they were okay, or he'd have called me.

The bar was full to the brim, crammed with sweaty bodies and grinding couples, most of them clearly out-of-towners. The tang of smoke, sweat, and expensive alcohol crawled into my nostrils. I snagged the only available stool at the bar and ordered Kieran's fancy drink and carrot cake. He knew this place, which meant he frequented it with my brother, Rhyland, and maybe their friend Tate. I tried not to think about how everyone around me had this glamorous, debauched, in-the-know lifestyle while I'd been stuck in a tiny Maine town serving over-fried eggs and watching *Peppa Pig*.

The bartender, a woman with a shaved head, two sleeves of tattoos, and a black crop top, slid my cake and drink across a sticky bar. "Enjoy."

"Is it always so crowded in here?" I looked around. I hadn't contemplated bar work in New York, but the tips must be through the roof.

"Happy hour." She grimaced, her jestrum piercing sparkling. "It can get pretty overwhelming at times." The sheen of sweat making her face gleam confirmed her observation. Her eyes were dull and unfocused.

I instinctively shot out my hand to clasp hers. "Hey, are you okay?"

She nodded. "Yeah."

I closed my eyes and tried to imagine my perfect career. I remembered Kieran's advice not to be practical, to be passionate. It came to me like a mirage, with vivid clarity.

Me. In a doctor's uniform. Making a change.

Ushering an injured child on a gurney. Into a theater.

Performing surgery. Steel hands. Cool-headed.

I reached for my drink with my eyes still closed, taking a sip. The whiskey prickled my tongue deliciously. I smiled. Another vision sifted through my jumbled thoughts.

Me. Making the rounds to see my patients, with a clipboard pressed to my chest.

Reassuring worried parents.

Comforting distressed children.

I want to be a doctor.

I'd *always* wanted to be a doctor.

It was there in the back of my head, a pipe dream that could never materialize.

I opened my eyes, and the first thing in front of me was the bartender, now clutching the edge of the bar. Her pupils were the size of soup bowls.

"Are you sure you're okay?" I asked.

"I'm feeling a little dizzy..." She blinked slowly. "Like my heart is beating out of whack." She reached for her head, and before I knew it, her eyes had rolled over in their sockets, and she was falling to the floor with a thud. The noise and the music drowned out her fall.

I immediately sprang into action. I jumped across the bar, knocking down my cocktail and my cake in the process, then I crouched down to check her pulse. There wasn't one.

Crap.

The bartender next to her—a man in his fifties—stared at me helplessly, holding two beers in his hands.

"Call 911," I ordered him.

He nodded, dropped everything, and took out his phone.

Luckily, I'd done a CPR course when Grav was born. I began alternating between chest compressions and mouth-to-mouth. The other bartender came to stand over me.

"Oh fuck, oh fuck. Faye is my best bartender. Is she going to be okay?"

"I don't know," I said honestly, timing my chest compressions. "Did you call 911?"

"Yeah. They asked me a bunch of questions. I…I told them to just come. They should be here any minute."

I checked her heartbeat against her neck again. This time, there was a faint pulse. My shoulders slumped with relief. The adrenaline coursing through my body made me feel almost drunk.

The doors to the bar flew open, and a member of the medical staff rushed in. The older bartender was too stunned to talk to him, so I had to explain what had happened. Faye was rushed out on a gurney, and I wondered if this was some kind of sign I needed to pursue my dream to become a doctor.

The bartender clasped a hand on my shoulder. "Thank you for doing that. *Shit.* I panicked. I can't believe I blurted out about her job when her life was in danger."

"No problem." I turned to smile at him, standing up. "People say weird stuff when they're stressed."

"Are you a nurse or something?" He eyed me curiously.

"Nope. Worked in restaurants my whole life, actually."

"So how did you know how to do…it?" He looked confused.

"What, CPR?" I chuckled. "I took a course before I had my daughter. You know, just in case."

He nodded. "Well, suffice it to say, your drink and your cake are on the house."

"Thanks." I glanced around. "So...do you need any help here? It seems busy, and you are one bartender short."

"Sure do," he grunted. "There's a recipe menu in the drawer right next to you. I'll pay you double what I pay hourly if you save my ass today."

I pushed up my sleeves and got to work after sending Rhyland a quick text message. The drinks were complicated and the recipes hard to follow—it was called the Alchemist for a reason—but most customers wanted the usual staples of beer or wine. The tip jar overflowed so many times we had to empty it into a bucket every hour. It was decent work that would help me finance a good, hands-on nanny for Grav while I worked.

Med school, though romantic, was no longer in the cards for me.

"Dylan," the bartender—who turned out to be the owner, Max—hollered at me. "Your shift ends in ten minutes. I'll Zelle you the money. You wanna take the rest of Faye's shifts for the week?"

"Text me the schedule. I'll see if I have childcare."

And then I was off, a thousand dollars less poor after the tip split. The clock read 6:45 p.m., and I knew I owed Rhyland a lot of answers and an apology.

I pushed the door open, about to pour myself out onto the street, when a hard body slammed into mine. My hands shot out to his chest. Muscular pecs that felt familiar beneath my fingertips bumped into me. My stare volleyed up like a bullet to his face. Patrician nose. Dark blue eyes I knew well, because once upon a time, they'd stared back at me every day.

"Dylan," he gasped.

"Tucker?"

Just when I thought the day couldn't possibly get worse.

"Wait." Tucker steadied me, clutching my arms and anchoring me in place. "D-don't go."

"What are you doing here?" I jolted away from his touch as though it were made of liquid fire. The father of my child—who wasn't really a father and acted *like* a child, hadn't seen her once since she was born, and had screwed off to God knows where—was here in New York.

Here in the bar I was visiting for the first time in my life.

Had he been here this whole time, right across the street? What were the odds?

Good, if Kieran knew he'd be here and orchestrated the entire thing.

"Babe, shit, you look so good." He stuck a hand in his hair, which was still lush brown, thick, and unfairly glossy. "I work here as a bartender." Tucker's eyes roved over me like restless hands. "Kieran told you to seek me out, huh?" He smirked smugly, and I wanted to kill him and Kieran and every man I knew. "I wanted to reach out—"

"But you didn't." I tried to stay calm, but it was hard to do when all I wanted was to claw his eyes out. "You ran away, and now you don't even know what your daughter looks like. What her hobbies are. Her dreams. Her allergies." I wanted to shoulder past him, to leave him here, stewing in this realization. If he even cared at all. Instead, a vicious thrill crawled through me, settling like a hand on my throat and squeezing venomous words out of it. "She has your eyes, you know," I sneered. "Big and blue and curtained with thick lashes."

His nostrils flared, mouth pressing into a thin line. Was he angry? Upset? Annoyed? Emotional? I couldn't tell.

I continued. "She's allergic to kiwi, just like you. She's athletic. Got it from both of us. Superfast and tumbles the best in her age group in gymnastics. She knows how to count to one hundred, how to read, how to draw a three-dimensional box. She'll be four in December and is already as advanced as a seven-year-old. She is *smart*. And cunning. I got a message from her sitter today that she extorted him twice." I didn't take a breath, didn't stop the rush of words from streaming out of my mouth like a troubled river. "She's so eloquent, so bright. She's beautiful and loving and warm—"

"I want to meet her." He reached out to touch me again. I zapped his hand away. A few people squeezed past us on their way out of the bar. "Dyl, *fuck*, you look so good. I missed you so—"

"Her name is Gravity." I ignored his words.

"I know," he said dispassionately, still eye-fucking me. "My parents told me."

His parents didn't stay in town after he ran away. They moved to Montana. They'd only seen Grav once.

Tucker's gaze broke away from mine, landing on my hand and the diamond that sparkled on my finger. Smothering darkness fell over his face. I knew this look. He was furious.

"Are you…" He didn't finish the question.

"Oh yes," I confirmed, waiting to feel triumphant, redeemed, or just a little less humiliated, but that victorious feeling never came. "I'm engaged to Rhyland Coltridge. Remember him?"

A muscle jumped in Tucker's jaw. I tried not to flinch. His anger always upset me. It was like a dark cloud following every decent moment in our relationship. And still, my big, feisty mouth couldn't help itself. I wanted to rile him up.

"I always thought he was hot. Had a thing for him growing up." A croupy laugh bubbled out of me. "Actually, remember that night we first hooked up? That was because he rejected me. It was always him. Everything worked out fine in the end."

It was the same night I went ballistic over Cal and Row having sex behind my back. Definitely something I wanted to forget.

"No, it didn't," he said tightly, his monotonous, clipped voice sounding extra harsh in my ears. "You belong with me. You and my kid."

Gravity, you asshole. That's her name.

"You're high if you believe your own words," I informed him.

He ignored me, shaking his head. "I deserve a second chance. I freaked out. I wasn't ready…"

Holding back tears, I jerked my trembling chin up. "Well, you can't meet her. You don't deserve her. Never have."

"Don't be a bitch. I'm trying to do the right thing here."

"Are you kidding me? A second ago, you were fine not knowing whether she was alive or not." I tried to sidestep him again.

"But now you're here, and—"

"And it doesn't change anything," I bit out. "You're still a stranger, and I still don't want you anywhere near *my* daughter." I squeezed past him.

"God dammit, Dylan, why do you always have to be so difficult?" He snatched my wrist as I fled, digging his fingers into my delicate skin and yanking me back.

My back crashed against the wall, the little stones in it digging into my spine. The pain knocked my breath away. I tried to jerk away, but it was too late. A ring of white-hot ache formed over the fragile bones in my hand. I looked up at him, shocked.

"I didn't mean to." He dumped my hand suddenly, and it crashed against the wall, which hurt even more. "Hey, don't look at me like I attacked you or whatever. You can't just up and fucking leave in the middle of a grown-up conversation, Dylan."

The pain still reverberated all over my wrist.

"You've always been so flighty." He chuckled to himself. "Anyway, so—"

I stormed off into the night.

Whatever calm I'd tried to maintain today evaporated like mist. My dreamless life had just turned into a nightmare.

CHAPTER FOURTEEN
RHYLAND

Her Highness returned to her apartment at 7:30 p.m. to find me slumped on the couch belly-down, her child sitting on my back making biscuits out of my hair. It was sometime around half an hour ago that I realized Gravity didn't know how to braid and was winging it, turning my hair into one giant knot. I'd have to shave my head completely after she was done with it. But being bald was a small price to pay to keep her calm and in the same spot for more than ten seconds flat.

"Mommy!" The child jumped up, stepping over my head in the process of running to her mother.

Dylan picked her up and flung her in the air, spinning her and nuzzling into her neck. They shared a five-minute conversation in high-pitched, ridiculous voices in which Dylan found out Gravity had spent her day eating McDonald's, getting temporary tattoos, scribbling all over her new bed frame, and watching *Family Guy*.

Dylan seemed strangely subdued and unaffected by my version of child-rearing, even when her child attempted to fart the alphabet using her hand and her armpit. Her eyes also looked puffy. I'd think she'd been crying, but I knew Dylan, and that bad bitch didn't even cry when her father died, when Tucker left her, or during childbirth. She was no crier.

"Did Uncle Rhyland give you a bath and dinner?" Dylan brushed her kid's hair with her fingers.

"Kentucky Fried Chicken!" the child gurgled. "Mommy, Mommy, he let me dunk my chicken in the beans and then in the milkshake, and we ate it, because he said everything ends up in the same place anyway!"

"Uh-huh."

"Oh, and I did bath with my Barbies."

"*So* cool. Why don't you brush your teeth and pick your bedtime story?" Dylan suggested warmly. "Mommy needs to talk to Uncle Rhyland a little."

Gravity charged toward the corridor, where she disappeared into her room.

"Where the fuck were y—" I turned to Dylan, fully prepared to give her a piece of my mind, but the minute her child was no longer in the room, her shoulders slumped and her face fell. The rest of the word perished in my throat. Her olive skin paled, her eyes sunk into two dark hollows, and her nose became red as tears drenched her cheeks.

Was this how a real parent behaved—mastering the art of prioritizing someone else even when they wanted to fall apart? I'd never seen Dylan like this. She was always the most stubborn, proud, fearless woman I knew. And I guess she'd stayed that way. But only for her daughter.

"What happened?" I demanded, a thunderstorm rolling over my temper. Up until a second ago, I'd been inconvenienced. Now, I was pissed. Row was going to rip me a new one if something had happened to his baby sister under my watch.

Instead of answering me, Dylan threw herself at me, burying her face in my neck and encircling me with her arms. She started sobbing uncontrollably, the kind of hiccupy, breathless bawling that ripped your heart out even if you didn't possess one. My knee-jerk reaction was to hurl her to the couch and bolt. I forced myself to stay still. She needed someone. Guess that someone was me. Soon my neck was wet and warm with her tears, and I couldn't help it: I wrapped my arms around her, bringing her close to my chest.

I'd never held a woman like this. Never been held like this either.

I was a stoic kid—independent, gruff, a rule follower, and above all, a selfish bastard. My parents weren't affectionate outside their own dazzling marriage, and the best lesson they taught me was that love had the tendency to quickly turn into an all-consuming obsession, a mutant of insanity, so I stayed the hell away from it.

Growing up, I didn't have girlfriends or relationships or anything that resembled intimacy. I had sex. Lots of it. But I'd always been up-front about what I was offering—a good time, a perfect date (if you could afford my rate)—nothing more, nothing less.

Her stomach grumbled between us. She hadn't eaten. Where the hell had she been for seven, almost eight hours?

I untangled myself from her, waltzing over to the state-of-the-art kitchen. "You need a tall glass of whatever the fuck has the most alcohol in it and a hearty meal." I tried to relax my jaw before it snapped and shot out of the Milky Way. I reached straight for the good whiskey in Row's bar cart, pouring a generous amount into two tumblers.

"I didn't realize you knew how to cook," she sniffled, and I caught her in my periphery wiping her eyes quickly.

"I don't," I reassured her, "but I am fucking excellent with my phone and the DoorDash app."

"I still need to put Grav to bed and take a shower…" She trailed off.

I spun around and handed her the drink I'd fixed for her. "Down a quarter. Now."

She took a shaky sip but didn't sass back this time.

"The child can wait."

"Stop calling her *the child* like she's something that needs to be extorted," she scoffed, the color returning to her cheeks. "And it's already past her bedtime. I promised her a story."

"I'll let her play a game on my phone."

"She doesn't know how to play mobile games."

"She does now," I confessed.

Dylan's jaw went slack. She looked ready to pluck my nuts with a pair of tweezers.

"Hey, I was in survival mode, okay?" I grabbed her shoulders and swiveled her toward the hallway, physically escorting her to the master bedroom. "Go take your bath—I'll order us food. I'll read the chil—*Gravity* a bedtime story." What difference did it make? I'd already wasted my entire day on the kid.

Dylan was reluctant to move, hugging her midriff. "She also needs a good-night kiss."

"Consider it done."

"And words of affirmation."

"Uh-huh."

"And…and…"

"Dylan." I clutched her shoulders, forcing eye contact on her. "*Go.*"

I read the child Gravity a surprisingly entertaining book called *I Need a New Butt*. As far as I was concerned, it was the height of literature. Fart jokes? Check. Crack jokes? Check. Stupid pranks? Check. The kid was draining, but at least she had good taste in books. I then threw a blanket over her like I was putting out a fire.

"G'night."

"Uncle Rhyrand, you forgot my good-night kiss."

Internally gagging like a cat with a hair ball stuck in its airway, I leaned down and pressed my lips to her forehead. She had that tiny-human smell, somewhere between baked goods and a warm, fluffy pillow. I stood up. She blinked back at me in the dark. *"Don't forget words of affirmation, asshole."* Dylan's words echoed in my head. Even in my head, she was busting my balls.

Also, *crap*. What should I say? I didn't know this child, and whatever I knew didn't exactly impress me.

"Let's see. You…uh, aren't too annoying for a kid?"

She tilted her head, searching my face through heavy-lidded blinks.

"I like that you are potty-trained," I offered. "I'd hate to change your diaper."

She curled her lips inward. "Mommy's better at this."

I sighed, searching my brain for something, *anything*, that was genuine and positive about her.

"You're funny," I sighed. "You make me laugh. You outran that greyhound, which was fuc—*fully* impressive. If I weren't so exhausted from today, I'd say it wasn't terrible."

She grinned, small white canine teeth flashing in the dark. "You wanted to say a bad word."

"No, I didn't. Now you're just projecting." Was I gaslighting a three-year-old?

"What?" She cocked her head on her pillow. The room still smelled of freshly shaved wood and crayons.

"Nothing. Good night, rascal." I tousled her hair.

When I turned around, Dylan was there at the door, staring at us, transfixed. I strode past her, ignoring whatever was stuck in my throat. Maybe I was allergic to children. I needed a Zyrtec if I was gonna babysit this kid on a weekly basis.

"Rhyland…" Dylan followed me, and I stopped at the dining table, ripping open the brown bag containing our DoorDash: triple burgers with crinkle-cut fries and two strawberry Oreo milkshakes. "Thank you for today."

"Don't mention it." I shoved four fries into my mouth, taking a pull of my milkshake. "Seriously. *Don't*. I'm fucking traumatized here. This is how people live with toddlers? Day in and day out? How are we not, like, extinct?"

She snorted out a quiet laugh, grabbing us plates and utensils from the kitchen. When she opened the drawer to grab a knife to poke through the sealed sauces, it pricked the tip of her finger. "*Ugh. Fuck me,*" she hissed, sucking the blood off her finger.

"Sure. Your kid'll probably hear us, but I'm more than happy to foot the therapy bill." I popped a fry into my mouth. "I'm chivalrous, which you'll learn to appreciate as our fake engagement progresses."

"Don't let your mouth write checks your ass can't pay," she sighed tiredly.

If you knew what my mouth was capable of, I'd be eating more than just a burger.

But she was right. We needed to be good and boring so as not to upset her grizzly bear of a brother. *Or* blow my impending deal. Couldn't risk a runaway bride.

We alternated between whiskey, milkshake, and food as she told me about Tara and Stassia and the way they'd degraded her for thirty minutes before sending her on her way. My blood boiled, then chilled to ice when she talked about how she'd saved the life of a bartender who'd had a heart attack and somehow ended up replacing her for the remainder of her shift.

The crux of the biscuit was the news Tucker was in town and working at the Alchemist.

"Did you know he worked there?" Dylan eyed me with suspicion, dunking two fries into her milkshake and tossing them into her mouth—which, I'm sorry, was the height of vulgarity. No one was perfect, I guess. Though Dylan came close, with those long legs and that peach-shaped ass. One couldn't expect her not to have such culinary quirks.

"No." I sipped my whiskey. "Whenever Row's in town, we go to the gastropub down the road."

"How come Kieran knew he'd be there? This wasn't a coincidence." Dylan frowned.

"He must've seen him the last time he swung by." I swallowed half my burger in one bite. "Kieran stays at the Plaza, not too far from here. Asshole probably thought he was doing you a favor by bringing Gravity's dad back into your life."

"He knows how much I detest him." Dylan sniffed.

"Kieran thinks he's smarter than God himself," I reminded her. "Just pretend that shit didn't happen, and move on with your life. Nothing good ever came out of Tucker."

"Other than Gravity," Dylan corrected, dipping more fries into her milkshake.

I visibly shuddered.

"Everything okay?" She frowned.

"You tell me. You dip your fries into your milkshake."

She shot me a steadfast look. "What's the problem? Weren't you the one who taught my daughter it all ends up in the same place anyway?"

"I said what needed to be said to make the little stinker eat. I don't know where she gets all that energy from. She runs on pissing me off and applesauce," I pointed out. "By that logic, it's okay to eat turd, because that's what your food turns into."

Her eyebrows shot to her hairline. "I see you've mastered the art of small talk. No wonder women pay a small fortune for you to date them."

That drew a snort out of me. "I'm off duty now. I can be my real self."

"They'd want someone else?" She studied me tiredly.

I wasn't in the mood to dig into my own bullshit, but taking her mind off her good-for-nothing ex was probably a good idea.

An indulgent smile puckered my lips. "They paid top buck, sweetheart. They got the fantasy. The real deal. I was the most attentive, sappy, possessive, gallant man on the continent."

"Did you sleep with all of them?" She licked her lips, tracing her tongue along a spot of mayo. I imagined doing it myself and stifled a pained groan.

"No, not all of them," I admitted. "And I was up-front about it with those I wasn't interested in screwing. Most of the time, though, they weren't interested in more than a fake relationship, too battered from whatever had made them hire me in the first place to want to sleep with another man." I sniffed. "Otherwise, yeah. I had sex with a lot of them and got paid for it. Low-hanging fruit is usually ripe and easy to bite into. And I didn't have the time nor the inclination to look for hookups after spending all my time playing pretend."

That is until someone took liberties I didn't offer.

"Anyway, have you decided what you want to do in New York?" I needed to nudge her into finding a job, because I was dropping her ass as soon as Bruce signed on the dotted line.

"Not yet, but I agreed to work at the Alchemist for a while."

"The fuck you did." I choked on my burger, coughing out a piece of pickle. "Tucker works there."

"Yes, I'm aware." She sat up straighter, the defiant zing returning to her dark eyes. "I'm not going to turn down a perfectly good job offer because of that bastard. I already lost so much because of him. Skipping this opportunity would be letting him win again."

"Dylan." I leaned forward, putting my hand on her shoulder to catch her attention. I didn't expect the jolt of electricity that ricocheted between us, nor the shudder that rolled across her skin and made her retreat from my touch. "I can't afford to subsidize your ass past the terms of our deal," I explained honestly. "I don't have those kinds of funds."

"I'm not expecting you to." Pink budded across her cheeks, and her right brow arched. "Which is why I took this position."

"Your ex aside? You need something sustainable, with regular hours. An actual profession. Go study something. Chase your dreams."

"No point. I'll never outrun them." She grabbed the empty paper bag, tossing our leftovers into it. "I had my chance, and I blew it. I could've had my pick of any college. I chose to serve sunny-side-ups and clean coffee stains from sticky floors. What's not to understand?"

"You're a bright kid. You have potent—"

"Please." She rolled her eyes, shooting up to her feet and walking over to deposit the bag in the trash. "Spare me. Studying requires money and childcare. I have neither. Being a single mom is like arriving to battle with one hand tied behind your back. I'll forever be in survival mode." She hugged herself, a brittle note to her tone. "You have no idea what it's like, to feel homesick for a place you've yet to create. To watch people fall in and out of love from the sidelines and know that part of life is off-limits to you. To double- and triple-guess yourself, because every decision you make also affects your kid. I'm just trying to get by. Bartending will help me do that. I can't afford to give up this work, because no one can promise me I'll get another chance at employment here."

It was then, when she was hugging herself, that I noticed it. The mauve-purple ring of finger dents circling her small wrist. It looked like the spot was going to become swollen too.

Her eyes followed my gaze, and she tucked her hand behind her back.

"Who did that to you?" My tone was deadly lethal, even to my own ears.

"Oh, this?" She snorted, massaging the spot softly before wincing in pain and dropping her hand. "It's nothing. I was in a rush and..." The rest died in her throat.

"And?" I coaxed, my tone so cold she shivered.

"I fell—"

"Never lie to me, Dylan," I warned. "I can tolerate a whole fucking lot, but I don't do well with liars. Why are there fingerprints on your skin?"

"It was a mistake, okay?" she hissed out. "Tucker's never hurt me before. Physically, I mean. Psychologically, he's murdered me about a hundred times." A humorless laugh escaped her.

"Tucker did this?"

"Accidentally."

"You can't be fucking serious." I didn't recognize my own voice, it was so thick and groggy. "He touched you? That motherfuck—"

"Leave it." She reached out to squeeze my arm. Our eyes locked. It was the first time I'd allowed myself to see her—*really* see her—since she came to New York. Normally, when we looked at people, we looked through them too. But not right now. My entire attention was on her.

Dylan, the rebel. The dreamer. The potty-mouthed kid who grew up to be Staindrop's hottest bombshell. Dylan, the smart. Dylan, the impulsive. Dylan, the mother. The daughter.

The sister, I reminded myself. *Your best friend's.*

But it was too late. Her hair was so richly dark it was burnished red under the superficial light, her beauty so violent it threatened to detonate like a supernova, leaving stardust everywhere. I couldn't help it. I wanted her in the same way a starving man wanted his next meal. Some men were into ass, boobs, or legs. Me? I was a spine kind of person. And she had plenty of it.

"Tucker can go fuck himself a million times over," she whispered, tapering her eyes. "If taking a job at this joint means I'll be able to afford a good nanny, nourishing food, and books for my daughter, a better future for her, I'll do it. No one—not Tucker, not Row, not my mother, not you—will stand in my way. There isn't a thing I won't do for my daughter. You'd best remember that."

CHAPTER FIFTEEN
RHYLAND

> Row: Are you taking good care of my sister?
> Rhyland: Good enough that I demand a raise.
> Row: What'd she get herself into?
> Rhyland: It's her story to tell.
> Row: Are you already this loyal to her?
> Rhyland: No, fuckface, I'm just too lazy/unbothered to type all that shit down.

I called Tate as soon as I left Dylan's apartment. He answered on the third ring.

"Do you have a minute?" I grunted out.

"No," Tate said flatly, "though I'm sure it won't stop you. It never has in the past. What do you want?"

"You still hold the majority of shares at Beaufort?" I cut straight to the chase, stepping into the elevator and trying to keep my temper in fucking check. Tucker had hurt Dylan. And while she wasn't my woman, she was still a woman, and he was still a man, and this whole thing was still majorly fucked up.

"Who wants to know?" Tate inquired taciturnly.

"Me, fucker. Who else?"

He made an uncommitted grumble. "How—or more importantly, *why*—should I help you with that?"

"I need you to get two people fired. Stassia and Tara from the marketing department. Low-level folk. Easily replaceable." I punched the button taking the elevator down, not up. My subconscious had already made a decision that would probably land me a night in the slammer. Ah well. You only lived once, and that was one experience to cross off my bucket list.

"I see." His icy drawl gave my ear frostbite. The crane descended down. "Not that I ever miss a chance to ruin someone's day, but may I ask what they did to earn such a visceral reaction from the laziest pothead I know?"

"They basically invited Dylan over for a job interview just to bully and belittle her," I blustered before considering Dylan might not want me to air her shit publicly. I usually thought things through before I spoke. This was out of character for me. But so was spending ten fucking hours straight with a three-year-old. If this was what they meant by "doing some growing," then no, thanks. I wanted to stay mentally fifteen.

"And you care because…" Tate yawned.

"Row," I scoffed. "I care because she is my best friend's sister, and he's riding my ass about taking care of her while she settles in."

"She's a big girl."

"Did I ask you for an observation?" I inquired.

"And as much as we like Row—which is not very much in my case and a decent amount in yours—you shouldn't care *that* much about his grown-ass sibling."

In the back of my head, I knew he had a point, but I refused to see it. Unlike him, I was selfish but not sociopathic. I still managed to feel bad for other people.

"Are you going to do it or not?" I snapped.

"I'll see to it, but you're going to owe me, and I always collect," Tate said crisply.

"Yes, I remember. Forty-two percent interest, right?"

"Fifty percent in your case, since I don't like your face."

I hung up before he could say anything else. I'd made a deal with the devil just to spite two meaningless bitches I didn't even know.

And I didn't regret it one bit.

I grew up as an only child. My parents loved each other too much to spare leftover affection for anyone else, so I never had the pleasure of dislocating anyone's jaw or nose for mistreating my sister. I'd always envied Row when he defended Dylan's honor. There was nothing quite as therapeutic as throwing a few well-earned punches after a long, hard day.

Another thing that was long and hard right now: my cock, after being in close quarters with my best friend's sister.

Violence was sex's ugly cousin, the Sweet'N Low to its pure, untainted sugar. But it'd have to do for now.

I pushed open the door to the Alchemist, slipping into the loud, darkened room. I spotted Tucker behind the bar. He hadn't changed much, save for getting more ripped and growing some stubble. He was mixing neon-colored drinks and flirting up a storm with a few leggy patrons. I found a place in the corner of the room, ordered a Peroni, and waited, watching him closely. Patience, I suddenly had. Bloodthirst too.

I grabbed my phone and sifted through some emails while I waited. Between junk mail, pleas from former clients begging me to un-retire so they could flash a fake boyfriend at a wedding or a funeral, and emails from potential investors was an email from Bruce's secretary. I clicked on it, my heart staggering its way out of my throat.

Dear Mr. Coltridge,

As per your meeting with Bruce earlier this week, Mr. Marshall has expressed an interest in hosting you and your fiancée at his farmhouse on the outskirts of Dallas three weeks from today.

Mr. and Mrs. Marshall would love to have your fiancée and her daughter as guests, show everyone some Southern hospitality, and discuss business as well as examine if you fit the Marshall Corp family and its uncompromised values.

You will be provided with private accommodation in Mr. Marshall's farmhouse should you accept.

Please let me know if the time and date suits you. If so, Mr. Marshall will see to your transportation arrangements.

Do not hesitate to contact me should you have any questions.

Faithfully,
Portia

Orgasmic triumph flooded me. *Finally.*

Marshall wanted to close the deal and wanted to spend more time together. I wasn't excited to pay Dylan for three more weeks, but I was sure as fuck thrilled to see the end was near, for both our sakes. I quickly typed out my acceptance of the invitation and opened a text box with Dylan. She'd had a crap-a-licious day, but not through my fault, so I didn't want to wait until tomorrow to break the inconvenient news to her.

Besides, I'd already filled my quota of being a great fake fiancé for the year.

> Rhyland: Just got word from Bruce. He invited us to his house for a weekend in three weeks. Save the date.
> Dylan: Seriously?
> Rhyland: I never joke about the prospect of becoming four hundred million dollars richer.
> Dylan: I hate it here.

> Rhyland: Tough luck, Cosmos. For the money I pay you, you should show up in a gingham dress with a homemade cherry pie, braids, two first names, and your knees ready to be scraped at a moment's notice.

My breath hitched. Was that last description really necessary? No.

Could I think about something that wasn't my cock inside her smart mouth? Also no.

> Dylan: That is a shockingly detailed kink.
> Dylan: I'm happy to report I do, in fact, own a gingham dress, know how to make a cherry pie, and give the best oral sex.
> Dylan: As for the braids, I'll have to charge extra for that. They make me look hella young.

My eyes rolled inside their sockets, my rock-hard cock muscling its way past my zipper, begging to break free. I'd thought eight years would dull out that incident when I almost took her in her tiny kitchen, but they hadn't.

> Rhyland: Forget the braids. Your hair will be in my fis

I erased the entire text message. What was I thinking? This couldn't happen.

> Dylan: Uh-huh. You typed then deleted. Dead giveaway you're breaking.

It didn't help that Dylan had the instincts of a panther and the bloodlust of a piranha. I stared at the screen and grinned like an idiot.

Dylan: The offer still stands.

Dylan: So is your cock, I'm willing to bet.

Dylan: No strings attached ofc.

Rhyland: I'm trying to do the right thing here for a change.

Dylan: Why? The wrong thing's always more fun.

I brought my fist to my mouth, biting it to stifle a groan. Checked my watch. Ten minutes before the bar closed and Tucker was let off. Good. I needed a distraction.

Rhyland: I thought you hated me.

Dylan: I do. I'm also horny and single. And I heard enemies-to-lovers is the best trope for sex.

Rhyland: Wouldn't know. Never felt anything for anyone I slept with.

Dylan: That's low-key sad.

No. What was sad was that we weren't having this conversation face-to-face so I could see her olive skin growing scarlet, her heavy eyelashes fanning her cheeks, and her chest rising and falling to the rhythm of her pulse.

Rhyland: Neither have you.

Dylan: Excuse me?

Rhyland: You've never slept with someone you love either, Cosmos. I know, because you told me you fucked Tucker on the day I acted like an ass to you (sorry about that, by the way. What was I to do? Tell Row my cock had bested my mind and I'd decided to get a piece of his sister?). And I know for a fact you haven't had anyone else since that asshole.

Rhyland: And you didn't love Tucker. Everyone knew

> that. Even you. He was just a way to pass the time that got complicated when you got knocked up.

I stared at the screen for a few minutes. No answer. I'd touched a nerve. I decided to dig a little deeper.

> Rhyland: Was he at least good in bed?

I was going to deserve the beating Row was destined to give me, no doubt. I'd just earned the first few punches, and I'd gladly take them if it meant prolonging this conversation a little. It was my version of "just the tip."

Technically, we were just talking. No touching was involved. The dotted line danced on my screen, and I momentarily forgot to breathe and blink.

> Dylan: He was actually surprisingly decent, which was why I stayed with him for so long.
> Dylan: Gave GREAT head.

My stare grazed the man behind the bar, envisioning him eating her out. Suddenly, I didn't want to rough him up a little; I wanted to dismember him into three-inch pieces and feed him to zoo animals.

> Dylan: What about you? Who was your best?
> Rhyland: I don't think I've ever had a best. All my hookups were the same level of adequate.
> Dylan: And they say romance is dead.
> Rhyland: It is, though, Cosmos. Think about it. Everything that represents love—flowers, hearts, swans, doves—dies eventually.
> Dylan: Cosmos is such a terrible nickname. I get that

you have to do this because of the fake engagement,
but can't you find something cuter?
Rhyland: Such as?
Dylan: Kitten? Baby? Sweetie pie?
Rhyland: You're not a kitten and you are not a baby
(thank fuck). I've also met limes sweeter than you.
Dylan: Whatever happened to trying to pretend to like
each other?
Rhyland: The rules don't apply to me.
Dylan: Why?
Rhyland: BECAUSE I'M THE ONE WHO IS PAYING AN
ARM AND A LEG HERE, CASABLANCAS.

Tucker rang the overhead bell, signaling the end of the service, and I slipped out of my seat and outside to wait for him. It took another twenty minutes for him to emerge from the entryway of the bar, a backpack slung over his shoulders and a ball cap covering his eyes. I effortlessly snagged him by the collar and dragged him into the alleyway between the Alchemist and a boutique realty building. I slammed him into a nearby wall with enough force to create an impact. His skull thudded against the stone, and he spurted a surprised, "Shit, man, what the fuck?"

"The fuck is you are a fucking fuckwad." I snatched the lapels of his shirt with one hand, using the other to throw a sucker punch to his right eye. I let my fist sail through, straight to his nose, hearing a small but prominent crack. He was going to have to get it repositioned.

Row never got the chance to do this when Tucker ran away from Staindrop, so I considered it a personal favor. I also wanted to put the message across that there would be no more finger imprints or blue marks on Dylan.

"That was from Row," I announced cheerfully, watching Tucker moan as he reached to clutch his bleeding nose—side effect of the black eye I'd given him. "And this one's for Dylan." I kneed his stomach, making sure to stomp on his nuts in the hope he wouldn't be able to reproduce anymore. This I considered a national service.

Tucker folded over, a squeak escaping his lips. "Enough!" His nose spurted blood that trickled down his neck and his shirt. He tried to push me off, but I only crowded him further. "Enough, *please*."

"And finally, this one's from me." My fist landed flat against his cheek, sending his head backward again, against the wall.

He collapsed to the ground like a LEGO tower, arms shooting to his face to protect it. He wiggled like a fish out of water on the ground, trying pitifully to get to his feet and run. I considered kicking him in the ribs to drive the point home, but he looked so pathetic, shrimping into himself in whimpers, that I decided not to overdo it.

"Look, man." He spat dirt into the gravel, eyes clenched shut, and in that moment, I realized he was a coward through and through. A coward who didn't step up when the girl he'd impregnated needed him. A coward who couldn't even look me in the face. "I get it. You guys are engaged. I saw the ring. She told me. But you can't keep me away from my kid. I know my rights."

That gave me pause. But of course, Dylan had been wearing my engagement ring—why wouldn't he have jumped to the conclusion? And why would she have corrected him? I was paying her to play the dutiful fiancée. Plus, throwing a new relationship in his face must've been satisfying. It worked for us both in maintaining our deception.

I hooked a finger around the back of Tucker's shirt, tugging him to his feet. He staggered to the wall, plastering himself against it, still flinching.

"Relax." I fixed the collar of his shirt, which was now red, not blue, thanks to the injuries I'd inflicted. "I'm done putting my point across. Word to the wise—I sincerely don't appreciate when people fuck with my shit. Dylan came back home with blue bruises over her wrist. I trust this is the first and last time you'll tarnish what's mine."

I used the derogatory language deliberately. Men like Tucker only responded to toxic masculinity.

He jerked his chin in a sharp nod. "I never meant to hurt her."

"Good. Good." I clapped his shoulder a tad too aggressively, a serene smile stretched across my face. "Accidents happen. I get it. Like, if someone were to mess with what's mine again, even though I'd warned them, I could have an oopsie too, you know. Chop their fingers off to ensure it was the last time they hurt a woman or disrespected me. Being theoretical here, of course."

Tucker rubbed his jaw miserably. Unfortunately, he was still handsome. Fortunately, no pretty face could fix the ugly on the inside.

"Dude, point taken. You want me not to hit on your girl, not to hurt her, not to bail on her." He studied me through silent fury.

I nodded briskly. "See? Row always said you were so dumb you couldn't pour piss out of a boot if the instructions were printed on the heel. I disagree. I don't think you're dumber than average, just more malicious. Which was why I felt the need to give you this little welcome despite Dylan begging me to forget all about it."

"So…Dylan didn't send you to hit me?" He worked his jaw back and forth, holding it in his fist to ensure it wouldn't fall off.

"Of course not. Doubt she even remembers she saw you today." I snorted, downplaying how pissed off I was at the prospect that it gave him hope. "This was all me."

"Well, you can't keep me away from my daughter. I wanna see her." Tucker lurched his chin up.

"Yeah? What stopped you until now?" I parked a hand next to his ear, leaning against the wall, and he instinctively flinched. I chuckled.

"I was going to. This Easter. Go back to Staindrop. I'm better now."

"Hardly fucking impressive, seeing as you can't do any worse," I muttered, rubbing my chin as I considered what to do with him. It was time to wrap it up. "Where were you until now?"

He shrugged, looking childlike. And, to my horror, a little like Gravity. Their lower lips stuck out in the same manner when they were going to cry. Only Gravity was actually fucking adorable when she did that.

You don't find her adorable. You find her annoying. What the hell are you thinking, Coltridge?

"After Allison got thrown in the can, I stuck around Maine for a little while so I could see her," he explained.

Allison was the woman he'd been cheating on Dylan with. It was the equivalent of breaking your diet to gulp machine oil.

Tucker's face clouded. "But then she'd get all difficult and snappy with me when I forgot to top up her inmate card or get her books and magazines, so I decided to travel for a while. Saved up, went to Australia, New Zealand, traveled the Far East by myself a little…"

"Single life is great, isn't it?" I drawled.

He recoiled again. "I was a kid."

"So was Dylan. She still stepped up."

"What do you want me to say, man?" he whined. "I screwed up. I'd do anything to make up for it."

I shook my head, realizing I wasn't the one he owed these answers to. Stepping back, I raised a finger between us. "Upset my fiancée again, Tucker, I fucking dare you. I'll finish the job without blinking an eye. You hear me?"

With that, I turned around and disappeared into the night.

CHAPTER SIXTEEN
DYLAN

Dylan: Hi. Tate?

Tate: Who is it?

Dylan: Dylan Casablancas.

Tate: How did you get past the security codes to message me?

Dylan: Row gave them to me. Hope you don't mind.

Tate: I do.

Tate: Also, I'm not interested.

Dylan: I'm not offering, you...you...

Tate: Asshole? Bastard? Waste of oxygen?

Dylan: All three.

Tate: Glad we settled it. Have a good life.

Dylan: I need your help.

Tate: I am not in the habit of giving it for free, and there is nothing you can offer me that I don't already have.

Dylan: If this goes sideways, Row'll drop everything, your mutual businesses included, to come to my rescue. So technically, it IS in your interest to help me.

Tate: What do you want?

Dylan: Advice.

Tate: Have you seen my life?

> Tate: I could think of 7.9 billion people better equipped to give you sound advice.
> Dylan: LEGAL advice.
> Tate: Shoot.
> Dylan: My ex Tucker is in town. We are about to work with each other. He wants to see our mutual kid even though he's never met her before and walked out on us. Does he have the right to see her?

Tate had passed the bar in New York sometime in the previous decade. He wasn't a practicing lawyer, but he seemed like the kind of man to know everything about anything.

> Tate: That's a complicated question. Did he ever abuse you? Hit you? Hurt you?

I thought about my bruised wrist. I was pretty sure if I went to the police, Tucker would be able to convince them it was all a big, fat mistake. That he was swept up, excited to see me, the mother of his child, and wanted to talk. And maybe it *was* the truth. Emotions had been running high. He'd never physically hurt me before.

> Dylan: No.
> Tate: Does he have a criminal record?
> Dylan: Not that I know of.
> Tate: The short answer is no, there's nothing you can do about it. He'll end up seeing your kid, even if supervised. The long answer is that you might be able to tire him out by making him retain legal counsel and jump through hoops. But it'll cost you time, money, and resources.

I set my phone down on the couch and closed my eyes. I was

in a terrible spot. Did I want to give my daughter the chance to connect with her biological father and trust that this might bloom into a healthy relationship, or was I putting her in harm's way with a man who'd violently grabbed me and left me in the worst possible circumstances?

> Tate: Where's my thank you?
> Dylan: In the same place I keep the fucks I give about what you think about me. Good luck finding it.

CHAPTER SEVENTEEN
DYLAN

The next day, I had a call with Cal and Kieran on FaceTime while Grav went down for her midday nap. They were both sitting in a cute, eclectic coffee shop in Chelsea, sipping macchiatos from tiny hand-painted cups in the lush back garden to avoid the paparazzi.

"I'm going to murder you." I pointed at Kieran. My actual rage was raging. Apparently, it was a thing. "Then I'm going to fertilize my ancestors' soil with your blood."

"I see you've spent a good amount of time giving it some thought." Kieran held up his hands, appearing genuinely sorry. "Look, I promised him I'd try to warm you up to the idea of seeing him. He's been dying to reconnect. Like, to a scary degree."

"Rewind," I whisper-shouted. "How did you even meet him? How did it get to a point where you guys were talking?"

"Last time I was in New York, I walked into the Alchemist, and there he was. At first, I gave him a piece of my mind, berated him and made a scene about what he'd done to you. But he never fought back. He kind of just…took it. Then he fell all over himself, begging me to talk to you about giving him another chance with his kid."

"For real?" I gasped.

"Dude, he was a mess. When I say he begged, I mean he *begged*." Kieran ran his hand over his trimmed stubble, frowning slightly. "I mean, he also asked me to sign his ball cap and then went on to sell it on eBay for four figures, but hey, that's just money on the floor. Point is he seems genuine, Dyl."

"What are we talking about?" Cal looked between us, her face a mask of confusion. She was wearing an adorable nineties getup of a white tee and a black spaghetti top. "Who wants a chance with who? And are you telling me I can make a thousand bucks for your signature? *Shit.* That's a start-up right there."

"Tucker." Kieran brushed invisible lint from his tailored Montauk polo, looking like a trillion bucks and some change. I really could kill him right now. Quite happily too, for that cunning setup. "Tucker works at the Alchemist, where Dyl is temping for a while," he provided.

Cal sucked in a breath, nails digging into Kieran's arm. "You're kidding me. You saw Tucker?" she squeaked at me. "Like, last night?"

"Thanks to our buddy over there." I tossed a hand Kieran's way, masking my dread and fear over this development. My wrist still hurt. "Yeah, there was a big reunion. Sorry, Dot, can you please punch Kieran for me? I'm not done being pissed at him."

"Sure." Cal drove a fist into Kieran's bicep, putting all her strength into it.

He groaned, rubbing at his arm. "You're lucky you didn't aim for my legs. They're insured for twenty million dollars."

"I'll aim for the balls when we meet," I announced. "You overstepped in a big way."

"I knew you'd never consider meeting him, and…well, it isn't just about you, Dyl," Kieran said defensively. "Though I agree the way I went about it was completely shit, and I take full responsibility for the messy outcome."

"How was it?" Cal ignored our back-and-forth.

I calmed down a little. Cal didn't know Kieran was gay. No one did other than me. And the fact that he trusted me with his most sensitive secret did make me feel instinctively closer to him.

I told her Tucker appeared extra douchey and aggressive, with a touch of sorry. That it was hard to get a vibe off him because of all the adrenaline rushing through my veins. I confessed I told him Rhyland and I were engaged. That drew a chuckle out of my BFF.

"What are you going to do if he really does end up being a part of Gravity's life? He's going to find out the truth sooner or later."

I waved her off. "I'll figure something out." But the truth was, subconsciously, I didn't believe Tucker would be present in Grav's life. He'd always been incredibly selfish, to the point of narcissism. "Still mad at you, Kier."

He folded his arms over his chest. "If I told you he was in New York and wanted to see his kid, what would you do?"

"Laugh and tell you to fuck off," I offered naturally.

"I rest my case." He opened his arms.

"Kieran, he cheated and abandoned me an—"

"I know." Kieran cut me off. "I'm not discarding all that. He's a ghoul who deserves every bad thing that's ever happened to him, and I'm sure the worst is yet to come. This is not me defending his ass. All I'm saying is it's not just you in the picture. You have to think about Gravity, on the off chance he might've changed. You owe it to her to at least try. She can't advocate for herself."

Cal was quiet beside him. I knew she agreed with him. And I hated that I did too. I would never forgive Tucker for what he'd done to me, but I couldn't deny Gravity a healthy father if he wanted to be a part of her life. As long as he behaved like an adult and not a little bitch like last time, of course.

"May I remind you that he also owes you, like, a trillion dollars in child support?" Cal chimed in righteously. "You can maim him with some legal shit while he reconnects with Grav. It'll be pretty satisfying, I'm sure."

"I'm not interested in his money." I flung myself over the couch, grabbing the remote. After being judged, talked about, and ridiculed in the small town of Staindrop for having a child out of wedlock with the asshole who had an affair behind my back, I wanted to prove to people—and to myself—that I could do it on my own. "And it doesn't look like he has much anyway. I just want him to be a good dad or to disappear again."

Not that I knew what a good dad might look like. Mine was a total waste of environmental resources.

I finished the call with Cal and Kieran and binge-watched a few more episodes of *Grey's Anatomy*. Something about that show soothed my soul, and I had the suspicion it was nothing to do with the hot doctors and the never-ending drama.

When Grav woke up, I decided to do something fun with her ahead of my shift at the Alchemist. Tire her out so Rhyland wouldn't have to drain her battery with walks, activities, and exercise. I took her to the playground across the road, and we made homemade pizza together. Grav wanted to experiment, so we tossed a ton of toppings on—pepperoni, bell peppers, onion, olives, and pineapple.

"Something smells good." Rhyland swaggered into my apartment in the afternoon without knocking—*again*—using the spare key Row had given him. I couldn't even be mad. Rhy was saving my ass on a daily basis and babysitting Grav even though I knew he didn't like children and had much better things to do with his time.

"We making a pizza!" Grav announced adorably from her stool, her face decorated with tomato-sauce stains and flour. "I want to add a cookiecumber."

"A *what*?" he asked, alarmed.

"A cucumber," I corrected.

"Nah, baby doll. That pizza smells just fine the way it i—" He sauntered over to us, peering at the pizza I was now slicing. "What in the fuck is this?"

"Potty word!" Gravity announced.

"Dang it all to hell." He fished for his wallet in his front pocket, tossing a five-dollar bill in her general direction. "This time, I brought cash. I knew I didn't stand a chance."

I stifled a laugh.

"Listen, little stinker, you can't go around putting pineapple on pizza like that." He crouched down to her eye level. "If you're a psychopath, that's fine, but you need to hide it."

Gravity batted her lashes and grinned at him, clearly delighted to see him.

Ugh, girl, same.

My stomach dipped and churned when his shoulder brushed my own as he lodged himself between us, peering at our dish more closely. "Listen, kid, pineapple is only good for one thing. Wanna know what it is?"

My daughter peered at him, soft and curious and trusting, and I vowed to never ruin this in her—the ability to trust-fall into people and actually believe they'd catch you.

"To throw in the garbage," Rhyland finished, plucking the hot slices of pineapple from the pizza and flinging them into the sink.

Eager to please, Grav did the same, twisting her nose and saying "yucky" every time she tossed a pineapple.

"Hey, children," I chided. "Don't yuck someone else's yum."

"That someone else needs to you-know-what, you-know-where." He eyed me meaningfully. "I'd say all the words, but the potty-word police are nearby." He jerked his head toward Gravity.

After they were done clearing all the pineapple from the pizza, Rhyland slid two huge slices onto plates and poured himself a cup of "grown-up juice" (read: beer) and apple juice for Grav.

"What does grown-up juice taste like?" Gravity piped up.

"Emotional numbness."

"Will I like the taste of emonamiss?" she squeaked.

"We all do, honey." He chewed thoughtfully. "When you're around seventeen, ask Uncle Rhyland, and I'll let you have a taste of your own beer."

I watched, transfixed, as they both ignored me for ten minutes straight, making conversation and eating their pizza without offering me any. It was clear the man was making no effort to change himself or talk toddler language for my daughter. It was also clear she was head over heels smitten with him. Fuck. This was really bad.

Finally, Rhyland swung his gaze to me. "Any reason why you're still here?"

Shit. I had a shift to go to, didn't I? I'd gotten lost in watching a man being adorable with my kid. It was more arousing than a *Magic Mike* show.

"Uh, her bedtime is—"

"Seven forty-five p.m., I know." He plucked a black olive from his pizza, tossing it into his mouth and chewing. "I read the manual. I know it better than the pope knows the Bible."

Gravity tried to pull off the same olive-to-mouth toss, but it hit her eye, and she squawked.

"What's with the attitude?" I tapered my eyes.

"Dunno. What's with the outfit?" The heat oozing through his light, playful eyes threatened to burn down the entire building.

My gaze slid down in confusion. I was wearing a black leather skirt and boots, along with a floral top. "I'm fishing for tips." I jutted a hip out, tossing my hair back defiantly.

"The NYPD might be fishing for bodies in the Hudson if the patrons don't watch themselves tonight," he murmured under his breath, ripping his eyes from me.

"That sounds possessive." I arched an eyebrow.

"Not possessive—*protective*," he corrected, standing up and sauntering over to me. He stopped when we were a breath away from each other, leaning down to whisper into my ear so only I could hear. "Trust me, Cosmos, if I wanted anything else, I'd be christening my best friend's bed by nailing you into it. You've given me every inclination you'd be game, the willing victim that you are."

Anger and shame flooded me. I sidestepped him, but not before stomping on his foot. "Try not to ruin her," I said, my voice steely.

To his credit, he didn't even flinch at my stomp.

"You tend to do that with everything you touch."

"Don't worry. I don't touch little girls." He winked me. "That's why I spared you."

God, he was infuriating. I wished I didn't need him quite so much.

For babysitting.

I tried to shake off the weird reverie I found myself in on my way to the Alchemist. Did I really put together an outfit for tips, or was it for Rhy? Maybe a little bit of both. Watching Rhyland's face as he took me in nearly undid me. It reminded me I was a woman—a conventionally pretty one—and that, in itself, brightened my mood.

I arrived five minutes before my shift was scheduled to start and was greeted by Max, who showed me the back end of the bar. The office was adjacent to the kitchen, home to a row of lockers, a desk with a computer on it, and a sole metal cabinet. The schedule for the week hung on a wall. I checked the timetable on a pinboard, relieved I didn't have to work with Tucker today. He was just finishing a shift. Maybe I could avoid him altogeth—

"Oh, great." His familiar voice slithered down my back like a cold, wet towel. "It's you."

Or maybe not.

I turned around. As soon as I saw his face, I choked on my saliva, coughing uncontrollably. "Oh my God." My eyes roamed his face chaotically.

He had two black eyes, a fractured nose that appeared crooked and out of place, a split on his forehead, and a busted lip. He looked like he decided to wrestle a pack of bears.

"Did you get in a car accident? What the hell happened to you?"

"Your fiancé happened to me," he sneered bitterly, yanking his locker open while pressing an ice pack to his upper cheek. "Don't play innocent."

"My wha—" Rhyland did this? But when? And *why*? And how come he hadn't mentioned it?

He could have mentioned it.

Dark, toxic delight filled my veins, thick and sticky. It was wrong to take pleasure in what Rhyland had done, but that didn't make me any less giddy. He'd hurt someone who had hurt me, tenfold. And I had a feeling Rhyland, despite his many shortcomings, was loyal to a fault.

Tucker shook his head, tugging out his backpack and his jacket and tossing the ice pack into the locker. I watched him, unsure of what to say. It wasn't my place to apologize. *I* hadn't messed up his face. Plus, he kind of deserved it.

"Already told you your wrist was a mistake. You didn't have to be such a baby about it," Tucker groused.

"He noticed my wrist by himself. I didn't tell him." Why was I explaining myself to this prick?

"Yeah, well, he made a whole stink about it."

"The fact that you left me for dead three years ago didn't help, I'm sure," I pointed out smartly.

Tucker fought an eye roll, seemingly eager to change the subject. "I told Rhyland I moved around after I left Maine." He returned his attention to his locker, speaking with his back to me. He slipped his bomber jacket on, and then his JanSport. "I had a horrible fucking time, okay? I couldn't go back to Staindrop because of Allison and her damn mess. Everybody judged me. I had to take random labor jobs everywhere I went. Australia. New Zealand. Japan. Working without a permit. I slept in hostels. My parents had to move to escape people's prejudice. It's not like I had fun."

"Wow, I'm so sorry running away from your family was an inconvenience for you." I put a hand to my chest and widened my eyes.

"That was always your issue, Dylan. You only think about yourself. Don't care about anyone else's misery," he accused, his eyes narrowing into slits—or trying to through the swollen skin around them.

"Holy gaslighting, Batman." I barked out a laugh. "You *did not* just make your Great Escape story about *my* selfishness."

"I forgot how sarcastic you are." He flattened his lips into a scowl. "Very unattractive."

"Good." I smiled brightly. "Only shit attracts flies."

"I'm ready to see my daughter now."

"Oh, it's about your schedule, is it?" I couldn't help but snap back. Kieran was right. I wasn't ready to contemplate the idea of Tucker and Gravity in the same room. "I'll let Gravity know. I'm sure she'll understand why you were absent her"—I checked an imaginary watch—"entire fucking life."

"I want to see my kid, Dylan." He screwed a ball cap over his head, ducking his head down. It sounded like a threat, which I didn't appreciate, but nothing about the words themselves seemed intimidating. It was his tone that didn't sit right with me.

He pointed at me. "And tell your future husband to keep his distance, unless he wants to sit behind bars."

The shift was long and busy but surprisingly rewarding. It felt good, doing something that extended beyond being a mother. My outfit proved to be a success in the tips department, but there were so many eyes on my ass I was half tempted to check if it had made it to Page Six's blockbuster list.

When the clock hit midnight and I slid out of the bar, I got a phone call. Rhyland's name stared back at me. I gulped in a breath and answered.

"What happened? Is she okay?"

"Jesus, relax." He sounded tired and annoyed and fed up with our arrangement. We were only a few days in. "Your kid is fast asleep." He didn't call her by her name—still refused to fully accept that she was human—but at least he'd stopped referring her as "the child." "I just knew you got off at midnight and wanted you to have someone to talk to on your way home."

I deflated now I knew my child was okay. "It is *literally* six minutes away," I protested.

"New York is unsafe."

"Thanks to people like *you*," I spluttered, trying to ignore the distinct feeling my heart was melting down into gooey, warm butter, settling between my legs, making me wet. Attentive Rhyland was a total panty dropper. "I saw Tucker's face."

"My condolences," he drawled.

"Seriously, Rhy, what were you thinking?"

Brief silence hung in the air before he answered. "I owed it to Row. This has nothing to do with you. He's been wanting to rearrange that man's face for four years now, almost five."

My buttery heart turned back into stone. Of course it was about my brother. Everything was.

"You could've gotten yourself into a lot of trouble."

"He wouldn't have told anyone," Rhyland maintained.

"How are you so sure?"

"He knew he deserved it."

I wasn't sure Rhyland was correct on that one. Instead, I guessed Tucker didn't want to start a war with a man like Rhy, who was connected to spine-chillingly ruthless billionaires with herds of lawyers at their disposal. Rhyland was definitely the nicest guy out of his crew, along with Kieran, but he also gave strong "don't fuck with me" vibes.

"Did she have a good evening?" I changed the subject.

"She did."

"Did she—"

"You know, Cosmos, we can have a conversation about something that isn't your daughter."

"I'm sure we can, but that would be pointless, because I want nothing to do with your ass," I said in a singsong voice.

"Are you still a big Swiftie?" He ignored my attitude.

"I am," I admitted begrudgingly. "You don't outgrow Taylor Swift—you grow *with* her. That's what the eras are all about."

It was one of the things I loved about her so much. No album was the same. She evolved right along with her music. Aside from med school, my dream was to go to the Eras Tour.

There had been plenty of almosts. Row purchased tickets for me once, a couple years ago, but Grav got a nasty ear infection and had to be nursed twenty-four seven.

A year ago, I decided to splurge and bought two tickets for me and a friend. But the friend's mother was hospitalized the same day. I had no backup to go with, so we ended up selling them.

"Are you still a big jackass?" I retorted. At this point, I was being mean to him just to remind myself he was off-limits, because that red line? It was blurring with each minute he spent with us.

"Huge, like everything else about me." Rhyland clucked his tongue. "Retiring from my fake-boyfriend business and quitting pot definitely gave me less room to misbehave, though. I still enjoy going out, drinking, a good fucking shopping spree. I've never really understood why men are so butt-hurt about going shopping—I love new shit. But I'm no longer unabashedly self-indulgent. I guess I'm in a phase where I'm trying to prove to myself and others that there's more to my existence than being hot as shit and fucking like a rock star."

"Don't forget being humble," I snorted, punching in the code to unlock the entrance door of our building. "By the way, I've always suspected rock stars are shit in bed, what with all the coke and alcohol pumping through their veins."

"I once hooked up with an *American Idol* contestant. She was pretty good. Stole my anal beads, though," Rhyland muttered bitterly.

"Hardly a rock star, Rhy." I suppressed a smile, pushing the elevator door and walking inside.

I'd kind of come to terms with the fact that we'd never be able to have a full five-minute conversation without bringing up sex.

"Hey, do you wanna see a mock-up of App-date?" For the first time ever, he sounded boyish, unsure. "It's pretty cool. You get to browse profiles of fictive AI users."

"Isn't AI super unethical?"

"Yeah, but, well…so am I."

This time, I *did* laugh.

"Honestly." He bristled. "Be thankful it's AI and not a trafficking ring or some shit."

"Sure. You can show me." As much as I hated to admit it, I was enjoying our truce. It was exhausting trying to hate the man just for rejecting me eight years ago.

The elevator door slid open. He stood there waiting for me in the hallway on the other side, looking fifty shades of perfect. Gray, low-hanging sweatpants and a white muscle shirt hung loose over his V-taper frame and broad shoulders. And when his mouth broke into a smile, I knew it wasn't the only thing that was going to break.

He was the sunset, burning bright on the cusp of something dark and forbidden. If he were a song, I thought wistfully, he'd be a ballad. Sweet and forlorn and full of hidden meanings. "Wildest Dreams," maybe.

I'd trained myself not to dream for so long, not to dare hope for something better, that Rhyland posed a threat to my very existence. He reminded me there might be something more to this life. And hope was like crack. Risky but addictive.

"Hey," he said breathlessly.

"Hi." I tucked a tendril of hair behind my ear, scurrying out of the elevator and into the apartment.

He closed the door behind us. "Wanna see?" He raised his phone up in his palm.

"Um, can I pee first?"

He rolled his eyes, downplaying his excitement. "I mean, if you must."

I went to the bathroom thinking he looked too thrilled to have me, an objectively ill-informed person when it came to mobile apps, view his work.

Had Row, Tate, and Kieran given him the time of the day—taken his idea seriously? I doubted it. Rhyland was always celebrated by his friends for being silver-tongued and handsome, but people naturally assumed all he had to offer was his charm. He wasn't outwardly talented at anything, like Row was with food, Kieran with soccer, and Tate with pissing people off.

After I washed my hands, I snuck in to check on Grav. She was sound asleep. I joined Rhyland at the breakfast nook, sliding onto the stool next to him. The mock-up app was already splayed on the screen of an iPad he must've brought with him.

"I thought I was going to see this on your phone." I grabbed the iPad from him.

"This'll give you the full experience. I made some tweaks to it after little stinker's bedtime story."

"What did you read?"

"*The Very Hungry Caterpillar*, for the fourth time." Pause. "In a row." Pause. "That caterpillar has untreated binge-eating issues. The book is romanticizing eating disorders. Parents should make more of a stink about it."

He was blabbering because he was nervous about the app. Which, at first glance, looked sleek as hell.

"Dude, are you, like, hardworking and shit?" I tilted my head, grinning.

He puffed up, his face twisting in abhorrence. "Please. I did this with Paint while dropping a deuce."

He'd brought his iPad so he could work here after Gravity went to bed. I didn't know why, but it made my heart squeeze. I scrolled through App-date. It looked like if X's elegance and Instagram's aesthetic had a baby, yet it was completely its own unique brand.

The logo was the app name in lowercase letters, along with an engagement ring, the diamond exploding into tiny, torn Polaroid pictures of loved-up couples. The slogan was "Your ex's pain is our gain."

"You went a little overboard with that slogan." I cleared my throat.

"The world runs on feelings, Cosmos. Every good marketing executive knows that in order to tap into people's emotions, you have to make them feel shitty about themselves first."

"You're literally so toxic I'm afraid to breathe in your direction," I muttered.

"Shh." He elbowed me. "Concentrate on the experience."

The background was probably one of the coolest features of the app. You had to choose where you were from, and the background immediately turned to a backdrop of your location, be it the New York skyline, the London Eye, or an open cornfield. The search engine was surprisingly specific. Location, age, gender, occupation, income, and exact goals. The app focused on people finding dates they could flaunt or play pretend with, not *actually* on finding love. But there were also broader searches for people who wanted to travel with like-minded individuals, befriend people with certain traits they missed in their exes, et cetera.

"It's different from Tinder and Bumble," Rhyland explained, licking his lips. "The goal here isn't to find a hookup or a partner. It's to have a strictly professional, quid pro quo relationship with someone willing to help you pretend like you've moved on. Or—and this is even more interesting—to find someone with the same traits as you to do something you already planned to do with your ex before you broke up. Like go on a hiking trip, backpack, and so on."

"Are there really that many people out there who want to *pretend* to have someone?" I turned to him, mesmerized.

He motioned with his hand between us. *Fair point.*

"Plus," he mused. "It's not just for fake dates and partners. It's a fill-in app. A place where you find a replacement to fill the gaping hole the person you broke up with left behind."

You could find anything on the app. A one-off date for an event. An entire fake relationship. A friendship between two heartbroken people. This app basically promised to be your best friend after a breakup. Which was ironic since Rhyland, its creator, had never had a girlfriend.

"Look, I'm not gonna lie, it's smart, sleek, and super freaking sophisticated." I pushed the iPad across the surface back to him. "But I get why Bruce 'Family Man' Marshall is hesitant. You're essentially promoting a lie."

"Am I, though?" He grabbed the iPad, sliding it into his messenger bag. "Who knows how these relationships will turn out? If two people are hell-bent on driving their exes nuts and like each other enough, through talking online, to flaunt each other, wouldn't you say they have a genuine chance of falling in love for real?"

"Um, no, because we're in a fake relationship, and the only real thing I feel is the need to spoon your eyeballs out every time you provoke me."

He snorted. "You wanna tell me, with a straight face, that you hate me the same way you did when we met on that curb a few days ago?"

"That doesn't count. You're literally helping me with Grav and money and—" The rest of my speech perished on my tongue. *Huh.* He had a point.

"And there you have it." He winked. "I don't think Bruce hates the idea of the app. If anything, it promotes informed consent around platonic relationships." He visibly shuddered at the blasphemy. "His issue is with me. With who I am. My reputation. That's why we need to ace this fake-lovers assignment, Casablancas."

I bit down on the side of my lip, glancing at the app again. "Fine. It's a good app. For what it's worth, which is probably nothing at all, I think Bruce would be mad not to invest in it. There's nothing sleazy or immoral about it. It would've been nice to have something like it when Tuck left me. In fact, you could monetize the shit out of this thing, because back then, I'd easily have spent a hundred bucks on signing up."

"We're looking at fifty bucks a year." He flicked my nose like I was an adorable puppy, standing up and collecting his things. "Besides, I'd have been your fake boyfriend free of charge. You'd be my pro bono."

Watching him move toward the door made my heart drop, and not in a good way. I didn't want him to go, I realized. But I just sat there and stared. What else could I do? I'd already monopolized so much of his time since I got here. I didn't want to overdo it.

When he got to the door, he slung his hand on the knob and swiveled his head to glance at me. "Dyl?"

"Yes, Rhy?"

Since when were we Dyl and Rhy? This change in dynamics symbolized the collapse of my self-defense mechanism.

"I found a really great daycare for the little stinker." He tucked a hand into his front pocket. "It comes highly recommended. Montessori method, with teachers specializing in mental development and shit. The waiting list is three years deep, but Bruce's wif—"

His words doused me like ice-cold water.

"How dare you?" I snarled.

Did he really hate spending time with Gravity that much? Did he think I was going to put her in care five times a week while I worked mostly night shifts and wouldn't get to see her at all?

"No one asked you to help me find a daycare. I don't want one."

"Nannies are unreliable." A muscle flexed in his jaw. He wasn't cowering away from the subject. "And once this app takes off, I won't have time to babysit her. Anyway, she is, like, fucking smart. Even *I* can tell, and she is legit the only three-year-old I know." His gaze snagged on mine, gritty and unwavering. "She needs to hang out with other kids. Make friends. Think about her."

"I *am* thinking about her." I stood up. A rush of panic and agony funneled through me. "I'm thinking she doesn't have a dad, so at least she can have a present mom."

I hated that my anger, my heat, my desperation, wasn't piercing through him. That he didn't shy away from confrontation when I expressed big feelings. That he cared enough to engage in a battle instead of walking off like Tucker did.

"All the same, I've gotten to know your kid, and I think you could both benefit from enrolling her, at least part-time," Rhyland maintained calmly. "You're going to go to school at some point. This bar gig ain't forever. And Gravity deserves more than a fake uncle who teaches her how to burp the alphabet and chuck pineapple pieces out the window to pass the time."

"There will be no school for me," I laughed. "New York is my one and only chance to escape living with my mother for eternity. I'm not gonna blow it by enrolling in college and risking financial demise. What do you think I'm going to do with your paychecks? I'm saving every penny." I walked over to the door, shaking with rage.

Did he think I was doing a bad job with my own daughter? That she wasn't being provided with enough stimulation?

"That's not—" he started.

"Get out."

He yanked on the handle, opening the door, those light, tranquil eyes still trained on me. But instead of getting out, he turned from the door sharply, taking one step and eating all the space between us. Suddenly, he was in my face. His heat radiated onto my body. His pulse drummed against my own. He leaned down so we were face-to-face. I felt like I was about to explode, and I didn't know if it was from want, need, or anger.

"Tomorrow. Ten thirty a.m. I'm driving." His breath skated along the column of my neck, his voice low and menacing. "I'm not Tucker, Dylan. You can't steamroll me. You can't make me run. You can't exhaust me into agreeing with you. Don't be late."

"I told you—"

"Marshall set it up," he snapped. "If this is a test, I wanna pass it. We're going."

"I hate you." I was acting childishly, I knew, but maybe it was exactly what I needed. Someone I could show my worst to, knowing they still wouldn't leave.

To my horror, a lone tear escaped my right eye.

This was why I was being horrible to him. My instinct was to push men away just to watch them leave. Only Rhyland hadn't left in the six days since we'd reconnected. *Yet.*

But I already knew he'd meet this challenge head-on. That was just who he was. He never shied away from hard work.

He used his thumb to brush my tear away. "Someone told me enemies-to-lovers tropes have the best sex." He popped his thumb into his mouth, tasting my tear.

"That someone sounds smart," I mumbled.

He nodded. "Hot too."

With that, he slid past me, his arm brushing mine in an erotic whisper, and walked away, leaving me in a pool of desire and anger.

What the hell just happened?

CHAPTER EIGHTEEN
RHYLAND

Dylan_loves_Rhyland4ever liked your reel.

Dylan_loves_Rhyland4ever commented: omg you look so much better my love! The green hue is almost gone. The doxycycline is working!! 👮

Rhyland Coltridge commented: Can't believe you're awake, babe. Thought you'd sleep off the hangover after that last binge.

Dylan_loves_Rhyland4ever commented: Burn in hell <3 <3 <3

Rhyland Coltridge commented: Ladies first <3 <3 <3

Dylan_loves_Rhyland4ever commented: Aw I love you so much I could strangle you.

Rhyland Coltridge commented: I want you so much I could suffocate you.

Tate Blackthorn commented: Wishing both sides success.

I'd always had mommy issues.

I once had a therapist who confirmed as much. Abandonment issues were secondary to my messed-up relationship with women, especially mothers.

Dylan tapped into my mommy issues like an erect dick on a perfect-peach ass. Everything about her triggered me. She was a hands-on, loving, fiercely protective mother. A constant reminder of what I didn't have growing up.

I'd always had a fantastic talent for destroying any constructive relationship I had with women. That therapist, for instance? I ended up fucking and ghosting her—a punishment in my screwed-up head for making me open up to her about my vulnerabilities. And I could feel myself teetering on the edge of doing something really goddamn stupid with Dylan. I didn't need her chef brother to know this was a recipe for disaster. All I needed was to feel in danger of opening up, of knocking down a wall or two, and I went into full-blown destruction mode.

And Dylan was dragging me out of my comfort zone kicking and screaming. Metaphorically speaking, of course.

Now here I was, tucked in my McLaren, my Tom Ford shades covering my eyes, waiting for Dylan and Gravity to come downstairs. I glanced at my Rolex. The one I was *definitely* pawning this week to come up with the money for our deal. 10:45 a.m. She was late.

Fuck it. Let her get there in Jimmy.

I kicked the car into drive, about to slide out of my double-parked spot. Just as the McLaren started moving, Dylan and her daughter emerged from the building door.

And my entire fucking existence buckled at the sight of her.

She looked so good I choked on my tongue. I always knew she was a bombshell, but now, in broad daylight, the sun playing on her raven hair and her smooth, tanned skin, her honeyed glow burning the edges of her frame, I knew I had a problem.

A ten-and-a-half-inch problem.

One that threatened to poke my steering wheel and activate the horn.

She was wearing a floral yellow chiffon dress with a big white bow in her long hair. Gravity wore a tiny, identical version of the dress, and they were both sporting a pair of Mary Janes. God, I couldn't fucking look away. The weight of my want for Dylan was pressing against my sternum, threatening to break my ribs clean.

She opened the back door, where Gravity's seat was already installed, and buckled her in. I stared at Dylan's cleavage through the rearview mirror, feeling my cock thumping against my thigh.

Then she entered the passenger seat next to me, the smile she offered her daughter melting into a scowl. "I'd say I'm sorry for being late, but I'm not. How's that chlamydia medicine working?"

"Fantastic. Your drinking problem?"

"Under control."

We had plenty of room to grow in the "playing pretend" department. I'd never been anything short of the perfect fake boyfriend. But then she'd come along and ruined a decade-long streak.

"You're going to need to behave yourself there," I warned. "The manager knows Marshall."

"Oh, I'll be a dream."

I floored it. This newfound revelation that her beauty affected me in a deeper way than "I want to screw her badly" made my stomach churn. I mean, I got the flutters out there for a second. Hopefully it was just the new protein shake I'd tried that morning. Kieran had warned me that shit was potent.

"Hi, Uncle Rhyrand," Gravity greeted sleepily.

"Hey, little stinker."

"She slept awful last night. Misses her granny." Dylan sighed, twisting her upper body backward to check on her. "My mom's coming next week to give her some TLC. Honey, why don't you take a nap while we drive?"

"I'm not tire—" Gravity started, but the protest turned into a snore midway. A second later, her head lolled from her seat, mouth hanging open as she napped.

Dylan tapped her knee rhythmically, glancing at me.

"What do you want?" I grumbled.

"A nicer fake fiancé," she shot back.

"Download App-date. You'll enjoy the variety."

"Of what? AI people who don't exist?" she taunted.

"Being in a relationship with something unreal should be familiar to you, judging by your vibrator collection," I snapped back.

"You went through my stuff?" she raged.

"I was looking for tweezers to remove a thorn in Gravity's palm. Most women I know keep vibrators in a nightstand drawer, not their bathrooms."

That shut her up. For all of five seconds.

"Actually, I plan on subscribing to your site once you launch," she piped up again, settling into her seat like a regal cat. "I'm going to be your first customer."

I'm going to ban every male from the app to ensure you don't match with anyone.

See, this was exactly the kind of risky train of thought I should be avoiding, especially after my intervention with Tucker.

Maybe if I didn't respond to her, she'd get the hint.

"Have I done something to upset you?" She eyed me in confusion.

You exist. That's enough to rile me up.

"Other than making me sell this baby so I could pay you for the pleasure of babysitting your brat all week?" I flashed her my Rolex. "Nope. You're a real fucking delight."

Her eyes widened in surprise. I immediately regretted both being a dick and indicating I couldn't afford our arrangement. She was about to say something when my phone started dancing in the center console between us with an incoming call. The screen said *Mom*.

She picked it up. "Should I answer that for you?"

"No!" I roared, so loud Gravity jolted behind us before falling back to sleep. *Shit.* What was wrong with me? "I'll get back to her later."

She put my phone back down, biting on her lower lip. "Look, I just made up a number. If ten K is too much…"

"It's not."

She needed the money more than I needed fifteen designer watches. And then, because for some reason I hated being an asshole to her, I added, "Look, just fulfill your end of the bargain to your best ability. If this thing with Bruce takes off, I'm going to make four hundred million bucks overnight and be on the fast track to becoming a billionaire. He's the best tech entrepreneur out there. His corporation is the mother company of all the big apps. Angry Turds, Verified Villains, Music Play, Telefind."

"Is this why you're letting him play you like a hockey puck?"

"I'm not—" I snapped my mouth shut, working my jaw back and forth angrily. "Sometimes you need to be smart, not right. Finding people who'll throw money at a good idea is easy. Finding people who can help you take that idea to the next level? Now that's hard. The promotion Bruce'd do in his own channels alone would garner tens of millions of downloads."

"How soon do you need this initial sum in your bank account?" She eyed me curiously.

"Yesterday," I admitted, feeling my ears go pink. "I burned through whatever money I made in the past few years, but I can sell some shit and stay afloat for a bit."

My phone came to life again. This time, it was my dad's name on-screen. What kind of fuckery had my good-for-nothing parents gotten themselves into now? A pyramid scheme? Insurance fraud? Had they gotten arrested for indecent exposure? I wasn't going to bail them out again—not after the last time they were caught bumping uglies on a public beach.

Dylan shot me an unsure glance. "Could be an emergency."

"That's what 911 is for." I ran a hand over my hair.

She stared at me, stunned. As far as she knew, my parents were great. My dad made a decent living. Mom was a homemaker. Truthfully, she made jack shit outside her outrageous demands. Still, my parents were prominent Staindrop citizens. They showed up to every event, participated in the Fourth of July pie contest. They were that lovey-dovey couple you knew would still hold hands well into their eighties.

Too bad they never bothered holding *my* hand.

Or, you know, showing up to my graduation. Which one, are you asking? Well, *all of them*.

"Okay. We're going to need to unpack this like it's an overflowing suitcase after a Thailand trip where you got to buy all the knockoffs." She circled a finger around my face.

"Blasphemy," I protested. "My fake fiancée wouldn't be caught dead with a knockoff bag."

"Yes, because she'll be living happily ever after with her full bank account and her fifty-buck Louis Vuitton bag. Now, tell me, what's wrong with your parents?"

"The better question would be what's not?" I huffed. "But it's none of your concern."

"Everything is my concern," she countered. "The more we know about each other, the better we can pretend we're a couple in Texas."

She wasn't wrong. Come to think of it, she was rarely wrong. I wasn't happy with her being both hot and whip-smart. Dangerous combo.

"In a nutshell, they were too busy screwing and courting each other to take care of me. I'm talking full-blown weekends away together by the time I was nine or ten. I'd *Home Alone* it like a pro, pretending there were other people inside the house, because I was shit-scared of imaginary burglars coming in. Date nights without proper care before I was fully potty-trained. When I was fourteen, my dad decided to teach me his trade—not because he took any kind of interest in me but because he wanted me to do his job while he and my mom took days off together. I was their little servant." My lips curled into a sneer at the memory. Glass half-full? Taking a trip down memory lane wilted my dick to a manageable half-mast. Plus, it reminded me why I could never, *ever* hit on Row's baby sister. Or anyone else, for that matter. Why love was not only a distraction but a self-detonating device used to forget yourself and people around you.

My parents' so-called love was my demise.

Dylan stared at me in shock. "Are you serious?"

"As a heart attack." I clutched the steering wheel harder. "Your mom used to send me home with sandwiches because she got tired of seeing my poking ribs."

My cheeks flushed as I remembered the day Zeta saw me playing shirtless with Row in their backyard, my ribs poking out, and decided to take it upon herself to feed me. "The first home-cooked meal I ever had that I didn't have to make myself was at your place. My last one too, come to think of it." I grabbed the green stick from my Starbucks coffee, rolling it across my mouth like a toothpick.

"Wow. I had no idea, Rhy."

"About my shitty childhood? Yeah, I didn't exactly advertise that shit."

"Mine wasn't the best either." She scratched an old scab on her knee distractedly. "My dad was a raging alcoholic who took his anger out on Mama and Row."

"Figured as much," I said quietly. Row and I never talked about it. I didn't want to embarrass him by bringing it up, and he'd never felt the need to discuss it, but I'd seen the welts. The bruises. "Still. Better a drunk dad and a great mom than two assholes who don't give a shit about your existence," I pointed out.

"I mean, if we're going to make it a competition…" She screwed her mouth sideways adorably. "My dad called me Dylan to spite my mom."

"Say what now?" I laughed.

"Yup. He knew she loved classic, gender-appropriate names like Ambrose. She named Row without consulting him, because he wanted to call Row 'Slater.' Filled in the paperwork before he could have a say. So he chose the most vindictive name he could think of for a girl." Her eyebrows shot to her hairline. "Dylan is hardly a classic for a girl. My whole existence is a fuck-you to my mom when you think about it."

"That is an impressive level of pettiness." I took a right turn toward the leafy Carnegie Hill neighborhood of the daycare. "My mother once forgot to pick me up from the hospital."

She gasped. "No!"

"Yup." I popped the *p*. "I was undergoing surgery for my leg. Got a direct blow to the knee during soccer from Kieran. When she finally showed up—after I had to borrow a nurse's phone to call her—she forgot my date of birth when she tried to discharge me and had zero paperwork to prove she was my mom. Police got involved. The staff was distraught on my behalf. It was the first time I realized there was something inherently fucked-up about my family. Child Protective Services got into the picture. It was a mess."

"Okay, fine. You win."

I bowed my head with flourish. "Thank you."

"Is that why you don't want children?" She cocked an eyebrow. "Because you saw firsthand that not everyone is equipped to become a parent."

"Among other things." I was opening up to her more than I intended to, but it didn't feel weird or forced. Of course, there was always a chance I'd mess it all up like I did with my ex-therapist. "I also know I'm probably as selfish as they are, and I don't want to ruin anyone else's life. I had a vasectomy when I was eighteen."

She clutched her heart. "You're kidding me."

I shrugged. "Condoms break. My resolve doesn't. I don't want children."

"That you don't want them I understand, but why are you so repulsed by them?" she insisted. "Grav is an objectively cute kid. Say otherwise, and I'll put you back at the hospital. And this time, your mom won't help."

Offering her a lenient smirk, I explained, "There's no reason to long for things you'll never have. It's better if I stay away from kids altogether." I was pretty at peace with that. Kids seemed like a lot of work without much return on investment.

"Can I ask you a question?"

"Sure, but in the spirit of full transparency, I tend to lie," I admitted.

"You literally told me lies are your hard limit." Dylan looked floored.

"Hey, I never claimed not to be a hypocrite," I said unapologetically. "Lying is a knee-jerk reaction from working in customer service with highly sensitive clients."

I was too used to telling not-pretty women they were pretty, untalented heiresses they were talented, and unlovable brats that love was just around the corner.

"Did you really never have a thing for me?" She cleared her throat. "Because I had a thing for you. Like, hard."

"I didn't," I told her.

But I do now, I thought. *And while manageable, it is extremely inconvenient.*

Even that wasn't the whole truth. She'd always been my biggest temptation. Sometimes I wondered if God created her just to make the only healthy relationship in my life—my friendship with Row—complicated, just to fucking spite me.

I found a parking spot right in front of the daycare and slid into it. The Broadway building boasted white columns, large arched windows, and two sets of bulletproof glass doors.

Grav was still asleep, so I unbuckled her and flung her over my chest, holding her as we stepped inside.

Dylan reddened. "I can do it."

"And block the view to your rack?" I sneered. "Yeah, I don't think so. It's the only thing keeping me going at this point."

We walked inside, where we were greeted by the bubbliest woman on earth—a redheaded fiftysomething in a pastel cardigan who introduced herself as Cherrie. "With an I-E, not Y!" She laughed at her own specificity.

Don't worry. I don't plan on writing you any letters.

She was the manager and good friends with Bruce's wife back in college, so I had to play nice. "It's an absolute pleasure to be here." I squeezed her hand warmly. "Thank you for giving us this tour. We've heard such great things about this school."

"Aww, thank you. And look at Daddy here, holding his sleepy girl." Cherrie clapped her hands, resting her cheek over them dreamily.

Dylan looked scandalized by Cherrie's words. "Oh, he is not the fath—"

I shot out my hand, lacing my fingers through hers and giving her a warning squeeze. "Sorry, my fiancée is a little intoxicated."

Hey, might as well keep this lie going since I'd already spread it online.

Cherrie blinked fast. "It's...eleven thirty in the morning?"

"Mimosa brunch. You don't choose who you fall in love with." I sighed.

I glanced around. The place looked like toddler heaven, with wooden shelves, toys and blocks, straw baskets laden with sensory toys, lots of drawings and art projects, and giant playground equipment.

"He's just joking," Dylan reassured in her best "me? I'm not mad at all" tone, digging her fingernails into my skin. "The truth is my fiancé is not Gravity's real dad." Pause. "I cheated on him with his best friend." She shot me a satisfied smirk.

"That is true," I said levelly. "My best friend is her older brother, by the way."

Check. Mate.

Dylan paled. So did Cherrie. I didn't know when exactly my need to out-crazy Dylan had overcome my need to secure Marshall's investment, but I needed to turn this ship around quickly.

"Obviously"—I cleared my throat—"we're just kidding. Grav isn't biologically mine, but she is my daughter in every sense of the word. And we're both on edge here, because the decision to enroll her in daycare is not an easy one. Up until now, she was watched by her grandmother and her mother, so this is all new territory for us."

The relief on Cherrie's face was immediate. "That is *completely* understandable. The adjustment period will be hard on everyone in the household. Well…why don't I show you around?" She clapped her hands, pasting on a ridiculously happy face.

Gravity chose that moment to stir awake in my arms. She blinked, drowsy eyes taking in her surroundings, before realizing she was somewhere fun and wiggling out of my embrace.

"Slides!" she exclaimed, climbing onto a wooden ladder and sliding off a slide backward on her tummy.

Cherrie parked her chin over her curled fists, grinning bigger. "Oh, how wholesome."

Wholesome, my ass. She didn't know the side of Gravity I was privy to—the one that could eat seven extra-large pancakes and sing *"Firework"* in its entirety through a burp.

Cherrie gave us a tour of the facilities while Gravity trailed behind us, stopping every now and then to take advantage of the toys and the indoor playground. I kept Dylan's hand clasped in mine. Both our palms were getting a little sweaty, but neither of us withdrew. It was a battle of wills, who would blink first, and I was determined to die glued to this woman's hand to prove my point.

"Here is our art room, and there's our splash pad and our indoor gymnastics. We offer dance, karate, yoga, Spanish, and art classes, included in the price."

"This is great. She speaks some Italian, and we've been working on art too." Dylan sounded breathless.

"It seems your daughter has taken a liking to our preschool, Miss Casablancas," Cherrie observed when Gravity decided to show off her monkey-bar skills. "This is usually a good indication that a child is ready for school."

"Honey, isn't that amazing?" I brushed my lips over Dylan's

temple. The subtext was: "I win. I was right. She does need this. Eat a dick. Preferably mine." I felt her stiffen at the gesture before forcing herself to relax.

"Yeah," she murmured. "Best news ever."

The more Cherrie showed us around, the more it was obvious this place made Disney World look like Rikers Island.

The school was a goddamn theme park. The staff were enthusiastic and kind. Gravity jumped into one of the teaching assistant's arms without a care in the world when the assistant offered her an applesauce pouch and a sticker.

I could tell Dylan was beginning to warm up to the idea when she asked Cherrie, "Can we do this part-time? Like, maybe three times a week to start with, so as not to overwhelm her?"

And you.

It was fascinating to me to watch a parent actually want to spend time with their kid. Mine had sent me by foot to knock on people's doors for spontaneous playdates when I was as little as five just to get rid of me.

"Certainly, we can." Cherrie nodded, frowning at an iPad in her hand. "Or, I should clarify, we normally can't, since we're at full capacity and committed to our current clientele, who always reenroll, but Jolene Marshall is my sorority pal, and she asked for this favor. I understand Daddy Rhyland here spoke to Bruce about you wanting to go back to school?" Cherrie smiled.

Dylan shot me a death glare. Completely off-topic, but I was willing to pawn my other Rolex and a kidney just to hear *her* call me Daddy Rhyland.

"I don't want you to feel deceived," Dylan answered Cherrie, her eyes still firing poisonous switchblades at me, "so I think you should know I'm not planning to enroll in college in the immediate future. It's just a thought."

"That's all right." Cherrie patted Dylan's arms, and that was when I realized we were still holding hands thirty minutes into this thing and that I wasn't hating it at all. "I'd be happy to accommodate you either way. Any friend of the Marshalls is a friend of mine."

Dylan turned to Cherrie. "Okay. What's the damage?"

Cherrie slid her iPad pen over the screen. "For three times a week, nine a.m. drop-off and two thirty p.m. pickup, you are looking at twenty-two hundred dollars a month. That includes a hot lunch, snacks, and three sets of school uniforms a year."

Dylan paled, and her jaw went slack. Yeah. This was…substantial as fuck. *Welcome to the Upper East Side.*

I got that she didn't want Row to pay her way. I did. I even appreciated that. But couldn't she suck it up and have him pick up the check while she studied for her future? This kind of money didn't even register to Row. He probably paid more per month for his fucking white truffle honey habit.

"That won't be a problem," I drawled.

"That *might* be a problem." Dylan shook off my touch, finally breaking our contact, and I hated that I already missed it—and hated even more that she wiped our joined sweat from her palm off on her dress. "I'll need to look into my finances. Can I have a day or two?"

"You can even have a week or three." Cherrie smiled at her with the infinite warmth of a mother who knew the struggles of expensive childcare. "I will need to know by the end of next month, though. Before summer camp begins."

"That's plenty of time," Dylan said. "Thank you."

The drive back to our apartment building was drenched in pensive silence. Gravity nodded off again as soon as we put her into her seat. I could hear the wheels in Dylan's head churning.

Finally, when we were just about to turn toward the building's garage, I said, "You need to bite your tongue and ask Row for a loan. If you don't secure yourself a good job now, you're going to regret it."

"You have no idea what it feels like to be the loser sibling."

"I have a pretty good idea of what it feels like to be the loser friend," I countered dryly. "Think about it. My best friends are Row, multimillionaire, famous chef; Kieran, the second coming of Jesus in the soccer world with literal fucking *movies* made about him; and Tate, who is marginally more powerful than God himself. And here I am, pawning my goddamn watches to afford a fake girlfriend."

"Fiancée," she corrected. "And it's not the same."

"It's exactly the same. We're both the wild cards. The ones who took a bad turn and didn't make it. But don't double down on one bad choice."

I hated that I sounded like a disapproving aunt, but I happened to know firsthand how cruising along where life took you could be dangerous. I bit down on my tongue.

Don't open up more than you have to, idiot.

Oh, the hell with it.

"Look, three months ago, I got sexually assaulted by a client." Bitterness exploded in my mouth. It was the first time I'd admitted it out loud. The first time I'd told anyone about it. My friends thought I quit because I couldn't be bothered anymore.

Dylan sucked in an audible breath, turning to look at me. The car glided down the road to the parking garage.

"We were at a weekend-long engagement party in the Hamptons. Her ex's. She wanted to pretend she'd moved on. She got drunk. I did too. We shared a room…" I felt my nostrils flare and my chokehold on the steering wheel tightening. A sheen of sweat was covering my forehead. What the hell was wrong with me? I couldn't stop oversharing with this woman.

"Rhy…" Dylan said softly, her hand palming my shoulder with a squeeze.

"I was taking a shower after a day of pickleball and mini golf with her pretentious friends and her awful ex. I was a hazy mess from the alcohol and the pot I'd snuck out to smoke when no one was looking. She slipped inside the shower."

My throat worked around my next confession as the car slipped into my allotted parking spot. I cut off the engine.

"As soon as I saw her in the shower, naked, I told her to please get out. I was calm but firm. I explained I didn't want her that way. That sex was not a part of our contract, and I wasn't open to renegotiation. But she insisted her friend, who'd hired me the year before, got the so-called full treatment. I clarified that certain *extra* was a case-by-case issue. But she crowded me, cupping my cock, kissing down my chest…"

I closed my eyes. *Fuck*. I always felt violently mad when I heard about women getting sexually attacked, because typically, it was near impossible for them to fight off their attackers, size- and strength-wise.

But seeing as I was a hulky, muscular dude, I couldn't stop thinking I could've prevented my assault somehow. Pushed her off. The victim guilt gnawed at me, chipping away at my self-worth and my pride.

"The worst part was that I let it happen," I choked out, transported back to that moment.

By the time she was on her knees, my stupid cock was already hard, my back pressed against the granite wall. I just stood there and watched as she sucked me off.

"The entire time, I felt like I was trapped in my own head, desperate to break free—to tear the chains. It was the longest ten minutes of my entire life. And in them, I realized a lot of it was due to the decisions I'd made over the years. I wouldn't say it was my fault, but…"

"No." Dylan shook her head, and when I turned to look at her, I was surprised to see frustrated, angry tears glistening in her eyes. She had the same look she sported yesterday, when I told her Grav should go to preschool. The look of a lioness ready to fight to the death. "Don't victim-blame yourself. None of it is your fault."

"I'm not saying it was. But *I* chose to drink on duty. I chose to smoke pot and get high. I chose to offer myself as a boyfriend-for-hire. I chose to sleep with ninety percent of my clientele. I inserted myself into a highly explosive situation. I could've put my business degree to use and worked on Wall Street. Hell, I could've still been working with your brother. He offered for us to co-own La Vie en Rogue before he opened it. I opted out. I didn't want the long hours, the mountains of paperwork, the endless sacrifices. I realized I'd been lying to myself this whole time by saying I enjoyed what I was doing." My mouth pressed into a thin line. "After it was over, in the shower, I grabbed my suitcase and left. Ubered it from the Hamptons back to Manhattan. That day, I threw away my pot. Made a rule to only drink once a week. Quit my fake-boyfriend business. I started looking into my finances and realized I'd been drowning myself not only in drugs and alcohol but also in big splurges that didn't match my income. I decided to turn a corner. Do something with myself. Provide people with the opportunity to have a fake date without putting any of the individuals involved into compromising positions."

"You should've gone to the police after the assault." Her lips twisted in fury. "This is ridiculous. What she did was illegal. She—"

I shook my head. "She was drunk off her ass and an emotional wreck. I'm not making excuses for her—I just didn't see the point. What can I say? I got a taste of the consequences of my own decisions, and I hated it. All this to say you can't fall back into working at a bar or at a restaurant in New York like you did back home. And trust me, I get that the familiarity of it is tempting. Not because there's anything wrong with it. There isn't. Some people thrive in these careers. But *you* don't."

She flinched, and that was how I knew I'd hit a nerve.

I dug deeper. "You've always wanted to become a doctor. You still can. Well-worth-it journeys tend to be uphill. If life's hard, it means you're doing it right. Don't pass up on this preschool. You owe it to yourself and to Gravity. If your kid doesn't see you chase your own dream, how do you expect them to chase theirs?"

"Rhy..." She clamped her mouth shut. Opened it again. "I'm really sorry—"

"Don't be." I put my hand on her knee, noticing her dress had ridden up on the way here. The touch of my rough finger pads against her smooth summer skin made a jolt of energy shoot up my spine. Something tightened behind my abs like a key twisting in its hole, unlocking something feral, and now I knew it wasn't the late-night burgers.

I had it hard for her.

I withdrew my hand casually, ignoring my rocketing pulse. "Instead of being sorry, take care of your future," I said stiffly.

"Okay, Daddy." Dylan rolled her eyes.

"Say that again," I groaned.

"No. I was being sarcastic. I'd rather stay an orphan."

I laughed. "Do you want help taking Gravity up?"

"No, thanks. See you in three days." She popped open the passenger door and rounded the car to get her daughter.

Shit. Her next shift was in three days? Why did it make me sad?

And why couldn't I wait for the days to tick by?

CHAPTER NINETEEN
DYLAN

> Cal: How's your fake fiancé?
>
> Dylan: Being a real pain in the ass.
>
> Cal: And Tucker?
>
> Dylan: So far, so good. Meaning I haven't seen him in a few days.
>
> Cal: Be careful, Dylan, okay? It's the same guy who bullied us in high school.
>
> Dylan: Trust me, Dot, there's nothing I want more than Tucker out of my life.

"Instead of wasting all that time and research on cybersecurity and flu strains, universities need to start looking into whether Nina Dobrev and Victoria Justice are the same person," Max mumbled, perched over the alcohol rack behind the bar, watching *The Vampire Diaries* on his phone.

My first time back after four days, and I was finally experiencing a graveyard shift at the Alchemist. It was officially summer, and New York City had decided to kick it off with a huge Central Park event laden with multiple live shows. Other than the random tourists staggering into the bar to purchase overpriced water, we were pretty much alone.

"They're not the same person, Max," I chuckled, browsing through my own Instagram for-you page, eyeballs glued to reels of people traveling the world. I especially loved the ones who lived in their vans. Here I was, being a salty bitch about my sweater getting caught in my door handle, when people actually had to drive to their gym to take a shower.

"How's Faye doing?" I asked.

"Better. Still not discharged, though. There's a recovery time they want her to take. Four, maybe five weeks before she can come back to work. You still fine to fill in for her?"

"As long as I have childcare," I confirmed.

"Let me know if anything changes. Well." Max yanked out his AirPods, stuffing his phone into his back pocket. "I'm heading out. Tucker will be here any minute to take over, so don't worry. You good?"

No. I was the opposite of good. I didn't want to see Tucker. I especially didn't want to spend one-on-one time with him. But it wasn't like I had a choice.

I gave Max a thumbs-up. "Sure."

"You can go when he arrives. Place is empty anyway."

"Roger that. Enjoy the rest of your day."

"You too."

After Max left, I decided to keep busy and clean some sticky tables and the underside of the bar to pass the time. I switched from Instagram reels to *Grey's Anatomy* for background noise. A part of me wanted to google premed programs in New York, but I stopped myself in time. I'd be better off sticking to this job for a few more weeks—months, if needed—before finding something suitable.

Finally, Tucker breezed into the empty bar. He wore a pair of jeans and a button-down black shirt. He was holding a donut box in his hand, a welcoming smile curving his mouth.

I slid an uncertain glance at him. "Um, hi."

"Hey there, Dyl! What's up?" He slid the donut box between us on the bar and flipped it open, gesturing toward a row of orange-glazed donuts.

I mentally checked the calendar. Nope. Fall was nowhere near us. The smell was overwhelming. Like I got lost in a pre-Thanksgiving Bed Bath & Beyond.

"What's this?" I peered into the box.

"Pumpkin spice donuts. I remember they're your favorite." He waggled his brows.

"You're remembering incorrectly." I folded my arms over my chest. Why was he being so nauseatingly nice?

His beam collapsed. "But when you were pregnant, you said—"

"When I was pregnant, I used to dip pickles in peanut butter. Pregnancy cravings have *nothing* to do with normal taste."

His shoulders slumped, his entire posture collapsing into a hunch. His face looked better, almost healed. Then his disappointment quickly morphed into fury, as it did when we were together. "What's your problem?" He puffed out his chest, rounding the bar predatorily, and I nearly cowered back from the force of his sudden anger.

Tucker used to either agree to do what I wanted to make me shut up or lose it completely, slamming doors and yelling. In my warped universe, door slamming and shouting weren't that big of a deal back then. I came from a household where my father would literally hit my brother and my mother for not answering his calls fast enough. But looking back, I couldn't imagine tolerating that sort of treatment with Gravity in the house. She didn't deserve to grow up thinking this was the standard. Didn't deserve an oopsie blue bracelet of pain around her wrist.

I grabbed a bottle opener from the counter and aimed it his way. "Take a step back before I disembowel you without anesthesia," I instructed with fake calm.

Tucker stopped a few feet from me, parking one hand on his waist and using the other to massage his temples. "Shit. You're right.

I'm just…take the donuts, okay? I had to go all the way across town to get them. They don't make this flavor at Krispy Kreme."

"I don't care." I angled the bottle opener toward his face, ready to put a hole in it. "I don't want your donuts."

"I'm trying to make an effort here," he said through gritted teeth, his flat mouth barely moving.

"Mission failed," I announced.

"See, this is why I left you. You always have an annoying comeback that spoils the mood."

Ignoring the way his words sliced through the muscle tissue of my heart, I retrieved a washcloth from the fridge handle, making a show of wiping the bottle opener clean. "I'm not here to become your friend. I'm here to earn money so I can provide for our daughter."

"Yeah. Okay. Let's talk about her." He pasted on an easy smile, and I got whiplash from the drastic change in his behavior every ticking minute. I used to tell myself Tucker being good in bed was proof he wasn't completely selfish. I now knew I was wrong. Bringing me to orgasm over and over was a way to stroke his own ego, to prove to himself that he could. My body was his toy. A means to an end. It was never about me.

"Yes?" I put the bottle opener down and immediately grabbed the paring knife, wiping it methodically.

"Am I going to have to get lawyers involved, or are you going to do the right thing here and let me see her?"

I examined the knife I was holding, reluctantly putting it back on the cutting board. "We'll need to make it gradual," I heard myself say. "I don't want to spring you on her out of nowhere. First, we'll do short visits. We'll introduce you as a friend of the family. Then, if everything goes well, we can tell her."

"Who's 'we'? You and that asshole?"

I blinked at him slowly. I meant me and *him*, but I didn't appreciate the attitude.

"Rhyland is doing more than you ever have for Gravity." This part was true.

"I don't like him."

"Good thing I'm the one who fucks him, not you." *If only.*

"How soon?" he demanded, his left eyelid pulsating, *twitch-twitch-twitch.*

"I'm not going to time it. When it feels right."

"That's not fair," he griped, giving me a look of disbelief. "I know my rights, Dylan. If you start posing too many difficulties, I *will* get lawyers involved."

"Awesome. I'd love to tell the judge you left me to raise her for three and a half years so you could get a tan on Bondi Beach." I turned to face him. "Oh, and I took plenty of pictures of the new bracelet you gave me." I raised my arm between us. "Nice gift, by the way."

"Look, I don't want any trouble," he said quickly, licking his lips. "I just want to be a part of your and Gravity's life. I think the fact that you came here, to this city, to this *bar*, is kismet. You can't tell me it doesn't mean anything. I mean, what are the odds?"

"Pretty good, considering Kieran sent me here."

"What are the odds I'd see Kieran here?" he insisted. "That he'd recognize me. That I'd tell him I was going back to Staindrop to take care of you and Gravity."

"Whoa there." I stumbled back, my ass hitting the counter. "I don't need you to take care of me. This is purely about Gravity. I—"

"C'mon, Dylan." He snorted, stepping forward, ignoring my discomfort. "You can't tell me you're really considering marrying that douchebag Rhyland. He's literally a man-whore. Like, it's the talk of the town."

Yawning provocatively, I gathered my hair and tied it into a messy bun. "Retired now. And all that practice made a particularly delicious perfect. I'm so thankful he introduced me to good dick." I winked.

Inside, I was reeling. Tucker's words had struck me like a thunderstorm. I couldn't stop thinking about the woman who'd abused Rhyland, imagining myself strangling to death the faceless, entitled piece of work who thought she could have him just because she'd paid him to accompany her. I didn't expect to take it so badly.

"Dylan. Dylan. *Honey.*" Tucker rushed toward me, and I tried not to flinch as he took my arms in his hands, peering down into my eyes.

I realized, to my horror, I could never hate him all the way, because he had my daughter's eyes and smile and dimples.

"It's your anger speaking, and I get it. I messed up. Let me make this up to you. We were so great together. Don't let one small mishap ruin this for us."

"Allison wasn't a mishap." I yanked my arms away, ducking under him and swiftly making my way to the back end of the bar. He followed me. "And neither were the last three, almost four, years. I can't, in good conscience, keep you away from your daughter if you plan to do the right thing by her. Better late than ever. But you and I have been done since the moment you docked back in Staindrop that Christmas and went to your mistress instead of to the hospital to see your daughter. This is still over, Tucker."

With that, I grabbed my shit from my locker and fled.

CHAPTER TWENTY
RHYLAND

> Bruce: Where are you?
> Rhyland: Home?
> Bruce: Why is there a question mark? You ain't sure where your fancy butt is, boy?

Goddamn boomers and their inability to decipher tone. I was close to losing my patience with the guy. He'd been jerking me around, making me wait for our Texas gathering before he'd make a decision. I knew business deals took time—Tate had warned me—but Bruce knew I was sitting on a gold mine and was playing hardball because... what, he knew I had a history of dating women for money?

> Rhyland: I'm home, why are you asking?
> Bruce: I'm coming over to hand-deliver you and your fiancée the invitation to my house.
> Rhyland: We already RSVP'd.
> Bruce: So?

My deep-rooted urge to knock Bruce's teeth down his throat morphed into panic. Truth was Dylan and I didn't live together, and one glance at my bachelor pad would confirm this. I had to think on my feet.

I knew Dylan was home, and in a purely convenient coincidence, her mom and soon-to-be stepdad were also in town, so she actually had a babysitter.

Dylan and I had been keeping our distance since the preschool tour, but it was time for her to earn that fat paycheck. I opened our chat box.

> Rhyland: Bruce is coming to hand-deliver our TX invitation. Let's meet him downstairs at Café Europa. Putting a show on for him would help me.
> Dylan: What'd you have in mind?
> Rhyland: Can I kiss you?
> Dylan: I'd literally rather eat my own eyeballs than pretend to enjoy it, but sure. Whatever gets you the deal.
> Rhyland: Sorry. This ain't working anymore. I know you've got it hard for me.
> Dylan: Hard-ly.
> Rhyland: Now you're just giving me a stiffy.
> Dylan: We can always do something about it.
> Rhyland: See? You are as consistent as a half-baked muffin.
> Dylan: I'm honestly repulsed by how much I'm attracted to you. But rest assured, I don't like you AT ALL.
> Rhyland: I'm attracted to you AND I like you. The liking you part is the problem though. I don't do relationships.
> Dylan: Aw. Are you afraid to catch feelings?
> Rhyland: Don't be so smug, Cosmos. That shit's contagious.

I shot Bruce a message to meet us downstairs because we were going on a mommy and daddy date. Then I lumbered into my walk-in closet and honest to fucking God had trouble deciding what I was going to wear. The options were dwindling by the day, seeing as I'd started selling shit online to keep afloat. I settled for a beige button-down short-sleeve shirt, olive chinos, and preppy tennis shoes. Then I proceeded to spritz on enough Valentino cologne to drown a small herd of kittens.

Did cats move in prides? Fat chance—they were solitary animals. Anyway, I was unnecessarily anxious because I knew I was going to kiss Dylan Casablancas today.

And I also knew I was going to fucking like it.

Things got progressively more pathetic when I took the elevator down and accidentally hit the button for Dylan's floor instead of the ground floor. I chalked it up to the fact that I'd spent a ton of time playing nanny to Gravity. Force of habit. Nothing more, nothing less. Still, I was already here, so I might as well say hi to Zeta.

I stepped out and knocked on the door. Zeta flung it open. She was wearing a red fitted dress and a matching lipstick, with an apron. She was a true MILF. A mature version of Dylan. Same high cheekbones, regal nose, thick, fluffy eyebrows, and an endless stream of thick black hair that ran down to her waist like a river.

"Rhyland! *Mio figlio!*" She threw her arms over my shoulders, octopussing me in a hug and dragging me past the threshold into the apartment. She kissed both my cheeks before grabbing my head and examining me. "You look good. Your mother and father are well?"

"Sure." *Who the fuck knows?* "You and Marty having fun in the Big Apple?"

"Yes. I just got back from a Broadway show. Now Marty went golfing with old college friends, and I'm baking a cake with Gravity." She licked her thumb, using it to wipe off the residue lipstick from my cheeks.

"Uncle Rhyrand!" Gravity's high-pitched voice rang around the apartment. The small human bolted from the kitchen stool she was standing on, climbing my leg like I was a tree. I squirmed as her little fingers dug through my waist, abs, and torso. She managed to get all the way up to my waist before I scooped her up and tossed her in the air until she almost hit the ceiling. With each toss, her giggling became squeakier and more enthralled.

"I told you," I said.

Toss.

"Uncle Rhyland."

Toss.

"Is a ticklish."

Toss.

"Bas—" I remembered Zeta was here. "Man."

Toss.

When I put her down, Gravity hugged my leg, staring up at me with her enormous dark blue eyes, her lower lip curled down to stop herself from crying.

"What's going on?" I ruffled her hair.

Where the hell was Dylan? Why wasn't she coming out? She must've heard me walking in.

"Uncle Rhyrand, I got a boo-boo cutting sugar dough." She extended her arm toward me.

"Let's see." I kneeled down on one knee and examined her arm. She was bullshitting me. Her pudgy forearm was pristine, with no scratch in sight.

Zeta chuckled above Gravity's head.

"Where is it, exactly?" I clasped her little wrist, turning it from side to side.

"Right here." A chubby finger pointed to a tiny beauty mark.

"Eh, I see." I nodded gravely. "Looks pretty bad."

"It hurts." Another pout.

"Gotta be honest, I don't know if you'll make it out of this."

That earned me a slap on the back of my neck with a kitchen towel from Zeta. I stifled a laugh.

"Go get the Band-Aids and markers. We'll fix you up."

Gravity nodded, dashing back to her room.

I stood up to find Zeta grinning big at me. I raised a hand. "Trust me, I'm hating every minute of it."

"*Mio caro*, you're growing up. You'll be a great dad one day."

"Is your daughter coming or what? We're going to be late to a meeting downstairs." I ignored her observation. I assumed Zeta didn't know about our fake relationship, so there was no point in explaining my existence in Gravity's life would be temporary.

"Oh yes. She jumped in the shower. She should be out any minute now."

"Can you go tell her to hurry up?"

"No. And neither can you. She's a lady. She needs time to prepare before going out."

I rolled my tongue along my inner cheek. Gravity returned, clutching a small tin with Band-Aids and her marker box. I got down on one knee, snatching both.

"Where is it again?"

The kid pointed to a beauty mark on a completely different arm. I did appreciate how committed she was to the lie. A lawyer in the making.

"There."

I opened the tin and grabbed a Band-Aid. I flattened it out on the uninjured spot, smoothing it over her skin. "Ink?"

"A giraffe eating a donut."

"Random, but I'll allow." I grabbed the markers and started doodling on her Band-Aid.

It all started when Gravity got a paper cut one day when I was babysitting her. She insisted I put a Band-Aid on it, but when she realized they'd run out of colorful, themed Band-Aids, she threw a fit. This resulted in me giving her a TED Talk about the decay of moral society through consumerism and the pink tax before concluding that anyway, it was best to buy plain Band-Aids and just draw what you wanted on them. We'd been patching her completely unblemished body ever since. I doubted Michelangelo was ever as busy as I was these days.

"All done." I dropped the brown, yellow, and pink markers back into the box. "You're as good as new."

"Thank you. I wove you." Gravity hugged me.

What was with the Casablancas family and being ultra-affectionate? And why couldn't Dylan touch me? She was the only one whose hands I wanted on me anyway.

I patted Gravity's back awkwardly. I still wasn't thrilled about befriending a toddler.

"Did you...draw smileys on her Band-Aid?" A voice coming from the hallway made my head snap up.

Shit. Now *this* was a sight worthy of being drawn in the Sistine Chapel.

Dylan, all made up, with a brown-and-white polka-dot summer dress offering a deep slit and a peek at her long, shapely legs. She'd done her hair in big, fluffy waves and put shimmer on her cheekbones, and she had that glittery thing on her lips and her inner eyes that made her look all dewy.

"It's a giraffe and a donut," I corrected matter-of-factly. "I will not have my work thoughtlessly disparaged by an amateur."

"I didn't realize we were...commissioning your work." Dylan swallowed a laugh.

"You ran out of fancy Band-Aids." I stood up slowly, since all my blood had rushed to my dick.

Dylan just stared at me with a mixture of awe and softness. It was the first time the grumpy woman had oozed warmth toward me, and not the kind that wished to set me on fire.

"Ready to hit the road?" I glanced at my lowly Cartier.

Finally, Dylan shook her head, snapping out of her weird reverie. "Um, sure. Mama, is that okay? It's five minutes from here and shouldn't take long."

"*Tesoro mia*, of course. You go have your fun. Make sure to drink a glass of wine. You deserve it."

CHAPTER TWENTY-ONE
DYLAN

Can you hear this sound, Dylan? It is the sound of feminism leaving your body. Because you just witnessed Rhyland Coltridge being amazing to your child.

Fatherly, even.

But you need to reel in your desperation. You've already made it clear you want to screw him, and he passed on the offer. Multiple times, in fact. And considering he's a sexual-assault survivor, it'd be nice not to treat him like a piece of meat.

"*Dylan,*" Rhyland hissed impatiently—for what must have been the thousandth time, judging by his tone.

We were in the elevator heading downstairs to Café Europa. I couldn't bear to look at him. Only now, it wasn't just because he was hot; it was also because this hotness was attached to a man my child absolutely adored.

But he was wrong. I wasn't catching feelings. I was catching hormones.

"Hmm?" I feigned boredom.

"I just gave you a rundown of the entire plan." He gave me a funny "what is wrong with you?" look. "Were you even listening?"

"Nope. Was too busy fantasizing about you moving out of the building. Repeat it."

He rubbed his hands together, boyishly focused. "We're going to beat Bruce there. He's a punctual motherfucker, but we're still early. So what we'll do is we'll kiss at the exact minute he walks in, and that way, he'll think he's walking in on us being lovey-dovey and shit."

"Remind me why he couldn't just bring the invitation to your penthouse."

"Because you're supposed to live there with me, and the most feminine thing I own is a life-size painting of Ursula Andress butt naked, and I don't think that counts."

That warranted me slapping his arm with my purse. "What's wrong with you?"

"Nothing. There wasn't a floor-to-ceiling-size painting, so I had to settle."

"Well, what if he's a few minutes late?" I challenged.

The elevator doors slid open, and we both stepped outside. The weather was glorious, the street flooded with sunrays and the sticky, heavy scent of flowers in bloom.

"Then you'll just have to suffer through kissing me for a little while longer." Rhyland heaved a long-suffering sigh. His fingers clasped mine naturally as we crossed the street to the pretty French coffee shop with overflowing pink-and-yellow flowerpots and white rustic tables.

"Don't ridicule my struggles. I might throw up. My gag reflex is super sensitive," I huffed.

"I'd love it if we could work on that."

Heat rushed to my cheeks, and I speared him with a look. He returned a languid expression.

"You don't have the balls to touch me," I taunted him.

"I'm literally about to fucking kiss you."

"And if Row finds out?" I inquired sweetly.

"I'll tell him the truth. That it was all for show. So we could have an audience. And that neither of us enjoyed it."

"I'm glad we're on the same page."

"We should probably practice before he arrives," Rhyland suggested.

"Practice?" My eyebrows slammed together, and he spluttered a laugh. "No, thanks. I already know how to kiss. I'm not entirely new to this, you know."

I hated that he knew how much I wanted him. Usually, it was the other way around. And sure, I knew Rhyland found me attractive, but Rhyland cast a wide net. He found a lot of people attractive. Didn't mean he'd give them the time of day.

"You're entirely new to kissing me." He waggled his brows. "It's not the same experience as kissing all the boys who came before."

He glanced at his watch again. So did I. It was ten minutes to.

"We don't have time to practice," I said.

"We won't need more than ten minutes. Actually, five will be sufficient."

He let go of my hand, grabbing my waist and tipping me against the wall, his own Leaning Tower of Pisa. A small gasp escaped me at his warm, possessive touch. He tilted me down, one hand on my waist, the other curling over the back of my thigh, as he brought his lips an inch from my own. He halted a breath away from my lips, and I could already taste him. Cinnamon, bonfire, clean male, and my demise.

"Famous last words before I kiss you?" he croaked.

"Man buns are ridiculous past twenty-five," I spewed out venomously.

With a sardonic, irresistible smirk, he dove down and kissed me.

CHAPTER TWENTY-TWO
RHYLAND

My stomach dipped as soon as our lips touched, a roller-coaster effect I'd never experienced before when kissing someone.

My hand hiked up, cradling her head, fingers threading along the locks of her hair of their own accord as our hot mouths fused together, suckling each other in desperation, as if we were gasping for breath.

She moaned into my mouth, and I seized the moment, slicking my tongue over hers, finding the heat of her and burrowing into it. She tasted like the sweetest nectar, and I found myself edging closer to heaven's gate, moving my mouth over hers softly at first, searching for the moans and the gasps, trying to gauge how she liked to be kissed—passionately? Sweetly? Ardently? Leisurely?—until I found the perfect pressure that made her ankle vine around mine, her sandaled toes curling.

Our tongues danced together now, and fuck, she knew what she was doing. She teased me with fast, shallow strokes, and every time our kiss got into a rhythm, she gave me a curveball, changing the angle of her head or biting my lower lip. She was playful and confident and *famished*. I could feel the tension in her muscles dissolving, how her trepidation melted away. She was putty in my arms, fierce but pliant at the same time, and I thought to myself that I'd been doing it wrong for the past thirty years. This was the real deal. The edge of something wild and dark and different.

This one simple kiss was better than a whole night of sex with someone else. It was—

Dylan broke off the kiss, slapping my chest away lightly. "Okay, horndog. That's enough practice."

I grudgingly disconnected my lips from hers, sulking—honest to God fucking *sulking*—down at her.

"You always bust my ass about having sex, but you won't even let me kiss you properly?" I gently brought her up and eased her body against the wall. Her nipples dug into the fabric of her dress like two bullets. Jesus. She wasn't wearing a bra. The little sasshole defied gravity too.

"That's different. Sex would be a mutually beneficial, tit-for-tat arrangement." She pretended to examine her nails in boredom.

There will be tits, all right.

The mere thought of it made my dick rigid and my balls heavy. I was very close to throwing caution—and a twenty-two-year friendship—to the wind and going for it. I wanted her. Bad.

"If I fuck you, will you let me kiss you again?" I blurted out.

"You're not doing me a favor." She snorted out a laugh. "And we can kiss again in two minutes when he arrives. Which reminds me, we need to get inside if we want t—"

"Are you kidding me? Two minutes is a lifetime. Let me kiss you again." I sounded like I was asking her for a first aid kit to sew my limbs back together. That was the level of desperation we were dealing with.

Pathetic, Coltridge. All you needed was one hit to get hooked.

She smiled incredulously, searching my face. "Oh my God. You're serious, aren't you?"

"I'm serious," I confirmed sullenly. "I want to make sure that first time was a fluke. No way is the next time going to be as good."

"What will you give me in return?" A gleam of mischief flickered in those dark eyes.

"Whatever you want," I croaked. "More money. Unlimited babysitting gigs." Pause. "You can never have too many kidneys."

She screwed her mouth sideways, scrunching her nose. "Mine work fine."

"How about I give you my penthouse for the length of the arrangement?"

Talk about pussy-whipped. Dylan laughed harder at this, and I didn't know when this whole thing had morphed from funny and light to decadent and tragic, but we were straddling that line like a stripper eager for a fat tip.

"No, thanks. But I would love it if you could take Grav to a Mommy and Me class once a week."

"Done." Small price to pay. "Can I kiss you again?"

"What's with you?" She seemed amused. "I mean, sure. Go for it."

I dove down again, desperate for that same rush and heat. For the way every cell in my body buzzed with adrenaline and greed.

Tragically, this time was even better. I threw out the handful of fucks I still gave about Dylan being Row's baby sister. Coaxing her lips open with the tip of my tongue, I met her velvety tongue with mine.

The kiss was playful at first, our tongues dancing together in a rhythm, thrust for thrust. Her hands slid beneath my shirt, nails raking up my torso, making my body break into uncontrollable goose bumps. I licked and kissed and bit the corner of her mouth, making up for...what, all the years I'd missed? All that time she was tucked away in bumfuck Maine, hidden like something precious and forbidden? I was grabbing her by the hips, pressing her core against my hard-on, wondering if we were going to get arrested for dry humping in public—and half hoping we would, since that'd mean more alone time with her—when a Southern drawl pierced through my skull like an arrow.

"Dadgum it, Coltridge, you're mauling the poor lil miss like a fox out for cattle!"

Dylan's lips stretched into a grin against mine. "I think your plan is working, family guy," she whispered into my lips.

It took all my self-control and a few other pedestrians' willpower to right her against the wall and smooth out my fake fiancée's dress. I turned to flash Bruce my cocksure smirk. He was striding his way over from a black Escalade. Luckily, my casual shirt was on the longer side, so it hid my enthusiasm for my newfound hobby of eating Dylan's face.

"Marshall." I nodded.

"Tomcat." He held a thick envelope, which he pointed at me with a wink. Each time I met him, he looked progressively more Southern, but today took the cake, with his cowboy hat wide enough to shelter an entire hockey team.

"Fine day, ain't it, Mr. Marshall?" Dylan's recovery was flawless. She met him halfway and thrust her hand in his direction for a handshake.

He grabbed it and tugged her into a hug, smacking a noisy pucker on each of her cheeks.

"Thanks a lot for the preschool tour. Looks like a great place."

"Sure is, Lil Miss. And would you look at that stone?" He pressed a rough finger pad to the diamond on her finger when their hands touched and turned her wrist to look at it with a nod of approval. "I say, Coltridge, you're not as hopeless as I thought you were."

I advanced toward them unsteadily, stopping beside Dylan and extending a hand to make him stop touching my fiancée. "Anything for my future wife."

"Gotta love two young lovebirds." He smacked the envelope onto my chest. "Here. All the details for the private flight and chauffeur that'll take you to us. The missus and I are looking forward to getting to know y'all better." His eyes bounced between us, assessing.

"Sounds good," Dylan chirped, unaffected by Bruce's obvious distrust. "Grav's met plenty of ponies in her lifetime, but this'll be her first stubborn ass."

Bruce elevated a brow. The little sasshole was giving him attitude. I was torn between kissing her and berating her.

"'Scuse me?"

Dylan batted her eyelashes innocently. "Cherrie mentioned you have a donkey—Eeyore?"

"Dang straight we do." His eyes lit up in delight. "Not many folks know this, but donkeys are smarter than horses. Don't get scared as easily." He stuck a red Marlboro to the side of his mouth, pulling a box of matches from his front pocket. He struck a match and held it to his cigarette, waving the match back and forth between us. "And lemme just give you a heads-up, I ain't completely sold on that app of yours. Been makin' some calls to people who know you through the grapevine, Coltridge. No one but Tate Blackthorn could vouch that you have any type of marketing and social media experience. And I trust Blackthorn just a tad less than I trust last year's weather forecast."

"Why's that?" I asked.

"Oh, got my reasons," he muttered darkly. "Five hundred and thirty million of them."

I gathered from this that Tate had screwed him over. Well, he was welcome to join the never-ending club.

"I don't like what you're insinuating, Marshall." I placed an arm over Dylan's shoulder. "I'd like to do business with you, but I'm not about to jump through unnecessary hoops to grant your investment. I have a good product that fills a massive hole in the dating-app market. I did all the legwork. All you have to do is put your already established platform to use and reap what I've sowed. If you're not interested in doing business, that's fine. Just tell me now so we don't waste our time."

"I'm not saying I don't want to work together. I'm just saying I need more time to study this app of yours." Bruce puffed his cigarette in my direction with a careless shrug.

It took everything in me not to lash out. I'd seen Tate and Row conducting business. They were always carefully unruffled. And to be fair, when I used to work with Row and when I worked as a fake boyfriend, I always maintained my professionalism too. It was only shit I cared about that riled me up. I cared about this deal greatly.

"That is fine." I smiled cockily. "If you have any questions, you know where to find me."

"Oh, I sure do," Bruce chuckled, turning on his heel. He took a few steps toward the black Escalade waiting for him before he stopped and tossed me a look over his shoulder. "Know what else I heard through the grapevine?"

I glared at him wordlessly. I had a feeling this one was going to hurt.

"That you're pawning your shit all around town. Are you losing your pants, Coltridge?"

Heat rose up my neck, spreading across my face. I opened my mouth, but Dylan beat me to it.

"I'm teaching him how to be less materialistic. He has no use for all those fancy watches and man jewelry. He's donating the money to children in need." She tossed her hair back.

"Which charity?"

"He's splitting it evenly between Children of America, Locks of Love, and Make-A-Wish Foundation. We won't be attending the latter's gala at the end of the month, but we're sending a check for both our plates and someone to do the bidding for us at the annual auction."

Holy fucking great liar. Was she a politician or something?

"What'll you be bidding on?" Bruce remained unaffected.

"The Damien Hirst skull."

She did not miss a beat. She was frighteningly good.

Bruce's face softened. "All right, Lil Miss. Either *you're* saying the truth or you're a fantastic liar. I can appreciate both."

"He's turning a corner, Marshall." Dylan patted my ass, and I could see the flare of her eyes when she realized my buns of steel could smash nuts, they were so tight. "I'm civilizing this man. A few more months and he'll be ready to join society."

"Careful, or I just might believe you." He saluted her, slipping past the door one of his assistants held open for him. "See y'all next week for the spice thingy."

"You mean the thing where you could've given us the useless invitation we've already RSVP'd?" I hissed sardonically.

He rolled down the backseat window with a shit-eating grin. "Yup. That's the one. I like to ensure my business partners are willing to drop everything and make time for me, as I tend to do the same for them."

When the Escalade pulled away from the curb, Dylan tipped her head back and moaned. "Don't pay me for next week. Send the check to the gala."

My brow furrowed. "Are you kidding me? You don't have to do that."

"Are *you* kidding *me*? Lying about giving money to charity? We don't need this kind of karma on our asses. Plus, he's not above checking if we secured seats with our names. And ten thousand is a lot of pants—it buys credibility that you have ten thousand in liquidity."

"You're right. Fuck. Thank God one of us is smart." And that someone wasn't me. I blew out air, delight trickling into my system. Bruce Marshall had fallen for it hook, line, and sinker. "We need to practice some more."

"That's what I've been saying since I got here. Look, I'm not a fan of reverse cowgirl or spooning, but any other position, I'm down." Dylan hiked her purse string up her shoulder, waggling her brows.

"I mean we need to get to know each other. He's going to ask us questions we don't know the answers to." I rubbed my stubbled jaw.

"Oh. Yeah. That's what I meant too," she mumbled, the apples of her cheeks pink now.

She was adorable on top of being sexy. I'd already come to terms with the fact that I was going to fuck this woman and bear the consequences. Even the complete demolition of my life was a price worth paying.

"Like, what kind of things?" She tossed her hair back from her face.

"I don't know. Favorite color. Favorite band. Favorite sex position."

"Turquoise. Panic! At The Disco. Sideways sixty-nine."

Precum pasted my crown to my briefs, my pulse hammering through the length of my dick. "Right. I think we should probably—wait, what's sideways sixty-nine?"

"It's the same as the regular one, but lying sideways so you can have eye contact. Pretty cool."

Not so cool that I imagined her doing it with Tucker and wanted to plummet my fist into his face until he looked like a defiled cherry pie.

"Right. Let's get inside and unpack all that." I rubbed my hands together.

"You mean…now?" She frowned.

"Yes. Now." I gestured to the café in front of us. "I promise to be a perfect gentleman."

"That's honestly not a selling point for me, but okay."

"Dylan, you have to stop doing this."

"Doing what?" She shot me a confused look.

"Being all funny and smart and sexy. Tone it down a little. Be, I don't know, more like Cal."

I liked Row's wife, but she was a disaster area who suffered from frequent bouts of verbal diarrhea and was almost cartoonishly clumsy. I could spend an entire lifetime fake engaged to her without yielding to temptation—or even being tempted.

"No, I can't." Dylan grinned cunningly. "If you find me so irresistible, stop resisting."

CHAPTER TWENTY-THREE
DYLAN

"So what's your favorite color, band, and sexual position?" I stared at Rhyland from across the round table between us. We were sipping champagne—*real* champagne, not prosecco—and sharing a mouthwatering flatbread with herbs and artichokes and honey drizzled on it.

I ordered steak for an entrée, and he ordered a chicken salad. This place was not a coffee shop at all. It was a restaurant, and a damn expensive one. There were candles between us, French ballads playing softly in the background, antique chandeliers.

I knew this date wasn't going to end up in the sack, so it was all a moot point. I didn't really need to find out things about Rhyland. I could wing it out of any situation by bullshitting my way through.

"Pink, Oasis, clear the table." He folded his hands, accentuating his crazy-buff biceps.

"Pink?" My champagne went down the wrong pipe, causing me to cough into my fist. "That's your favorite color?"

"What's not to like about pink? It's the color of nipples and pussy—both my favorite things." He squinted at me from behind his champagne, taking a slow sip as his lips spread into a taunting smirk. "Do I sense prejudice here? What's wrong with a man loving on pink?"

"Absolutely nothing. You just give purple vibes."

"Why do I—" he started. Then he shook his head, looking amused. "You know what? No way is he going to ask us about our favorite colors or sexual positions. He probably thinks anal play is the equivalent of signing a lease on a new condo in hell with your dick."

"Fair enough. Let's try to narrow down what he might ask about." I snorted. "Probably how we got together and when."

"We need to come up with a story." He snapped his fingers, pointing at me. "Help me out here. You're the one with the big brain and great ideas."

I loved that Rhyland made me feel smart and reminded me of it so frequently. No one else ever did. Not because I wasn't smart but because people hardly noticed it. I didn't fit into the stereotype of a smart person. I was just a single mom with a bar job.

"Well, we need to keep it real. He knows you used to entertain for money." I bit into the flatbread, which was orgasmic, and chewed with gusto. "I think our safest option is to make our romance short but intense. Like, we hooked up last Christmas and decided we couldn't live without each other."

"Who hit on who?" Rhyland asked, noticing I was plucking the black olives from the flatbread and helping me out with the task.

"You hit on me, obviously." I rolled my eyes. "We need to make it believable. Authenticity is key, Coltridge."

"When are we getting married?" He passed me the olive-less piece of flatbread he was working on.

"Sometime next year." I waved him off. "Best to put a buffer to allow sufficient time for the breakdown of our engagement."

"Who's going to break it off?"

I pointed to myself. "I already thought about it. We need something to make you look like the good guy so your professional relationship with him doesn't suffer. I'm going to leave you for two werewolf shifters named Dolph and Claws."

"I think we have two different ideas about what 'authenticity' means." Rhy squinted, and I laughed.

The waitress stepped between us with our plates, slipping mine onto the table first before setting his salad in front of him with a beam. "Hi, Rhyland."

"Hey, Wendy."

Wendy licked her lips, looking between us awkwardly. She was objectively gorgeous, with an irresistible pout and long platinum hair that reached her lower back. "You, um, haven't answered my texts?"

I pressed my lips together to keep myself from laughing. Rhyland's salacious lifestyle was biting him in the ass, and I had a front-row seat for the occasion.

To his credit, Rhy didn't seem too ruffled by her accusatory tone. "I wanted to tell you face-to-face." He reached for my hand as I was grabbing another piece of flatbread, bringing my knuckles to his lips from across the table. The flatbread dropped between us. "I'm engaged now. It was all very sudden, but I met the one." He made sure she got a good look at my rented engagement ring.

"Oh." Her face closed off, her shoulders squaring. Her gaze scooted to me, and she forced out a smile. "Congratulations. That's great."

"Thanks."

When she scurried away, disappearing into the kitchen, I shot Rhyland an inquisitive look. "Wow. That was cold."

"She's been bombarding me with text messages and emails for weeks," Rhy explained. "I've been trying to let her down easy for a while now."

"Rhyland Lucas Coltridge, did you take me here deliberately to break a girl's heart?" My jaw dropped to the floor.

"Not really, but it was a nice bonus."

"Is there any female in this zip code you haven't slept with?"

"Pfft, of course." He popped cubed chicken into his mouth, parking his elbows on the table. "First of all, there's you." He gestured toward me. "And I barely made my way through Forty-Fourth Street and Fourth Ave."

"I can't believe I'm saying this"—I dug into my juicy steak—"but I feel kinda bad about cockblocking you."

"Don't," he croaked.

"Why?"

"Because variety doesn't equal freedom." He popped a piece of chicken into his mouth. "And if I had the freedom to choose, I'd still choose you." His eyes scurried back to his dish, and he took a forkful of a bite. "As a fuck buddy, of course."

"Then why are you holding back?" My pulse gathered above my eyelid, *thump-thump-thumping* like a hummingbird. "There's literally nothing at stake. Row's not going to know."

"Maybe, but I will, and I'd never forgive myself."

I had nothing to say to that. I didn't want to push him around. Not that he couldn't take it—Rhyland was a big boy.

But then he added, "But I'm beginning to see that I'm fine living with the guilt if it means I can have you."

"What do you mean?" I blinked.

"After those two kisses, I'm starting to think we're inevitable. I think we always were. Since you were eighteen." A tiny pulse of silence. "Fucking is baked into our fake engagement if you want it to be. As long as you understand it's not contingent on you getting paid."

"I get it."

From this point on, we both pretended to focus on getting to know each other. I found out he was part of a bridge club and a thriller book club and that he'd won a few mini golf tournaments. That the woman who bought his penthouse for him hadn't hired him to be her fake date at all—she was actually an elderly widow who felt lonely, and he still saw her twice a week for a game of bridge and some bickering about thrillers they buddy-read together. Only now he was doing it for free.

I found out he went to see Row in London at least once a month and that he'd never done anything with his business degree, because at first he'd wanted to help Row set up his businesses and travel Europe, but by the time he moved to New York, the fake-dating business was booming and demanded only a fraction of the time he'd have had to invest in working in finance. It was the easy way, and he'd taken it.

I, for my part, told him about my perfect 1600 SAT score, the colleges that had come knocking on my door, and that Mom was the reason I decided to stay in Staindrop. I told him things I had no business sharing. Things that had nothing to do with our fake engagement.

Like the night Gravity was conceived. I was on the pill but also taking antibiotics for a sinus infection. I confessed to Rhyland about the crushing disappointment I felt when I took the pregnancy test and held it in my hand, perched on the closed toilet seat, and my reaction when the second line turned blue. How I'd collapsed on the floor and fallen apart, because the day before I bought that test, I'd received an acceptance letter from a college.

Dad was dead. Mama was recovering. I was finally ready to spread my wings and fly. And then this happened.

When a waitress—not Wendy, who'd disappeared into the ether—came over with the dessert menu, Rhyland didn't even take a look at it. "Get us one of each for the table."

Soon, I found myself wolfing down orange-sauced crepes, tarte Tatin, and crème fraiche meringues.

"My favorite one is the tart," I moaned around my spoon.

Rhyland pressed his lips hard together to avoid a dirty joke, and I grinned back at him.

"Go on—you know you want to."

"Nah. The only way I can see myself coming inside my best friend's baby sister without hating myself is if I treat her like a lady." He sat back, watching me.

"I guess it's good that you had a vasectomy, but I want you to know I'm also on the pill. And this time, I know better than to disregard antibiotics." I rolled my tongue along my upper teeth. "We do need to give each other clear health sheets though."

"I'll get mine tomorrow." His upper teeth scraped at his lower lip, and I knew exactly what he wanted to ask me.

"You're wondering why I didn't terminate my pregnancy with Gravity." I set my spoon down.

A lot of people wondered. I'd been accepted to a good college on a full ride. I was about to leave Tucker. I was on the brink of a turning point.

"Yeah." He tapped his clean spoon on the table. "I kinda do."

"My mother is a devout Catholic, and I knew it would destroy her if I terminated my pregnancy. But that's not even why I decided to keep her. I kept her because the truth is I fell in love with her way before I knew her. After the shock and hurt subsided, I felt... *enthralled*. By the idea that I would have someone of my own. Someone to mold, to take care of, to protect."

He stared at me with rapt fascination but not an ounce of sympathy, and I appreciated that he didn't feel sorry for me. So many people did.

"You're not eating." I cleared my throat, changing the subject.

"The only thing I'm hungry for is currently hoovering her dessert."

Butterflies flapped behind my rib cage. "Does this mean we're heading up to your apartment after this?" Because let's be real, this wasn't a romance book, and I was uncomfortably full. To the point where sex would only be possible if he was okay with missionary while I fought my reflux each time he pressed home.

His cock seemed impressive too, from our brief encounter when he'd pressed against me during that fake kiss. No. The kiss wasn't fake. The feelings attached to it were. And I knew Rhyland joked about ten and a half inches, but honestly? It seemed legit.

"No," Rhyland said gravely, his voice gruff and a little strained. "As much as I want to take you home and fuck you to oblivion and back, I've decided I'm going to do it the right way. We'll let it unfold organically."

I pouted. "You and your stupid rules. Just remember not to fall in love with me, because I don't do relationships."

"I'm going to try my best here, Cosmos. I mean, who doesn't like a woman who busts their balls on an hourly basis?"

The date ended too soon, with Rhyland picking up the check and leaving an impressive tip. I never judged a book by its cover, but I always judged people by the gratuity they left. You can learn a lot about a person from the way they treat service providers.

As soon as Rhyland and I entered the elevator, he gave me a playful shove, crowding me against the wall. He boxed me in with his hands on the railing behind me, one hand coming up from the banister. He used his finger to tilt my chin up to meet his gaze.

"Hello, smart mouth."

"Hello, assh—"

He drowned the rest of my words with a hard, luscious kiss. There was brutal greed in the strokes of his tongue, in the way his whole mouth covered mine. His palms slid from the railings to my butt cheeks, fingers curling around my flesh as he hoisted me up to sit on the railings. My legs spread open of their own accord, the slit of my dress exposing my entire lower body, save for my modesty, which was protected by black satin panties. Yes, I'd bought new panties as soon as I arrived in New York. I'd manifested this entire thing, getting lost in this forbidden, tantalizing man.

Even through my panties, I could smell my lust for him, the sweet earthiness of my desire. I was soaked beneath the flimsy fabric. His mouth slid down my chin, the tip of his tongue teasingly descending along my skin until he reached my breasts. He gave my upper boob a soft bite, and I shuddered, fingers twisting in his hair, ruining his man bun.

"I'd love to fuck you like this. In my favorite position." He thrust himself between my legs, his cock pressing against my drenched underwear through his pants, and even though his head was blocking my view, I swear, it *was* ten and a half inches. God help me, I was going to need an epidural before our first time.

I reached between us, giving him a firm stroke. His dick twitched, leaning into my palm like an excitable pet. A tremor tore through me, and our lips collided again, our kiss deep and urgent as I pressed my tits to his defined pecs.

"Fuck me," I begged into his mouth. "Please, Rhy." I wrapped my legs around him, rolling my hips to bring the point home.

The elevator dinged, and the doors slid open. I was sure he was going to let the doors close and take me up to his penthouse. Instead, he grabbed me by the waist and put me down, shoving me out. I whipped my head around to look at him in shock and found him standing there with an unaffected smirk and a messy bun. The only telltale sign that this hot make-out session hadn't been entirely in my head was the bulge latching onto his upper thigh. He was so long and thick it splayed all the way across to the other side of his hip. My mouth was parched.

"Later, Cosmos."

"Later, dickwad."

His laughter rang out across the entire building as the doors closed and I trudged my way to my apartment.

CHAPTER TWENTY-FOUR
RHYLAND

> Rhyland: Don't forget I'll have to get handsy with your sister tonight bc of Marshall.
> Row: Not too handsy. She is saving herself for marriage.
> Rhyland: SHE HAS A KID.
> Row: She found Jesus.
> Rhyland: You've lost your plot.
> Row: Don't take advantage of the situation, Rhyland. I mean it.
> Rhyland: You don't trust me?
> Row: With my finances? Yes. With my sister? NO.
> Rhyland: Would it really be the end of the world if I were your brother-in-law?
> Row: Now you're just begging to be punched.

Three days later, Row's seasoning line, the Grill Deal, launched at Times Square. It was a celebrity-filled bash. Viral chefs, culinary influencers, and Food Network personalities glided up and down the red carpet, smiling big for the cameras and taking selfies.

Each guest received a goodie bag that included Row's special spices: a collection of grill rubs for poultry, steak, seafood, pot roast, and pizza. The bougie kit would go for ninety-nine bucks at retail price—unheard of for a bunch of dried herbs. It was a total sellout move, another way for him to amass even more millions than he already had, but I could hardly blame him. Gotta hit the iron while it's hot, and Row had already confided in me he wanted to retire early and spend all his time with his wife and daughter.

Speaking of hot things, I didn't look too shabby in my Kiton suit. I'd skipped the dress shirt, going for a buttoned blazer that showed off my crazy-sculpted chest. I stopped on the red carpet to give the cameras a dazzling white smile, one hand casually tucked inside my front pocket. Out of the corner of my eye, I spotted Row and Cal speaking to a hotshot TV executive I'd once fake-dated to get her parents off her back. Row was wearing an all-black three-piece suit, and Cal was wearing… What the fuck *was* she wearing? Some kind of burgundy velvet dress that blended in with the carpet, with two giant roses covering her tits.

Don't get me wrong, she was a knockout by anyone's standards, but I wasn't a fan of the super-quirky style.

Row caught sight of me on the other side of the carpet and made his way over. He gave me a bro hug and a side chest pump. We sauntered back to Cal. The TV executive caught sight of me, remembered how she'd ended up in my sheets with her best friend, and lumbered toward a Food Network domestic goddess before our paths crossed. Kieran and Tate joined us.

"Thanks for being here, guys," Cal squeaked.

"You're most unwelcome. I have stock in Row's brand. It is in my benefit that this line doesn't crash and burn," Tate drawled monotonously. "I'm not doing it out of the goodness of my heart."

"I know," Cal chirped. "Because you don't have one."

"Long time no see." Kieran clapped my shoulder. "How're you doing, Rhy?"

"Never been better," I lied. My entire future, hopes, and dreams hung on Bruce Marshall, and I was becoming poorer by the nanosecond. "How 'bout you? Up to more destruction this month since leading Dylan to the bar her ex works in?"

"Come on, Rhy. We need to let her figure it out on her own." Cal made a sympathetic face. "Now Dylan has the chance to have Tucker help her raise Gravity."

"A chance she never asked for. You okay with this shit?" I cut my gaze to Row. The way he worked his jaw back and forth in response told me he wasn't.

"Maybe he's changed," he muttered noncommittally.

"Sure. Nothing says 'redemption' like deciding you suddenly wanna take a part in your kid's life when your ex walks in looking like sin on legs," I snarled.

"Someone's taking their fake engagement pretty fucking seriously." Tate gave me a less bored once-over.

"Hold on a minute. Something's missing." Kieran frowned at me.

"Probably his balls," Tate drawled. "He's been fake-dating this chick for less than a month and is already whining about her ex."

"Watch it," Row warned Tate, but I kind of wanted Tate to take it further so I'd finally have an excuse to rearrange his face like I did Tucker's.

Kieran tore off his horn-rimmed shades, cocking his head sideways and folding the arms of his glasses. "You cut your stupid ponytail."

"Man bun," I corrected. "And hold the press—we found this generation's Sherlock." I craned my neck, searching for Dylan. We hadn't come here together, because she'd had an early shift at the Alchemist. She was making good money. At least one of us was.

"Has Tucker seen Gravity yet?" Row asked.

"No," Kieran and Cal answered in unison.

That was a relief. I hadn't asked Cosmos about it—I made a point not to take an interest in Gravity when she wasn't right in front of me—but I didn't trust that bastard with the kid.

"Mr. Casablancas." A woman holding an iPad and a headset mic approached us. "They're ready for you to take the stage." She slid her finger over the screen. "Do you remember the verbiage? 'Grill or no grill, I'm happy to unveil the Grill Deal'?"

Row nodded at her in reply.

Tate sneered. "When does the name becomes less cringy?"

"Never is my guess." Kieran winced.

Cal shot them both warning looks.

As it turned out, Dylan didn't make it to the Times Square event. Neither did Bruce and his wife. But I watched as my best friend killed it with the crowd, signing his cookbooks, taking pictures with fans, and selling five thousand units of that ridiculous kit, before we all folded to the after-party at Row's eatery, Casablancas, in Bryant Park, a rooftop restaurant he'd opened last year as an homage to his wife, who was craving—sit down for it—fish fingers.

The bistro had a more modern feel to it than La Vie en Rogue, with cracked turquoise marble for floors, dimmed lighting, and an entire semitransparent wall that was also an aquarium containing some of the most colorful and rare fish in the world. It was dark, moody, and sexy.

I was the last to walk in, since I'd actually driven here and didn't have a chauffeur like all my billionaire friends. When I got in, I saw all of them seated at a long table in the farthest corner of the VIP section, sipping drinks and laughing. Bruce and Jolene were there too, chatting to Cal and Kieran animatedly. Tate had another faceless model on his arm. The place was jam-packed. I moved through the mass of bodies, searching for my fake fiancée.

"Sorry, passing through. Passi—"

Gentle hands scrapped my back from behind, and when I turned to look at the person trying to cut in front of me, Cosmos was staring back. She was breathtaking in a powder-pink dress, her tresses cascading down her shoulders. Her mouth fell open as soon as she saw me.

"You cut your hair."

"Yeah."

"Why?"

I felt my face heating up. "Because you didn't like the man bun."

She cupped her mouth. "What? When did I say that?"

"Three days ago, before I kissed you."

"Jesus, Rhy, I was just giving you shit. That man bun made my lady bits tingle."

I sighed. "I'll add some extensions."

She laughed. "No, you won't."

Yes, I probably fucking will, because you like it.

The thought frightened me. Since when did I care about making anyone other than my dick happy? But I hadn't seen her in a couple days in a bid to prove to myself I did not seek her out more than absolutely necessary. Now she was here, and it was time for our charade to resume.

"You look amazing, baby." I reached down to kiss the edge of her shoulder, which was still hot from the leftover sunrays outside. She smelled of her body lotion—coconut and a sandy beach.

"I know." She tossed her glossy hair back. "To be honest, I should've charged you extra just for letting you look at me tonight."

I bent down, my stubble sailing over the smooth skin of her cheek, raising goose bumps all over her body. "Careful with that mouth," I whispered into the shell of her ear. "Or I'll have to fill it with something long and thick to shut you up."

"Really?" She tipped her chin up to stare at me, her heavy-lidded sex eyes zeroing in on mine. "You think they serve cannoli here?"

That earned her a bark of laughter from me. I couldn't help it.

I wrapped my hands around her waist, the tip of my nose gliding down the slope of hers. "Bruce is here." My lips moved over hers sensually, and her body sought mine, enveloping me instantly.

"I see." She knotted her arms around my neck. "So this is all a big, fat ruse."

"Watch where your hands are going, Coltridge." Row's predatory gaze locked on us from across the VIP room, eyes darkening into two pools of tar. "Or I'll have to make sashimi out of you."

"Stop it, Row," Dylan chided, breaking free of my embrace. "I'm not a child."

"You do call me daddy sometimes." I frowned.

Row was about to pop an artery.

Bruce, suddenly there, coughed into his fist, half laughing, half choking. "Why'd you mind that he kisses your sister, Casablancas?" Bruce enquired. "They're engaged to be married. Even I'm not that strict."

A muscle twitched in Row's jaw. He licked his lips. "Having a hard time letting go, I guess. I helped raise her, see."

"Who's taking care of Gravity?" Jolene, Bruce's wife, asked.

I could tell by Cosmos' smile she appreciated that the woman had remembered her daughter's name. "My mom's in town, and she doesn't like big crowds, so she's home helping me out." Dylan stuck out her hand at Jolene, but the latter flung her arms around Dylan.

They hugged, immediately chatting about preschools with Cal.

"Tell me, Dylan." Jolene clutched her hands. "Are you taking care of yourself? Do you use face masks? Paint your nails? Have a set time that is completely yours? Taking care of yourself is a part of taking care of others."

Dylan nodded but didn't answer. I knew why. Truth was she didn't have that time for herself. Her nails weren't painted, she never had a minute set aside just for herself, and for some ridiculous, messed-up reason, I was feeling guilty about it, even though I hadn't been the one to knock her up.

Bruce and I shook hands. My grip crushed his, and I could tell by his surprised face he wasn't expecting that. "How're you doin', son?"

"Good. And about to get better once you sign the contract I emailed you ten minutes ago."

Bruce's brows shot up his forehead. "Putting the cart before the horse, I see. I didn't accept anything y—"

"You will." I cut him off. "As soon as we leave your house after our upcoming test drive. You know it. I know it. It's a good deal." Tate helped me draft it, which meant I was bulletproof and could screw Bruce six ways from Sunday if anything went wrong. Of course, I didn't expect it to. Bruce had an entire floor to house his litigation team. But I was also sure they were all nepo hires from his small town, so who knew their level of incompetence?

We joined the others at the table. Expensive liquor, cocktails, and food began to flow to our corner of the room steadily. Lobster rolls, Maine crab cakes, shrimp alfredo, and stuffed lobster butter croissant. I sat next to Dylan and put my hand in her lap, giving her a squeeze. Truth was keeping busy these past couple days hadn't helped with pushing her out of my mind.

"What's the estimated annual profit margin on App-date?" Tate buttered a bread roll. He was playing this all out for me. He already knew all the deets.

"We're looking at twenty billion revenue the first year," I said. "Eight less than TikTok in 2023. Not too shabby for a so-called niche."

"Really? People want a fake relationship that much?" Jolene sounded doubtful as she sipped her Bloody Mary.

"You'd be surprised." My hand traveled up Dylan's thigh, my tone cool and calculated. "It's not the niche market you think it is. People need dates for weddings, parties, work events. People want to find other like-minded individuals to go on vacation with. Have deep, philosophical conversations that delve deeper than what apps like Tinder and Bumble offer. The sexiest thing about my app is that it isn't about sex. It forces the participants to actually get to know each other. I think it'll breed more married couples than all the dating apps combined," I said confidently, knowing it was what she wanted to hear.

Bruce nodded absentmindedly. "I can see it. It's like forcing people to go on real dates without the expectation to sleep together afterward."

"Exactly," I said.

"Can't remember the last time I heard about an app predicted to have a revenue of more than three billion in its first year," Tate commented dryly, taking a sip of his whiskey.

Up close, I recognized the woman on his arm. A Netflix actress who had a smash hit playing a vampire Cleopatra.

"This is a steal, Bruce," Tate said.

"And you would know, as a thief." Bruce patted the corners of his mouth with his napkin.

My hand settled on the crux between Dylan's hip bone and her pussy, grazing the edge of her panties. They were satin, like last time. She arched into my touch while discussing something with Cal. She sounded distracted, which amused me.

"...Taylor Swift Eras concert in September," I heard Cal say excitedly. "Would you be able to make it?"

"Oh my God, are you kidding me?" Dylan shrieked as my pinkie grazed her panties, back and forth. She cupped my shoulder, and there was something so intimate and familiar about it, like we'd done it hundreds of times before. "Rhy?"

"Hmm?"

"Would you be able to babysit Grav on September thirteenth?"

"Sure."

"This is important. If you can't do it, I'll ask my mom—"

"I said I can."

"Right, but see, I need you to lock it down. Cal and I are going to the Eras Tour."

"And we have VIP seats." Cal danced in her seat. "Taylor's sweat is practically going to *drip* on us."

"Weird kink, but this is a no-judgment zone." I yawned.

Technically, this would be past my arrangement with Dylan, but

I didn't mind a one-off. Especially as I knew what a hardcore Swiftie Cosmos was.

"I'll put it in my calendar now." I made a show of plucking my phone from the table and blocking off 5 p.m. on September thirteenth, showing it to the ladies. "Happy?"

"You have no idea." Dylan's eyes glittered, childish delight painting her face. Feeling Bruce's eyes on me, I cut my gaze to him.

He gave me a nod of approval. "I think I'll use your contract as reading material tonight."

"Perfect sleeping material, I bet." Kieran smirked.

"There's actually some spice in it," Tate assured him. "Clauses 33A to 43B, Rhy fucks him over good if he withdraws for no good reason."

I picked up my drink and saluted Bruce.

"I can't believe I'm going to the Eras Tour." Dylan reached to squeeze Cal's hand. "Thank you."

"So how did y'all find out you were in love?" Jolene's eyes ping-ponged between us. She patted her stiff updo to ensure no hair was out of place. "That must be a story for the ages."

My hand froze under Dylan's dress. We'd discussed it on our fake date but never agreed on anything I was comfortable with. To be fair, Dylan had deranged ideas.

"It is!" Dylan cooed, her smile brightening the entire fucking universe. How had I never realized how stunning she was? How funny? How strong? "Honey, mind if I tell her? You know I always love talking about it." She put her hand in my lap.

"Go ahead," I grunted.

Row's eyes narrowed, darting between our faces.

"He literally *cried* he was so desperate to date me." Dylan put a hand to her throat.

I was going to kill her.

Fuck her first, but then kill her.

Kieran choked on his cocktail, pressing his knuckles to his lips.

Tate smirked behind his whiskey. Row and Cal looked equal parts amused and confused.

"Oh, bless his heart." Jolene slapped her chest. "You mean, with tears and everything?"

"Jolene, he was bawling like a baby." Dylan rolled her eyes. "Hyperventilating. At some point, I considered giving him half a Valium from my dog's ACL rupture surgery."

Now she was making up a whole-ass pet with a whole-ass surgery. I didn't know one man on this earth who was able to handle—let alone tame—this crazy, brilliant woman.

"Do tell us the story." Bruce rubbed his hands together.

"Yeah, tell us." I slipped my pinkie under her panties, and Dylan gasped, sitting up straighter.

"I-it was right after Christmas dinner. Rhy came to say hi to everyone. I'd been dating someone else. He spent the holiday with us. We were getting pretty serious. He was a doctor."

"Wow." Jolene's eyes rounded in fascination.

"Actually, he was a surgeon. And an amateur pilot."

My pinkie rubbed the hot, sleek slit of her pussy, which was bare. All the blood in the room rushed to my dick. Was it normal that I was jealous of a fictional boyfriend? Probably not.

"I mean, how small does your dick need to be for you to compensate by being a surgeon *and* a pilot?" I piped up.

Jolene choked on her Bloody Mary.

Tate looked affronted. "I'm a self-made billionaire and a pilot, and I have nine inches and some spare."

Now wasn't the time to tell him I was bigger. Actually, it was, but I refrained, because I also happened to want to be a billionaire, and I was pretty sure disclosing my dick size would send Jolene to the hospital.

Dylan rolled her eyes like she wasn't growing wetter by the nanosecond under the table while my finger teased her opening and grazed her clit. "Anyway, he came to say hi. Chad was just helping my mom dry some dishes in the kitchen…"

Chad. She wasn't even trying to make it sound real. Kieran snorted, and Tate pressed his lips together to suppress a wry smile.

"Rhyland and I bumped into each other under the mistletoe. There was a pause. I always knew he was pathetically in love with me, but I decided to spare his poor, fragile heart. I smiled, embarrassed, and was turning to walk away when he fell down on his knees, hugging my midsection. 'I can't do this anymore,' he started crying. 'If I can't have you, my life has no meaning anymore.' I thought he might do something to himself. It was really scary."

I slipped a finger into her, finding her drenched and warm and perfect. Her muscles squeezed my index finger for dear life, and I hissed out, imagining her tightness wrapped around my cock.

"Look at him," Jolene laughed. "He looks anguished!"

You have no idea, lady.

"So you gave him a chance?" Jolene turned back to Dylan, whose eyes rolled—and not from attitude for a change. I was bringing her to the brink of a climax while everyone was watching.

"Y-y-yes." She barely spluttered out the word.

I was semi-fucking her slowly under the table with my finger, punishing her for her little stunt. If she thought she was going to get awarded with an orgasm, she had another thing coming.

Her cheeks were bright pink, her lips parted in desire, every muscle in her body clenched tight. "I-I gave him a ch-chance. And he c-came through." Her hips rolled, desperate for more of my touch. She was close. I could feel it.

"Well, one of us had to, sweetheart." I kissed her cheek casually, giving her swollen clit a flick with my thumb before withdrawing from her panties in one go. She actually yelped in frustration.

"And you, Ambrose?" Bruce turned to Row. "How'd you take their coupling?"

"Not well," Row grumbled darkly. "But I love my wife and daughter too much to spend the rest of my life in prison for first-degree murder."

"Honey, you have to taste this special sauce." I ran the finger that was just inside Dylan along the alfredo residue on my plate, bringing it to her lips.

Her nostrils flared in annoyance. "I'm not hungry."

"Alfredo is your favorite sauce, sweetheart. Isn't it, Cal?"

"Uh…yeah," Cal confirmed, confused.

Dylan shot me a heated glare but wrapped her lips around my finger nonetheless. There was barely any sauce and a whole lot of pussy juice.

"Taste good?" I rasped.

"Uh-huh."

"Well, we'll be off. Early flight into Dallas tomorrow." Bruce stood up, adjusting his belt over his stomach and screwing his cowboy hat on.

"Hope you forgive us for not staying for dessert." Jolene smiled apologetically, assisted to her feet by her husband.

"Not at all," Cal assured her. "Do what you gotta do."

As soon as they left, Row turned his focus on his sister. "What's that shit about you working at a pub, Dyl?" he demanded.

While I was glad that was the first thing to catch his attention, I didn't like his tone. Neither did Dylan, judging by the way her spine snapped to attention.

"It's a bar," she corrected primly. "And I need to subsidize my life as well as my kid's. You know, food, clothes, tuition, extracurricular activities."

"I can take care of all that." Row's brows grooved into a deep scowl. "You should be focusing on your future. On going back to schoo—"

"I'll do that on my own, thank you," Dylan clapped back. "You're doing more than enough for me. I want to succeed because of me, not because of you."

"You're being ridiculous," Row bristled. "You think rich kids who go to Harvard because Grandpa donated a fucking wing tell their families, 'Oh no, I want to bust my ass for a scholarship or go to a community college. I don't want to use my connections'?"

"I don't know what those kids say, and to be perfectly honest, I don't care. I'm *me*. The girl you left behind to live your glamorous life and advance your amazing career. The girl who was always less-than. Who was known as somebody else's sister. You don't know what it feels like, Row. To be the spare, not the heir. The talentless, unremarkable one."

"What are you talking about?" Row was practically foaming at the mouth. "You're a genius."

"Not many people know that, though," Dylan said. "I don't want to be indebted to you or to anyone else. I don't want anyone to question if I had any shortcuts. I want to prove the people who underestimated me wrong, and I want to do that independently so that my daughter learns that no matter what your starting point in life is, you can always fight your way up." She took a quick breath, cheeks flushed. "And while I am grateful for the privilege of house-sitting for you because I get to live in Manhattan, I won't let you pay my way through life."

"Row." Cal put a hand on her husband's hand gently.

"No, Dot. She needs to hear it. You're of the same mind as me. She is wasting her life away. Rhy." He cut his gaze to mine. "Talk some sense into your fake fiancée."

"Sorry, pal. I jumped on that feminism bandwagon when they started offering free condoms in college." I sprawled out in my chair, soothingly toying with Dylan's hair. "I'm letting her call the shots on her own future. Radical, I know."

Row dug his big, rough finger pads into his eyelids, massaging them. "Traitor."

I ignored him. "You know, I'm starting to warm up to the theory that women's brains aren't actually smaller than ours. I'm still not fully sold on giving them voting rights, but, like, some of them have profound shit to say."

Kieran snorted. Row was fuming, his ear tips red, neck flushed, eyes luminous with wrath.

Kieran excused himself. "Sorry, this toxicity shit is bad for my chakras, and I need to take a call from my agent." He gestured to the lit screen of his phone, disappearing behind the aquarium wall.

Coward. No wonder Dylan never gave him a chance when he pursued her. He half-assed his entire life. Anything that wasn't soccer got the narcissistic jerk treatment and was promptly neglected.

"I'm staying right here," Tate informed no one in particular. "Wouldn't miss a public meltdown for the world."

"Quit." Row fixed his gaze back on his sister. "I don't want you near Tucker. I don't want you in a slimy bar. And I don't want you—"

"I don't care what you want!" Dylan shot to her feet, slamming her palms against the table. "Get it into your thick skull—you're not my dad. Even if you were, I wouldn't listen to you. I am my own person. Your concern, your love, your devotion, is suffocating. Because it's always your way or the highway." She visibly gulped, pupils dancing in their sockets. "The road to hell is paved with good intentions, and you're living proof of that. Seriously, thank you for always having my back. Thank you for being protective of me. But I can handle Tucker." She stormed away from the table, toward the restrooms.

Silence fell over us all.

"That went well." Tate was the first to shrug off the past few minutes, tossing a shrimp into his mouth.

Cal shifted uncomfortably in her seat. I gave Row a scathing look.

"What?" Row barked my way. "I said what everyone at this table thinks. My sister is a fucking genius. Why can't she—"

"Because she wants to look back and appreciate the journey, not just the fucking destination," I roared. I was on my feet now, even though I couldn't recall my brain giving my legs the order. "Take it from someone who spent the majority of his twenties as your sidekick—not everyone wants to live in your shadow, even if that shadow offers sweet perks. You should be proud of her for wanting to do this on her own. You're right. She is brilliant. But not only because she's book smart or some shit. Because she is fiercely independent."

"Rhyland is right." Cal bit down on her lower lip. "You've gotten so used to protecting Dylan since the time your father was alive, somewhere along the way, you forgot it was time to let go."

Row said nothing, staring me down with murder in his eyes. "You remember it's all fake, right?" he asked me. "If not, I can always remind you, and I'm not going to be so nice about it."

Shaking my head, I left the table and ambled to the restroom to look for Dylan.

Taking a turn behind the huge aquarium wall, I entered the dark corridor leading to the restrooms. I skidded to a halt when I came face-to-face with a silhouette of Dylan and Kieran embracing each other, Dylan's lean frame draped against the wall, him covering her.

My blood roiled in my veins, my body a live wire of high-octane anger.

"Get your hands off her before I break both your legs like chopsticks." The blade of fury in my voice cut through the air between them, making Kieran stumble backward and break the hug.

"Jesus, Rhyland, not you too." Dylan's face was saturated with disappointment as she shook her head at me.

I turned to Kieran, struggling to keep my temper in check. "She's not going to fuck you, buddy. Move along."

To this, he responded with a chuckle. "Ah. I guess I am destined to be a prop in the jealous-douchebag kit. First Row, now you. I'm starting to see a pattern."

There was a hot minute when Row thought Kieran was after Cal the year they got together. He hadn't appreciated the competition, and Kieran sported a slightly crooked nose as a reminder of that episode.

"Leave us," I ordered, steely.

"The hell I will!" Dylan threw her hands up. "I'm going to stand here and give you a piece of my min—"

"Not you, Cosmos. *Kieran.*"

"Oh."

"Do you want me to leave?" Kieran turned to Dylan. "I won't if you don't want me to."

She nodded. "It's okay. I can take him down. I'll aim for his balls." She curled her fists. But once Kieran had scurried back to the table on the other side of the aquarium and it was just me and her, she dropped the charade and pressed her forehead to the cool fish tank, closing her eyes and blowing out a breath. "Oh God."

"Is he still hitting on you?" I leaned a shoulder against the marine wall, studying her.

"No." A wry chuckle left her mouth. "Even if he did, you and I made a promise to each other we'd be exclusive for the length of this arrangement."

Her eyes were still closed. Maybe it was time I stopped worrying so much about her porking other people and more about the fact that she seemed upset. I was still new to this "giving a shit" business.

I pinched my lower lip between my fingers. "You know Row was only trying to be helpful in his own backward, ooga-booga, me-a-tough-big-ape, you-a-small-cute-ape kinda way, right?"

She pushed off the aquarium with a sigh, her forehead leaving a smudge on the glass. "Yeah, I know. But it doesn't change the fact that I still feel fourteen sometimes. Like I'm not fully in charge of my own life."

"Because Row is an overbearing prick?" I frowned.

"Because my family doesn't trust me to do the right thing by myself and by my daughter. I'm like a fish in a tank." Her finger traced the path of a bright orange discus fish over the thick glass. "Swimming aimlessly, pretending to be free, but very much a prisoner in my own beautiful golden cage."

"Well, you know, that's just like, uh, your opinion, man," I blurted, bringing my palms to rest atop my head.

She turned to give me a funny look.

"Are you *Big Lebowski*-ing me after my big emotional speech?" Her eyes widened.

"Are you getting a reference from a nineties movie?" I lit up. "Impressive."

"I'm Calla Casablancas's best friend. I know everything about the nineties."

"What I mean to say is you might feel like a fish in a tank, but trust me, you're more like…a shark in a pool."

"Meaning?" She slanted her head to study me.

"Yeah, your brother is domineering, but you're just as stubborn and opinionated as he is. You don't let him push you around. You're made of the same cloth, so it's not like he has the upper hand. You guys are just butting heads. You always end up doing whatever you want anyway."

"I hadn't thought of it that way." Her lips twitched with a small smile. "I *am* just as stubborn and bossy."

"You could use someone to boss you around. It'll give you a chance to let go a little. I bet you'd like that." I studied her intently. "Being a little more submissive in bed."

From the color in her cheeks, I knew I was heading in the right direction. My pulse drummed its way up to my throat.

"Come here." I curled a finger her way.

She did, pushing off the aquarium and erasing the gap between us in three strides. She stopped, waiting for more directions. My dick twitched. I slipped my hands inside my front pockets, clinging to my nonchalance as if it were a goddamn anchor.

"Are you wet?"

She snorted. "You wish."

I *tsked*, giving her a slow once-over. "Flip your dress up, and show me your panties."

Her satisfied smirk disappeared, and she looked at me with uncertainty. I knew she was wet.

"What will I get if I do it?" she bargained.

"The orgasm I denied you back there, when you made up a whole story about me sobbing to take you out." I jerked my thumb behind my shoulder.

She gulped. Grabbed the hem of her dress, slowly hiking it up a millimeter at a time. Didn't matter, because by the time her pink satin undies were on full display, I could see the stain of her arousal where the slit was. Her eyes traveled up to meet mine, her blush deepening.

"God, you are gorgeous." I grabbed the back of her head, tilted it up by fisting her hair, and kissed the fuck out of her.

We were in the corridor. The only thing standing between us and our group of friends was the half-see-through aquarium wall. It was risky and illicit, and I found myself throwing caution to the wind. At the end of the day, what were humans if not mere animals—impulsive, egotistical, and emotional? I took an AP class in psychology before college, so I knew damn well I was rationalizing to myself an excuse for why my thumb was currently brushing the junction between my best friend's baby sister's inner thigh and underwear. Even before I made it to the center—to the slit, the main event—I could feel her wetness. Every fiber of my body and soul wanted to take a knee, dunk my head under her pretty rose dress, and feast on her pussy like a starved man.

Our tongues were at war, and I walked her over to the crook between the aquarium and the emergency exit, the darkest corner of the restaurant. Our friends' table was right in front of us. I could see their faces from the other side of the aquarium in my peripheral. If one of them walked toward the bathroom, they'd be able to see my broad back as I crowded her but not what I was about to do next.

I broke off our kiss, licking a path down her jawline, traveling south to the column of her neck. She tipped her head back, giving me full access, one hand gripping the back of my neck and the other clutching my erect cock through my slacks. She gasped at my size.

"How is this thing going to fit into my vagina?" she moaned.

"It'll fit." My tongue swirled its way down as I peeled off the corset of her dress, freeing those magnificent tits that didn't require a bra. "It'll fit your pussy." I kissed the top of her right breast. "Your smart little mouth." I kissed her lips. "The space between your wonderful tits." I scraped my teeth over her left breast. "And your ass too." I used my free hand to squeeze her ass cheek, my hand traveling down and forcing her thighs open for me from behind. I reared my head back to study her bare breasts. *Fantastic*. Pear-shaped, heavy, and tan. Her nipples were light brown, tiny, and on point.

I dove down to swirl my tongue around one areola. She hissed, rolling her hips to meet my crotch, her grip on my cock tightening through my slacks.

"Look how sweet and pliant you are," I murmured into her breast. "Not so tough now, are you, Cosmos? Touch yourself until you're ready for me."

"Rhy, I'm already too—"

I bit the tip of her nipple gently. "More masturbating, less mouthing back."

She groaned, bringing her hand into her panties and playing with herself.

I turned to give my attention to her other tit. It was just as delicious. Then I kissed her again, using the palm that was cupping the junction between her ass and her slit from behind to apply delicious, taunting pressure to her pussy, my fingertips grazing hers as she worked her pussy faster and harder. She had three fingers inside herself. Good, but not nearly enough. Past experience had taught me that women—especially narrow women like Dylan, judging by the finger I put in her earlier—needed proper prepping before I fucked them.

"Rhy, I can't take this anymore. I'm embarrassingly soaked," she moaned into my mouth.

I looked down to examine her panties. *Jesus.* They were ruined. It looked like she'd sat in a fucking bucket of water. Not gonna lie, the fact that she was so responsive made my dick harder than the Empire State Building.

"Take me out," I ordered her, trying to keep the strain away from my voice.

She eagerly unbuttoned and unzipped me, pushing my Armani briefs down. My cock sprung out like a freaky clown from a jack-in-the-box. It was thick and long, with a fat crown glistening with precum and a natural curve that made it too easy for me to hit my partner's G-spot.

Dylan gasped at the sight. "I'm never going to walk again."

"Come on—we need to be fast. Put it in your underwear, but no penetration," I ordered.

She stared at me, aghast. "Are you serious?"

"I'm always serious when I have my cock out in a public place and a pretty woman by my side." I was downplaying the entire thing. I'd never done anything half as crazy as this with anyone else. And she was more than pretty. She was a work of art.

"I'll die if you don't fuck me."

"Trust me. I'm prepping you now for next time, when we exchange clean health bills and things get serious." I grabbed my cock and slid it into her panties.

Her pussy immediately made a slurping noise. My dick leaked more precum. This was bad. I mean, it was great, but I wasn't sure how I was going to last more than five seconds once we did the dirty. Plus, the health-bill talk was bullshit. We'd already done enough to catch a whole lot of STIs.

Not that I cared. She could literally shoot me in the femur, and I'd say "thank you."

Holding the base of my cock, I slid it up and down from the

edge of her ass crack until my wet tip flicked her clit. Dylan threw her head back against the wall and moaned so loudly I wouldn't be surprised if she woke people in Rhode Island.

"Rhy."

"Shh, baby." I pressed my palm over her mouth. "We need to be quiet. Now, take my cock and do what I just did. No penetration."

She nodded eagerly, taking over, sliding the tip of my cock from one corner of her pussy to the other, up and down.

"Can I play with your ass a little, baby?" I nibbled on her earlobe, kissing the side of her face and enjoying the slurping sounds we made together.

"Yeah," she mewed.

I retrieved the hand that was grabbing her ass, spat onto my index and middle fingers, and returned it, teasing her tight hole while Dylan quickened her pace with my cock.

"I'm going to come just from this," she said breathlessly. "Oh my God, that's never happened."

I slapped her hand away from my cock with my spare hand, and she purred in protest—until she realized what I was doing. Tapping the crown of my cock over her swollen clit, withdrawing every now and then to slide just the tip into her before teasing her clit again.

"Yes," she panted. "Yes, just like that."

We both looked down, watching with fascination the imprint of my dick through her drenched panties.

A cry of panic and disbelief sounded behind my back. I shot a quick glance over to our table. Everyone was there, Kieran included.

"Get the fuck out of here," I growled to whoever was behind us. From the sound of clinking heels, they took orders better than my fucking fake fiancée.

"I'm coming," she announced.

Thank fuck.

"So am I."

A few seconds later, her entire body convulsed, her jaw went slack, and she closed her eyes, rocking to the rhythm of the pleasure rushing through her body. My own orgasm followed suit, in the form of my balls tightening and tingling, followed by shooting my load right inside her panties. Health bill, my ass. We couldn't keep our hands off each other for the duration of one meal. We hadn't even made it to the entrées.

I pulled back, steadying her. She looked a mess, and I knew it was going to be damn near impossible to explain why we both looked like we'd been hit by a train.

"Holy shit. I need to get rid of this underwear before it wets my entire dress." She grabbed the elastic of her panties, tugging them down her thighs.

I clutched one of her thighs, giving it a squeeze. "Keep them."

She stared up at me, horrified. "Are you serious?"

"Yes. I want your pussy to swim in my cum while you eat your dessert."

Her nostrils flared, her pupils dilating. She opened her mouth to refuse, so I cut in, "You said you want to let go of some of your control. You deserve a little filth in your life, Dyl. You've been on the straight and narrow for too long."

Taking a ragged breath, she nodded and pulled her panties back up with some struggle. They were too wet and knotted together.

I watched the small river of transparent white cum in the gusset. *Fuck.* Her pussy was going to be dipped in my cum all night.

"We need to get back to the table." I grabbed her hand.

She didn't budge. "Rhyland?"

"Yeah?"

She seized my wrist and slipped it under her dress, running my fingers through her dripping cunt again. I shuddered. She raised my wrist and brought it to my lips. It was full of our cum. I sucked on my index and middle fingers hungrily, and she pulled me in, her lips fusing with mine against my two fingers, both of us licking them like we were sharing a lollipop. The scent of her heated my blood. I could feel the pulse inside my cock as it strained against the fabric of my slacks again.

Dylan leaned back on the balls of her feet, and I knew—just *knew*—she loved that I was taller than her even though she was a tall girl. "A hundred bucks says you'll end up jerking off to what happened between us tonight as soon as you get home." She smirked brazenly, combing through her hair with her fingers and smoothing her dress over her legs.

I took my phone out of my pocket, my thumbs flying over the screen.

"What are you doing?" She readjusted the shoulder straps of her dress.

"Venmo-ing you two hundred bucks."

"I said a hundred," she laughed.

"Yeah." I scratched my jaw. "One time won't be enough."

CHAPTER TWENTY-FIVE
DYLAN

OMFG.

CHAPTER TWENTY-SIX
RHYLAND

Even though I wanted to give Dylan a ride home—and maybe get a blowie on the way as a bonus—it wasn't in the cards for me. First of all, she'd arrived here with Jimmy, her half-dead car. Second, our friends were already suspicious, seeing as we'd spent twenty minutes away from them. And third, Tate had asked me to stay back after everyone dispersed.

"What do you want?" I sulked at the lean patrician man, watching Dylan happily walking out of the restaurant with her brother, her sister-in-law, and Kieran.

I still didn't trust that fucker Kieran.

"Let's take it to my private suite." Tate jerked his chin toward the elevators.

I scowled. "What are you talking about? This is an office building. You don't have a private suite."

"I have a private suite on every block in this city."

We made our way down to the fourteenth floor—a half condo, half office setup with sleek, modern couches, sexy lighting, and sparse, modern furniture. Tate fixed us drinks, and we settled in recliners on the balcony, both of us staring at the view.

"My date caught you fucking Row's baby sister when she went to the restroom." He cut straight to the chase.

Shit. When I did an inventory to check who was at the table, I forgot Tate's latest conquest.

"We weren't having sex," I said wryly, twirling the tawny liquid in my beaker, watching the golden glow of it intensifying like the heart of a flame. "And if this is about upsetting your business partner—"

"Christ, no." Tate's facial expression was carved in stone. "If you think I give a fuck about anyone's feelings, you haven't been paying attention. I'm talking strictly business."

"This fling between us is constructive to my deal with Bruce," I lamented.

"It is," he agreed brashly, "and I'm not opposed to you fucking her a few times before whatever this thing is runs its course. But it is my duty to warn you that you don't want to get tangled up with someone with a kid and a bag full of issues."

I snorted. "You can't be serious. Me? Monogamy? Kids?"

"I see the way you look at her," Tate said tersely.

"Yeah, and how is that?"

"Like she's a pied piper about to lure you to the edge of a cliff."

Clicking my tongue, I shot up to my feet. "Is that all?"

"No." Tate remained seated. "Bruce is playing you. There's no reason for you to sit around and wait for him to sign the contract. For fifty-five percent of the company, I'll offer you the same seed money as Bruce and ten million in ad budget."

My jaw nearly hit the granite of his balcony. It was a good offer. And it was an offer that could pull me out of the financial trouble I was currently swimming in. My fridge was emptier than Tate's chest. It took me a second to think it through.

"No," I said.

"Fifty-one percent," he bargained, standing up now too and looking at me like I'd just pissed in his soup.

"Tate, I want Bruce. He can take me to the next level."

"*I* can do that too." Tate, like all billionaire playboys, had a really hard time hearing the word no.

When I got into my car, I noticed a few text messages I'd missed when I was with Tate.

Mom: Where are you, Rhyland? We need you.
Mom: You're so irresponsible for ignoring our calls.
Mom: We know where you live, you know.

Nothing said motherly love like Mafia tactics.

Mom: Fine. Have it your way. You'll regret not answering us.

CHAPTER TWENTY-SEVEN
DYLAN

A day later, I woke up to the chime of the doorbell. I dragged myself to the door, still half-asleep. Mama was already in the kitchen, making herself and Marty sandwiches ahead of her scheduled flight back home later that morning. I tossed the door open, expecting a package or a neighbor in need of a cup of sugar, only to find a delivery guy holding a peculiar bouquet.

"Dylan Casablancas?"

"Unfortunately," I groaned. *Damn hangover.*

"Can you please sign here?" He handed me a small touchscreen device.

I did, accepting the bouquet from him. There weren't flowers in it but arranged pieces of what looked like newspaper.

"Who is it?" Mama called from the kitchen.

"Oh, just one of those artistic bouquets…" My fingers searched for the card attached to it, finally finding it nestled between the curled shreds of paper.

Good moaning, Cosmos.

Hope you had a great night. I'll see you very soon.

—Rhyland's cock.

I stifled a snort, taking another look at the bouquet to see what was printed on those pieces of paper. There were lots of them. The first thing I noticed was that they were all the same. Meaning it was the same page printed over and over again. I walked over to the kitchen counter, pulling pieces of it out to try to put together one full page, like a jigsaw.

When I realized what it was, a laugh escaped me.

It was his clean health bill sheet to show he didn't have any STIs. *This* was his stab at romance.

"Why are you laughing?" My mother turned to look at me, confused.

I immediately grabbed the bouquet, shoving the papers back into it. "Nothing. Rhyland is just being…Rhyland, I suppose."

"That boy always had a thing for you." Mama snorted distractedly, returning her attention to the bologna and mayo she was slamming onto pieces of bread.

I took a shower, got dressed, and said goodbye to Mama and Marty. Grav cried when they left, which made me feel shitty. What made me feel even shittier was the knowledge that Tucker was finally coming over at ten in the morning to meet Gravity for the first time. Suffocating panic clogged my throat. I was going to be there the whole time, but I was still uneasy about this entire thing.

"Mommy, when is our new friend coming?" Gravity trotted to the kitchen, clutching Mr. Mushroom close to her chest.

I'd told her Tucker was a friend from Staindrop who'd been traveling the world for the past few years and wanted to meet her. I wasn't going to tell her he was her dad until he proved to be a balanced and reliable individual.

I checked the clock on the wall. "Oh, in ten minutes, actually. I'll fix you a snack beforehand. Apples and peanut butter?"

"Yes, please." Gravity hoisted herself onto the couch, grabbing her iPad and flipping through the pictures on it, grinning.

"What are you looking at?" I started slicing an apple for her.

"Uncle Rhyrand and I drew faces on my toenails and made a TV show about them. They are all different characters."

I snorted. I should probably be more worried about how completely and thoroughly this man was now woven into my life, but he was the only good thing that had happened to me in a really long time.

I handed Grav her apples and peanut butter and checked my phone, hoping to find a message from Tucker announcing he wasn't going to come over after all or from Rhyland saying…well, anything at all.

But all I found was one message from Cal.

> Cal: I'm not crazy, right? There's something going on between you and Rhy. I could feel it sizzling between you two.

I bit down on my lower lip, suppressing a smile. I felt bad for not confiding in her about my enemies-with-benefits situation with Rhyland, especially considering she'd been extremely transparent about her love story with Row when they started dating. But I knew she'd never keep a secret from Row, and Row would kill Rhy if he found out. For once, I wanted something just for myself. My thumbs flew over the screen.

> Dylan: Nope. Being a mess is our entire personality. Of course we're being cheeky with each other. But there's nothing going on.
> Cal: Okay…

The doorbell rang. *Tucker.* I opened the door with a ten-ton anchor in my stomach, dread coursing through my veins. He was dressed as though this were a date, in a crisp white button-down shirt and smart navy pants. His hair was slicked back, and he was holding flowers and chocolate.

"Hey, babe." He smirked.

My nose tingled like I'd smelled something foul.

"Hey," I said dispassionately, taking the flowers and the heart-shaped chocolate box without so much as thank you. It would have been nicer if he'd brought something for Grav.

Meanwhile, my little girl bolted from the couch, wedging herself between my legs to peer at Tucker with a naughty grin.

"Hi, Uncle Tucker. I heard you're Mommy's friend." She flashed him her tiny white teeth.

I drank in his reaction as he took her in. The cold, unaffected way he scanned her face, almost like he was searching for imperfections, before his mouth settled into a grim smile.

"Hi. You must be Gravity."

"I am!"

He extended a hand to her. "Tucker. Nice to meet you."

"Nice to meet you too."

Awkward silence blanketed us. He was still on the threshold, and honestly, I wasn't eager for him to come inside.

"I was thinking maybe we could all go to the zoo today," I said finally. "The weather is amazing, and Grav and I have been meaning to check out Central Park Zoo. There's a cheetah exhibit. Grav loves cheetahs."

"They're my favorite!" Grav clapped, delighted. "Uncle Tucker, did you know that cheetahs don't roar? They meow! Like kitties!" She curled her chubby fingers into claws.

"Hmm." Tucker looked between us distractedly, smoothing out his fancy shirt. "Kinda hot outside, no? Wasn't planning on getting sweaty."

I stared at him, dumbfounded. We were not getting off to a good start. "Your shirt'll survive," I said dryly. "I'll grab my bag and her sippy cup. Stay here."

Things got progressively worse when I parked Jimmy outside

the zoo and we entered. Tucker complained as if he were the toddler, not Gravity. About the heat, the long line for the tickets, the stroller we rented for Gravity that had one wonky wheel. After seeing the cheetah exhibit and feeding birds in small cups, we stopped for lunch. Gravity accidentally squirted ketchup on his shirt trying to squeeze it onto her fries, and he nearly yelled at her. He kept trying to strike up conversation with me, not her, and I wondered if I was being harsh with him, since he literally had no experience with kids, or if he was just being a straight-up unredeemable asshole.

"So your brother... Doesn't he want to expand his businesses here in New York?" Tucker asked while I watched the minutes tick by on my phone, praying for salvation.

"I don't know," I answered tersely. "I don't talk shop with him."

"But what if I sent him a business propos—"

"Uncle Tucker, do you think dolphins can brea—"

"I'm talking, Gravity," he snapped.

His tone slapped the spirit out of her, and I watched her recoil. My blood zinged through my veins. In that moment, I knew I was capable of physically assaulting him for how he was treating my daughter.

Tucker turned back to me on the bench where we'd taken our lunch. "I was saying, if I were to send him a propo—"

"If you were to send him a proposal," I started taciturnly, my voice frighteningly cold, "he'd use it to wipe his ass. Like me—and like Rhyland, Cal, and anyone who ever got to know you—he loathes you. Let me be clear once again about what this is. It's about the one mutual thing we have in common." I didn't dare utter her name. As it was, she was busy using a fry to draw something in the mountain of ketchup on her tray. "You'll get nothing else from it other than a relationship with that person. I don't want you. Row doesn't want to work with you. It is solely about her."

Tucker's face clouded with rage. I could tell his pride had taken a hit, and even though I didn't particularly care, that same uneasiness, the sense of danger looming in the air, washed over me.

"Understood," he clipped out. "How about we take it back to your place? I don't think I'm the best version of myself when I'm overheated."

What was he—a fucking sponge cake? Nonetheless, I happened to notice Grav's cheeks were flushed under her sunscreen too, and it was almost time for her afternoon nap.

"You can't stay more than half an hour," I warned. "It's almost her naptime."

"Fine."

We loaded ourselves into Jimmy and made our way back to the apartment. I was a ball of anxiety when I opened the door and invited him in. It felt too much like letting the devil into my den. For his part, Tucker tried to ask Gravity about her toys and stuffies. He shot me a disapproving glance when she introduced Mr. Mushroom to him. I watched them hawkishly, every muscle in my body ready to pounce in case he made a wrong move.

Tucker was on the carpet next to Gravity, doing a puzzle with her, when he shot his head up to eye me. "Where's your boyfriend?"

"Fiancé," I corrected. "And at work."

"Mommy doesn't have a boyfriend!" Gravity announced, leaning on her palms to grab a faraway piece of her *My Little Pony* puzzle. "She says boys are bad. But she lets Uncle Rhyrand babysit me, because he is okay for a fuckboy." Pause. "What's a fuckboy, Mommy?"

Oh. My. God.

Gravity had obviously been doing some intense eavesdropping on my conversations with Cal and Kieran when I thought she was asleep. It was time to reevaluate her naps altogether.

"I said *fun* boy." I cleared my throat. "Rhyland is a fun boy. Because he likes to do fun things, right?"

"He is!"

Tucker twisted his entire body toward me, lifting his right eyebrow. "You're not really engaged," he said matter-of-factly.

"Of course I am," I snapped. "She doesn—"

"My parents sniffed around with their old Staindrop friends." He cut me off. "Your mom had no idea what they were talking about. She said you and Rhyland are just neighbors. I can't believe she was right."

I clamped my mouth shut. I really didn't want Tucker to sit on this kind of ammo against me. "The engagement is...*complicated*," I said vaguely. "But we are dating for real. We just haven't said anything yet, because my brother would kill us."

This wasn't technically a lie.

Tucker stood up from the carpet, seemingly forgetting he was in the middle of bonding with his child, and walked over to me. I got up on my feet, refusing to cower in front of him.

"I knew it wasn't over." He flashed me a chilling smile, moving his hand to touch my face.

My hand shot out to block him, every instinct telling me to push him away, when I heard a key turning in my door, and it was flung open.

"Honey, I'm home."

CHAPTER TWENTY-EIGHT
RHYLAND

Maybe it was my destiny to walk into situations where other men were trying to seduce Cosmos.

She and Tucker were standing there in the living room, with Gravity at their feet doing a puzzle.

Only I knew better than to think Dylan actually wanted him here.

"Tucker," I greeted with a devil-may-care smirk, letting the door slam shut behind me for the full effect. "I didn't realize you were in the mood for hospital food."

"Why would you say that?" he sneered.

"You're standing too close to my fiancée for my liking."

He stepped back. Gravity shot up and ran toward me, and I picked her up midrun, tossing her in the air.

"Uncle Rhyrand!"

"Little stinker," I greeted back.

She giggled, and I didn't know why, but I wanted to rub it in his fucking face. So I hoisted her up on my shoulders and walked toward the kitchen. Her head nearly scraped the ceiling I was so tall. She shot her little hands up, laughing uncontrollably.

"Rhy, you're going to give my kid a concussion," Dylan warned.

I opened the fridge, making sure he knew I was right at home in this place. "Nah. I'm never gonna let anything bad happen to her. Right, little stinker?"

"Right!" Gravity hugged my neck from behind, resting her cheek on my head. "I'm sad I can't pull your hair like a horsey now," Grav murmured above me. She missed the man bun.

"Run your cheek over my hair. It'll give you a fuzzy feeling."

She did. My hair was buzzed and very straight, so the sensation was satisfying.

I grabbed orange juice from the fridge and gulped it straight from the carton.

"Me too!" Grav piped up from above my head. I reached to give her some, and she held the carton clumsily. Orange juice poured down my face and onto some of my Prada shirt, and for once, I didn't care.

I turned around to Dylan and Tucker, chuckling. "Grav decided my shirt should be orange, not white."

Dylan's expression was whimsical, charmed, almost pained. "It suits you," she croaked softly.

My eyes flashed to Tucker. I saw the stain of ketchup on his shirt and immediately understood.

"Tucker, it's time for you to leave," Dylan said.

He opened his mouth, about to argue, then glanced at me and groaned. "Fine. Gravity, come say goodbye," he barked at her. Like she was his dog or something.

"Grav needs to go down for her nap," I informed him unflappably. I knew her schedule by heart, thanks to our time together. "Bye, Tuckwad."

That made Gravity giggle even though she didn't get the reference.

I took her to her room to tuck her in and rolled down the blackout blinds. Kissed her forehead. Gave her some daily words of affirmation. "You're cute. You're smart. You keep Uncle Rhyland from saying bad words because he can't afford your fees." I winked.

"Oh, I wove you, Uncle Rhyrand."

"I like you too, little stinker." And as I left her room and closed the door behind me, I realized that wasn't even a lie anymore.

Dylan was waiting for me in the living room with two tall glasses of white wine. I checked my watch. I'd already sold all my Patek Philippe, Rolex, and Cartier, and now I was sporting an embarrassing Michele Deco Madison. At this rate, I was going to show up to Bruce's place with a fucking Apple Watch.

"It's only two," I pointed out.

She shrugged. "I needed something stronger than coffee."

"I'd have volunteered my dick." I sauntered over to her, grabbing a glass of wine from her outstretched hand and taking a sip. "Did you like my flowers today?"

She grinned. "I did. Mine hasn't arrived yet, though."

I waved her off. "You could be carrying the Spanish flu and I'd still tap that."

She pressed her face to my shoulder, breathing me in, and I instinctively curled an arm around her, kissing the top of her head. "Was it that bad?"

"Oh, worse." She kissed the exposed sliver of skin peeking through my shirt. It gave me a glimpse at who Dylan could've been if Tucker and her dad hadn't collectively shat on her trust in men, and I was low-key mad at them for doing that.

She'd have made a great *real* fiancée. Not that I was looking for one.

"He tried to pitch me a restaurant idea and asked if he could send Row a proposal. Every time Grav tried to speak to him, he either ignored her or barked at her that he was speaking. And before you came in, I think he meant to kiss me, even though I flat out told him I'd rather die than give him another chance."

"Hey, you gave it a try, and it turned out he is as much of a failure as a dad as he is as a partner and a human." I hitched a shoulder up. "At least you tried."

"It's not that simple. He can obtain visitation rights with or without my consent. Especially in New York. I looked into it. It makes more sense for me to play along and give him supervised access to Grav. I've a feeling he'll tire out once he realizes he won't be able to get his hands on Row's money or my ass."

I tensed, the realization he was here to stay in their lives chilling me. "Well, I want you to call me every time he's here so I can help you supervise him."

She let out a chuckle. "Come on, Rhy. You have your own life. You can't babysit me."

"Life's about priorities, Cosmos. And my priority is not to hear about you getting assaulted by that prick."

We sipped our wine, and I let her vent about Tuckwad for a while before Dylan announced she needed to take a shower.

"I took one earlier today but got sweaty at the zoo," she explained.

"Cool." I looked around, searching for something to do. "Netflix and chill afterward?"

She gave me a weird look. "I was thinking more…mutual shower and porking?"

"Oh." I tried to mask my pathetic delight. "Sure. Fuck *Baby Reindeer*. Let's go."

On our way to her en suite bathroom, we peered through Grav's door. She was fast asleep, snoring softly after a long day at the zoo.

We kept the bedroom door open but locked the bathroom and undressed. I flicked on the rain shower and watched Dylan put her phone on the vanity to get undressed. It was the first time I'd seen her completely naked, and I couldn't goddamn take it. This young, gorgeous woman needed to make up for the sexless time she'd lost during those years of hibernation. And I was happy to be of service.

I got rid of my underwear and socks until I was stark naked in front of her. She turned to me and whimpered, watching me stroke my already hard cock.

"Seriously, Rhy, how is it going to fit?"

"Trust the process." I chuckled. "By the way. Ass play? Anal? Yes? No? Maybe?"

"I'm willing to do anything fun." She gathered her hair into a high bun.

"Oh, it's fun." Pause. We both grinned at each other. "Get into the shower, and lather yourself in soap." My tone turned businesslike.

She flushed with excitement, hurrying into the shower.

I leaned against the vanity, watching her squirt liquid soap into her palm. She cupped her tits and moved her hand all over her body sensually. It was like a slow striptease for me, and I used the opportunity to stroke my cock and get used to the glorious sight of her so that I wouldn't come when I was halfway inside her. I usually lasted a long time. But I usually wasn't fucking my absolute goddamn fantasy.

"Join me," Dylan coaxed, smushing her tits together. Her body was insane. Long, lean legs, a round ass, and the faint outline of abs.

"Kneel in front of the granite bench." I pushed off the vanity, opening the steamed glass door and stepping inside.

She did, the pearly cobblestones of the tiles digging into her knees.

I sat in front of her, my cock twitching in front of her face. She stared up at me with those dark, sexy, upturned eyes that had always symbolized power and strength to me. She went in to suck my cock but I *tsked*, reaching between her legs like I was fishing for something at the bottom of my bag, my fingers penetrating her pussy. She was already soaked, but not enough to take me.

"So wet. Good girl." I gave her pussy a few degrading pats. "Now take this cock in your mouth, and show me how much you want it."

She grabbed me by the base, flattening her tongue and taking not even a quarter of it in, using her hand to pump my length up and down with a swirl, before I put my hand on hers.

"Did I say you could use your hands?"

"Ah…"

"Masturbate with both hands while you suck me off. One hand on your clit, the other inside you."

She complied, sucking my tip and masturbating. My dick swallowed her whimpers.

Because she had nothing to anchor my dick with, it kept swinging in her face, slapping her cute pink cheeks and slipping from her mouth. Her back arched, and she rolled her waist like a pro, and I knew—just knew—I had to come at least one time before I could fuck her properly and last. Through the noise of the pounding water, I heard the slurps of her pussy. I didn't want her to come. Not like this. And I was close.

"Use your hands on my cock," I instructed. "I want to come on your face. May I?"

She nodded eagerly.

My balls were already throbbing, tightening up, my muscles flexing, abs contracting.

"God, you're so big and thick," she moaned, holding me like an ice cream cone, licking me hungrily, sucking me, kissing the tip.

"Faster," I rasped gruffly.

She picked up the pace.

And then I felt the tickly butterfly sensation starting from the base of my cock.

"I'm coming," I grunted, grabbing my cock and aiming for her eyes, her mouth, her cheeks. White strings of cum covered her face. She opened her mouth, taking in as much as she could.

When I was done, I used the tip of my cock to drag a smear of cum from her cheek into her mouth. She closed her mouth over the tip immediately, sucking it clean with an innocent smile.

Our eyes met.

"Thank you." She kissed the slit of my penis.

Oh god. I was going to marry her for real if she continued this way.

This gave me the few minutes I needed to recoup. I scooted to the edge of the bench, lifted her by the ass, and hoisted her over me so her legs were slung over my shoulders and she was sitting on my face. I leaned against the quartz wall, internally acknowledging that I had the audacity to fuck my best friend's sister in his own shower, in which he'd probably screwed his own wife countless times, and still I was beyond shame. Past redemption. The crux of my existence, it seemed these days, was to fuck Dylan as much as I could for as long as I could. And I wasn't even inside her yet.

"I'm unsteady." Her palms flattened against the wall as I nuzzled her clit, rubbing it in circles with the tip of my nose. "What if I fa—ahhh."

I licked her, butt crack to clit, gathering a fair helping of pussy juice to coat my tongue with. Fuck, she was delicious. Earthy, musky, sweet, and a little salty. Generally speaking, pussy tasted like a penny, but Dylan's pussy tasted like the four hundred million I was going to make from Bruce Marshall.

"Ohhhh..." She began to ride my face shamelessly, no longer worried about falling off my shoulders.

I grabbed her ass in a death grip to keep her balanced, my pinkie traveling into her ass every now and then for a tease. I used my nose to swirl her clit, fucking her with my tongue. Nature had been kind to me and given me a long, strong tongue—one that could reach the tip of my nose...and serve as a good cock substitute. My tongue mercilessly thrust in and out of her as she cupped the back of my head and rode me like a cowgirl. I was already at half-mast again.

This woman was either going to be the death of me or the love of my life. No in-between about it.

"I'm coming." She squirmed, trying to dodge my tongue, the sensation too much, too acute, for her.

"Yeah, baby. Come all over my face."

I felt her muscles spasm around my tongue, her legs shaking

along my back, toes curling against my skin, and I knew that sex with her was going to be like nothing I'd ever experienced before.

I brought her down gently after she came, holding her by the waist and setting her on my lap while I was still on the bench, her legs spread open on either side of me. She looked drunk on lust. I kissed her hard, claiming her sweet mouth, tasting my salty jizz on her plump lips.

"I cannot wait to claim that ass, sweetheart." I reached between us to check how wet her pussy was. She was ready now. But I still needed a few minutes. "First, we'll get your pussy adjusted to my size. Then we're claiming this." I pushed my middle finger gently into her tight hole.

She writhed and groaned, sinking her ass into my touch. The water grew colder around us.

"Ugh. The boiler's a mess," Dylan said apologetically. My finger was halfway inside her ass, and she was moving around to give it space, letting it stretch her out. "Sorry about that."

"It's fine." I kissed the side of her neck. "Let's move it outside. It's probably better that we turn off the water in case Grav wakes up."

She stilled in my arms, haunted eyes searching mine.

I frowned. "What?"

"You care."

"Of course I care. I'm not a fucking monster."

"I never said you were, but a few weeks ago, you were adamant you hated children."

"Listen, Cosmos, I'd love to have this conversation with you, but maybe when I don't have my finger up your ass and my dick begging to be inside you."

She laughed, swatting my chest.

We hobbled outside, and I bent her over the vanity. Her fingers curled around the edges of the copper vessel sink.

"Are you sure I'm ready for it?"

"You gave birth," I chuckled, taking my dick in my hand and guiding the fat, thick crown into her pussy from behind. I was counting on hitting her G-spot and making her forget about how big it was.

"I had a C-section," she said. "I still have an ugly scar as a souvenir."

"Nothing about you is ugly." I pressed into her, and she hissed, arching toward me nonetheless.

"This okay?" I groaned. She was probably the tightest partner I'd ever been with.

She nodded swiftly. "Yup. Yeah."

But I could tell she wasn't breathing. Still, I pushed in some more, until I was halfway through.

She clenched around me, and my eyes rolled over.

"I need you to relax before I come my entire body weight into you," I warned softly.

She laughed, her entire body trembling, which made her pussy unclench a little and allowed me to slide the rest of my cock into her.

"How do you feel?" I asked.

"Full," she croaked.

"Can I start pumping?" I moved her hair across one shoulder, bending down to kiss the side of her neck.

"Yes."

I grabbed her by the waist with one hand and started pumping lazily, watching myself in the mirror in front of us. My abs flexed with each thrust, and it was the most satisfying thing I'd ever fucking done in my life.

"You look like you want to high-five yourself," Dylan moaned from underneath me.

"True story," I chuckled.

I withdrew, slamming into her again. Nothing should feel this good in life. I hoisted one of her feet up off the floor by tugging at her waist, turning her slightly sideways for deeper penetration, and when I pressed in again, I knew I was hitting her G-spot from the shuddering and uncontrollable whimpers of pleasure coming from her.

"Oh, Rhy—"

I spat onto the tip of my forefinger and slid it into her ass. It slipped in so effortlessly I could tell I'd already managed to stretch her a little. "You are doing so good, sweetheart. Taking it all in like the perfect girl that you are. Grab your tits and lick them for me, okay?"

She did just that, and it was a miracle each time I drove into her without coming.

Suddenly, her phone started dancing on the counter in front of us. She grabbed it, letting go of her tits.

"Oh, shit. It's Tuckwad." Dylan's eyes met mine in the vanity mirror, and we both shared a private laugh. I liked that the nickname had stuck.

"Answer him."

"Are you kidding me? What if—"

"That's the point." I smashed into her from behind again, the slap of our flesh meeting making my balls tingle. "I want him to hear me fucking you into submission."

Her blush deepened, and she slid her finger across the screen, clearing her throat. "Yes?"

Thrust.

"Tucker?"

"Hi. Uh, it's me." His little bitchy, sulking tone filled the bathroom as I rode Dylan's pussy like it was a carousel. "I was going to check when's the next time I can see my daughter."

Thrust.

"Anytime during a weekday next week."

Thrust.

"We're flying out to Texas for the weekend from Friday to Sunday," Dylan explained.

"Are you...are you jogging?" He sounded confused.

Dylan slapped a hand over her mouth, stifling a giggle as I picked up speed, gathering those ass cheeks and giving them gentle slaps of appreciation.

"Stick to the point," Dylan managed to moan breathlessly. "What day do you want to see her?"

Thrust.

"You know, actually, I didn't authorize this little trip of yours." Tucker sounded butt-hurt.

"Oh, please." Dylan's temper flared, but she also sounded like she was about to come. "Don't give me that bullshit. You've been—"

Thrust.

"—MIA—"

Thrust.

"—for four years—"

Thrust.

"—and I managed to keep her alive."

Thrust.

"She doesn't—"

Thrust.

"—even—"

Thrust.

"—like you."

The other side of the line went deathly still to the point I thought the call had disconnected. I was almost there, on the cliff of a mind-blowing orgasm, and with the way Dylan was panting with abandon, gripping the sink for dear life, I knew I wasn't the only one.

"Are you fucking him as we speak?" Tucker asked finally after a long pause. Disgust dripped from each and every one of his syllables, and I wanted to give him a piece of my mind. But I let Dylan have the honor. She never disappointed when it came to put-downs.

"No." She was done trying to be quiet, moaning loudly, like in a porno. The thwack of our skin slapping together rang in the air. So did the wet sounds of her pussy and the soft thud of my balls hitting her lower ass cheeks. "For your information, he's fucking me."

More silence. My chest rumbled with a chuckle.

"His finger is up my ass now," Dylan reported, crying louder. "God, he is so good, Tuck. I thought what we had going was great. I was *so* wrong. I've had four mini orgasms in the past three minutes alone, and I'm about to ride the really big one."

More silence. I started to laugh, still fucking her from behind. We both came together, moaning and grunting and panting in unison.

Throughout the entire thing, the other end of the line was quiet.

After Dylan gathered herself, she cleared her throat and asked, "So Wednesday okay? Around three p.m.? I have an opening. Are you still there?"

"Whatever," Tucker bit out and killed the call.

She fell into my arms, both of us laughing.

CHAPTER TWENTY-NINE
DYLAN

Dylan_loves_Rhyland4ever commented: Siri, play "Marry You" by Bruno Mars.

Rhyland Coltridge commented: Siri, play "The Most Beautiful Girl in the World" by Prince.

Dylan_loves_Rhyland4ever commented: Siri, play "Lollipop" by Lil Wayne.

Rhyland Coltridge commented: Siri, play "34+35" by Ariana Grande.

TheRealKieranCarmichael commented: Get a room. 🗿

How did you know when you were a sex addict?

How much sex was *too* much sex?

I couldn't quantify that. All I knew was that for the rest of the week, Rhyland and I bumped uglies at least three times a day, excluding mutual oral. We went through all my favorite positions, then his. We had sex during Grav's naptime, after she went to sleep. When Cal came over with Serafina, I insisted I had an urgent OB-GYN appointment to attend, instead going upstairs to have my vagina destroyed by Rhyland Coltridge.

Addicts always said they could stop whenever they wanted.

Unlike them, I was beginning to see it was going to be pretty hard to say goodbye to this magnificent dick, and to the man attached to it, when all this was over.

So on the Thursday before our trip to Texas, which would probably mark the end of our arrangement, I decided to broach the subject with Rhy.

It was ten o'clock at night. Grav was fast asleep after Rhy took her out for a carriage ride and some Union Square Donuts. He'd tired her out real good in order to make sure he could have her mother all to himself afterward.

"Rhy." I pressed my stomach and breasts against his bare back, lying on top of him.

"Hmm?" His cheek was pressed against my pillow, and he was half-asleep. He never stayed over when we hooked up. It was one of those invisible lines we refused to cross.

"Are we going to stop…you know, *this*, when the arrangement is over?"

"You mean fucking?" he asked groggily.

I smiled, and I knew he could feel my cheek stretching against his skin when I did. "Yeah."

"Not if it's up to me." He flipped himself over onto his back, hugging me so I wouldn't fall off the bed. We were now in a woman-on-top position, my hands on his pecs. His fingers ran up and down my back soothingly. His eyes met mine—green, blue, and mesmerizing. "But I'll respect whatever you decide."

"You're insane if you think I'm quitting the D train." I rolled my eyes.

He laughed, kissing my nose. "Good to hear, because I wasn't planning on stopping, you know, that part of the arrangement."

I licked my lips, trailing a finger over his collarbone. "Are you still going to babysit Grav when I go to the Taylor Swift show in September?"

He offered me a scandalized look. "Duh, dude. What the fuck? She's my girl."

There was something about the way he said it—*she's my girl*—that made me struggle not to cry.

"I'm also down for the occasional babysitting gig. You know, here and there." He smoothed my hair back gently. "But you'll have to figure out a permanent arrangement. I'm going to be neck-deep in working on the app. Probably going to sleep at the office most nights."

"I know," I said distractedly.

Rhy elevated one eyebrow. "Have you spoken to Cherrie at all? Let her know your decision?"

"Not yet."

"You need to if you want to secure Grav's spot."

"Still thinking about it," I said vaguely, scurrying up to wrap myself in a robe.

I was no longer on the fence about the preschool itself—it was amazing, and it had crazy-good reviews on Yelp out of hundreds of reviewers. My issue was the tuition. I'd saved a really good amount of money, but I knew I'd forever be playing catch-up with the fee once my savings ran out.

I padded to the bathroom to brush my teeth, with Rhy stretching out on the edge of the bed before following me inside. When he entered the en suite, his cock was still at half-mast from sex a few minutes ago, and he was scratching the side of his ass, and it struck me that this was what domestic bliss looked like. Only we weren't a real couple, and he was way out of my league even now, on the cusp of being a millionaire but not quite there.

"Hey." He hugged me from behind while I brushed my teeth. Our eyes met in the mirror.

"Hi," I murmured around white foam and the head of the toothbrush.

"You're not mad, are you?"

"No," I scoffed. "Why would I be mad?"

It wasn't his fault I couldn't afford anything in this god-awful city.

Maybe Tucker could babysit Gravity for some of the time I needed for work. Yesterday, when he came to see her, he wasn't completely awful. Still cold and detached, but they watched TV together and ate Italian wedding soup in silence, and she seemed cool about it. Not rabid like she was with Rhyland, but definitely comfortable.

Rhyland shrugged, burying his face in my throat. "I don't know. Just checking. Do you want me to leave?"

I should say yes. We'd already had sex twice today. It was late, and I'd see him tomorrow morning anyway for our Texas trip.

"No," I heard myself say.

"Do you want to have sex again?" He grinned cheekily against my skin.

"Yeah, in a little bit." I spat foam into the sink, flicking the water on. "If you're up for it."

"I'm always up for it." He thrust his now fully erect cock between my ass cheeks. "All puns intended."

I was wrong.

I wasn't a sex addict.

I was a Rhyland addict.

CHAPTER THIRTY
DYLAN

Grav was equal parts excited and frightened for our plane ride. I couldn't blame her. There was something deeply unsettling about entering a metal tube someone else was in charge of that soared through the sky. She'd been on airplanes before, when we went to visit Row and Cal, but back then, she was too young to understand what was happening.

I dutifully distracted her with snacks and *Bluey*—every parent's emergency kit for the distressed child.

Throughout the flight, Rhyland looked right at home on the private plane, working on his laptop and occasionally goofing around with Grav. It was a reminder that our lives weren't the same. Not really. In a few days, he'd return to his glamorous existence with his billionaire friends, and I'd keep busting my ass in a bar to make ends meet and bickering with a good-for-nothing ex about supervised visits with our daughter.

The flight passed quickly, and we were greeted by a huge black Escalade that took us to Bruce and Jolene's ranch on the outskirts of Dallas. Grav was glued to the window, nose smushed to the glass, oohing and aahing at the sunflower and strawberry fields. Rhyland and I were kind and impersonal with each other, as we always were around my daughter. I didn't want her to get the wrong idea. To get her hopes up. To get *mine* up.

It was an hour before we reached the ranch-style house, which appeared surprisingly modest. Gray brick, with open red shutters, overhanging eaves, and a wide, open-plan porch. Surrounding it were cattle grazing freely. Cows, elk, and sheep with shepherd dogs running around.

An intense pang of realization stabbed at my chest. This was what I wanted for my daughter. This carefree, natural lifestyle.

Bruce and Jolene were waiting on the porch with sweet iced teas, sitting on rocking chairs and talking easily. They stood up as we poured out of the vehicle. The golden glint of an unforgiving summer glazed every surface—the ground, the walkway, the heat rolling off the concrete walls of the house—and Gravity, who in her excitement forgot to be shy, dashed outside, running everywhere, trying to play with the dogs.

"Grav," I laughed nervously, trying to snatch her back to me. "Careful, sweetie. You don't want—"

Rhyland scooped her up even though he was holding both our suitcases. "No way, little stinker. We're going to ride horsies together now."

Bruce and Jolene approached us, and we exchanged pleasantries. They were obviously impressed by the deep, genuine connection Rhyland had with my daughter.

"Hey, Lil Miss." Bruce tousled Gravity's hair affectionately. "Does Mr. Rhyland right here take you to do fun things?"

"Yes!" My daughter's eyes widened with delight. "We do all the fun things together. And he makes me waffles."

Rhyland sent Bruce a satisfied smirk, and it occurred to me his relationship with my daughter could be part of a grander, more sophisticated scheme. The thought made me shudder.

Jolene and Bruce showed us around the house. It was an open-plan, one-story, L-shaped house with two wings. Their bedroom was on one side, ours on the other, and there was a huge living room and two dining areas in between.

"I raised my five kids in this place." Jolene touched her cheek longingly as we weaved in and out of comfortable, generously furnished rooms that smelled of farmland, with dancing curtains and folded quilts and the intense, pleasant feeling of home.

"You have *five* kids?" I shrieked. I had one kid—not a particularly difficult one—and still found it overwhelming.

Jolene laughed. "I sure do. I kept having boys and wanted a girl."

"And did you get one?" I hoped she had. Hell, I was half considering giving her mine, she seemed so committed to the task.

"I did!" Jolene said brightly. "Our fifth one is adopted. Her name is Lorelai. She lives right down the street from us."

"That's amazing," I breathed.

We followed Bruce and Jolene to the backyard, which had a huge, gated pool and an impressive play area, including a tree house, swings, slides, and a sandbox. Gravity lunged into the sandbox without even asking for permission, doing the breaststroke in the hot sand.

I snorted out a laugh, shaking my head. "Sorry. This'll make a mess, but I'll clean it up."

"You will not," Jolene chided, grabbing my hand and squeezing it. A rush of gratitude coursed through me before she caught my gaze and said, "This weekend is not only about business, Dylan. It's also about you. I'll take care of Gravity. I have ten grandchildren between my children—I know what I'm doing. And you'll always be within reach, close enough to see her. We'll shadow you while Bruce shows you around. There are so many things to see here."

My knee-jerk reaction was to refuse. I had a hard time letting other people take care of Gravity. But I needed to let go if I was serious about going to school at some point in the near or distant future.

"Okay." I nodded, my voice grainy and heavy with emotion. "Thank you."

We started off with pony rides for Gravity and exploring the property. The Marshalls had owned this land since the 1800s, and every generation was engraved onto it, worked it, and cared for it.

"We Marshalls never did too badly for ourselves," Bruce explained with a piece of straw wedged into the side of his mouth. "But it wasn't until I worked for a technology company and came up with Telephonication that I saw a real big buck in my bank account." Telephonication was the app everyone used to make video calls and have unencrypted conversations all over the world for free. "I sold the app, and since then, I don't know..." He massaged his chin with a frown. "Never put my hand on a venture that was a bad idea. I know a hit when I see one. And you." He turned to Rhyland. "You have a good idea right there. I'm starting to warm up to you."

Rhyland looked pensive, deep in thought. He'd been like this since we boarded for Texas, and I wondered if there was something on his mind that didn't include our little weekend charade. Maybe something to do with his parents, whom he refused to speak to.

The last stop in our grand Marshall estate tour was off the main pathway leading to their door, beyond the ranch itself. It was an old, round well made of heavy black stones. With a galvanized metal jug hanging on a frame under its wooden roof, it looked like something out of a Grimm Brothers tale, and I pressed Gravity hard to my chest, afraid she'd wiggle off and launch herself into it.

"And this is the family wishing well." Bruce stopped to pat the hot stones with a proud smirk. "I ain't superstitious or anything, but this wishing well has made quite the name for itself over the past couple centuries. We stopped utilizing it for water in around 1900. My great-great-grandfather fell ill during that time, and his wife, Bertha—she was a nurse—thought he'd never get out of it. The doctors gave him a few days. Folk traveled from all over to say goodbye to the old man. One night, she sat on the edge of the wishing well, dropped a coin in, and prayed he'd get better. The next morning, he woke up feelin' like a trillion bucks!" Bruce's eyes gleamed with juvenile enthusiasm. "Since then, people from all over Texas come here to drop a coin and make a wish. This lil baby has helped countless people." He smacked the stones again. "Get married, get pregnant, overcome illnesses, gather the courage to do something new. You should try it sometime."

"Charming, but people under the age of fifty don't carry cash on them, let alone petty cash," Rhyland said brutally.

I elbowed him. What was wrong with him? I knew there was some tension between him and Bruce, but the latter was finally opening up.

"Don't be a cynic," Bruce said. "Where there is no belief, there is no growth. Doesn't matter who your god is. Could be justice, hope, or the Big Daddy in the sky. You have to believe in something, or you have nothing to live for."

When we got back to the main house, Jolene suggested Gravity help her make cornbread. Rhyland and I retired to our room, adjacent to Gravity's bedroom. For all their conservativeness, Jolene and Bruce had allotted us one bed even though we weren't yet married.

When Rhyland unzipped his suitcase on the bed, I went in for the kill.

"What's up with you?" I hopped onto the mattress. "You've been surly."

"Nothing," he muttered, tugging out expensive polo shirts and designer briefs.

I'd never seen Rhyland in a bad mood. In fact, up until now, I wasn't entirely sure he was capable of one.

"If I wanted a bullshitter, I'd have stayed with Tuckwad." I frowned. "You're obviously upset. Is it about Bruce? Is it abou—"

"Yesterday, I mortgaged my apartment." He flicked his empty suitcase shut, tossing it to the floor.

My jaw loosened with shock, and I shot to my feet, placing my palm on his cheek. He looked the other way sharply, hissing with humiliation as the pink flush on his neck crawled up to his face.

"I've been such a fucking idiot for years. Recklessly spending all my money. Thinking I could live like my much richer friends. Every bad idea I ever stumbled into, I took. I got a fucking six-million-dollar penthouse basically for *free*..."

Holy shit, his place is worth six million?

"And I managed to lose it."

Guilt gnawed at me for charging him an insane amount of money for our fake relationship.

"You haven't lost the apartment," I whispered. "Mortgaging means nothing. I mean, I heard some people do it for better rates or whatever!" I was really talking out of my ass now, since I'd never owned anything more expensive than a Dyson hair dryer and had no idea how those things worked. "And look." I licked my lips. "Forget about my fee. I'll pick up more shifts at the Alchemist..."

"No," Rhyland said decisively, shutting down the idea. "Paying you so you can take care of yourself and Grav is the least stupid thing I've been doing with my money. This has nothing to do with you."

"But, Rhy—"

"No." He grabbed my shoulders, squeezing as he peered into my eyes. "Stop making this about our arrangement, okay? It's not you I'm mad at. It's myself. It took me all these years to figure out how to live my life, and now I'm playing catch-up."

"If it makes you feel any better, you're doing a pretty awesome job." I smiled at him tentatively.

He gripped my waist and jerked me to him, giving me a peck on the lips. We'd been careful not to be handsy in front of Gravity. "Would you call yourself a fan, Cosmos?"

"Of my nickname? No. Of you? Absolutely."

We swayed slowly to a soundless rhythm only we could hear. I pressed my cheek to his chest, feeling his heart beating all over the place, knowing mine was doing the same thing and that this was going to end in tears.

Most likely mine.

It was as if Rhyland had decided to go on a quest to destroy my ovaries that day. After Grav had spent time with Jolene, I gave her a bath, braided her hair, and did some coloring with her before dinner. After supper, we tucked her into bed, and the little traitor turned to me seriously and said, "Mommy, I wove you, but I want Uncle Rhyrand to read me a story."

I pretended not to be offended and used the time to unpack my suitcase. But after ten minutes of waiting around, Rhy still hadn't left Gravity's room, and she still hadn't yelled for me to come kiss her good night. Despite myself, I peered through the crack of the adjacent door, spying on them. Rhyland was sprawled out next to her in her floor-level princess bed, her head tucked into the crook of his arm, flipping a page in their book.

"…then Pooh said, 'But I love honey,'"—he made a…was it a German accent?—"and Eeyore replied, 'Yes, we know.'" He pinched his nose theatrically when he narrated the donkey, and Gravity giggled.

I leaned against the doorframe and grinned.

"Finally, Piglet laughed, 'So do I!'"

Each character had its own voice and accent. Sometimes, Gravity would ask Rhyland to read the same page over and over again, then she'd laugh until her tummy hurt. I was shockingly disturbed by how hot I found it when my upstairs neighbor made silly faces, crossed his eyes, and attempted different accents.

Finally, they finished the book, and Rhy dropped a kiss on my daughter's head.

"Words of affirmation?" he offered her.

She nodded seriously.

I loved that he'd remembered. I loved too many dang things about this man. My entire body liquified into something warm and delicious and content at his voice, his words.

He stood up, tucking the book between the bed frame and the mattress and covering her with her blankie. Mr. Mushroom was pressed close to her chest. "You are my favorite girl in the whole entire universe."

"Even more than Mommy?" Grav gasped.

Rhyland's eyes met mine from across the darkened room, and I realized he'd known I was there all along. He smirked. "Mommy is my favorite woman. It's not the same category, little stinker."

"What's a caddegory?" She rubbed her fists over her eyes.

"I'll let Mommy explain." He slipped out of the room, and I sat down on the edge of my daughter's bed and kissed her good night.

"Mommy?"

"Yes, baby?"

"Is Uncle Rhyrand staying with us forever? Will he always be our neighbor?"

That simple question pierced through my skull like an arrow, making my head throb.

No, he wasn't. In fact, soon enough, he wasn't going to see her a few times a week—maybe not even a few times a month. He was going to live the new life we were setting up for him now.

I tried to keep my composure. "I'm not sure, sweetheart." I stroked her braid's flyaways from her forehead with what I hoped was an easy smile. "I mean, we'll always see him. He is good friends with Uncle Row and the family. But sometimes you see a person a lot, and other times…not so much." This was the nicest way I could think of telling her not to get attached.

Gravity pouted. "Well, I want to see him all the time. I wove him a lot. Maybe even as much as Granny."

Girl, tell me about it.

Fine. I didn't love him, but I had reconsidered my entire "no men ever" rule for him, which was a lot.

I closed the door behind me softly and pressed my back to it, closing my eyes. I was in trouble. Big trouble.

"Hey, Cosmos."

Rhyland's words pulled me out of my weird mood. I opened my eyes. He was standing in front of the mirror, getting dressed.

"I'm taking you out tonight."

"But Grav—"

"Is already asleep," he finished for me. "And Jolene insisted on babysitting her. Come on." He made a face. "It's time to look lovey-dovey. For my deal, yeah?"

I nodded. He needed this win desperately.

I got ready and slipped on a tight red dress. When we walked out of the house, we looked like two awkward teenagers passing Jolene and Bruce in the living room. They were watching *Wheel of Fortune* like it was 1993.

"Have fun, kids!" Jolene called out.

"Keep it in your pants, mister," added Bruce.

A chauffeur drove us into the nearest nondescript town, where we drank our beers silently. We could both feel it all coming to an end. Bruce was pacified. The deal was likely going through. And there really wasn't any point in doing more bonding.

Rhyland's phone danced on the counter of the bar. His mother again.

I sighed. "You're going to have to deal with your parents sooner or later."

"Wanna bet?" he drawled sarcastically, taking a pull of his beer. "They fucked me over real good and nice. Now it's my turn. Whatever they want, it's a favor. And I'm fresh out of fucks when it comes to their problems."

"What if one of them has health issues?"

Rhyland shook his head, holding his beer by its neck between his index and middle fingers, eyes wandering to the football game on the screen above our heads. A rerun. "If one of them was about to kick the bucket, they'd spend all their time together and not invite me to say goodbye. Ever since I was a kid, they've always had this...

possessiveness toward each other. I remember Dad always butting into our hugs every time I embraced my mother. He wouldn't really let me touch her. And as I grew up, I think he kind of...almost competed with me for her. Teaching me his craft, passing along his skills, was mainly to keep me busy and away from her."

"That's sick," I said quietly.

He nodded. "I grew up feeling like a voyeur in my own home. Love and affection were a currency, and I was hella poor." No wonder, then, that he'd grown up becoming richer from that very same coinage.

Three beers in, we called it a night and stumbled back to our waiting car.

"I could get used to this." I put my head on Rhyland's shoulder and closed my eyes, only for a few seconds. When I opened them again, we were parked in front of the ranch.

I moaned groggily and scooted out of the back seat of the Escalade, murmuring my thanks to the driver. Rhyland snatched my hand in his and led the way. At first, I thought we were heading for the door, but then he took a sharp turn left, and we were stomping on dry summer land and mostly eaten grass.

"Where are you taking me?" I yawned into the back of my hand.

"You'll see." His voice sounded strangely strained, and that woke me up from my power nap.

We trudged in the pitch-black, Rhy lighting the way with his phone flashlight. Then I saw it, like a beacon in a sea of nothing.

The wishing well.

Rhyland's grip tightened on my hand. Then we were right next to it, the now-cold stones pressing against the front of my thighs. The metal jug jingled softly to the swoosh of the wind.

He placed his phone screen down on the lip of the well so that the light touched the silhouettes of our faces. There was urgency in his expression.

"Bruce was right," he said solemnly.

"About me being the perfect woman?" I purred. He'd said that earlier today when I helped Jolene do the dishes after dinner while Gravity hung from my neck like a little monkey.

"That too." Rhy palmed the coin pendent on the chain around his neck, ripping it from his skin in one go and flattening the pad of his thumb over it. "You have to believe in something, and I believe in nothing, so I might as well take a leap of faith. Here." He grabbed my hands and squeezed, brushing his thumbs back and forth over my skins soothingly. "It's the only coin I have."

"I'm pretty sure this thing is a part of your DNA." I tried to inject some laughter into my voice, but the truth was I was choked up with emotion. He had one wish to spare, and he was giving it to me? "I've never seen you take this thing off."

"Silver Washington quarter. Rare coin." He smirked, ignoring my rush of incoherent words. "My grandfather gave it to me before he passed away. I used to spend summers with him. We were close."

I shook my head vehemently, gulping. "I'm not throwing that away, you psycho."

"If you won't, I will. And I'll wish for something really spiteful." He assessed me for a moment. "That your perky boobs will go saggy or something."

"You wouldn't." My eyes tapered.

"You know I would. It's classic me."

True. Rhyland was that level of stubborn, just like me. We weren't yin and yang; we were two fucking yins that still managed to complete each other.

He dangled the coin in front of my face slowly, mock hypnotizing me. "You're getting very sleepy, and you want to use this to make a wish, because I decided that's what needs to happen, and I always get my way."

"Ugh." I snatched the pendant from his hand.

Clutching it, I peered down at the dark nothingness of the well and took a deep breath. The summer air hit the bottom of my lungs.

I knew what I wanted, but I was afraid to ask for it. I'd spent the past four years training myself so well not to want, not to wish, not to dream, that it was hard to admit I wasn't happy. That my sweet, bright child wasn't enough.

I squeezed the pendant harder. No matter which direction my thoughts skidded to, I was met with a wall of anxiety.

Med school? Financial insecurity, long hours away from my daughter, the possibility of failure.

Rhyland? Heartbreak, insecurity, past trauma, crushing betrayal that was to come, because it *always* came. Other than Row, there had never been one man in my life who hadn't disappointed me.

"Go nuts, Cosmos," Rhyland urged in the background. "Ask for your wildest dream."

I stretched my arm, letting the coin fall into the well. A soft *clink* sounded as it hit the still water.

"What did you ask for?"

You.

CHAPTER THIRTY-ONE
DYLAN

Bruce and Jolene smiled at us when we scurried into the house.

"Had a good time, lovebirds?"

"Yup." Rhyland slung his arm over my shoulders.

As they both stood up to excuse themselves to their bedroom, Bruce's gaze halted on Rhy's neck, where the pendant used to be, and he nodded to himself in approval. He knew. And just like that, I wondered if Rhyland sacrificing his pendant for my dream had been about me or about *him*.

Asking outright would be foolish. I wasn't supposed to care. Why couldn't it be both?

I thanked the couple for taking care of Gravity and padded into my room to check on her through our shared door. She was fast asleep. I closed the door softly. When I turned around, Rhyland was standing in front of me, partially naked and completely hard.

"Oh." I raised one eyebrow. "That's fast."

"Literally *never* heard that from a woman."

I smiled, but the truth was I wasn't in the mood. No matter how filthy and decadent our sexual encounters were, to me, they still meant something.

"What's up?" He sauntered over to me in just his briefs, hugging my midsection.

I shook my head.

"You look troubled."

"Nothing. It's just…"

"Yes?" He lifted one brow expectantly.

I decided to just go for it. Miscommunication was such a dumb way to sour a relationship.

"Us? This?" I gestured between us with my finger. "It scares me."

"Why does it scare you?" He looked genuinely puzzled.

"Because I'm breaking my rules for you."

"I'm breaking my heart for you," he said without missing a beat.

"What?" My mouth went dry, my heart pounding inside my chest. Had I heard him correctly?

He licked his lips, grabbing the back of his head and turning his back on me. "Look, maybe I'm saying this wrong, but trust me, this thing we have going? It's not easy for me either. I'm playing fucking house with the hottest woman I know when I *know* I can't give her everything she deserves. It's doomed, and it's fucking killing me, because in another life, in another scenario, we could've been really good together." His throat rolled with a swallow. "We could've been the best thing that happened to me."

"Why?" I tried to keep the desperation from my voice. "Why do you think you can't give me what I need?"

"Because I don't know how to love," he answered simply. "And because the only example of love I've ever witnessed was toxic as hell and made me swear away from it."

I wasn't a girl who cried about boys. Never. Even when I found out Tucker had left me with a day-old baby, I'd shrugged it off and kept my head high. So it was curious that now I felt like crying.

Still, I nodded calmly, twisting in place and raising my hair. "Mind helping me with my zipper?"

His fingertips glided down my back as he helped me out of my dress. The shoulder straps fell to my waist, and I shimmied out of it. I wasn't wearing a bra, but instead of cupping my breasts from behind, Rhy kissed my temple, his hands roaming over my stomach.

"I meant what I told Gravity."

"You mean my vibrator is a fancy microphone?" I asked playfully. It was such an artful save. When she found it, I thought I was going to choke.

"Well, yes. That too," he chuckled into my skin, making my whole body feel soft and warm and safe. "But also that you're my favorite woman in the whole world, and I hope when we part ways, you'll remember that."

When we part ways.

"Mm-hmm." I knew that if I spoke now, I'd cry.

He trailed kisses from my neck down to my shoulder. Then he turned me around, falling to his knees and grabbing the elastic of my undies from each side of my waist. He slid them down slowly, pausing when he saw the tiny C-section scar we'd talked about the other day. He pressed his mouth to it. Breathed it in. I shuddered, cupping his head and closing my eyes.

"You're perfect." He kissed it again. "One day, I'm going to see you with your new husband, sit across from you at a table in some event Row invites both of us to, and loathe my entire existence."

Now it was my turn to slide down to my knees. I grabbed his face and kissed him, tasting my tears in that kiss, the saltiness of broken promises that were never made and the bitter disappointment of who we were. Two people who could never let go of the past. Who could never build a better future for themselves.

This time, the sex wasn't feral and wild. It felt a lot like making love, with Rhy laying me down on the carpet and kissing me as he entered me missionary-style, my legs wrapped around his narrow waist, fingers toying with his now-short hair. We maintained eye contact, communicating an entire silent conversation. I rocked onto his cock, kissing him softly, so softly, as he hit the most sensitive spot in my body over and over, bringing me to a quiet, shuddering orgasm. Then he came inside me, staying inside for a while, bracing himself on his arms.

Finally, Rhyland blinked at me as if he'd just woken up in a completely new place.

"Friends?" He offered me his pinkie between us.

God, it was the worst lie we'd ever told each other. It really felt like we were spiraling into something dark and messy. I wanted more, and I knew if I couldn't have it, I'd implode.

I mustered a smile and curled his pinkie in mine. "Friends."

CHAPTER THIRTY-TWO
RHYLAND

"Damn, son. If I knew you could shoot like a Texan, I'd have signed that contract a decade ago." Bruce whistled low, squinting at the log on which a Snapple cap had sat just a second ago. "How'd you learn to aim so well?"

I lowered the Remington 870, rolling the gum in my mouth from one side to the other. "My old man taught me."

"Are y'all close?" He stuck his thumbs inside the loops of his belt, putting one booted foot on a chopped log in his backyard.

Bruce had woken my ass up at six in the morning, first for a run ("you can tell a lot about a man by his physical capabilities"), then for a shooting session. I suspected we were going to finish off the day by hunting a bear with our bare hands, and I wasn't looking forward to it.

Good thing we were at the last dregs of our visit, a breath away from boarding the private plane in the afternoon and going back to New York. I'd marked this whole thing a success, mostly because Dylan and Gravity had brought their A game and were both endearing and agreeable to a fault.

"He's back in Maine, but we try to catch up as much as we can."

Once every couple years or so.

I walked over to the logs, fishing for bottle caps in my pocket and putting one on each of the four logs in front of us. Bruce propped his shotgun up. I sauntered back next to him.

"Did you read the contract?" It had been some time since I sent it.

He fumbled with the shells in the box beneath him, pretending not to hear me. After reloading, he aimed the barrel at one of the caps. He was off by at least a few inches. I sighed.

"Watch your stance, Marshall. Feet should be shoulder-width apart, knees bent, slight forward lean. C'mon—it's not amateur hour."

"I've been hitting the range my whole life, boy." He took the shot and missed.

"Here." I ignored his sulks, coming in from behind him and cupping his elbows to push them up slightly and better his stance. I kicked his feet open from behind. "One cheek on the stock, hold it tighter to your shoulder," I instructed, tilting his head just right. He wasn't terrible, but he wasn't great either.

He took the shot with me behind him, and the bottle cap soared through the distance, snapping in two midair.

Bruce lowered his shotgun and turned to me. "You know, Coltridge, patronizing your potential investor is bad for business."

"Not taking good fucking advice is worse," I said dryly.

He studied me through bloodshot eyes. He didn't look like a man who slept too often, and I wondered if his life was as fucked up as mine under all this wholesome pretense.

"I can't figure you out," he said. "You seem like a happy-go-lucky guy in company, but every time it's just the two of us, I get the distinct feeling you're predatory and dark."

"I'm both," I said laconically. "I've spent my life perfecting the art of being exactly who I need to be at any given moment. Which is why you'd be a fool not to get into business with me. I know exactly what you need. Now, answer my question—did you read the contract?"

"Yes." He took his hat off, using the back of his hand to wipe the sweat from his forehead. "I sure did, the night at the restaurant."

"And?" I didn't want to seem eager, but I was drowning financially.

He sighed. "Tate helped you draft it, didn't he?"

"What makes you say that?"

"Because you are fucking me over real good if I fail to push it down people's throats."

"Shouldn't be an issue if you plan on helping me make it big."

"You should be very wary of Tate Blackthorn." He changed the subject.

"And why's that?"

"He's shadier than the Mariana Trench at midnight. Dangerous too—I'm talking underworld stuff. And you know what it's like. When shit hits the fan, everyone in close proximity gets dirty."

I'd always suspected as much about Tate. His suits were clean-cut, but I saw the ruthlessness lying underneath them. However, I found his expertise and balls of steel valuable to my endeavors. And it had to be said: he had yet to let me down.

"Thanks for the heads-up. So? Will you sign the contract?"

Bruce pressed his lips together, gave me a puzzling look. "Do you love this woman?" he asked.

What does that have to do with anything?

"Lil Miss," he clarified. "Are you going to be a family man and treat her and her daughter right? Keep your nose clean and your ass outta trouble? Not run off with my money and resources to seek refuge on a Bahamian island?"

I took my turn to raise my shotgun. I leaned into my shot, focused on my target, and slowly pulled the trigger. The cap danced in the air before falling to the ground.

"Yes," I lied. "I love her."

I'd told more brazen lies in my lifetime.

I didn't love Dylan.

But there was no point in denying it: she was no longer just Row's annoying, albeit hot, little sis.

These days, I found pieces of her everywhere. On the radio in my car when a Taylor Swift song was on. In tired, happy moms chasing after their kids in the park. In the scent of garlic and tomato wafting out of the Italian restaurant across from my dry cleaner.

"Why do you give a shit about my personal life?" I growled.

Bruce ran his knuckles over his white stubble, ill-contained rage thinning his lips. "The one and only time I entered into a business relationship with a young, single man, it blew up in my face." He gave me a sidelong glance that dug into my conscience, like he was talking about me.

"Explain," I instructed, watching him reposition himself to take a shot. This time, he did good.

"I'm talking about Blackthorn," he barked out.

"Tate never mentioned you two worked together."

Then again, how much did I really know Tatum Blackthorn? How much did anyone? He always felt like an extension of the three of us—me, Row, and Kieran—never fully integrated into the group.

"That's the one." Bruce dug the barrel of his gun into the ground. "He was a spring chicken back when we first met, in his early twenties. I was riding my fourth exit high. I was richer than God. Had everything I ever wanted. Tate tried to force my hand into business with him—first directly, and then, when I shot him down, in roundabout ways. Through hostile takeovers of companies I worked with, getting on the boards of corporations I was considering taking over myself."

That sounded about right. Tate Blackthorn didn't take no for an answer. Sometimes I thought his entire existence was about pissing other people off.

"Okay," I said. "And that was enough to get you so riled up?"

"I wasn't finished." Bruce bared his teeth, jaw stretched tight across his skin. "He spent three years butting into my shit, to the point I was fantasizing about taking out a restraining order against him. Then my father passed away after a long battle with cancer."

We slung our shotguns over our shoulders, making our way to the shed.

Bruce ran his tongue over his upper teeth. "My father's dream was to be buried on Slipdown Mountain. He used to take us hikin' there when we were kids, me and my six siblings. We'd camp there. The place holds some of our most precious memories. But Slipdown Mountain is a tourist attraction. There were little private lots for sale there."

I knew where this was going, and my blood curdled. I had a ruthless streak, but I was by no means a sadist. Tate was.

"Tate purchased all the private lots?" I guessed.

"Sure did." Bruce offered a brief nod, kicking the door to the shed open. It wasn't one degree cooler than it was outside. If anything, the air was stuffy and still on top of being hot. "Every spare inch of land."

"Did he sell it to you at an insane price?" I asked, put off by Tate's behavior and general existence. I could be a top-notch asshole when prompted, but I'd never understood Tate's unabashed desire to hurt people.

"He didn't want to sell." Bruce's jaw twitched. "I offered him well above the going rate, allotted three real-estate firms to try to get him to sell, rent me out a spot—anything."

We hung the rifles over the wooden wall.

"He wanted my business, not my money. My connections. My trade secrets."

"Did he end up getting them?" I eyed him warily. I already knew the answer. Tate stopped at nothing to get what he wanted.

"Yes," Bruce admitted, his voice cracking midword. He bowed his head. "He got everything he wanted from me. He extorted me, used my knowledge and means, and went on to build an empire bigger than mine just to throw it in my face. I sold him something far more valuable than companies, materials, or land." Pause. "I sold him my *soul*."

We were quiet for a moment. I finally understood why Bruce Marshall had played me around. That day a few months ago, when I first approached him with my idea, I threw Tate's name around as a mutual acquaintance, thinking it would give me legitimacy, since there wasn't one businessman in the entire world who didn't know Tate personally. I hadn't taken into consideration his notoriety. Nor his ability to make anyone an enemy.

"Then why did you go to Row's event?" I asked. "You knew Tate would be there."

Bruce headed toward the door, and I followed. "I refuse to show him I still care."

"Even though you clearly fucking do," I chuckled.

"Even though I clearly do," he agreed. "But I am very suspicious of people who consider themselves his friends and show the same behavioral patterns as him."

"I don't think Tate sees anyone as a friend, me included," I said honestly. "And I'm nothing like him."

I jerked the door, about to go outside, but Bruce slammed his shoulder against the wooden thing, trapping us in together. Our eyes locked. I knew I could take the old man down easily, but I wanted to see where he'd take this.

"Son?" he asked.

"Yeah?"

"I'll sign that contract, but you are going to prove to me you are nothing like your hellion friend. Understood?"

I nodded. I didn't appreciate being treated like a child, but I was also so close I could practically taste victory on the tip of my tongue.

"If you let me down, I'll be the Tate in our story," Bruce elucidated.

I smirked indulgently. "Sure."

He could think what he wanted.

He was going to make me filthy rich.

CHAPTER THIRTY-THREE
DYLAN

It was not a soft landing back in New York.

First of all, Max called me on my return flight to announce Faye was doing a lot better and was scheduled to come back to work this coming week. While I was happy to hear she was doing well, I also knew it meant fewer shifts for me. I dreaded going back into the unemployment market and suffering through job interviews—if I even got invited to any.

Second, three days after we were back, I came down with the mother of all flus.

It wasn't an ordinary virus; I seemed to sport every single symptom available, including ones that were brand-new: congestion, fever, a cough, a sore throat, an ear infection, and two pink eyes. My muscles ached, and my head felt like the home of a hundred-ton metal.

It was the first time in my life I'd found myself unable to take care of Grav properly.

Problem was I didn't actually have any help available. Cal and Row were in London, Mama was in Staindrop, and my go-to person, Rhyland, was holed up in an important technology conference for the next three days. I knew he'd shelled out money on a booth for App-date to get some prelaunch hype, and he had back-to-back meetings with investors, so he couldn't afford to get sick.

I also knew he literally couldn't afford milk these days, so he *needed* this to hype up his app.

I had no choice. I found myself calling Tuckwad.

I rationalized to myself in a million different ways as I put the phone on speaker, holding it close to my mouth. I watched Gravity run aimlessly around the house, bored and cabin-fevered, begging for someone to entertain her.

He was going to stay here with us, not leave the house, so I'd be able to supervise them. And his last visit hadn't been a complete disaster—they'd seemed to tolerate each other. Besides, maybe he needed to be thrown in at the deep end. That was what parenting was all about. Plus, I didn't really care if he caught whatever plague this was.

He finally answered, sounding smugger than Conor McGregor getting ready for a bar fight. "Hey, hot stuff."

God, I hated him.

"Hi, Tucker. I have a favor to ask…"

"Wow," he bristled. "You sound like shit, dude."

"Thank you." I took a deep, steadying breath, willing myself not to scream. "I happen to feel it too. Which is why I'm calling."

Silence. I waited for him to pick up on the unspoken request. Instead, there was silence, punctuated by, "And?"

"I'm calling because I know you don't have a shift today, and I need help with Grav. Like, it would be great if you could come here and spend a few hours with her while I draw myself a bath and call in a doctor."

Normally, I was too cheap not to drag my ass to the clinic, delirium and high fever be damned, but my instincts told me Gravity and Tucker weren't ready to spend time with each other alone.

"Oh…" He trailed off, sounding put off by my request. "Well, this is kind of awkward, but I have a date today."

Was he fucking kidding me? This was about our daughter and defining and establishing his role in her life.

"Tucker." I bit down on my lower lip, the inside of my head hot and throbbing. "I could really use some help here. Gravity needs some human interaction. Soon enough, she's going to figure out her mommy can't really take care of her properly. It'll freak her out."

I was sweating, ice-cold and burning at the same time.

"Aren't you being a little dramatic?" Tucker asked with faux sympathy. I hated when he did this—cooed at me while saying something really cutting. "It's just the flu."

"Know what?" I huffed. "Forge—"

"Fine! I'll come, I'll come." He sounded supremely inconvenienced. "I'll cancel my date for you."

Somewhere in this universe, a woman owed me her life for sparing her from this asshole.

"Thanks," I said tightly. "Your altruism doesn't go unnoticed."

"Can I just ask one small thing in return?"

"What?" Words could not describe how much I suffered each time I had to communicate with the bastard.

"I'm a little strapped for cash, and I would love it if your brother could—"

"Goodbye, Tuckwad." I hung up in his face.

Tucker wasn't coming.

Nobody was, and things got progressively worse.

I tried to watch some *Grey's Anatomy* under the blankets while Grav sat next to me on her iPad, but I couldn't focus on anything past my state of misery and exhaustion. Grav was completely helpless, and when I accidentally complained that her twitching was making me dizzy, she even almost tried to make me a cup of tea, but I talked her out of it.

At some point, I dragged myself to the bathroom and filled myself a bath, bringing her along with me. I sat her at the foot of the claw bathtub with some toys and made her swear she wouldn't leave my side. The idea turned out to be one of my worsts, though, as I accidentally dozed off in the tub, and I would have slipped under if it weren't for my daughter screaming at me, "Mommy! Mommy! Wake up."

"I'm okay." I somehow managed to crawl out of the lukewarm bath and gently collapsed naked on the floor, unable to gather the energy to pull myself together.

Gravity sat on the other side of the bathroom studying me with her big, frightened eyes, and I hated that I couldn't give her the most basic thing she needed: a balanced and strong adult to lean on.

"What can I do?" she whispered to me. "Tell me what to do, Mommy."

Sweetie, I am so sorry. This was a big mistake. I cannot do this alone. As soon as I get better, we're going to pack our things and move back with Grandma.

The words sat on the tip of my tongue. It took everything in me not to utter them out loud.

"Can you grab my phone from the coffee table in the living room, baby?" I croaked finally. I had to bite the bullet and call Tucker again. I'd figure out the situation with Row. Maybe let my brother turn him down personally so he'd shut up already.

Gravity ran out to the living room, and I fought to keep my eyes open, mainly for her.

"Slowly!"

A few seconds later, she returned, wobbling carefully along the corridor, my phone pressed to her ear. Who was she talking to?

"...yes. And then she took a nap in the tub!" Gravity snorted, covering her pink strawberry mouth with her chubby fist. "Silly Mommy! I had to wake her up."

The person on the other end of the line was talking. I was anxious it was Tucker. And I was even more anxious he was going to say something idiotic, as he did so often.

"Now? Now she is being sleepy on the floor!" Gravity was at the bathroom door, still pressing the phone—which looked so big in comparison to her—to her ear. "I think she needs a grown-up. Yes, I can give her to you." She passed me the phone. "It's Uncle Rhyrand," she whispered.

Horrified, I put the phone on speaker, too exhausted to hold it. "Hi," I groaned.

"What's this shit I'm hearing about you fucking dying and not calling me to come help?" he demanded, enraged.

Okey-dokey, no speaker next time.

"Are you dying?" Gravity cried out in horror. "Mommy, is that true?"

"No," I whimpered. "No, honey, it's a figure of speech. Tell her, Rhy."

"No, little stinker, Mommy isn't dying. I was being dramatic." Pause. "But Uncle Rhyland wants to kill her for being so stubborn. I'm on my way now."

I heard the steady flow of busy conversation and mic announcements in the background and remembered he was at an important work thing.

"*Don't*," I protested desperately. "I'm feeling better. I'm going to take more Tylenol right now."

"No offense, Cosmos, but your stubbornly self-reliant ass is the reason I have trust issues."

"Rude." I tried to laugh, and my ribs screamed with pain.

"Just hang in there. I'm on my way."

"Rhy, your conference…"

I'd already interfered in his life so much with all the babysitting, I didn't want to be the reason he lost out on business opportunities too.

"Boring as shit," he completed for me. "Plus, the booth is manned by two engineers and a PR guru I hired to mesmerize the crowd. They're working their charm. There's a twenty-person line waiting to see us."

"Oh wow," I whimpered. "That's amazing."

It didn't escape me that both Tucker and Rhyland needed money. But whereas Rhyland spent every penny he *didn't* have on paying me a salary for a made-up job so I could take care of my child (when he'd paid for a vasectomy as a teen), Tucker was constantly begging me to hook him up with Row so he could make a quick buck or borrow one. Tucker was also burning through his money in get-rich-quick schemes, I suspected, because he tended to receive upsetting texts that ruined his mood whenever I was around. The difference was staggering.

"So I'll see you in a bit, yeah?" he asked.

"Yeah."

"Hang in there."

Thirty minutes later, Rhyland was feeding me wontons and chicken soup on my couch. He propped some pillows up so I could sit down comfortably, blowing gently on the spoonful of soup before bringing it to my lips.

Gravity sat in the breakfast nook across from us, enjoying a bento box from the same takeout place, with fries, teriyaki chicken, and fruit. We hadn't eaten all day. I was so grateful I was close to tears.

"Motrin kicked in yet?" Rhy blew on my soup before guiding it to my mouth again.

I nodded. "Yeah, I think so."

"You need to alternate between Motrin and Tylenol for best results. The doctor should be here any minute."

"Rhy, I'm so sorry—"

"Please shut up." He looked a little pissed off, and I wondered if it was because of the conference or because I was mortifyingly embarrassed about him being here. "If I were in the same condition, I'd expect you to drop literally everything and wipe my ass."

"Why? We don't have that kind of relationship." I blinked lethargically.

"Yes, we do," he said. "I wasn't gaslighting you back in Texas. We're friends now, Cosmos. And friends show up for each other." His nostrils flared. "I'll always show up for you."

A few minutes later, the doctor knocked on my door—a tan, lean, balding man who prescribed me some antibiotics after checking my throat. The doctor recommended I take another lukewarm bath to bring down the fever before bedtime. "This time with supervision," he chuckled, because of course Grav had shared with him the fact that I fell asleep in the bathtub.

Rhyland put Gravity to bed, read her a good-night story, then drew me a bath. Having been pumped with antibiotics and Motrin/Tylenol the second half of the day, I felt significantly better. I sat in the tub, Rhy perched on the edge of it, and closed my eyes, giving in to the small pleasure of having him there.

"At least your conference went well." I perked up, opening my eyes.

"About that…" Rhyland gave me a rueful smirk. "I lied. I didn't want you to talk me out of coming here. There was no PR guru and no twenty-person line waiting to see my app."

We were both quiet for a moment while I digested all this. For the first time in my life, I wanted to ask my brother for a loan. Not for me but for Rhyland. Only I knew he'd never accept it.

"But, I mean, it wasn't terrible." He forced out a smirk. "Some people came by. I exchanged business cards with a ton of tech bros, and those who stopped by my booth showed *actual* enthusiasm for the app, so we'll see."

"How can I help?" I asked.

"You can't," he said too quickly. "Bruce'll sign the contract any day now—his lawyers are going over it right now—and then I'll be gold."

But the statement lacked the confident shine with which Rhyland usually delivered his words.

"Oh, by the way, I found out why he's so traumatized by fuckboys." His fingers swooshed the water, gently caressing the tips of my nipples. I was way too comfortable to be self-conscious in front of him.

"Yeah?" I purred with my eyes closed. "Why?"

"Tate. Apparently, he fucked him over by buying the lot he knew Bruce wanted to bury his dad in."

"That's disgusting." I made a face. "Also, I wouldn't consider Tate a fuckboy. A demon? Yes. A ghoul? Absolutely. The reason humanity doesn't deserve nice things? Sounds about right. But not a fuckboy."

"You're probably right."

"No. I'm *always* right."

"Sassing back, I see." His hand cupped my boob, dipping all the way into the water, and I moaned, instinctively arching myself, on offer to him. "Means you're all better now."

"Thank you for taking care of me." I tipped my chin up, searching for his lips, and he leaned down, giving them to me in a gentle, unhurried kiss.

"Thank you for letting me," he said. "I know how hard it is for you to let go."

"You can take care of something else if you're so inclined." My hips bucked under the water, and I smirked at him. I was still feeling under the weather, but I wouldn't say no to some good ole fingering. And Rhyland really knew how to strum my body strings like a guitar.

"Say no more, baby."

He dove in, and I wondered when our bubble was going to burst.

Because it was pretty obvious something this good wasn't meant to last.

CHAPTER THIRTY-FOUR
RHYLAND

"No," I announced simply, slamming the door to my penthouse.

It was eight o'clock—too early for anything that wasn't morning sex, finding out you'd won the lottery, or both. I hadn't even had my first coffee yet. I wasn't equipped to deal with this shit.

I strolled casually toward my open-plan kitchen, flicking the expensive espresso machine to life and withdrawing my MacKenzie-Childs mug. The doorbell chimed once, twice, three times in urgent succession. This time, I dutifully ignored it. I grabbed my phone from the quartz countertop and shot Dylan a quick message.

> Rhyland: Hi, it's your favorite dick owner. Just checking in to see that you feel better.

And because Dylan was mom to a toddler and those fuckers tended to wake up at six in the morning like they had some busy, hot shit to do, she answered immediately.

> Dylan: I feel so much better. Thanks. Grav and I are enjoying bagels and cream cheese on the patio if you want to join us.
> Rhyland: I'm good. I'll check in later though.

It was a good idea not to waste all my time with someone I was hardly going to see in a few weeks. And it was cruel to let Gravity keep forming an attachment to me when I had no intention of sticking around in her life in any serious capacity. Besides, I had to draw the line *somewhere*. When I found out Cosmos was sick, I dropped everything and ran to her. While it was nice in theory, it was a disaster in reality. I didn't do relationships, monogamy, or loyalty. I was a hot fucking mess. Thanks to the people on the other side of my door, who were now banging on it with their fists, refusing to get the hint.

"Rhyland!" my mother chided in a rage. "Open up!"

The coffee machine tutted, and I slipped the mug inside, fixing myself a macchiato. I readjusted the elastic of my low-hanging gray sweatpants, saying hello to my morning semi, and scrolled through the headlines of the *Financial Times* on my phone.

"Rhyland." It was my father's turn to reproach me sternly from behind the door. "This is ridiculous. Not opening the door is not going to stop us from telling you the news. We're just going to send you a long text about it." Pause. "Worse, we're going to voice message it to you. In five parts. Each three minutes apart. I know how much you loathe voice messages."

True story. People under eighty who left voice messages were not fit to join polite society. We needed to banish them without parole. Who even did that?

Still, I wasn't sold on the idea.

I sipped my coffee, sliding my ass onto a counter stool.

"You know." My mother's cunning tone arrived next, and God, I'd forgotten how much I hated her. How much her presence in my vicinity made my skin crawl. A coping mechanism after spending half my lifetime trying to get her to hug me, to say a good word, to accept me if not validate me. "A journalist person called me the other day. Someone from Tech World—"

My head snapped up from my phone. It was the biggest tech site in the world, frequented mainly by industry insiders.

"She told me you're about to launch a huge app and asked if I'd be willing to talk about my soon-to-be-billionaire son. I said I respected your privacy." She took a strategic, deliberate pause. "I might not remain so respectful, though, if you refuse to even open the door for your own *mother*."

I checked the time on my watch—Apple, the absolute lowest of the lows—and groaned. Yup. It was not even 8:30 a.m., and I was already being blackmailed by the woman who birthed me.

I hopped off the stool and made my way to the door. Flung it open. My parents were standing exactly where I'd left them, my mother wearing one of her hippie tunics with leggings and a criminal number of bracelets and chains and my father wearing whatever the fuck she told him to wear. The control she had over this man had him in a choke hold. It was another reason why I was allergic to relationships. I liked my balls where they were, thank you very much.

"What do you want?" I asked tiredly, sipping my coffee.

"Aren't you going to invite us in? Offer us some coffee?" My father glowered.

"No," I said evenly. "Now answer my question."

Then I noticed something. They were holding a dog each in their hands—one of those insufferable breeds that was tiny and loud and cost about the same as a luxury car. A Pomeranian, I think. The canine version of Farrah Fawcett, if you will. The minute my gaze landed on the two canines, I knew. I just *knew*. Suddenly, the reason my parents had sought me out in recent months finally made sense.

"No," I said, resolute. "No way. I'm not doing it."

To their credit, my parents didn't even attempt to deny what this was about. "Oh, come on, son! We have nowhere to put them," my father chastised.

"They're not fucking accessories, Dad. You're not supposed to put them anywhere. You're supposed to take care of them." My voice rose, and I hated that I was showing emotion. I never did with them.

There was no point. "What made you think you'd be fit to become a dog owner? You did a shit job with your only son."

"Here we go again." My mother slapped her own thigh, shouldering past me and stomping into my apartment. My father followed suit. They put the tiny dogs down, letting them roam my living room unsupervised. One immediately ran to the kitchen island, raised its tiny leg, and took a piss on the leg of my Italian stool. My teeth slammed together, blood boiling. I closed the door, forcing myself to take a deep breath.

"You always seem to be complaining about the job we did with you, but you turned out fine, didn't you?" My mother fixed herself and my father some coffee, making my place her own without asking. "Nice job, beautiful apartment in Manhattan, lots of friends. You want for nothing, Rhyland," she huffed with a shake of her head.

I folded my arms over my chest, leaning against the counter. "What's my job?" I asked tonelessly.

My parents exchanged blank looks. My teeth dug into my inner cheek. Even though I knew damn well they'd never made an effort to get to know me, this was next-level shocking.

"Don't start," my mother warned, aiming a teaspoon at me.

"No, I'm serious. What's my job?"

"You studied business," my father provided cautiously, as if this in any way showed they'd been involved in my life in the past decade—or before it. "You work in…finance?" He stared at me helplessly.

"Yes, finance." My mother nodded, oozing bitter elegance. "And now you have this app thing going on."

"I'm a *whore*," I lied. Well, half lied, really. Maybe quarter lied. I was retired now.

My mother choked on her coffee midsip. My father shot me a horrified glare. The damn dogs jumped up on my leather couch, and by the smell of it, one of them was in the midst of taking a shit.

"Rhyland," my mother warned, clutching her pearls in a death grip.

"It's true." I shrugged. It was the first time I'd verbalized my previous profession for what it was. I dated for money. I romanced for money. I fucked for money. I sold my body, my heart, my soul, for a quick buck. This was the truth. And every day I *didn't* do that was a healing process. So fuck the money. Or, in this case, the lack thereof. "It's the honest-to-God truth, *Mother*. I worked with Row for a few years, back when my escort business was just taking off, but this is my main gig. Being a male prostitute. Business is booming. Thanks to you, I guess." I gestured to my sculpted six-pack, to my height, to my face. "This apartment was paid for by one of my clients."

Again, not a lie.

There was silence for a moment before my mother collected herself and sat up straighter on the stool. "So what?" She pouted haughtily. My mother was a classically beautiful woman, but she didn't have that glow that came from within. She looked like a lifeless symmetrical drawing. "Men aren't sensitive about such things. So what if you have sex for money? You're probably having fun doing it. You're right—you *should* thank us. Not many men have the opportunity to do this. We gave you the good genes to have a successful gigolo career."

"Genes were the only things you gave me," I seethed. "And even that only because you didn't have a choice. Nothing else, *Mother*. Nothing at all."

Her words aggravated me, and I wasn't even sure why. None of this was news to me. But somehow, even after all these years, it still cut deep to see them completely disregarding my life, my choices, my feelings.

"Listen, son, we're not here to judge you." My father raised his palms. "We only want to make sure you're doing well for yourself. You *are* doing well for yourself, right?"

I had a feeling they were about to break some more bad news, which I didn't think was possible, since they were already here with a task. My mouth curled in annoyance. My nostrils twitched.

Yeah. That damn dog had definitely taken a dump on my designer couch.

"I'm doing all right. Why?"

"We sold off the house, the cars, and all our possessions," my mother announced laconically, but the quirk of her mouth gave it away. She wasn't neutral about this at all. She was having fun breaking the news to me. "I'm sorry, Rhyland, but we won't be in a position to offer you anything inheritance-wise."

I'd never counted on their inheritance money. The Staindrop house was worth about $400K, give or take, and the cars, furniture, insurance maybe another $200K. In the grand scheme of things, if I got my way, $600K would be small-fry for me. Still, it was the thought that counted. They were now *explicitly* going to leave me penniless.

"Yeah?" I yawned, taking another sip of coffee. "What happened? Sold it all off and joined a cult?"

"My goodness, how did I create someone so crass?" My mother pressed her fingers to her mouth. "For your information, we decided to sell all our possessions and go travel the world. Enjoy our retirement money instead of hoarding it. You only live once."

"And in some people's cases, even that's too much," I muttered under my breath.

"This is why we need to leave Fluffy and Mittens with you." My mother ignored my sarcasm but looked eager to leave now that she'd finally unloaded the news off her chest.

"Fluffy and Mittens?" I snarled. "Who the hell are they?"

"Our little doggies." Mom made a baby sound. She smacked her lips together cooingly, and they ran to her, barking happily, wagging their tails. She leaned down to kiss them, and they licked her nose enthusiastically.

A scream lodged itself in my throat, because they'd had more affection in ten seconds than I received in my entire childhood.

"Well, *your* dogs now, really. We're leaving tomorrow. That's why we're here."

"I'm not taking your dogs." I shook my head.

"We have no one else to turn to," my father said in an accusing voice.

"Sounds like you could've done with making a few friends instead of drowning in each other and ignoring the world."

"We don't have the heart to put them in a shelter."

"I will then." I shrugged, meaning it. I was not getting one dog, let alone two. I traveled a whole fucking bunch and wouldn't be home regularly once App-date launched.

"What you do is on your conscience, sweetie, not mine," my mother tutted—which, in her warped mind, was true. She really thought this cleansed her of all responsibility. She was a narcissist. And most likely, so was I.

She started for the door, and my father followed her, coffee mugs still on my kitchen island, poop still on my couch. They didn't even tell me where they were going.

I knew the dogs were staying—until I dumped them in a shelter.

"Hey," I called out to their backs, internally acknowledging how deeply messed up it was that they'd barged into my life after years of radio silence, discarding their dogs with me and telling me my inheritance was gone. This wasn't neglect. It never had been. It was *abuse*. It was the systematic action of breaking your child's heart and spirit. "When can I drop by your house and collect my boxes?" I had some stuff left there that I wanted. High-school sports trophies, diplomas, certificates, school photo albums. Basically, my entire history before I moved to New York four years ago.

"Oh." My mother halted but didn't turn around to look at me. She didn't turn around to take one last look at her so-called beloved dogs either. Her hand fluttered over the doorframe. "Pity you didn't tell us. We got rid of everything while we were cleaning up. The house sold so fast. We had to."

"You threw away my shit?" My breath caught in my throat. How many more times could she make me feel like I was nothing to her? How many more times could I be surprised and fucking gutted by it?

"Don't judge us." She swiveled toward me swiftly. "It's not like we didn't try to reach out to you. We tried for months."

"You could've texted," I clapped back.

"Why would we?" She jerked her nose up snootily. "You didn't even take our calls. You ghosted us. Why should we be held to a higher leve—"

"Because you're the parents!" I snapped, completely losing it. I was shaking now, my heartbeat out of control.

Suddenly, I wasn't Rhyland Coltridge, twenty-nine, a playboy and soon-to-be billionaire; I was Rhyland Coltridge, five, a boy who desperately wanted to know what he'd done wrong and why his parents couldn't love him.

"Parents are held to a different standard. Parents understand. Parents show up. Parents let their kids make mistakes. They let them learn, try, *feel*. You and I are not the same. Our roles are vastly different. And recently, I had a front-row seat to an actual healthy relationship between an incredible parent and her child." I thought about Dylan, how she prioritized Gravity over anything else—including herself.

My mother stomped. Actually stomped. "I was never good enough for you. So what if I'm not a lovey-dovey person?"

"You are." I pointed at the dogs. "Just not to me."

That sobered her. "You were a mistake, Rhyland," she said quietly. "You came after we were married, but…you weren't in our plans. I wanted to complete my degree in art. Your father wanted to become an architect. We never could recover from having you…" Her eyes crinkled sadly. "And yes, we were young. And angry. We shouldn't have been. But ever since you were a teenager, all you wanted was to leave the house. You acted like we were hitting you or something! Like we were abusing you in some way."

"You were," I said flatly. "You can destroy someone without lifting a finger at them, and you did that to me."

And then, because there was nothing more to say, I finished with, "Anyway, this is not goodbye."

"Why, thank yo—"

"This is good riddance. I don't want to hear from you ever again."

"Son—" my father started.

"Never." I held up a hand. "Not if someone gets sick, not if someone dies, not if someone needs help."

My mother shook her head, looking disgusted with my existence. She finally had the audacity to let her true emotions play on her face. "Have a good life, Rhyland." She slipped through the door. Before she banged it behind her, she stuck in her head. "By the way, Fluffy has a liver disease and needs an important leg operation. Make sure you tend to that."

After I cleaned up dog shit, gave the two dogs water and some pastrami, and ordered harnesses for them both on Prime, I crouched down in front of them. They were standing shoulder to shoulder, staring at me with urgency, like I was Moses coming down from Mount Sinai with an update from God.

"Okay, assholes, which one of you is Fluffy?"

One of the dogs cocked its head sideways, opening its mouth in a smile and showing off a pink tongue. This was Fluffy, I supposed. I looked between its legs. Male. Well, *barely*.

"So you're Mittens." I glanced at the other dog, peering between its front legs. Female.

She barked her approval.

"I'm sorry, folks, but you can't stay here. It's not personal. I'm just not built for responsibility."

Fluffy whimpered as though he understood me.

"Yeah, I know." I ruffled his fur on a sigh. "They screwed up my life too. But you're expensive, good-looking dogs. You'll do fine. People'll line up to adopt you."

Fluffy and Mittens exchanged doubtful looks. "C'mon. I got thrown out too, and I turned out all right." Pause. "Okay, I didn't. But what doesn't kill you makes you stronger."

The harnesses arrived. I took them down for a walk to do their business—there was nothing quite as humbling as picking up tiny dog shit with a plastic bag and hunting for a trash can on a busy New York street—then I packed them up into my car and drove to the nearest no-kill animal shelter.

The closer I got to the shelter, the more nauseous I felt. My mother had mentioned Fluffy had some health issues. What if he couldn't find a home? And what if they split these motherfuckers up? They seemed close, constantly giving each other tongue baths and chasing each other.

I remembered growing up how bummed I was about not having a sibling. Someone to confide in and lean on. Row came the closest to it.

And you've been fucking his baby sister on the down-low for over a week now. Some friend you are.

But this was exactly why I couldn't be with Dylan: I was a narcissist, like my parents.

By the time I'd parked in front of the shelter, my head was a mess. I grabbed the leashes from the passenger seat and twisted around to clip them onto the dogs' harnesses. They complied without complaint, hanging their dumb, innocent gazes at me.

"Don't look at me like that." I scowled.

They blinked in unison.

"You don't fit my lifestyle. I didn't choose this. Not any of this crap."

Silence.

"God dammit." I unclipped the leashes, dumping them on the passenger seat and rubbing my face.

By dropping these little shits at a shelter, I *was* becoming my parents. An emotionally stunted, self-centered human without one redeeming bone in his entire body.

I knew lots of people. I could get them rehomed somewhere nice, with people I trusted. Tossing them in a shelter was the easiest, coldest, most immoral option. It was the wrong thing to do.

I blew out a breath, dropping the back of my head to the leather seat. "Fluffy?"

He whimpered in response.

"I'm sorry, buddy, but we're going to have to hit the vet next. But first, there's something I need to do."

I called Dylan. She answered on the first ring. I tried not to read too much into it.

"Do you want me to grab Grav for a couple hours? I'm heading to the vet, and I'm sure she'll like this experience. Figured it'd give you more time to recoup from that flu."

"Did you catch what I have? I know I called you a horndog, but I did not mean that literally." Dylan sounded skeptical.

I grinned. "My parents dropped their two dogs with me earlier today when they came to tell me they're fucking off to travel the world and that they sold the house, burned my inheritance money, and got rid of all my childhood memorabilia."

"Jesus," Dylan hissed out. "I'm so sorry. I wish I could've been there to give them a piece of my mind."

"You'd have given them a piece of your fist too. Admit it." I immediately felt lighter as I pulled off the curb at the shelter, talking to Dylan.

"I'd never lay a finger on an elderly couple. I'd have insulted them to their demise, even if it took days."

I laughed.

"Just, you know, as a homage for my brother, of course. Not because it's you or anything," she added.

She was trying to keep this below surface level, the way I did when I rearranged Tuckwad's face.

"Yeah, we both care for your brother so much. So how about that vet?" I asked.

"Yeah, she'll be excited, and it'll give me some quiet time to look for work."

Five hours later, I was eight thousand dollars poorer thanks to the vet fees I'd paid for Fluffy's upcoming cruciate ligament repair. I also had to get them both shots so they were up to date, chip them, and pay for blood work, dental cleaning, and a ton of other shit to make them good candidates for adoption. The vet said they appeared to be between two and three years old, and although they were in good health, they had been obviously neglected. No surprises there.

Grav was a trooper throughout. I told her I'd buy her ice cream if she helped the vet. The vet gave her mundane tasks like cleaning the same spot on the metal counter over and over again, throwing things into the trash, and washing her hands a thousand times. I treated her to three scoops afterward and taught her to drink the dregs of the ice cream like a milkshake through the tip of the cone. I considered it my contribution to humanity.

By the time I brought her back to her mom, Gravity was pooped. Dylan opened the door looking like my favorite meal, and I was glad when her kid ran to her room to do something that wasn't asking us five hundred questions a minute about doggy heaven. The dogs were upstairs in the penthouse, but their scent clung to me.

As soon as Gravity was out of our way, Dylan crushed me with an all-consuming hug. "I'm so proud of you," she murmured into my neck.

"That makes one of us. I spent almost ten thousand dollars on a pair of pets I don't even own." I disconnected from her, waltzing over to the wine room to grab myself a drink.

"You're becoming a person you'd want to befriend." She followed me.

I poured us both generous glasses of wine. "What about you? How was your day?"

"It was good. I…" She bit down on her lower lip as her cheeks stained scarlet.

"You?" I tilted one brow up.

"Looked into some premed programs around the city. But before you get all excited, they're all pretty intense. It's not even about the money. I'd need constant help with Gravity, and I'm not sure either of us is ready for something like that."

"Your kid's a rock star," I said, realizing I meant it. Grav was a bad bitch, just like her mom. Well, a bad puppy, really. "She'll do well at that preschool." It was on the tip of my tongue to offer my own services, but I bit the words back. I couldn't commit to this. I couldn't.

It was in this moment it dawned on me that if the deal with Bruce Marshall fell through, I was basically homeless. I had no income. My apartment was mortgaged. I'd already sold most of my valuable stuff. My parents' house was gone, so I couldn't crash there—even on the off chance they'd have let me. Row would give me a roof for a few weeks—unless he found out I was screwing his sister—but I would never ask.

I couldn't offer more of myself to Dylan even if I wanted to, for the simple fact that there wasn't much to give.

"I don't know that I can do it without any help." Her upper teeth sank into her lower lip. "I mean, maybe if I found somewhere cheaper. Or…or if Cal moved back here for a while."

I pursed my mouth shut to keep from offering my help. Could I take Grav to the office with me a couple times a week or come home a little earlier to babysit her while I worked remotely? Probably. But the truth was Dylan's presence in my life meant more complications and inconveniences.

"I was thinking." Dylan tucked a raven lock behind her ear. "Maybe if we—"

My phone buzzed.

It was Bruce Marshall, the man of the hour. Of the day. Of my century, really.

I held a finger up. "Sorry. I need to take this."

She clamped her mouth shut. I pressed the phone to my ear. I didn't want her to witness it in case he came bearing bad news.

"Coltridge?"

"Yeah?"

"I signed the papers. App-date is a go."

Dylan must've interpreted the good news on my face, because hers lit up like a Christmas tree, and she started jumping and clapping excitedly, swallowing down whimpers of happiness.

It was happening.

I was launching the next dating app.

Only on a bigger, better, more lucrative scale.

I was going to trick people into making their fake relationships real.

And I was falling into the same goddamn trap in the process.

Bruce was spitting out some details at the speed of light. It took everything in me to process them. The money. The fucking *money*. I was about to become filthy rich. The kind of rich my friends were.

When I hung up, I was too stunned to speak. Dylan, however, kept cheering for me. The noise drew Gravity out of her room.

"What's going on?" she grumbled.

"Uncle Rhyland got good news from work!" Dylan announced. "We're taking him out for tacos and margaritas."

And before I knew what was happening, they were both hugging me.

Kissing me.

Melting me.

I was so screwed.

CHAPTER THIRTY-FIVE
DYLAN

A week after my flu from hell and Rhyland's news that he was becoming a billionaire tycoon whose barely incorporated company was on the verge of going public, my brother and my BFF came to New York.

They were here only for a few hours for Row to sign some contracts, but Cal brought over her nanny, whom we trusted to babysit both Gravity and Serafina while we went out.

Cal insisted we go to a club, even though I was pooped from working shifts at the Alchemist, putting together my college applications, and monitoring Tucker's meetings with my daughter. Rhyland had still been babysitting Grav. He claimed we needed a four-week buffer of him continuing to pay me and babysit for me in case Bruce needed more proof we were together, but I knew he just wanted to keep paying me so I'd have a good amount of money saved up for school.

I was getting there, though. $60K meant my tuition was paid for one year. Too bad I needed seven of those.

"Aren't you happy I talked you into going out?" Cal cooed in front of the mirror in the hotel they were staying at. She'd let me borrow a Valentino sequin minidress in a shade of green that complimented my olive skin.

Cal hugged my shoulders from behind, grinning at me in the reflection.

"Yeah," I admitted with a smile. "I think I needed some grown-up time. Thanks."

"How's your fake romance going?" She kissed my cheek.

"Surprisingly well," I confessed.

Though I felt guilty about not telling our friends we were hooking up, I also knew it wasn't my decision to say so.

"Rhy really helps me out with Gravity. Turns out I really like him."

"Good, because he's coming with us to the club." Cal winked. "Tate too," she said apologetically before I could process the first bomb she'd thrown at me.

"Cal, it was supposed to be a girls' night out," I moaned. "There'll be more testosterone there than in an NHL locker room."

"Row wasn't feeling comfortable about the two of us clubbing alone in the big city." My best friend winced apologetically. She was ethereal, gorgeous, and sweet—but a total people pleaser. "But he also wasn't feeling super comfortable tagging along alone like some kind of grumpy bodyguard."

"That's literally what he was our entire adolescence," I argued.

"Yeah, so I guess it wasn't fun for him like it was for us."

In the end, we all crammed into a limousine. Rhyland and I took opposite seats and tried hard not to eye-fuck each other. I still needed for us to finish our conversation about my school and our babysitting arrangement, but I'd chickened out. It didn't look like Rhyland wanted to offer his help, and now, with his business taking off, I was one hundred percent sure he wouldn't have time for that.

"Everyone's looking like a million bucks." Cal looked between us as we tipped our champagne glasses in the air, clinking them together.

"No need to hurl out insults, Calla," Tate said taciturnly. "My suit is not that cheap."

That asshole thought a million-dollar suit was cheap? The man was so high maintenance I was surprised he'd agreed to share oxygen with mere mortals.

"Speaking of big bucks..." Row's glare traveled from Tate to Rhyland, his arm slung protectively over his wife. "Congratulations are in order."

Rhy smirked, lounging back and tipping his champagne in the air.

"Surprise," Tate said in the driest voice possible, tossing something into Rhyland's hands. "This is your business-deal gift from me and Row, and this outing is our celebration."

I shot Cal a furious look. "They were always coming, weren't they?"

Cal shrugged. "We didn't want you to tip Rhy off. I love you, but you do have a big mouth."

"Lies. Her mouth is just the right size for my di—" Rhy started, then he realized what he was saying and clamped his mouth shut.

Oh my God. This idiot. He wasn't even drunk.

"Come again?" Row said slowly, slipping his arm from behind Cal and leaning on his elbows, examining Rhyland more closely.

"I think that was the premise of his entire statement," Tate said unhelpfully.

"It was a joke," I ground out tightly. Row had no right to tell me who to fuck. But he had expectations from both of us, and he'd been nothing but generous and loyal to me and Rhyland. "You know? Funny ha ha." I rolled my eyes.

"It wasn't fucking funny," Row informed me, "and there was no ha ha."

"She's not your daughter," Rhyland said evenly, and I noticed he wasn't denying the fact that his dick really had been in my mouth at least a hundred times since I moved in downstairs. "Even if she was," Rhyland continued, a note of darkness in his tone, "I don't take well to your overbearing behavior. She can fuck whoever she wants, whenever she wants. And if we happen to want to fuck each other, there's nothing you can do about it."

The temperature dropped about a hundred degrees in the limo. Bile burned a path up my throat.

"Unless you're into watching," Rhy drawled, bored. "I'm a charitable man and a sworn extrovert." He winked.

Row launched himself at Rhyland. Cal and I, who were bracketing Row from each side, pushed him back to his seat. But Rhy looked about ready to fight him, and that scared and thrilled me in equal measures.

"What are you saying?" Row spat, back in his seat, panting hard.

I knew this wasn't the right time or place to break the news that we were hooking up—if there even was a right time to say it—and decided to steer the conversation to safer waters.

"He's just telling you to tuck the crazy inside. You're being hella overprotective," I snorted. "Seriously, chill. Rhy and I got chummy because of the fake engagement thingy. Of course your behavior grinds his gears."

"Just remember, that ring isn't real." Row pointed to my engagement ring.

The words punctured my soul and poured all the hope and happiness out. I'd gotten used to the weight of it on my wedding finger—to the way it sparkled and shined when I worked at the bar scrubbing toilets, doing dishes, pouring drinks.

"I know," I said quietly.

"Stop being an asshole." Cal swatted her husband's thigh.

The place we were going to was called the Forbidden Fruit Club, a decadent hot spot in the East Village. Tate had crowned it as his family business, which made little sense, since it didn't appear he had any living family members and he usually spent his Christmases working.

"The Forbidden Fruit Club." I tasted the name in my mouth, happy to change the subject. "Why did the owner decide to call it that?"

"It's a twenty-four-hour-operation joint," Tate explained, and

I think it was the first time he'd acknowledged me directly in the entire three years we'd known each other. He was icy and expressionless, and there was something frightening about his eyes. They were so dead I couldn't even figure out their color. "In the mornings and afternoons, it's a place for finance people to fuck their lowly staff. Kind of a hotel, but with a restaurant and a happy hour. At night, it turns into the place with the best DJs in the world, crafted cocktails, and enough drugs to sink the *Titanic*."

"It sounds like a horrible place." I made a face.

"I know. I love it." He wasn't being sarcastic for a change.

"You said the owner is family. Who is it?" Rhyland cut into our conversation, and I wondered if he was jealous. I wanted him to be. Even though I recognized how pathetic it was.

"*Like* family," Tate corrected. "And it's a secret. I am actually quite good at keeping those. Right, Coltridge?" A sinister smile slashed his face.

I remembered Rhyland telling me after our hookup at Row's restaurant that Tate's date had caught us. Tate hadn't breathed a word to anyone. Now was the first time I noticed.

"Whoever he is, he's making a great buck," Row mused, back to nuzzling into his wife's neck.

"They sure do," Tate said.

CHAPTER THIRTY-SIX
RHYLAND

The Forbidden Fruit Club looked like hell's waiting room.

Everybody was a fucking heathen. Women ground against obvious Mafia dudes in three-piece suits like it was the fifties. Semi-familiar models in waitress getups weaved in and out of the crowd holding trays laden with fifty-buck cocktails. There were VIP pockets surrounding the huge dance floor, each manned by a bouncer and bracketed by red velvet ropes. The floor was black and the ceiling high, with neon-blue lightning cracks for lighting, though there weren't very many of those at all. It was almost pitch-black, probably to cover for the sinister things that went on.

As soon as we walked in, Tate was ushered to a VIP table behind a rope. Apparently, he *really* knew the owner. I didn't want to know what the fuck that meant—my nerves were already shot from the exchange with Row. I didn't even fucking know why. The expiration date for this affair was fast approaching, and Dylan looked ready to murder my ass if I outed us.

"This is your celebration, Coltridge." Dylan pierced through my brain fog, sliding a blue cocktail my way from across the table. "Celebrate!"

"You're usually the king of the dance floor." Row flashed me a dark scowl—the only expression in his arsenal. "Yet here you are sulking the night away. What's up with your ass?"

"Yes, Rhyland. Please share with the table." Tate's lips twitched into something that resembled a smirk. I'd never seen him smile, let alone laugh.

"First of all, it's been five fucking minutes since we walked in here." I took a sip of my blue drink, whatever the hell it was. "Second, this place isn't ready for my moves yet."

"It sure as hell ain't ready for your bullshit," Row snorted.

"Well, we're going to dance." Dylan grabbed Cal by the hand and dragged her to the dance floor.

"And I'm going to supervise," Row grumbled.

The girls were already deep in the thick mass of human bodies. I was reassured by Row's presence there. He wouldn't let some guy from the Outfit snatch them, which seemed like an actual possibility in a place like this.

Tate stared at me wordlessly.

"What do you want?" I knocked down a whiskey—fuck the raspberry cocktail—and stared into the bottom of my empty tumbler.

He didn't say anything.

I needed to rein in my temper. Tate had helped me a lot with my Bruce Marshall deal. Yes, he'd fucked him over, and yes, he was going to cash in on the favor in due time, but he'd never wronged me before.

"I didn't say anything," Tate said.

"Bruce told me why he hates you." I turned to face him.

Not a muscle twitched in his blank face. "And?" he asked dryly.

"Why'd you do it?"

"I needed the business with him," he replied blatantly. "And I had a tech company in need of a PR facelift. I managed to turn a corner with it after Bruce agreed to cooperate. It helped create a veneer of legitimacy with my high-tech ventures."

"You're a ghoul."

"You say that like it's a bad thing."

I turned to look at the girls on the dance floor. "Hypnotize" by Alesso bounced over the walls, making the floor tremble. Dylan and

Cal were in the zone, flipping their hair, grinding against each other, shouting the lyrics, lost in this moment. Everyone was looking at them—and not because of their dance moves. The men were gaping. I couldn't blame them.

But I sure as hell could be pissy about it.

"Everyone's staring," I commented to Tate, gesturing to Dylan and Cal.

Tate redirected his gaze begrudgingly to the dance floor, one arm slung over the headrest of our black leather booth. "Yeah, well, Row's wife looks like she's having a fucking seizure."

"They want them." I ignored his distasteful joke.

"Maybe," Tate drawled. "But Calla isn't up for grabs. Dylan is."

No, she wasn't. She was mine. In every fucking way that counted.

Her pussy was mine.

Her laughs were mine.

Her funny observations.

Her tears. Her fears. Her worries.

Well, not everything. Her heart wasn't mine. We'd made a promise to each other to keep that organ out of our arrangement.

I stood up and walked to the dance floor, cutting in between Cal and Dylan. Cal shrugged it off and danced her way over to a horrified-looking Row, swaying her hips to the music and knotting her arms around his neck. He didn't do dancing.

I grabbed Dylan by the waist, staring into her eyes. "Every man in this club is eye-fucking you."

"Maybe." She grinned, raising her arms up and moving her hips seductively. "But only one of them is dick-fucking me, and that is you. You hungry?" she asked.

I raked my gaze up and down her delicious body.

She rolled her eyes. "Get your mind out of the gutter, Coltridge."

"Why? You love it filthy."

"We should order something for the table." She ignored me. "Something savory."

"I'll show you savory." I grabbed her by the ass and hoisted her up, then spun her around. Her laughter carried on the air. In that moment, I really couldn't give a shit if Row had something to say about it.

We danced for a while, until we were sweaty and spent, twirling and laughing and spinning. I was having fun, even though initially, coming to her was a way to piss on my territory and make sure everyone at the club knew not to go near her.

Finally, Dylan sighed and pushed my chest. "Okay, I'm going to pee."

"I'm going to come." I slid my fingers through hers, holding her hand.

She shot me a confused glance. "Wow. Everything *does* turn you on."

I barked out a laugh, leading her to the restrooms, and noticed Row and Cal making out against the wall on our way there, lost in each other. The line to the bathroom was three people deep.

"You think they're snorting coke?" Dylan turned to grin at me.

I reached to wipe sticky locks of hair off her sweaty forehead. "No, baby. They're snorting coke in plain sight at the tables."

"This place is insane."

"So is the guy who brought us here."

When it was finally Dylan's turn, I walked in right along with her and locked the door behind us. She turned to me, confused.

"What are you doing?"

"Thought we'd have a quickie since we're already here." I waggled my brows.

Her eyes flared, but a spark of mischief ignited inside them. "What if we get caught?"

"Well, it'd be someone's lucky day."

"Let me just do my business." She crouched down right in front of me, squatting in the air as she peed, hiking her minidress up and sliding the side of her panties.

It was so hot to see her doing this in front of me I couldn't even control myself. I staggered with my back against the door and unzipped myself. She flushed, tugging the dress down when I put a hand over her wrist.

"No. Leave it as it is. Turn around and grab the coat hanger."

She did as instructed. The hanger was a little high up on the door, but she was on the tall side. So was I. We matched in so many fucking ways. Her panties were still pushed to one side when I grabbed my cock by the root and tapped her ass with it, smearing a bit of my precum on her skin. I took my time bunching her panties into a thong inside her ass crack and teasing her tight little asshole with it.

"I'm ready," she panted, bending over and offering me both of her holes by spreading them open.

"Let's see." I parked the crown of my cock in her asshole—just the tip—reaching down to run my fingers along the slit of her greedy cunt. She was dripping for me. With a sigh and a shudder, I positioned myself at her entrance from behind.

"Come on." She arched. "Just do it."

"Say please," I instructed, biting the side of her neck softly. "You're a hell-raiser outside, but when I fuck you, you're my good little girl."

"Please," she moaned, pressing herself into me, sinking my dick into her.

"Better." I grabbed her hair, my other hand holding her waist as I began pounding into her. "So, so much better."

Better turned into orgasmic way too fast, though, because after only a few thrusts, Dylan started making porn noises. She was always vocal in bed, which I loved. She usually pressed a pillow to her face when I ate her out to drown out her whimpers, and when we fucked, I let her bite my shoulder or my hand, depending on our position. This time was no different. I pushed my index and middle fingers into her mouth, letting her suckle on them while I rode her faster and deeper from behind. My dick was slick with her juices, and the possessive, jealous side of me wanted to test her limits.

"How close are you?"

"Close," she murmured around my fingers.

"Can I fuck your ass?" I asked. "I think you're ready. And there's enough lube."

I thought she'd freeze for a few seconds. Mull it over. But then I forgot who I was dealing with.

"Yes," she growled. "Please, fuck my ass hard."

Say no more.

I began playing with her anus, pushing my middle finger in and out, filling both her holes at the same time. I did it often to help her get used to the sensation, and she immediately made happy noises around my fingers and pressed deeper into me, clenching around my finger ravenously, asking for more. It was when she was close to climaxing that I entered my second finger into her. Things got stretchy at this point, and a groan of discomfort escaped her as she rocked against my dick.

"Should I stop?" I asked gently.

"No, no," she said breathlessly.

Somewhere in the back of my head, I was aware of voices coming from the other side of the stall, of the pounding on the door, the demands that we evacuate because it had been ten minutes, but I didn't care.

It took everything in me not to come when she climaxed on my cock. By then, I had three fingers in her ass. I spread them out too. Made sure she was completely ready. Her asshole vibrated, asking for more. I leaned in to kiss the side of her neck again. I didn't know why, but I was particularly fond of that place.

"When I fuck your beautiful, tight hole, it's going to hurt at first. The pressure will be uncomfortable. You might feel like you need to go to the bathroom. You might release some air. If you want to stop, just let me know. I won't be disappointed."

Understatement of the century. She'd already fulfilled every single one of my fantasies by merely existing.

Dylan clutched onto the coat hanger harder, her knuckles whitening. "Just get inside, Rhy. I don't care if I fart on you—I want my ass fucked."

Holy shit. Was I falling in love?

I slipped out of her pussy, pressing home into her asshole. I did it gradually but also not so slowly as to make it excruciating. I had no idea what organ my dick was hitting by the time I was fully settled inside her. I just knew it felt like a slice of heaven.

I tipped my head back and closed my eyes, groaning. Nothing in this world was supposed to feel this good.

"How're you feeling, Cosmos?" I asked groggily. I was going to come as soon as I stopped holding my breath. That was how intense the pleasure was.

"Good. So good," she purred, wiggling her ass a little, making my balls tickle. "This hits so different. I can't believe I've never tried anal before."

My eyes snapped open. She'd never tried anal before? I didn't know why it shocked me. Maybe because Tucker seemed like the kind of asshole who'd want it all. Maybe because she'd been open to it from day one, never voicing any concern. I was prepping her for my size, not the experience itself. Whatever the hell it was, a delicious feeling spread in my bones.

I grabbed her by the waist with both hands and started fucking her ass. I knew I wouldn't last long, and neither would she—the pleasure was too much—so I took full advantage of our position to extort her.

"Cosmos?"

"Hmm?" she cried, her cheek pressing against the door people were pounding on as I drilled into her again and again.

"I have a job offer for you."

She grunted in response. I doubted she was of sound mind right now. I knew I wasn't, considering what was about to leave my mouth.

"Is this really"—*pant*—"the time?" *Pant*.

"I want to extend our fiancée-for-hire arrangement for six months at a set price of $100K per month. After the six months are up, we'll break our engagement and announce it to Bruce. Good for my business. Good for your med school. Good for everyone."

Other than my bank account, but I needn't worry about it, now that Bruce had signed the contract.

"I'll have to think about it."

Thrust.

"What?"

Thrust.

"I said I'll have to think about i—"

Thrust.

"No, I heard you fine. I just can't believe I did. I'm offering you a fucking gold mine here."

Thrust.

"Don't let our dynamics in bed fool you, Coltridge. I'm not a charity case. We're equals. And I'll decide when and where I want this to end. Now fuck my ass and shut up."

My thrusts became quicker, jerkier, more punishing. What was she thinking? I was taking all her goddamn problems away, putting her through med school, and she was turning it all down.

My head was a mess, but the rest of my body was pretty clear on where it stood. I shot my load inside her asshole less than a minute after in an orgasm that ripped through me like a hurricane. She came too. We rocked that climax together. I made sure I emptied out inside her, then I rearranged her panties over her asshole and her cunt.

She glanced at me over her shoulder, still scowling. "Aren't I going to drip from there?"

"Pucker that asshole tight, sweetheart." I gave her ass a friendly tap. "And if you manage to keep it all in, when we get back, I'll eat it off you."

CHAPTER THIRTY-SEVEN
RHYLAND

We wobbled back to the table looking exactly like two people who'd been fucking each other as if the world was ending for the past twenty minutes.

"Where the hell were you?" Row's eyes followed my every movement from his spot in the booth.

"Rhyland wanted to show me the upstairs facilities." Cosmos smoothed her hair back from her face, her voice casual. We hadn't exchanged one word between our fuck and now. We took our seats on opposite corners of the booth.

"Yeah? Did you like the antique billiard table?" Row turned to his sister.

She started at him point-blank, not a muscle in her face moving. "Yeah. I thought the old-school finish to it was a nice touch."

"Yeah, it's my favorite too," Row agreed.

"Right?" She smiled.

"Sure. I love shit that doesn't exist."

Silence fell over the table.

Cal's eyes darted between me and Dylan. "Okay, Dyl, we love you, but this is getting ridiculous."

"Fine. We didn't look at the facilities. We were fighting," Dylan sighed.

"That, I can believe." Row appeared satisfied. Like he wanted us to not get along. The look Cal gave him showed she knew he was in deep denial. We reeked of sex.

"Your stubborn sister doesn't want to carry on with this charade for six more months for a hundred K a month." I gestured to Dylan. "Tell her she's insane."

"Smart girl." Row patted his sister's shoulder. "Don't tie yourself up with his bullshit. Go meet a nice, respectful guy who'll take care of you. Build a family. Live your life."

My fists curled under the table. I was about to kill my best friend if he didn't shut up.

"Maybe she can keep the charade and date around on the down-low?" Cal snapped her fingers like this was a good idea or something. "That way, she doesn't, you know, miss out."

"No." I shut her down savagely. "I pay a hundred thousand fucking bucks, she doesn't breathe in anyone else's direction unless I say so. Clear?"

"Wow. You're really selling it to me now." Dylan's signature eye roll made a comeback, and she snatched a cocktail from the table, taking a sip.

"Too bad," Cal sighed. "My favorite trope is why choose."

"Choose, because otherwise all the candidates will die at my hands." Row flashed her a polite smile. "Is that a good enough reason?"

"Know what?" Dylan stood up. "I was about to grab a bite here, check out the restaurant, but I think I'll just eat something at home. I'm tired."

"I'll grab a cab with you." I shot up to my feet.

Dylan glared at me in disbelief. "*You're* the reason I'm leaving, asshole."

"Is there a point somewhere in your sentence?" I arched a brow.

"They loathe each other." Row swept invisible sweat from his brow. "Now I can relax."

Dylan and I were in the middle of a no-blink match. She lost.

"You can't leave." She threw her hands in the air, exasperated. "This whole party is for you."

"The point of the night is to do whatever I want," I explained to her slowly, "and what I want is to bicker with you to death in our Uber, which arrives in about"—I glanced at my phone clock (fuck the Apple Watch—I'd rather go commando)—"three minutes, so we need to hurry the fuck up."

"You called us an Uber?" Her jaw dropped in shock.

"Would you rather walk in those heels?" My glare dropped down to the two needles that supported her. "Because I'm fine watching you squirt."

"What did you just say?" Row growled.

"Squat," I lied.

"No, you didn't," Row accused.

Dylan snickered. That was what I wanted. To get a smile out of her.

"Yes, I did. Okay, we're out of here." I saluted everyone, placed a hand on the small of her back, and herded her outside.

Once we were in the fresh air, I immediately dropped the smart-ass façade. "Fine. I fucked up. I shouldn't have assumed." I raised my hands. "It's just that...Cosmos, you're so much better than whatever job you're aiming for these days. I'm not saying that in a patronizing, I-know-better-than-you way. I'm saying it because I know, deep down, you agree with that statement. You were born to do something great. And I want that for you. I *really* want that for you." I rubbed my cheekbone. "Like, I don't even know why I'm so invested in this."

"Maybe the wall of ice around your heart is finally thawing." She knotted her arms over her chest.

"You're right. That might be it. Fucking global warming."

"Sorry I got super mad at you," she sighed. "I'm a little prickly about, you know, the future."

The Uber arrived in perfect time. The temperature between us dropped to something manageable. We both slipped into the back seat and greeted our driver.

"So do you wanna come over to my place for that…um, thing you promised me?" Dylan turned to look at me, blushing.

Fuck, I wanted to. There was nothing I wanted more than to eat her cum-glazed donut hole. Even if it meant I might spend the night there. I wanted to explore it. What can I say? She'd broken me. Or maybe it was the opposite. She'd pieced me back together into someone who actually wasn't shit-scared of relationships.

"I can't," I found myself grunting. "I need to take Fluffy and Mittens out. They never do their business on their pads. Vindictive assholes, just like my parents."

"I still can't believe you own dogs called Fluffy and Mittens," Dylan snorted.

"I don't own them." I glowered. "I'm putting them up for adoption."

"You let them sleep in your bed."

"It's the only way they don't whimper and let me actually fucking sleep," I protested.

"You're a big softie." She curled her lower lip adorably.

I grabbed her hand and put it on my dick through my slacks. "Take that back or feel his wrath."

"Now you're just encouraging me to misbehave."

We both laughed drunkenly, and I leaned down to kiss her, biting her lower lip teasingly. I made a mental note to download Uber's competing app, since I was definitely going to get kicked out of this one after the inappropriate sexual display.

"I'll take them out for potty and then come back down to see you. Deal?"

"Deal."

"Did you manage to hold it all in like I asked?" I fussed, running my nose along the tip of hers.

"Yes," she said proudly. "Every single drop."

My cock was about to burst out of my pants. I pressed her head to my chest.

I'm falling. I mouthed the words silently across her temple, feeling the unspoken confession soaking into my skin. *It's wrecking my life.*

CHAPTER THIRTY-EIGHT
DYLAN

I woke up with my limbs tangled in Rhyland's and a hangover from hell.

Also, my anus felt like a herd of elephants had blasted through it on the way to freedom.

Last night's events trickled into my conscience like a leaking faucet. I groaned, flinging an arm over my eyes.

Oh God. It was getting serious with Coltridge.

There was no other way to explain what was happening. It was more than a fling, and he must have felt the same way, because he'd come up with that weird idea of paying me for six more months to be his hookup and date. While I loved being both, I wanted more than to feel like we were exchanging currencies.

I wanted to date him and fuck him because we liked each other.

It was time for the talk, wasn't it? The one I never thought I'd have to have with my big brother's best friend.

My bedroom door was flung open, and in ran my daughter, clutching Mr. Mushroom, sporting an unusual shade of green. "Mommy! Mommy!" she cried out.

Shit, I thought. *Shit, shit, shit.*

She was not supposed to find Uncle Rhyland in her mother's bed, let alone mostly naked. Rhy had briefs and the duvet covering most of him, but still.

"Oh, hey, sweetie!" I greeted extra-loud, kicking his feet in the process to jar him awake so he could make a hasty exit—or, at the very least, help me with the damage control. I opened my arms wide for her. "What's going o—"

But I didn't have the chance to finish my question. As soon as my daughter reached the foot of the bed, she keeled over and vomited all over my duvet, Rhy's foot, and the bed frame.

Warm, sticky, partially digested noodles and chicken nuggets swam in an ocean of yellow and orange over the bed. I sprang into action, scooping her up and bringing her into my en suite, where I peeled the vomit-soaked pajamas from her little body.

"Mommy." She flung her arms around my shoulders, weeping. She hadn't even noticed Rhy. "I feel so bad. My tummy...it is hurting."

"I can tell, sweetie." I stroked the back of her head, filling her a bath. I checked her temperature with my hand. She definitely had a fever. *Crap.* She seemed to have caught what I had a few days ago. Poor thing.

"Baby, I'm going to run you a bath and give you some Tylenol and some water, okay?"

She nodded sulkily.

The claw bathtub was filling. I squirted some liquid soap into it so she'd have some bubbles. She was now naked, sitting on the edge of the vanity, dangling her feet. She still looked green. I felt so horrible for her.

"Little stinker?" Rhy pushed his head between the door and the frame, glancing inside. He looked sleepy.

"Uncle Rhyrand!" She perked up immediately at seeing him.

He pushed the door open and walked inside, tousling her hair. "How're you feeling, little one? Your tummy's giving you trouble?"

"Yeah." She pouted.

"Don't worry, baby. It'll pass soon. And know what? Uncle Rhyland is gonna take Fluffy and Mittens on a walk and get you a surprise."

He was keeping her engaged while I filled the bath and ran to the kitchen to get the Tylenol, all with puke on his foot, and for that, I was grateful. When I came back, Grav took the Tylenol, and I put her in the bath.

"I got it now." I rubbed Rhy's arm, smiling. "And...thank you."

"No problem. I finally get to fulfill my potential as a toddler's sick bag." He hesitated, about to leave. "You want me to come back after I take the two furballs out for a walk?"

I shook my head. I honestly didn't want him to do more than he was already doing for me. Already, he was the one pulling most of the weight in this relationship.

"Nah, I got it."

"But you have a shift today."

He remembers.

"I'll call Tuckwad to help out. He needs to make himself useful at some point, right?"

That made Rhy stiffen and his jaw tense. I studied him carefully, waiting for his reaction.

"You're not going to leave him with Grav alone, are you?"

Why do you care? I wanted to ask. *Have you changed your mind about kids being the devil's work?*

"No." I smiled instead. This was neither the time nor the place to have a big talk about our relationship and the meaning of all this. "I'm going to be here with them. I'll call Max and tell him I can't make it. I just think it's a good idea for him to take care of her. Maybe those fatherly instincts will kick in."

After Rhy left, I took Grav out of the bath, put her in new jammies, and made her tea. I made her a small fort on the couch, put on *Bluey*, and gave her some cuddles. Then, when I saw the Tylenol had kicked in, I excused myself to the kitchen and called Tucker.

"Yeah?" he asked, almost smugly. "Asshole dumped you, so you decided to lick your wounds with me?"

God, I hated him. He claimed to want to be a part of his child's life until it was time to actually help out with her.

"Your daughter's not feeling well," I ground out between my teeth.

"What's wrong with her?"

"Nothing is *wrong* with her, Tuckwad." Screw it, I was making his nickname a thing. He'd earned it. "She caught a stomach bug slash virus. I had the same thing. It goes away in forty-eight hours, but it's brutal."

There was a slight pause in his response before he asked, "Do you want me to come take care of her?"

Finally, he was saying something that didn't make me want to claw his inner organs out.

"Yes, please. I need to clean the apartment, shop for groceries, and research premed programs."

Tucker snorted. "Yeah, right."

I despised him. I really did.

"When can you come?" I asked, businesslike.

"In, like, maybe four hours or so. I have some stuff to do first."

"Uh-huh. See you then."

"Hey! If I come, can you ask Row about giving me that loa—"

But it was too late.

I'd already hung up.

CHAPTER THIRTY-NINE
DYLAN

Five hours and three vomit bouts from Grav later, Tucker arrived, and he looked none too pleased about it. The only ray of sunshine in this entire crap-a-licious day was that my daughter was probably done puking, and I'd managed to get some chicken noodle soup into her.

"Yo."

Yo? Was he twelve?

I stepped sideways to let him in.

He peered around, spotted our daughter on the couch, and approached her with his hands shoved deep in his pockets. My breath caught in the back of my throat when he crouched down and tapped her knee.

"Hey, buddy. Heard you aren't feeling too well. Care for some company?"

Well, this wasn't that bad at all. I released the trapped air in my lungs.

Gravity nodded. "Can we draw a little bit?"

"Sure. Yeah." Tucker looked about him.

Something clenched behind my rib cage.

"I...I'll go get the colors and the paper." I cleared my throat, making myself useful and trekking over to her room.

As I gathered the washable crayons and paper, I allowed myself to hope Tucker was finally turning a corner. I'd figure out the logistics of staying in New York and studying here if he stepped up. I'd plan my entire existence around Grav's happiness.

I gave them the colors and got started on cleaning the apartment. Every now and then, I checked in on them. They were doing surprisingly well together. First, they drew. Then, Tucker helped her color in her drawing. They made M&M cookies together (with prepared dough) and consumed the sticky rice and chicken nugget lunch I made for them without complaint.

When it was time for me to go downstairs for some groceries, I was torn. On the one hand, they seemed to be getting along fine. On the other, he was still…Tucker. Rhy was right to ask me about leaving them together. It seemed incredibly premature.

He is literally her father. They share the same DNA. He's said he wants to be a part of her life countless times. And this is their sixth time hanging out together.

Yeah, Tucker was Tucker, but I didn't think he would physically hurt her.

What he did to me that night was violence. But he also said it was a mistake. And he'd never used violence against me before. Besides, it was literally going to take me fifteen minutes—I only needed the basics. And Rhyland was in the building if they ran into any issues.

Just make a decision already.

"Grav, why don't you come with Mommy to get some shopping done? It won't take more than twenty minutes, and Uncle Tucker will wait for us." I smiled tightly.

Her head lolled up from the book they were reading, and she looked at me wearily. "Mommy, can't I just stay here?"

My stomach turned. *No, you can't*, I wanted to say. *Please come with me.*

"Baby, you could use some fresh air," I said desperately, hating the twang of desperation in my voice.

"Seriously, Dyl, I can take care of her for twenty minutes." Tucker looked at me like I was crazy. Maybe I was. And Rhyland did say I needed to let go when it came to Grav.

"It might be a little longer than twenty. I'd just feel more comfortable if—"

"Mommy, I'm too tired to go out."

"No worries!" I said brightly. "I'll just Instacart it."

"*Dylan.*" Tucker stared at me, his expression drenched with horror. "Jesus, I'm capable of taking care of my ki—" His eyes widened, and he quickly corrected himself. "Of *a* kid for less than half an hour. I used to babysit my sister's kids all the time. You were there with me."

He was right. And they'd all survived, as far as I was aware.

I kissed Grav goodbye and scurried away before I could change my mind. My instincts screamed at me that this was the wrong thing to do, but I forced myself to ignore them. I had to give this a chance, for Gravity's sake.

I finished my trip to the grocery store at record speed. I spoke to Kieran on the phone all throughout while he encouraged me to breathe and not have a public panic attack. I forgot a lot of things on my shopping list and ran back home.

As soon as I stepped out of the elevator on my floor, I heard the screams from the apartment.

I bolted there, discarding my shopping bags on the floor. My hands shook as I unlocked the apartment door and rushed inside. I found Gravity on the couch crying hysterically, her face, hair, and clothes full of vomit and Tucker's shirt and pants covered in puke.

"Thank *fuck* you're here." Tucker hurried my way, gesturing to his stained clothes. "She freaking puked as soon as you left the building. Jesus Christ, it's everywhere! My clothes, my hair…"

I shoved him out of my path to Gravity, picked her up, and held her close to comfort her. She didn't usually cry this badly, if at all, when she vomited.

"Mommy, he s-started shouting." She hiccupped, clinging onto me with desperate little fingers. "I-I-I only did it by accident. It just came out!" She hung her big eyes at me apologetically. "Am I in trouble?"

No, but he is for making you feel this way.

"Honey! Not at all. You don't have to explain yourself. People vomit. It happens all the time. Everything is okay." I carried her to the main bathroom, Tucker chasing after me.

"Is he mad at me?" Gravity looked broken as, for the second time today, I peeled off her soiled clothes and filled the bath.

I don't know and I don't care, I wanted to say. *That asshole doesn't deserve you.*

"No, baby, of course not." I kissed her forehead. It was burning again. I missed Rhyland. Rhyland would take charge. Clean the couch. Help out. Crack a joke to lighten the mood. "He was just a little surprised. Uncle Tucker doesn't spend a lot of time with children."

"He pushed me," she whispered into my neck, clinging tighter to me.

My whole body went rigid and cold. I froze.

"I hurt my head, Mommy."

My fingers immediately shot to her head, and I began to gently search it for blood or bruises. I found a small bump on the right side of her skull. She hissed when I touched it.

"There, Mommy. There."

I was going to kill him.

God help me, I needed someone to intervene. Because I really was going to kill him.

"Dyl, can you help me here?" Tucker leaned against the bathroom door, arms and ankles crossed, oblivious to the fact that I was about to slam a steak knife between his eyes. He was flicking chicken nugget pieces from his shirt, sneering. "I look a mess."

"Tell me something I don't know," I muttered, tossing yellow rubber ducks and pink boats into the bathtub. I needed to keep it cool. I couldn't fall apart in front of Gravity. First, I'd deal with this. Then I'd deal with him.

"Can I take a shower here?"

"No," I said coldly, picking half-digested rice and chicken nuggets from my daughter's dark curls.

"Dude, what am I supposed to do?" he groused. "I can't go out of here like this!"

"Figure it out."

"It *stinks*." He sounded just about ready to cry. "And I—"

"I don't care." I twisted around sharply, snapping at him. I barely managed to keep my voice contained, and even that was only for Gravity's sake. "I really could not care less, Tucker. I don't think you understand. This isn't about you. All of this"—I gestured to the room—"was never about us. It's about—"

The main door opened, and Rhyland's voice filled the room. "Little stinker? Cosmos?"

"Uncle Rhyland!" Gravity wiggled out of my embrace, butt naked, and charged toward the living room.

For the first time since he'd walked into my apartment, Tucker and I were alone.

I flashed him a glare full of fury. "She said you pushed her."

He looked stunned but didn't say a word. Dread spread across my body. So he did do it. Not that I didn't believe Gravity, but somehow, the confirmation in his silence undid me. The signs were there. That time he hurt me at the bar. The bruise he left on my wrist.

"You hurt her head," I said.

He sputtered, making a guttural, nasal sound. "No, I didn't." He threw his hands in the air. "And don't act like I hit her or something. The second she started puking on me, I instinctively pushed her off me, and her head bumped the wall *very* lightly. Like, just barely. And I said sorry immediately and asked her if she was okay, but she was probably screaming too loud already to hear."

Panic clogged my throat. I'd put my daughter in harm's way by trusting her with this...this...*monster*.

"You don't freaking push a kid off when they throw up. You soothe them, rub their back, help them."

Tucker snorted, shaking his head like I was full of it. "C'mon, Dylan. Get off my ass, will ya?"

"Excuse me?" I was on the verge of gutting him with my daughter's lice comb.

"Taking care of sick kids is a woman's territory. Men don't have these kinds of...I dunno, maternal instincts or whatever. I did the best I could in the given situation. It's civilization, baby. Mother Nature. We're meant to hunt, not clean rice and chicken nuggets off the floor."

My mouth hung open, and I stared at him silently. He meant it. He seriously thought it wasn't his job to take care of his sick kid. The water streaming from the faucet drowned out the throbbing thoughts swirling in my head.

"So what *is* your role—you know, as a big, macho man with big, macho biceps?" I folded my arms.

"Provide shelter." He crossed these things off with his fingers.

"Didn't see much of that these past four years." I circled a finger around his figure skeptically.

"Well, no, but if you give me a chance—"

"How much money did you contribute toward Gravity's upbringing?" I continued.

"That's not fair." His eyebrows slammed together. "Your family's loaded! Your brother's a multimillionaire. If anything, *you* should be the one helping *me*—"

He continued talking, but I muted him out. I was losing my mind listening to his idiocy. I turned off the faucet, checked the temperature of the water, and grabbed the door handle. I walked out to the corridor, pouring myself into the living room. There I saw my naked daughter wearing Rhyland's much-too-big biker jacket. He was crouching before her on the floor, doodling a tattoo on her arm after pushing the sleeve of his jacket up.

"...no one will mess with you after they see this. To be honest, even I'm a little scared," Rhyland said. Gravity made a roaring sound, baring her teeth, and Rhy chuckled, shaking his head. "You're a biker, remember? Not a tiger."

"Oh." Gravity giggled. "What sound do bikers make?"

Rhyland rapped a wooden piece of furniture with his fist. "Hey, bartender! Get me a beer."

A smile broke across my lips. I strode onto the scene, wagging my finger at him. "Don't corrupt my daughter."

"I'd never, Miss Casablancas." Rhyland stood up, grabbed me by the waist, and tugged me to him. "I'm not even done corrupting you," his lips murmured into mine. "Came to check in on you and Grav. Got us some pho. How's everything going?"

I tried to push him off me, knowing Tucker was in the bathroom and could walk out at any minute. Rhyland dove down for a kiss.

"Rhy, not now."

"Why? Grav already knows," he murmured into the shell of my ear.

"Tuckwad doesn't."

Speak of the devil. He strode out of the hallway and looked between the three of us.

"Coltridge." Tucker gave him a swift nod.

"Tuckwad."

"Any chance I can borrow some clothes?" Tucker asked boldly, gesturing to himself. "Gravity had an accident."

"Gravity doesn't have accidents. She graces us with her sometimes unexplained art," Rhyland corrected. "And sure, I'll grab you something to wear from upstairs. But it's not a borrow. Those clothes are contaminated once you touch them. I don't want them back."

Tucker's throat bobbed with the nasty words he must've swallowed down.

I scooped up Grav and got rid of the jacket on her. "I'll go give her a bath."

"I'll take one in your bedroom," Tucker said, ignoring the fact that I'd clearly told him he couldn't.

"You'll stay right here until I come back with those clothes," Rhyland corrected him.

We split to go our separate ways. Gravity was too tired to play with her duckies and her boats. I quickly got her into pajamas. She skipped the pho (said she wasn't hungry), drank some water, and asked to go to bed. Since her fever was down, I decided to forgo the Tylenol and just check on her in an hour. Hopefully by then, she'd have sweated the rest of it out.

When I walked back to the living room, only Rhyland was there. He was scrubbing off the remainder of the vomit on the couch, but everything else was squeaky clean and back in order. For the millionth time, I thanked God for creating Rhyland Coltridge.

"Where's Tucker?" I asked tiredly.

"Taking a shower in your bathroom," Rhyland replied, sounding none too pleased about it. "How's Grav?"

"Out cold," I sighed, wiping my brow. I could use a warm bath myself. And maybe a small nervous breakdown.

"Poor thing." Rhyland grabbed my ass cheeks, tugging me so I was flush against him, pressing against his erection.

"Me or Grav?"

"Both of you." He leaned in to give me a tantalizing, sloppy kiss that made all my troubles disappear, even if for one moment. "Now, you can tell Tuckwad to fuck off, and we can salvage your day together."

But just like always, we couldn't keep our hands off each other, and soon, his hand was in my shirt, my palm rubbing his bulge between us. I desperately needed a distraction, because thinking about what had happened with Tucker was putting me at risk of doing something very, very stupid.

"Fuck, sweetheart. I can't wait to bend you over the couch and fill your two holes with my dick and my fingers." Rhy hoisted me up to wrap my legs around his waist, walking us forward until my back was pressed against the wall.

"Please," I moaned into his mouth. "Fuck me, Rhyland."

We heard a noisy and deliberate clearing of a throat over my left shoulder and both turned to see my ex staring at us, his cheeks stinging with fury. In the eyes I'd lost myself in countless times, I now found nothing but wickedness and malice. His nostrils flared, and his mouth barely moved as he spoke.

"Please don't tell me you guys are fucking serious about this hookup."

A shiver ran down my spine. Rhyland put me down carefully. It was in this moment everything clicked for me.

That time Tucker hurt me wasn't accidental. He'd wanted to leave a mark. He'd wanted me scared and small and frightened. Tucker wasn't a good guy, and there was no redemption arc for him. Whatever had made him warm to the idea of reconnecting with our daughter had nothing to do with altruism; she was just a pawn in his very twisted chess game.

"What we are and aren't is none of your business," I said coldly, walking over to him. He was wearing clothes of Rhyland's I didn't recognize. Pink Bermuda shorts and a long-sleeve yellow button-down with a llama print on it. He looked absolutely ridiculous, and I had no doubt Rhyland had put effort and care into ensuring the outfit was as disastrous as possible. "You really upset my daughter today."

"*Our* daughter," Tucker corrected.

"No," I said calmly. "Mine. Being a sperm donor does not make you a dad. You are no father, Tucker. And if you want visitation rights, then I suggest you retain a lawyer, because I'm going to fight you on it every step of the way."

"You can't be serious." He raised his voice, not paying heed to the fact that our child was asleep in the next room. "This is an insane overreaction. You can't do that."

"I can, and I am. Now get the fuck out of my apartment before I call the police and tell them about the bruise you left on my arm and the way you slammed our daughter's head against the wall."

Rhyland's face swiveled my way, his expression astonished. "What did you just say?"

"When Gravity puked on him, he 'reflexively' pushed her. She bumped against the wall," I explained.

"You're making it sound so much worse than it really was," Tucker exploded.

"I'm saying it exactly as it is."

"Tucker." Rhyland turned to him, eyes ablaze, a war raging inside them.

Dread trickled down the back of my neck. He looked like he was about to murder Tucker. Not in a figure-of-speech kind of way. In a what-the-hell-do-we-do-with-the-body kind of way.

"You'd better get out right this minute, before I rip out your intestines and wrap them around your neck until I cut off your oxygen supply," Rhyland said slowly, methodically, *calmly*, which made everything so much worse somehow.

"Okay, okay, I'm leaving!" Tucker walked backward, face red with shame.

"You're never coming back," Rhyland said, not asked. "I mean it, Tucker. I'm not responsible for my actions if I see you on the same street as Dylan and Gravity again."

Tucker looked between us, shocked and annoyed. For a moment, I thought he was going to argue, but then he took another look at Rhy, thought better of it, and stomped out of my apartment.

The first thing I did was lock the door and press my back against it, heaving.

He hurt my child.

He.

Hurt.

My.

Child.

The second thing I did was break down in tears, sliding off the door and falling apart.

And the third thing?

I was put back together by Rhyland Coltridge.

CHAPTER FORTY
DYLAN

Ping.
Ping.
Ping. Ping. Ping. Ping. Ping.

The annoying sound tapped its way into my skull like a beak in impressively quick succession. Sunrays filtered through the shutters, warming up my skin. Birds chirped outside my window.

I stretched in my bed, last night's events slowly trickling their way back into my consciousness. Tucker hurt Gravity. I'd cried close to all night in Rhyland's arms. Then, when I finally managed to get my shit together, he asked if he could stay over, and I said no.

Why did I say no?

Because you are falling in love with him, and sooner or later, he is going to break your heart. No part of him wants a relationship. He's made that very clear. And the last thing a newly minted billionaire who looks like a Greek god needs is a single mom, a toddler child who's not his, and the baggage you come with.

This thought was punctuated by six more pings. My phone was blowing up on the nightstand. I reached to grab it and was immediately alarmed by the river of text messages that kept on flowing in real time. I saw Row's name as well as Cal's and Kieran's.

Row sent an attachment.

> Row sent an attachment.
> Row sent an attachment.
> Row: Explain??
> Row: Why do you want me to commit murder, Dylan? You know I'm a family man.
> Cal: THIS, from a woman who claims to be my bff.
> Row: I'm flying back to New York RIGHT. FUCKING. NOW.
> Cal: I am never going to not be mad at you for keeping this from me btw.
> Cal: I am so disappointed you didn't tell me.
> Kieran: You are in so much trouble, sweetheart.
> Kieran: Offer still stands if you want to do some damage control by marrying a man who is not the biggest man-whore on the planet.

Heart pounding, sight blurry, I clicked on the attachments my brother had sent. Three pictures came into focus. They were almost identical and showed me and Rhyland in my living room yesterday, my legs wrapped around his waist, his hand shoved down the front of my jeans, obviously fingering me. My fingers were greedily clutching the back of his head, bringing him in to deepen our dirty, tongue-filled kiss.

With a sigh of exasperation, I fell back on the pillow, covering my eyes with my arm and groaning.

My entire social circle had pretty much seen stills of a sex tape of mine.

And then another.

> Row: How did Tucker get my number?

My guess was that the picture had been sent to the three of them simultaneously. Tucker knew my closest circle—Cal, Row, and

Kieran. He must've grabbed their contacts during one of the million times my phone was there in plain sight when we had a shift at the Alchemist together, still unlocked from when I'd been messing with it. He was just waiting for the opportunity to do something like this and ruin things for me.

Tucker knew this was going to detonate my world, and he felt vengeful.

An incoming call from Cal made my phone dance in my hand. I swiped the screen, holding my breath and bracing myself.

"Young lady, explain yourself," my best friend demanded.

"It's nothing serious, okay?" I said grumpily, rubbing my eyes with a yawn. "We played pretend for Bruce Marshall, and somewhere along the way…well, we decided to enjoy the perks."

"Is getting shot in the ass a perk?" my brother demanded from beside Cal.

Oh great. I was on speaker.

"Because that's the kind of bonus Rhyland's about to deal with."

A part of me—and not a small one—wanted to apologize for my behavior. For the elusive betrayal. But a much, much bigger part of me knew that doing so would simply give my brother more power than he already had over the situation.

I was an adult. I made decisions. Not all of them were great. But all of them were *mine*.

"I will hear no criticism from you." My voice was an ice cube dragging over skin, it was so cold. The other end of the line was silent. "I did not break any bond with you, any secret bro code. I am your sister. I love you to death, Ambrose, but you have to stop pretending you have control over my life. You don't. I will fuck whoever I want, however much I want, wherever I want. I will not ask for permission, and I sure as hell won't answer to you. Are we clear?"

My brother grunted on the other end of the line. "Fine. *Fine.* I'll stop pushing. It's just…it's hard, okay?" Another dark growl. "It's a force of habit. I spent my entire childhood terrified Dad was going to hurt you. Somewhere along the way, I convinced myself that if you listened to me, things would be…okay, you know?"

"I know." My voice softened, but my anger remained. "Still, Row. Enough is enough."

"I've been doing very well these past few years, though, haven't I? I barely boss you around."

"You shouldn't be bossing me around at *all*."

"Well, there is my shitty personality to take into account."

Cal snorted. "How'd it all start—this thing with Rhy? Is it serious?"

"We just…I don't know, got very comfortable around each other," I confessed. The alternative—telling them I propositioned him the day I got here—was not ideal. "And no, it's not serious. Rhyland is gearing up for some big things, and so am I. A relationship doesn't fit in with them."

"Does this mean what I think it means?" Row asked.

"Yeah," I said, biting down on my lower lip. "I think. It's time I spread my wings, you know? Go to college. Even if it's hard, it'll give me and Grav a better future. And it'll teach her to chase her dreams."

"I'm so fucking proud of you." Row's voice cracked. "But I'm still going to kill Rhy, FYI."

Cal squealed. "I've always wanted a doctor in the family! I have so many shady spots on my body. And I could really use a monthly boob check for lumps."

"I check your boobs for lumps twice a day," Row protested.

"Um, no, honey. If you did, you wouldn't be concentrating solely on the nipples."

"Way too much info." I cringed. "Besides, I haven't been accepted for anything yet."

"You will be," Cal said confidently. "You're the smartest person I know."

"Da fuck, Dot?" Row protested.

"You're the hottest, sweetie."

"So…" I stood up and padded out to the hallway, dropping my voice so as not to wake my daughter. "Are you guys…not mad anymore? Because I didn't really give you much of an explanation, just told you to screw off."

"You're off the hook in my eyes," Cal confirmed. "Of course, I owe you from that time I banged your brother behind your back when we were teenagers."

"Too true. You did that too, Row."

"I'm aware. I was there," he allowed grumpily.

I entered Grav's room. Pressed a hand to her forehead while she slept. It was cool and dry. *Thank you, Jesus.*

"As I said, you're off the hook, but Rhyland isn't," Row lamented. "He broke the code and deserves a good beating."

I sighed. "Can you please refrain from ruining his face? He's too pretty."

"Clearly. That's what got us into this whole mess."

No. What got me into this mess was the fact that he had an amazing personality on top of being handsome.

"Any other requests?" Row asked.

"Yeah." I toyed with a lock of my hair, putting it between my lips and chewing. "Protect the crown jewels, Row. I really like them."

"Too late. I'm going to dethrone the motherfucker."

>Rhyland: We need to talk.
>Dylan: Please don't tell me you're pregnant. I'm really not ready for this kind of responsibility right now. I can't even commit to a gel manicure.
>Rhyland: Okay, rude. For one thing, I don't chip after, like, five seconds.
>Dylan: Do I want to know how you got all this manicure knowledge?

318 L.J. SHEN

Rhyland: I made a career pretending to be an attentive boyfriend. I know all about women's woes.

Dylan: I'm guessing it's about our leaked sex tape.

Rhyland: There's a video too?!

Dylan: A reel. But Row tells me Tucker only shared it with friends and family.

Rhyland: He has neither.

Rhyland: Are you downstairs?

Dylan: Getting ready 2 leave. Taking Grav to the park. Fever's down. She's feeling better.

Rhyland: I'll join you.

Dylan: 👍

Rhyland: Need me to bring anything?

Dylan: Nope. My camel toe is huge.

Rhyland: False. Your pussy lips are as perfect as the ones upstairs.

Dylan: CAMO TOTE!!!

Rhyland: Sure, Jan.

Dylan: I'm never using voice to text again.

Rhyland: Why? Your oral skills are fantastic.

Dylan: You're not humping.

Rhyland: I've a feeling I will be tonight...

Dylan: HELPING!!!

Rhyland: You know, predictive text says a lot about the words we use on an everyday basis.

Dylan: I hate you.

Rhyland: Was that autocorrect?

Dylan: No. That was a fart.

Rhyland: Bless you, Cosmos. I'm glad we've reached that level of intimacy.

Dylan: FACT.

Rhyland: 😊😊😊

CHAPTER FORTY-ONE
RHYLAND

Dylan was getting her cardio when I got to the park, in the form of chasing after her daughter from the swings to the slides and roaring at her not to do things Grav then proceeded to do with an evil giggle. I smirked to myself as I swaggered toward them. They were chaotic and messy and a whole fucking lot but also kind of adorable.

Fluffy and Mittens were wobbling at my side on their leashes. I figured I could use the chance to take them out on a walk. I was still in the process of finding them a home. Two people had emailed me back after I sent a mass email with pictures of them attached, saying they were interested in adopting them, but I was waiting to see if there were any better candidates before I replied.

"Don't run into the street!" Dylan was screaming now, so of course, Gravity dashed straight into the fucking traffic. I blocked her way to the busy road, tucking the leashes of the dogs into my pocket and football-tackling the kid. She giggled and wriggled her feet in the air.

"Uncle Rhyrand! What are you doing?"

"Bribing a three-year-old, apparently," I muttered.

"What?" She continued squirming as I led her back to the depths of the park and away from the street.

"How about we make a deal, little stinker? If you play nicely and refrain from trying to kill yourself for the next twenty minutes, I'm going to buy you a whole-ass Barbie house. How 'bout that?"

We were nearing Dylan, who was standing with her arms crossed and a face that said she knew I was using language I shouldn't with her daughter.

"I don't like Barbies anymore." Gravity blew a raspberry.

"What do you like, then?"

"Dinosaurs."

I forgot she was her mother's daughter.

"Right, well, I can't buy you one of those, as they've been out of stock for, er, let's see...sixty-six million years. But I can buy you a big dinosaur stuffie."

"Uh-huh."

"So you'll play nicely?"

"Yes."

"Do you promise?" I hedged.

"No."

We were already close to Dylan, so I had to take whatever I could from this arrangement.

"All right, stinker. Go play." I put her down and patted her shoulder, watching her bolt back to the slides, and—of course—climb them in reverse while closing her eyes. She was so much like her mother it was frightening.

Dylan and I shared a peck on the lips. "How're you feeling?" I asked. After everything that had happened with Tuckwad last night, I wanted to make sure.

"Mad as hell." Dylan tipped her chin up. "I'm determined not to let Tucker anywhere near Gravity after what he did. Oh, and the asshole sent Row, Cal, and Kieran pictures of us making out. As I'm sure you're aware."

"Yup. Row already told me to update my will."

"Was he very mad?" Her bottom lip was pinned to one side by her teeth.

I pulled out my phone and showed it to Dylan wordlessly.

> Row: You have some nerve. Dylan is like a sister to you.
> Row: ANSWER MY CALLS, FUCKER.
> Row Casablancas Unsent a Message.
> Row Casablancas Unsent a Message.
> Row Casablancas Unsent a Message.
> Row: Cal told me to unsend the messages that could land me in jail, so I guess you'll have to see what I have in store for you when I arrive in New York.
> Row: (which is in three hours, by the way)

"Hmm." Dylan stared at the screen, notably blasé about the fact that her brother was going to skin me alive. "And I thought I was the one with the anger issues in this family. Did you answer him?"

"Not yet. I wanted to see where you and I stood before I had that conversation with him." I searched her face.

Her spine stiffened, and she looked momentarily startled, as if a huge grizzly bear had walked into the playground and she couldn't move. She forced herself to roll her shoulders.

"What do you mean? We both agreed it'd be casual."

"Does this feel casual to you?" I assessed her frankly. I'd never been eager to enter a relationship—never, in fact, been in one before—and I had a feeling I would definitely find a way to fuck it up with Dylan. But unlike past instances, I actually wanted to try.

The sex was incredible, she made me laugh, she was smart as hell, and though the idea of Gravity certainly appeared to be baggage, in practice, she was kind of hilarious. The only drawback I could think of was that if I did screw this up, it'd affect my friendship with Row.

If I still had one, that is.

"It, well…" She rubbed the back of her neck, peering around us. "I mean, it's definitely more intense than I anticipated."

"Understatement of the fucking century." I tried to keep my composure about me. "I thought I'd get you out of my system after three fucks."

Okay, that *definitely* sounded better in my head.

She started to laugh. "Wanting to have sex with someone doesn't make a good reason to start a relationship with them."

I took a deep breath. "I don't only want to fuck you. I also want to talk to you. Like, all the time."

"I do too," she admitted miserably. Her gaze skittered to her daughter, who was now picking up flowers and sticking them in Fluffy's and Mittens's fur beside me. "What are you saying?" She dared look up at me again. "That you want to give it a try?"

"I mean, why not? We're already exclusive, and we have fun together, the sex is insane, and we're neighbors, so it's convenient. What's the downside?"

"That we're both extremely damaged and have never been in a healthy relationship?" She laughed.

"Good. So we're starting this marathon together and can help each other out."

"Might be a sprint." Dylan shrugged, but the sassy mirth was gone from her voice. She licked her lips, staring at the tip of her sneakers as she drew circles in the sand. "Look, I find it really hard to trust men. Allowing myself to feel is betraying my own heart. I promised myself I'd never hurt it again."

"Is it happy being numb?" I challenged, smoothing her hair out of her face. It was always everywhere. Like a flock of ravens. "Is it happy being guarded by a thousand fucking walls? Were you happy the past few years?"

"Yes." Her brow furrowed in outrage. "Of course I was happy. It's been challenging, but Grav—"

"Is only one facet of your life." I cut into her speech. "And you know it. You have needs too. You have a life. Dreams. Don't tell me you forgot about them, because I won't buy it. You're still a dreamer. You've *always* been a dreamer." I grabbed her cheeks and pressed her forehead against mine, my lips moving over hers. "You've never stopped dreaming, and that's why staying away from you has been so goddamn hard."

We were both panting even though we were standing perfectly still. The dogs beneath me looked like a bouquet, but Gravity was true to her word and didn't interrupt us.

Finally, Dylan broke free from my touch. "Trial relationship." She erected a finger between us warningly. "That's all you get."

"Does this mean I'm getting my money back if I'm unhappy with the product?"

She punched my arm. I laughed.

"Take it or leave it, mister."

"I'll take it."

She balled her fists, resting them on my pecs. "This is a gentle reminder that you should treat me like a blue jay with the sass of an eagle. I act all tough, but I'm flighty and get easily scared. So, you know…" She trailed off, shaking her head and chuckling at the awkwardness between us. "Just…don't fuck it up, okay?"

"Trust me, I'm going to try my fucking hardest."

"Potty word." Gravity's head snapped up from the dogs. "Ha! What do I get for not telling Grandma about it?"

"Nothing." I gave her an incredulous look. "Your Grams is not *my* mother. I don't care if she knows I use potty words."

I was still embracing her mother, holding my breath that she wouldn't say anything bad about it, like "get your filthy hands off my mommy, bozo."

Instead, Gravity shrugged and said, "I want my dinosaur."

Dylan shot me an inquisitive look.

"I bribed her so I could talk to you."

"With a prehistoric creature?"

"With whatever it'd take to get a moment alone with you." I locked her chin between my thumb and index fingers, tilting her head up for a kiss. "Gravity?" I asked.

"Hmm?" the small child answered, back to tucking flowers behind the canines' ears.

"I'm going to kiss your mommy now. Can I do that?"

"Only if I get two chocolates and an ice cream."

"You drive a hard bargain, but I'll take it."

Then I leaned Dylan back and gave the entire playground a display that almost landed me in jail.

CHAPTER FORTY-TWO
RHYLAND

Figuring I still had some time to burn before Row arrived to deliver my well-deserved punch, I decided to hit the building's gym. I frequented it every morning, and today was no different, but I needed to release some steam before this conversation.

I hit the StairMaster for twenty minutes before winging an all-body workout (I usually followed an A/B plan with two-day stretches and yoga to lengthen those godly limbs). It was toward the end of my workout when disaster struck. Sweaty and spent, I was reaching for the forty-pound dumbbells when someone grabbed a fifty-pound dumbbell from behind me and dropped it on my fingers. Pain exploded all over my knuckles. I hissed out, arching my back and tugging my fingers from beneath the crushing weight.

As it happened, I had help. Row—who I now spotted behind me in the mirror—grabbed me by the back of the neck and walked me toward the opposite wall, a snarl on his face.

"Hello, *bestie*." He slammed my back against the wall.

I dodged his fist when he sent it straight to my face, grabbed him by the base of his throat, and gave him a hard "don't fuck with me" squeeze.

Yeah, I'd messed up with Dylan, but other than this one transgression, I'd been an impeccable friend to him. In fact, if it weren't for me helping his wife with her grand gesture before they got married, he'd still be pining for her ass.

Row curled his fingers around the arm that was squeezing his throat, trying to pry my touch off. "You have some fucking nerve, hitting me back," Row growled.

I released him, and he stumbled backward, looking flushed and pissed off.

"You came all the way to New York to take a cheap shot?" I shook my head. "Do you have no goddamn life at all? I wouldn't come to personally hit you if you fucked my own mother."

"First of all, you hate your mother." Row erected one finger. "Second, she's not my taste." A second finger. "Third, I warned you not to touch her." He now raised his middle finger, sticking it in front of my face. "Fourth, I was already on the way to a business meeting. Now, kindly tell me what in the ever-loving shit is going on here."

I frowned down at my fingers, extending and curling them to make sure they weren't broken. What a prick my best friend was. Who did something like that? He knew this was my jerk-off hand.

"Christ, Row. You're insane." I shook my head. "You could've broken all my fingers."

"Are you going to apologize for screwing my sister?" Row growled.

"No," I said honestly, looking up at him finally.

"No?" His eyebrows jumped up. He was not expecting that answer.

"No," I confirmed. "I've already pulled one shitty stunt on you by keeping this a secret. I'm not going to lie to you again. I'm not sorry it happened. In fact, I would do it all over again in a heartbeat. I would die a thousand deaths at your hands from now until eternity and still not regret the briefest touch I shared with your sister, so you might as well punch me now. You've sure as hell earned it."

I thought this little speech would at least earn me a second of grace, but no. Row tilted his head back and laughed hysterically, as if I'd just told him I was joining the circus as a goddamn contortionist.

"Drop the charade, Rhy. You can't catch feelings. They're not transmitted via blow jobs."

"Well, sorry to disappoint, but I do like your sister." I sidestepped him, my shoulder crushing his purposely.

"Like her or love her?" he enquired.

"Like her enough to be mindful with her feelings. I give a shit, okay?"

He stalked out of the gym behind me. "Giving a shit is the bare minimum. And it's usually enough if there're two people involved. But my niece is in the picture too. Did you ever stop to think about what you were walking into?"

I punched the elevator button and ground my teeth in annoyance.

Row clipped my shoulder. "No, seriously, Coltridge. I—"

"No. You listen to me now, asshole." I swiveled around sharply to face him. "I get it. You love your sister. You're protective of her. You have this shared, fucked-up past, blah, blah, blah. But in case you haven't noticed, she is a ball-busting hard-ass who'd happily wrestle a shark for a bet. And *win*. To you, she is your baby sister. To the rest of the hetero male population, she is sex on fucking legs, with a smart mouth and funny tidbits and interesting observations to boot. You love her because she is your family. I lo—*like* her for all she is. You and I are not the same." I pushed at his chest.

He stumbled backward, his face a mask of shock.

"And yes, I am aware she has a daughter. I've been spending a lot of time with both of them. We're both fucking grown-ups, and it's time you deal with that."

"I told Dylan I'm backing off and letting her live her life," Row said charitably, as if he had a choice in the matter. "But that doesn't mean I'm not going to warn you off. She deserves the world."

"I will give her the entire goddamn galaxy," I retorted.

The elevator pinged open, and I stepped inside.

"Just stay the hell out of my business, yeah?"

With that, I clapped his shoulder with a polite smile, let the doors slide closed, and went up to my penthouse.

CHAPTER FORTY-THREE
RHYLAND

Dylan_loves_Rhyland4ever posted a new picture.

Rhyland Coltridge commented: We look so hot together.

Dylan_loves_Rhyland4ever commented: It's only a picture of me??

Rhyland Coltridge: Oh, I'm inside. IYKYK.

TheRealAmbroseCasablancas commented: Watch it, Coltridge.

Dylan_loves_Rhyland4ever commented: Row? Since when do you have Instagram?

TheRealAmbroseCasablancas commented: Since you two ruined my life.

The next three weeks were pure bliss.

Since the contract had been signed, I got a rush of money into my bank account. This time, I wasn't being stupid about it and blowing it all on designer shit. I hired the financial firm Tate used and opened several investment portfolios. I also continued paying Dylan for her fake fiancée services while we sported an impressively wholesome real relationship. Tuckwad slipped under the radar and kept his head low. He still shared some shifts with Dylan at the Alchemist, but they'd stayed out of each other's way. Cosmos said he'd been giving her creeper vibes, but that was pretty much his default mode, so I wasn't too worried.

In those three weeks, a lot of things happened. Dylan and I started doing sleepovers, including at my penthouse. I bought Grav a princess bed and assembled it from scratch. She went nuts when she saw it. Dylan applied to premed programs for next year. I found an office space ten minutes away from the penthouse and hired a PA and three developers on top of the team Bruce had sent into New York to help throw App-date into high gear.

Fluffy and Mittens were not yet adopted.

I refused to part ways with the little fuckers unless I knew the place was legit. And really, it wasn't too bad. I brought them into the office every day. My new PA took them on walks. Employees snuck treats under the table for them. They slept in Grav's princess bed every night, which made her happy. Life was good.

Too good, maybe. I was beginning to suspect a curveball was waiting right around the corner. And fate did not disappoint, as usual.

I was in my office when I got the call, scrolling through thirst-trap AI profiles of fictional people looking for a fake friend to go on a fake coast-to-coast trip with. Fluffy and Mittens were at my feet, chewing lazily on their squeaky toys. It was Bruce.

"Yes?" I asked briskly.

"How's the app coming along?" Bruce drawled in his southern accent. He sounded chirpy, which immediately put me in a bad mood.

"Fan-fucking-tastic."

Better than expected, actually. We were launching in one month, and four hundred thousand people had already subscribed to the service without even trying it, since we'd run a promotional price through an ad campaign that was all over cable TV and Times Square billboards. The competitors were shaking in their boots and announcing they'd be offering similar services.

But they'd never be able to be the OG. What we had was unique, and everyone knew it.

"Good, good. My people are telling me you're burnin' the midnight oil at the office." Bruce sounded impressed. Or at least he didn't abhor my existence, which was progress.

"Yeah." I sat back, staring at my screen, wondering where the shit he was going with this. I ran my hand over my head. My hair was growing out. Thank *fuck*. I was never taking things Dylan said literally ever again without asking her first. She missed the man bun. And I missed all the times she could've tugged on it to navigate my head exactly to the spot she wanted licked when I gave her oral.

"I also heard your pretty little fiancée is visiting you frequently." I heard the grin in Bruce's voice. "Bringing you food and whatnot. Very sweet."

"Not that I don't appreciate you stating the obvious over and over again, but is there a point to this conversation?" I enquired, not so politely.

"There is," Bruce said. "I've decided to throw a little publicity junket at the ranch ahead of the app launch. Invited all them fancy-schmancy industry people we need to chummy up with. There'll be interviews, after-parties, presentations. All the stuff."

"Sounds good." I was a social fucking butterfly. I thrived around people. "When's it happening?"

"Tomorrow."

"You're fucking kidding me."

"I don't have a sense of humor, son."

"No sense of time either," I groused. "You expect me to drop everything and just go?"

"What's the problem?" Bruce munched on what I guessed was a cigarette or a straw or my raw fucking nerves. "I've seen you work a crowd. Should be no issue for you."

"I need to go over the presentation."

"It's the same one we showed the investors. Interactive enough and puts the point across. 'Sides, it's only for three darn days."

"Let me see if I have the time cleared up," I groaned, double-clicking my digital calendar on my MacBook. Sure enough, three days from now was Dylan's Eras Tour concert with Cal. The one for which I'd promised her I'd babysit Gravity. I'd been slacking on this part of our deal in recent weeks, since I started working on the app, and I wasn't going to let her down.

"Can't do the last day." I *tsked*. "Dyl has a concert, and I need to take care of Grav."

"You're sayin' she has a concert like she's Dolly Parton herself."

"I'm not doing the last day," I maintained, my tone not leaving room for negotiation.

"Tell her to change the date," Bruce fired back.

I chuckled wryly. "I don't think you understand the situation, Bruce. Dylan is going to the concert—that is a fact. The junket taking place? Now, that's fucking optional." I leaned back in my chair, resting my feet on my desk leisurely. "So let's unpack what's about to happen. I'm going to drop everything and go to Texas on a whim because your disorganized ass has asked me to, and I'm a good sport like that. I will be leaving first thing Saturday morning, though, to make it back to New York on time for my fiancée."

"The flight's not that long. You can leave in the afternoon," he grumbled.

"I need more time. I promised I was going to help her make friendship bracelets."

"You're pulling my leg."

"No. That's probably one of the wild animals you're raising in your backyard."

"You leave at one p.m., right after the last after-party. Can't beat that deal with a stick."

I pinched the bridge of my nose, holding myself back from biting out what I was about to beat with a baseball bat.

Bruce continued. "Come on now. I've paid a pretty penny to fly celebrities out here."

I dreaded to guess who he considered a celebrity but braced myself for washed-up country singers and nineties models. The latter could've been fun if I weren't taken.

"Noon, I'm out of there," I countered. "And I'm borrowing your private jet to make sure I make it in time."

"You have some nuts on you," Bruce complained.

"I'll bring an EpiPen with me if you're allergic to those."

"Fine. But you bring me your A game. You don't sit there and mope around watching the clock till it's time to make friendship necklaces."

"*Bracelets*," I corrected. My fucking goodness. I had to cup my crotch to make sure my balls were still intact.

"Yeah, those."

> Rhyland: Change of plan.
>
> Dylan: Are we going to the Italian place instead of the Burmese place? 👀
>
> Rhyland: No, we're still going to the Burmese place, it took me three months and a goddamn sexual favor to secure a reservation!
>
> Rhyland: (don't worry, the sexual favor was flavored condoms from Japan I still had a pack of that the manager wanted)
>
> Rhyland: (besides, the most important meal of my day, YOU, is still happening)
>
> Dylan: That's a lot of side notes. Hit me with the bottom line.

Rhyland: I'm going to Texas for the weekend to mingle and entertain Bruce's journo and celebrity friends to help the app take off.

Rhyland: BUT I'm going to make it here in time for the Taylor Swift concert + make friendship bracelets with you.

Dylan: Thanks for clarifying. I was THIS close to going upstairs and destroying all your belongings.

Rhyland: LOL.

Dylan: I'm not kidding.

Rhyland: I'm not going to disappoint you, baby.

Dylan: OMFG what is wrong with me? I totally believe you.

Rhyland: Is this a love declaration?

Dylan: Depends. Am I talking to your dick?

Rhyland: Yes.

Dylan: Then yes.

Rhyland: And if you're talking to the man attached to it?

Dylan: Getting warmer, but not yet.

Rhyland: Burn, baby, burn.

CHAPTER FORTY-FOUR
RHYLAND

I spent Thursday kissing so much Texan ass I was worried my breath would smell like manure and smoked brisket.

Bruce Marshall had really worked me like his busiest call girl. There was a junket, a press release, a virtual conference, and a dinner with all the investors tied to the project. By the time I walked into my room, it was two in the morning. I sent Dylan a quick message to let her know I was still alive, albeit barely, before crashing.

Friday started at 6 a.m. First, I subjected myself to a ninety-minute yoga session with youth-obsessed tech moguls who bragged about being so flexible they could suck their own dicks. Then there was breakfast with the press, a brainstorming session with Hollywood PR gurus, a professional photo shoot of me and Bruce looking like we were reenacting *Brokeback Mountain*, then another dinner, and another party.

This one was different from the rest. Bruce had decided to clear out the entire backyard, all two acres, and had gone guns blazing on the Texan experience. There were mechanical riding bulls, long wooden tables laden with southern comfort food, cowboy-boot-shaped beer glasses, and donut stands. A live band took the makeshift stage. There was a lot of media present. Photographers, influencers, and bloggers roamed the place, taking pictures in the App-date picture booth, downloading a sample app, mingling, and having fun. I had to admit, he'd gone balls-out and garnered at least five pieces of traditional press for the company, not to mention endless social media posts and reels.

And the celebrities? He'd actually managed to pull in a few A-list actors, including the hottest actress on Hollywood's current roster, Claire Larsen, who was helming the blockbuster *Bratz* movie. She was, in truth, every man's fantasy. She looked like a cross between Megan Fox and Scarlett Johansson. And she was fast approaching me from across Bruce's manicured lawn while the bastard was talking my ear off about ways to monetize the app.

"Well, I'll be damned. Claire Larsen's comin' to talk to you," Bruce murmured, mouth pressed against the rim of his beer bottle. She wore a white waistcoat with nothing underneath, the slit coming all the way down to her belly button. I'd seen more clothes on a Victoria's Secret runway model.

"You mean *us*." I knocked back the rest of my whiskey.

"No, you," Bruce chuckled. "I'm an old, married man. You're a young, handsome one. Ain't no ring on your finger yet."

"She'll be wasting her breath," I said tersely.

I meant it too. There was only one woman these days who could get my rocks off, and she was probably busy wrestling an almost-four-year-old into the bathtub right about now.

"Claire doesn't know that." Bruce patted my back. "And I paid her two hundred K to make an appearance here, so while I'm fixin' to go to the courtyard, you keep her entertained and flirt up a storm, eh?" He winked.

"You want her entertained, you go flirt with her," I offered dryly. "What the fuck happened to being a family man? To wanting to work with other respectable men?"

"Ain't nothing disrespectful about smiling for the camera with a pretty woman on your arm," Bruce maintained seriously. "I've done that plenty a times to push a product."

"I love that you judged me for being a man-whore when all along, you were just as bad," I said frankly.

"Now listen here, pretty boy." Bruce dropped his relaxed grin in a nanosecond, clapping my shoulder and squeezing. "You be nice to this woman and have your picture taken with her so this event makes it to Page Six and *the Daily Mail*, or we're gonna have a problem, you hear me?"

My lips curled in revulsion. I stared him down, ready to strangle him, but reminded myself that this time tomorrow, I'd be back home weaving colorful beads into strings and making Dylan pregame cocktails. The thought was strangely reassuring.

"Respectfully, Bruce, go fuck yourself." I smiled cheerfully. "Next time, a 'please don't waste the photo op' will be sufficient. Rest assured; I like money just as much as you do. Now go check on your cow."

He made a face but screwed right off. Just in time for Claire Larsen to park herself in front of me, offering me a dazzling smile.

"Rhyland Coltridge. We finally meet."

She stretched her hand for me to kiss. I lowered it between us and gave it a stern shake. My smile, however, was blissfully charming.

"Does my reputation precede me?"

"Oh yes. In fact, two years ago, I was on the brink of giving you a call." She ran the fingertip of her index finger along my chest, and I smoothly changed positions to angle myself backward and escape her touch. I was a master flirter. But I also had no interest whatsoever in more than a few pictures in the *Daily Mail* crowning me as a new tech mogul.

"I went through a nasty breakup from Tim McFadden," she explained. McFadden was a rock star. "I needed a PR facelift. A friend of mine who did Broadway at the time—Farah Singh—told me you did a great job for her when she needed a fake wedding date so her parents wouldn't fix her up with the next-door neighbor."

"I remember Farah." It was hard to forget, when she'd paid me $20K for a sex-a-thon weekend in Santorini. "Good girl," I mused.

"I can be a good girl too. Or bad. Depending on what you're into." She pouted sassily, her body almost flush with mine.

I felt the camera lights flashing across my face as the photographers started asking her questions.

"Claire, is this your new beau?"

"Larsen, is there anything you want to share with your fans?"

"Does this mean you and McFadden are done for good this time?"

"Are you planning to download the app? Is there hope for the average Joe?"

This was a trap, I realized. Claire had come here looking for a photo op too, to show her ex she'd moved on. With the industry's biggest whore—*me*.

"What I'm into is my fiancée, whom I am tragically in love with." I gave her a lazy grin. "So I'm afraid you're both out of luck and options, but I'm happy to help you open an account on App-date if you need someone to tease McFadden with."

While Claire's face went from indulgent to furious and she stomped away from me, something depressing occurred to me. I wasn't lying. I was one hundred percent in love with my Dylan. I needed her like air.

She was it. She was everything. The beginning, the end, the best part of my day. Losing her was my worst fear. She added dimension to my otherwise flat life. With her, I could tackle anything. Without her, nothing was worth doing.

And I loved her. Loved her, loved her, loved her.

I needed to tell her that.

Now.

No, not now. Now would be premature and awkward. I couldn't tell her over the phone—she'd probably think I was drunk. I needed to tell her as soon as I got home tomorrow. And if she didn't say it back…well, I had an entire lifetime to make her fall in love with me. I was a stubborn bastard too.

This time, it was three in the morning by the time I checked my phone.

> Dylan: Are you still going to be able to make it tomorrow?
> Dylan: Totally okay if not. I've still got time to ask Row to come with Cal and babysit Grav. Serafina is staying in the UK with the nanny.

Like hell he would. First of all, she was downplaying how much my being there meant to her, and I knew it. Second, I'd rather feast on my own bowels than look like a bad boyfriend in front of Row.

> Rhyland: I'll be there.
> Dylan: You really don't have to.
> Rhyland: Why are you still up?
> Dylan: I could ask you the same thing…

I peered down at the semi behind my jeans. *Touché*. The mere thought of her staying up so she could talk to me gave me a chub.

> Dylan: I know this weekend is super important to you.
> Rhyland: No. You're super important to me.

She was typing, deleting. Typing, deleting.

> Dylan: You're just saying that bc you want your dick wet before I go to the gig.

I groaned. Dylan still struggled with words of affirmation when they weren't directed at her kid. But I wasn't gonna take the L. I'd wear her out. I'd make her as obsessed with me as I was with her.

> Rhyland: And? Is it working?
> Dylan: Yes.

Rhyland: Good night. See you tomorrow, Cosmos.
Dylan: See you tomorrow <3

CHAPTER FORTY-FIVE
DYLAN

> Dylan: Hey! Are you on your way?
> Dylan: I tried to call but it threw me to voicemail.

I stared at the unanswered messages, willing myself not to freak out. Cal and Gravity were sitting at the dining table making friendship bracelets and drinking hot cocoa, even though it was a thousand degrees outside.

We had to leave in about three hours. Every instinct in my body told me to brace myself for the worst. That he was going to disappoint me, break my heart, never show up. After all, that was what happened last time Tucker went on a fishing boat. He never returned home. Decided he was better off without me.

Rhyland is not Tucker. Snap out of it, bitch.

This was just residual trauma from the other times I hadn't gotten to see Taylor, that's all.

Standing up from the couch, I made my way on wobbly legs to Cal and Gravity, who were chatting animatedly.

"…and then Uncle Rhyrand looked at his clock belt…" Gravity said animatedly.

"Clock belt?" Cal lifted her head from the colorful beads. She'd been relentlessly looking for the *Y* so she could spell my name.

"Yes. When you have a clock on your hand." Gravity pinched her wrist, frowning seriously.

Cal threw her head back and laughed. I smiled too.

"And then he said he will be here to help us make bracelets, and he didn't, so now he needs to buy me all the candy and all the toys and all the dinosaurs."

Cal threw me an apologetic look. "I'm sure he has a good reason."

"Yeah, I know." I coughed around a lump in my throat. That good reason better be a stab wound or alien abduction, though. Anything else would not be sufficient.

"I'm *fine*," I insisted.

I wasn't fine.

I was far from fine.

Cal stood up and rushed over to hug me. My lips trembled as my arms encircled her body.

"Hey," she whispered into the shell of my ear, running her fingers through my hair, squeezing me harder. "Go take a shower and get dressed. He'll be here."

"How do you know?" I moaned into her rich chestnut hair. The tips were turquoise blue.

"Because he is crazy about you," she reassured me. "And because I'll rip off one of his arms and beat him with it if he breaks your heart," she added in her whimsical, sunshine voice.

I snorted.

She disconnected from me, patting my ass. "Now go put something slutty and wonderful on, and let's get this show on the road. Taylor Swift, baby!"

After I'd had a shower, washed and dried my hair, and put on a red satin gown, I painted my lips burgundy, going for the man-killer look, even though it was totally the wrong vibe for the show. On my way out of my bathroom, I picked up my phone from my nightstand and checked it.

Nothing.

With a grunt, I perched my ass on the edge of the bed and logged in to my Instagram to see if he'd updated his stories. He hadn't. Then I figured I'd check his tagged section, see what he'd been up to.

My heart flipped painfully in my chest.

No.

No, no, no, no, no.

But there it was. In full color, and through a blue checkmarked account of the one and only Claire Larsen: sex symbol, Hollywood starlet, and fashion icon. She'd captioned the picture of them, *Gonna tell our kids we are Bonnie and Clyde.* 😉

The picture—of her gliding her finger along his chest while he stared down at her through his green, mysterious eyes—had 3.2 *million* likes, and it was only posted yesterday.

Pinkywinky commented: omfg your children are going to be gorggggg.

Annika9237 commented: excuse me? Is this a long-lost Hemsworth brother? either way I AM SAT.

Jaystern commented: Why am I so invested in this??? What's his name? We need a ship name.

I ran to the bathroom and vomited straight into the toilet bowl, clutching it with my trembling fingers. Cal heard me and ran inside.

"What happened?" She was panting. "Oh God, food poisoning?"

Rather than answering her, I tossed my phone across the marble floor. She picked it up, frowning at the picture.

"There could very well be a good explanation for this." She measured her words, which were empty of weight or conviction.

"Could there now?" I huffed.

Silence. She and I both knew the truth. Rhyland had a history of being a womanizer. And the fact of the matter was we were supposed to leave in a few hours, and he still wasn't here.

Cal's red-striped Superstar sneakers padded across the bedroom and into the bathroom. She put a comforting hand on the edge of my spine. It was that simple gesture that made me completely break. I plastered my forehead to the cool marble and heaved out as tears streamed down my cheeks freely. I wasn't a crier, and I made it a point not to cry over a boy. Ever.

But Rhy wasn't a boy—he was a man.

A man who'd shattered my heart.

The ache I felt seized every nerve ending in my body. It hurt so much I couldn't breathe. I was fighting for air, gasping at the sensation. The jealousy, the anger, the disappointment, the sadness—it all slammed into me at the same time like a freight train. Yet tossed inside this cyclone of negative emotion, I still couldn't find it in myself to regret every kiss, every hug, every moment I writhed beneath him.

Because Taylor was right.

The high really was worth the pain.

CHAPTER FORTY-SIX
RHYLAND

I woke up to the fucking apocalypse.

Thunder cracked outside my window. It sounded like a leather leash whipping at skin.

My phone alarm hadn't buzzed yet. I tapped my screen, checking the time. 5:15 a.m.

Rubbing my eyes, I peered through the window. On top of it raining like a motherfucker, patio furniture was swirling in the air, curling upward to the sky before crashing onto the ground. I heard shouting and screams, muffled by the shrieking winds, and squinted to focus on the figures of Bruce and Jolene, all bundled up and weighted down by big jackets, herding their cattle into the stables.

I bolted out of the bed as if my ass were on fire, not bothering to put on a shirt, and skidded across the hallway. The front door splintered off its hinges as I ripped it open and ran barefoot to Bruce. He was locking up the stables and pushing heavy furniture against the door, his wife nowhere in sight now.

"Coltridge, son, good to have you here. Come help me push this bench against the door." He seemed completely unbothered by what was happening, which begged the fucking question: Was I in business with a goddamn psychopath?

I grabbed the large wooden bench in one hand and angled it against the door handle, my eyes unwavering from Bruce. "Is this doomsday?" I demanded. "Because if so, I need to get home even faster to be with Dylan."

"I'm afraid ain't no one flying out anywhere in this weather." He squinted up at the gray sky, the downy cotton balls he called hair dancing in the wind.

"What?" I felt the life draining from my fucking body.

"I said, ain't no one flying out anywhere in thi—"

"I heard you the first time." I grabbed him by the collar of his puffy jacket, fisting my fingers around the cloth and tugging him to me so my nose crushed his. I was beyond furious. I was somewhere between feral and murderous. "How long is this shit going to last?"

"May I suggest, son, that you release me before your whole darn future goes down my overflowin' drain?" He squinted.

I released him so suddenly he stumbled backward, his ass landing in a pool of mud. Turning around, I stalked back inside. I needed to check the weather report. Then I needed to get a car and drive out of the eye of this tornado to the nearest operating airport. Ideally, a private one with a plane I could charter.

Bruce got up to his feet with a loud grunt, chasing behind me. "It's going to be like this till five, I'm afraid, but it'll clear out soon. It was completely spontaneous."

"So is your upcoming death." I made my way to my room—the same one I'd occupied with Dylan and Gravity five weeks ago.

Dylan.

She was never going to forgive me for letting her down if I didn't make it to my babysitting gig. Cal was already on a plane alone, en route to New York, and they had no backup plan. Just me.

I flipped my suitcase open on the bed, shoveling my clothes into it haphazardly.

"What do you think you're doing?" Bruce got in my way, trying to stop me. I pushed him so hard he slammed against the closet.

"What does it look like? I'm packing."

"The airports are closed."

"I'm driving out to Irvine."

"It's a two-hour drive." He snorted. "You can't drive in this weather."

"Wanna fucking bet?"

"I'll rephrase. No one in this retreat is going to give you their vehicle to drive yourself into sure death. Just call your lil miss. She'll understand."

"She won't." I slammed my suitcase shut. For the first time in my life, I felt powerless. I turned to look at him, heaving. "She won't understand, because she has a concert she needs to get to. It's the first fucking thing she's done for herself in four years, since her daughter was born, and maybe it seems trivial to you or silly, but it means the world to her. And to *me*. I'm getting there in time no matter what. You understand?"

His eyes were as big as saucers as he raised his palms up in surrender. I shook my head, contemplating calling her and telling her about this mini tornado sweeping its way through rural Dallas, but then I decided against it. I wasn't going to make excuses. I was going to show up and not bother her with this bullshit, like I'd promised.

I pulled my phone out and called Tate, putting him on speaker. Bruce watched me intently the whole time, the flash of anger and betrayal passing over his face when Tate's low baritone filled the room like black smoke.

"What is it?"

Yeah, he wasn't winning any congeniality awards.

"Are you in the States?" I demanded.

"Christ, no. I'm in New York. What would I do inside America?"

Tate Blackthorn was an obnoxious snob. But he was an obnoxious snob with a 747–8 VIP. His private airplane included a fourteen-seat boarding room, two Jacuzzis, and full-size bedrooms.

"I need to borrow your jet," I gritted out, bracing myself for all the shit he was going to give me. A favor from Tate always came with a hefty price tag. The exterior was hedge-fund baby, but the interior was Napoli-style Camorra.

"Where are you?" he demanded.

"Dallas."

"Isn't there a tornado there right now?"

"*Mini* tornado," I corrected. "And I promised Dylan I'd be home before five."

"Is this the part where I'm supposed to care about your fake relationship with your fake fiancée?" he drawled.

Shit, shit, shit.

Bruce heard him and immediately perked up, his shoulders squaring, expression honing into fury. "Tatum," Bruce boomed.

There was a beat of silence from the other end of the line before Tate sighed. "I forgot it was hick o'clock CT."

Bruce ignored the quip. "What did you say about Miss Casablancas being Coltridge's fake fiancée?"

Tate didn't miss a beat. "I did not say that."

"Yes, you did."

"Prove it."

"You know I can't."

"Oh, well then."

Tate was a ten-out-of-ten gaslighter. Unfortunately, Bruce had already heard him the first time.

Actually, I wasn't even that bothered. Fuck the deal, and fuck Bruce Marshall. I'd bent over backward for him. If this was what made him pull out of the contract, then he really was a piece of shit.

"Tate." I snapped him back to attention. "I need that jet."

"I'm not flying my precious four-hundred-million-dollar private plane to tornado-stricken Dallas just because you found a moderately good pussy to sink your dick into." Tate spoke slowly, like you would to a stubborn child.

"Irvine is out of the danger zone. I can drive there and have the plane wait for me."

"What's in it for me?"

"I'll owe you one."

"You already owe me six," Tate ricocheted back. "I'm keeping your secrets, drafting your contracts, firing assholes who mistreat your precious Dylan. Next, you'll ask me to wear a pencil skirt and bend over your executive desk."

Taking a deep breath, I closed my eyes and slammed my teeth together. "What do you want?" He knew he had me against the wall. Knew I was going to give him whatever the hell he wanted. Now all I could do was hear what I was about to lose.

"I want twenty-five percent of your shares in App-date."

Motherfucker.

My whole body was shaking, and I was sweating, cursing the very day I met this asshole. He'd wanted his hands on this app since the night at Casablancas when he tried to outbid Bruce. Tate was simply biding his time. And as always, he'd succeeded.

Bruce groaned. "Don't do it, son."

I turned to him. "Then *you* lend me your plane."

"I would." Bruce gave me a panicked look. "But it's in Dallas. It can't fly out of there."

Dammit. He was right.

"Fifteen percent," I bargained into the phone.

"Twenty-eight," Tate countered, a hint of cheerfulness slicing through his unbearably smooth tone. "Every single time you try to negotiate, I'll up the ante."

"Are you kidding me right now?" I spat out.

"No," Tate said. "I don't waste my precious humor on people I don't want to fuck."

"Do you waste your humor on people you do want to fuck?" I asked doubtfully.

"Good point. I never developed one. Might attract unwarranted affection," Tate muttered. "That's a risk I can't take. So do we have a deal?"

"We're keeping it at twenty-five, and you are giving me the option to purchase it back for the current rate."

"0.2 percent rate, and you've got yourself a deal."

Considering there were triple-digit millions on the line, 0.2 percent was atrocious, but I knew I couldn't get anything more from him. "Fine. I'll text you the name of the airport."

"Text it to Gia." Gia was his PA. "I'm entirely disinterested in doing more admin than you've already assigned me." He hung up.

That left me with one thing to sort out: a car to take me to Irvine.

I glanced out the window. It was pouring harder than before, the wind shrieking and whining, pounding on the windows like a soul-sucking ghost. I shook my head. What the hell was wrong with this state? It was as hot as sweaty balls yesterday.

"Did you just..." Bruce pointed at my phone, then at me, tilting his head sideways in confusion.

"Did I just what?" I barked impatiently, searching through car rentals online on my phone. Everything was closed.

"Hand over twenty-five percent of your shares to that devil?"

I looked up from my phone, dead-ass serious. "I need to get to New York before that concert starts."

"Fine. Take my car." He pushed his hand into his front pocket, rummaging for his keys and tossing them into my hands.

I caught them midair. It was a Ram. Less likely to blow in the wind. Silver linings and all.

"But I have to warn you, Coltridge. There's a good chance you won't make it to the airport in one piece."

"That's a chance I'm willing to take."

CHAPTER FORTY-SEVEN
RHYLAND

I floored it all the way from Bruce Marshall's ranch to Irvine, relying on road signs since my internet was down, and so was my phone network. The tornado—mini or not, that motherfucker was not friendly—caught the Ram a few times, throwing me off the road twice and making me skid into the opposite lane once. Luckily, I was the only insane bastard on the road and therefore didn't collide with anyone.

Since I wanted to arrive in New York in good enough shape to take care of a toddler, I had to pace myself and drive at a reasonable speed to avoid veering off to the next planet. That added forty minutes onto my journey to the private airport. Once I got there, I found out my phone network was still down in the majority of the Dallas-Fort Worth area due to the weather.

I cursed in seven languages, even though I was only fluent in one, and asked a random airport worker for his phone to call Dylan. Her phone went straight to voicemail. I checked the time. She was due to leave for the concert in two hours. I was failing her.

But I still wanted to get there as soon as possible so I could grovel into the next lifetime.

"Mind if I text my girlfriend?" I held the guy's phone in a death grip. By the look on his face, he minded very fucking much.

"Actually..." He was rubbing the back of his head, thinking of a plausible excuse, when I saw Tate's onyx-black private jet rolling across the tarmac.

I chucked his phone back into his hands, already walking in that direction. "Never mind. Keep your iPhone 13, cheapo."

"Hey!" he called after me. "It's called vintage, okay?"

I practically ran across the tarmac like a madman. I forgot my suitcase in the Ram I discarded in the parking area of the airport. I had a one-track mind, and it was to get there as fast as I could.

Leaping onto the plane, I took the steps two at a time, foaming at the mouth when I walked inside. There was a landline phone there, and I immediately tried to use it before realizing it wasn't working.

Two Blackthorn Company flight attendants and a pilot greeted me at the door.

"Good afternoon, Mr. Coltridge. It is a pleasure to have you—"

"Yeah, yeah, just floor it." I collapsed onto the couch, staring blankly at my phone and waiting for the signal to return. This was what it felt like to live in the Middle Ages, I assumed.

I keeled over with my elbows on my knees and gripped the back of my head.

I wasn't going to make it.

I was going to disappoint the only woman I'd ever wanted to impress.

All while trying my hardest not to.

The plane took off, and I spent the majority of the time pacing from wall to wall, waiting for my signal to return. According to one of the flight attendants who'd arrived here from New York, the signal should be restored in about forty minutes. I waited with bated breath. And when the signal finally returned, I immediately called Dylan.

She didn't answer. I called again. Nothing. I started sending her text messages.

> Rhyland: I'm sorry I missed the show. I can explain.

> Rhyland: There was a tornado.
>
> Rhyland: I drove inside it for two hours to get to a private airport.
>
> Rhyland: I sold Tate 25% of my company so he'd lend me his plane to get to you on time.
>
> Rhyland: I will never, ever, EVER disappoint you again.
>
> Rhyland: I love y

My phone died.

And I didn't have my charger, since I'd discarded my suitcase in the Ram.

With a howl of frustration, I hurled the phone at the wall. It shattered on the floor, splitting into all the small pieces that made it work.

Great fucking going, idiot.

Suddenly, I was claustrophobic.

I wanted out of here. To claw my way out of this flying airplane, to hurl myself into sure death, to run away from my own consciousness to avoid the consequences of what just happened here.

Losing the deal with Bruce Marshall would've been disastrous.

But losing Dylan was un-fucking-fathomable.

I couldn't allow it. Wouldn't. I would do anything I needed to regain her trust.

But trust was an abstract idea; it wasn't wealth, fashionable clothes, or an expensive vacation. Unlike materialistic things, it wasn't something you could accumulate once you'd lost it.

"Sir?" One of the flight attendants put a tentative hand on my shoulder.

I stared at her, unblinking. Her gawk shifted from my shattered phone back to me.

"Is…is there anything I can get you? A drink? Something to eat? A blanket?" *A fucking Valium?* I was sure the words were on the tip of her tongue.

"Your phone." My baritone was so low it sounded like it was emerging from the depths of hell.

"E-excuse me?"

I uncurled my fingers, opening my palm in her direction. I suddenly understood with sharp clarity why Tate was as ruthless as he was. When you wanted something—really wanted something—you stopped at nothing to get it. "Phone. Here. Now."

"I…" She stumbled back, her spine hitting the wall. Her eyes kept skirting from my broken phone to me.

"I'll get you fired if you don't," I warned evenly. "I've done it before. Ask your boss."

She flinched before withdrawing her phone from the pocket of her uniform, slowly placing it in my hand.

"Password?"

"Zero nine, zero six."

"Happy birthday."

"Ah…thanks." She blushed.

I started making some calls, ignoring her for the rest of the journey.

Dylan had to know I'd tried.

She had to.

CHAPTER FORTY-EIGHT
DYLAN

"Oh my gosh, girl, looking fierce!" Three girls shrieked when I squeezed my way toward my seat, an hour late and my sanity short.

Cal had gotten us VIP tickets a breath away from the stage, but I was relieved to see everyone was standing up, as I intended to do. I peered over my shoulder, thinking they were referring to someone else who hadn't spent the past couple hours weeping uncontrollably and trying to pick up the pieces of her broken heart.

"I'm talking to *you*." One of them covered her mouth, giggling. "Seriously, the dress? The makeup? Vibe unmatched. You look like a movie star."

A rush of angst decanted into my veins when I thought about the *real* movie star my so-called boyfriend had been cozying up to last night. My last relationship ended with Tucker running away with the town's nepo bimbo. It had hurt, but it hadn't burned. Claire Larsen, though? I couldn't compete with her.

"Th-thanks." I shoved a piece of tissue that was falling apart into my nostril, sniffling. I had panda eyes, and I'd missed the two support acts, but I'd showed up. No part of me had wanted to leave the house. Cal had insisted I go alone.

"It's your dream. You've always wanted to see her. No way are you letting a boy ruin this for you. Besides, I don't want Grav to see you so upset. It's going to be bad for her psyche."

It was the last reason that made me evacuate the apartment. I couldn't stomach the idea of my daughter seeing me ripping at the seams of my own existence over a man, like an injured animal picking at the stitches of a fresh wound. So I ran off, leaving Cal to babysit her. I couldn't think of anyone I trusted more than my best friend.

I studied the girls in front of me, forcing myself to engage in something that wasn't my own insecurities. They were all in their early to midtwenties, one blond, one redhead, and one with black hair. They were all stunning and wore cute denim and sequined crop tops, glitter adorning their temples and cheekbones. They kind of looked like cheerleaders.

"No, seriously, your whole vibe is vibing." The redhead circled my face with her finger.

"Thanks. I'm Dylan." I stuck out a hand.

"I'm Sadie." The redhead grabbed it and tugged me into a hug.

"I'm Alix." The blond pointed at herself.

"And I'm Gia." The last girl hugged me too. She had an English accent and the impeccable posture of an athlete. She seemed vaguely familiar, but I couldn't pinpoint where from.

I unzipped my Ziploc bag, handing Gia a friendship bracelet with the words "Dylan Thomas" on it. "Nice touch, amiright?" I winked, gesturing toward myself.

"The best."

They gave me bracelets too.

I hurt my back moshing to Taylor Swift.

John Mayonnaise.

I am the exception.

Yes, I thought to myself. *I've found my people.*

Even though it wasn't the same without Cal, I forced myself into easy conversation with the three friends—all college friends who came together once each summer to do something fun for the weekend, this year a TS concert—and ignored the constant pinging of my phone in my pocket, signaling Rhyland's text messages from an unknown number begging to be heard.

I was going to hear him eventually, but not soon, and definitely not today. He'd publicly humiliated me by openly flirting with Claire Larsen—what was he thinking, doing that in front of Bruce Marshall?—and he clearly missed his scheduled flight, which means something kept him busy over there.

It was a reminder that men could not be trusted. Even if they gave you butterflies, feathery kisses, and the best orgasms of your lifetime.

For the next three hours, I drowned in the show, screaming the lyrics to "Look What You Made Me Do" and weeping to "cardigan."

"Is your phone blowing up too?" Gia checked her phone for the millionth time. She, like me, wasn't entirely focused on the show. She groaned at her screen, shaking her head, one thumb flying over the screen as she typed out a text.

"Everything okay?" Alix put a hand on her shoulder.

"Yeah. Just Tate being...Tate."

"Ugh." Sadie made a face. "That's the worst state for him to be in."

"I'm quite sure the worst state for him to be in is the one *I'm* physically in. Unfortunately, we're both currently in New York. He lent his friend a private jet, because there's a mini tornado in Texas and loads of flights got canceled. The friend is apparently trashing it because he's going through some kind of mental breakdown?" Gia's delicate eyebrows pulled together. "How is that my fault?"

A mini tornado?

Flights canceled?

My blood froze in my veins.

"Your boss is Tate Blackthorn?" I shifted my full attention from Taylor onstage to Gia.

"Hey, don't hold that against me." She scrunched her nose. "The benefits are great, and every time I try to quit, he raises my salary. Do you know him?"

"He's friends with my boyf—" No. Rhyland wasn't my boyfriend. We'd never discussed our official titles. "My neighbor."

"That pause right there was giving," Alix laughed.

"And…" I grimaced, feeling guilty for a reason beyond my grasp. "Did you say mini tornado? In Texas?"

"Yeah, it's all over the news," Alix said. "No casualties or people injured, thank God, but it's looking awful. I've been checking the news hourly. Lots of damage to property."

Fear gripped every bone in my body.

Was Rhyland okay? Was he safe? I didn't even care about the Claire Larsen thing. Even if he screwed her seven ways from Sunday, I still wanted him to be safe. To be *happy*. Jesus, what was wrong with me? I should be furious, not worried.

"I think he's the one trashing your boss's jet," I heard myself say. "Do you know if it's out of the danger zone?"

"It is. It should land any minute now. Would you be so kind as to tell your neighbor to stop?" Gia slanted her head, giving me a perplexed look. "He's acting mental, and Tate's driving me bonkers."

"Yes, yes." I rummaged around in my purse for my phone. I was still upset with Rhyland, but I also recognized he probably *was* coming back to see me, and he *did* feel bad about what happened—whether it was standing me up for the babysitting gig, cheating, neither, or both—and that he was now razing someone else's private property because of those feelings.

When I pulled out my phone, I had fifty unread messages from the number he'd texted me on and about a hundred missed calls. It was too noisy to call him. I clicked on the message block, watching as the text tumbled down when I reached the last message. It was sent twenty minutes ago.

Driving toward the stadium. See you there.

He'd already landed. Safe and sound. Relief washed over me.

I looked up from my phone. "He's left the airplane."

"In one piece?" Gia winced.

"That's to be determined."

I was about to tuck my phone back into my purse, feeling significantly lighter now that I knew he was alive and well, when a message from Cal popped through.

And that was when I realized it was not her first or even her second text message.

She'd been calling too. It was just lost in the shuffle of Rhyland's chaotic rumbling.

> Cal: He took her.
> Cal: I'm so sorry. I am SO SO SORRY.
> Cal: I couldn't stop him. I tried. I called the police.
> Cal: I called Row. Your mom. Everyone. I'm so sorry, Dyl.

CHAPTER FORTY-NINE
RHYLAND

I landed back on New York soil, with Tate greeting me on the tarmac. He was surrounded by two bodyguards, a standby PA who wasn't the girl he was obsessed with, and three tan men in sharp Italian suits who reeked of hostility. The general vibe was that someone was going to get murdered. Preferably me.

Tate turned to one of the men, saying something in Latin. The man responded with a brief shake of his head. From the way their heads eyed my movement, I knew they were talking about me.

"I heard you made a scene and confiscated my employee's phone," Tate drawled.

I halted a few feet away from him.

"Didn't peg you for a gossip." I reached out to smooth the collar of his dress shirt, just to piss him off.

He snapped my hand away, ripping his shades from his face. "Don't fuck with me, Coltridge."

"Don't threaten me, Blackthorn," I retorted. "I broke my own phone and a goddamn vase—which, by the way, who the hell keeps a vase on a *plane*?" Every minute I wasn't in a taxi on my way to Cosmos was a minute wasted. "And yes, I asked your employee for her phone to reach Dylan. Don't make it what it's not. Now, tell me why you're here, because it can't be because you've missed me, and I have a woman to go grovel to."

Tate snapped his fingers, and his Gia replacement—an

unremarkable blond woman who looked like an extra in a porno—unzipped a leather folder bag and retrieved a large stack of papers. She gingerly handed it over to me, along with a pen that probably cost more than her entire goddamn outfit.

The asshole had drafted and printed out an entire contract to reflect the twenty-five percent ownership deal in a couple hours. Who did something like that?

"I'm in a hurry." I cut my gaze to Tate, ignoring the outstretched contract and pen. I sidestepped him. "Email this to me, and I'll get my lawyer—"

Tate stepped forward, blocking my path toward the waiting cab. "That makes both of us. I have business to conduct in the Dominican Republic and will be out of the state for the next two weeks. Sign the papers, Coltridge."

A lick of danger pebbled my skin when our gazes clashed, and though I was unperturbed, I knew with unyielding clarity that Tate Blackthorn could very well kill me if I didn't sign the contract.

"Anastasia." He motioned the woman with his finger.

"It's Rebecca." The blond woman shifted beside him.

He waved a dismissive hand. "Show our guests into the plane, and run an inventory of everything that's been damaged."

"Yes, sir."

She handed him the contract and the pen before ushering his companions onto the plane, conversing with them in perfect Italian.

"You know, Rhyland." Tate buttoned his suit slowly, eyes never wavering from mine. "You should always judge a man by the quality of his enemies."

"I don't wish to make you an enemy," I said calmly. His macho bullshit didn't impress me. I just wanted to get this show on the road and be on my way to Dylan.

"Oh, you won't. You're not worthy of the title." Tate handed me the contract and the pen. "Sign the papers, and you can go get the girl. No papers, no girl."

His flight attendant's phone started ringing in my pocket. I glanced at it. It was Dylan's number.

I wasn't going to have this conversation in front of this bastard.

"I'm not going to sign a contract before I read it." Every muscle in my body burned to flee and be with her. "And I need to get to her."

"Time is a currency you presently do not possess." He uncapped the blue pen, handing it to me. "Oh, I forgot to mention. I sent your cab back home. The taxi behind us? It's my driver. Your only way to Dylan—or anyone else you care about, for that matter—is signing the contract."

Fury splattered inside me like a detonated body. The level of hatred I felt for this man scared me. Yet I knew he'd somehow avoid the consequences of his actions. He always did. He'd managed to worm his way into Ambrose's closest circle after fucking him over in business. Tate had always had this talent for keeping the people he'd hurt around.

I grabbed the pen and scribbled on the dotted line with a savage growl.

"Now your initials on every page," Tate lamented with boredom. "On the bottom right corner, kindly."

"Your driver better floor it to the stadium," I rustled behind clenched teeth, hating that I had to ask him for more favors.

"Iven is quite good at keeping me punctual," Tate said charitably. "Oh, and my assistant will send you the bill in the mail."

The motherfucker.

"I hate you." I slammed the signed contract into his chest.

"I'm flattered." A ghost of a smirk hovered over his face, never truly making an appearance.

With that, he brushed past me onto his private jet.

Dylan: Call Cal.

I stared at the message in the back seat of Tate's seashell crème Bentley. She hadn't picked up when I'd tried to call her back.

Why the fuck?

It was purely by chance that I remembered Row's wife's number. It happened to be the same as Row's, with the last digit changed from three to seven. Cal picked up on the first call, sounding out of breath.

"Yes? Who is it?" She sounded hysterical, even more so than her usual jumbled self.

"Rhyland. Dyl asked me to call you. What's up?" I was on my way to the stadium to try to catch Cosmos, but the rusty knot of dread twisting in my gut told me she wasn't there anymore.

"Tucker kidnapped Gravity."

"*What?*"

The word boomed so loudly it filled the car, the neighborhood, the fucking universe. Tate's private driver flinched, the car veering sharply to the side before righting itself back on the road.

I sank my fingers into my thigh to stop myself from screaming, bile hitting the back of my throat. That visceral reaction was partly due to the fact that I knew Dylan was now in bad shape and partly, I realized to my horror, because I'd grown to care deeply about the little stinker.

"What do you mean, kidnapped?" I rumbled.

"He, he, he, he…" Cal stuttered, hyperventilating, her breaths shallow and fast and out of rhythm, wheezing each time she tried to suck in oxygen. "He just showed up. I-I-I thought it was you. I thought you came back and knew you had a key."

The background noise was unmistakably a busy Manhattan street. People conversing, laughing, drinking, and cars honking. She was walking around aimlessly. *Not* a good sign.

"He barged in. I tried to fight him. I tried to push him. I swear, Rhyland, I tried everything. I nicked his cheek, but it only made him angrier. He rattled off about no one being willing to help him.

About Dylan being a frigid bitch and Row always looking down on him, even when they were together. Just…nonsense. Insane stuff. And then he took her. And when I tried to stop him, he…"

Silence.

All my blood rushed to my head, making me dizzy.

"He what?" I demanded.

Silence.

"*He what?*" I barked louder.

"I think he broke my arm," Cal finished, brittle.

I closed my eyes. "Do you know where he went?"

"No."

"Did you call the police?"

"Yes. And Row too. Dylan knows. She's on her way back. I'm just walking aimlessly, looking for him… He couldn't have gone far, could he?"

"You *need* to get medical attention."

"No. I won't. I can't." Her voice was high-pitched, emotions flooding it again. She burst into a sob. "This all happened because of me. I need to fix this. Oh my God, poor Grav. What is he doing to her? And Dylan. She must be hysterical."

Dylan, Dylan, Dylan.

What was she thinking right now?

What was she going through?

How the hell did I fix this?

And then I knew. All of a sudden, I remembered.

Because I was a possessive piece of shit.

Because I craved control.

Because I was naturally suspicious and cunning and—well, yes, a bit of a bad guy, really.

I did something I shouldn't have. But it just might pay off.

"Cal?"

"Yes?"

"Go to the hospital. I got it."

CHAPTER FIFTY
RHYLAND

As soon as I made it to the apartment building, I took the elevator up to my penthouse. There were three police cars parked in front of it, and Row texted me that an Amber Alert had gone out with the car model and license plate of the vehicle Tucker rented a few hours before. Goddamn amateur stopped at Budget *before* breaking Cal's arm and kidnapping his own kid. He really was committed to being a grade-A loser.

When I got home, I bolted to my bedroom, unhooking my iPad from its charger and bringing it to life. A few weeks ago, when Tucker began visiting Gravity regularly and before things detonated between him and Dylan, I'd inserted a tracking device in Mr. Mushroom. I figured if Grav was that attached to the little chub, she was going to carry it everywhere with her. The device had an advanced GPS map that was wired to satellite software, so not only could I see the location, I could even see the street.

I stared at the iPad as I clicked onto the app, watching it gathering information about the location of the stuffie and praying to high heavens it wasn't going to show up in this building.

Please, baby. Tell me you took it with you when Tucker snatched you from your bed.

The map appeared on the screen, the red dot indicating the stuffie's location blinking as it moved slowly past streets.

My shoulders slumped with relief. She'd taken it.

Attagirl.

The location showed somewhere in Brooklyn. The address pointed to a warehouse. I grabbed the iPad and took the stairs down to Dylan's apartment. The door was open, the place swarming with policemen and detectives. Dylan sat on her couch, crying into her hands. Three women I didn't know were standing next to her.

Actually, one of them I *did* know.

It was Tate's PA. The one he was obsessed with.

But that was the last thing on my fucking mind right now.

"I know where she is," I announced.

All eyes spun to me. I held up the iPad in my hand.

"Dylan, baby, please don't kill me, but when Tucker started seeing Grav regularly, I put a tracking device in Mr. Mushroom. Behind the zipper that conceals the batteries." Because of course, Mr. Mushroom vibrated.

"I don't fucking care!" Dylan said impatiently. "Just tell us where she is."

I handed the iPad over to one of the police officers. She studied it along with her colleague, then nodded briskly. She pressed the police radio to her lips and gave reinforcement the address and directions.

"Suspect may be armed and dangerous. Assaulted the young woman babysitting the child when he took her."

Speaking of assaults, I was goddamn sure that as soon as Row touched ground in New York, he was going to kill Tucker six times over. The first time to make a point and the other five for what he did to Cal.

"I'm going there," I announced to no one in particular.

"I'm coming," Dylan said.

"I'd strongly advice against it," the policewoman said.

"We strongly don't give a fuck," I answered in the same serious tone.

Dylan trailed behind me outside. We left her new friends in the apartment. The elevator ride down was silent, and so was the first half of the drive to the warehouse in Brooklyn. Luckily, there was barely any traffic.

Finally, Dylan spoke, her eyes still on her phone. "Poor Row is stuck on a plane. He can't wait to get to Cal."

"I'm sure."

Silence.

"Do you think Tucker did something to my daughter?"

A wave of fresh fury drowned out my swirling thoughts, and my fingers tightened over the wheel. "No," I answered, unsure if I was giving her the truth or my own wishful thinking. "He's a lowlife who is incapable of making one decent decision, but he loves himself too much to get into *that* much trouble."

"He needs to be behind bars after this," Dylan said shakily.

"He will be," I reassured her.

"How do you know?"

"Because it would be his better option. The alternative is being killed by me."

We got there in record time. It was a warehouse on the outskirts of Brooklyn, a two-story redbrick square, with arched black doors. Night had fallen over the city, and the wide, pebbled road was empty of cars. It appeared to be abandoned, and the mere thought of Gravity—so tiny, so precious, so innocent—somewhere so nefarious made my skin crawl.

There were also no police cars anywhere in sight. Though to be fair, I'd gotten here faster than expected on account of not following traffic laws.

I pushed the driver's door open and rounded the car, opening Dylan's door. "You're going to walk in behind me," I instructed, rolling up my sleeves and making my way in through the arched, rusty door. It felt like today had stretched into an entire century, and I was ready for it to end with Gravity safe and sound, Dylan's forgiveness, and Tucker twelve feet under.

Dylan nodded briefly. This was one of the first times she hadn't sassed back.

I shoved the door open with my shoulder. It was heavy but unlocked. Abandoned, just like I'd thought.

The minute I stepped inside, the stench of cigarettes, alcohol, piss, and decayed human flesh filled my nostrils. The scent was unbearable. I tugged my shirt over my nose, grabbed Dylan's hand from behind, and proceeded into the dimly lit open space.

Inside, there were exposed brick walls, sleeping bags scattered on the dirty floor, and needles on the ground. Shadowed silhouettes of people danced across the windows and the walls, created by the pale, filtered light borrowed from streetlamps outside. Dylan clenched my arm, fingers digging into my wrist, as we both moved slowly, peering into people's faces to try to find Tucker and Gravity. It felt like swimming against a stream.

This was no place to take a child. Little stinker was in great danger. Dylan understood it just as well. Her body rocked and trembled next to mine as she bit down on her sobs.

I studied faces through squinted eyes, searching for Tucker and Gravity. Some people cursed at the invasion of their privacy. Others were asleep, half-dead, or too far gone to care. And then, in the far corner of the hayloft, nestled under a ladder to shield them from view, was a very small, weepy girl clinging onto her pink Mr. Mushroom and Tuckwad.

The relief I felt was immediate. She was here. And she was okay.

I tugged on Dylan's arm and pointed at them, pressing my finger to my lips to signal for her to stay quiet. Dylan gasped, her eyes veiled behind a curtain of unshed tears.

Tucker was shushing and berating Gravity. "You have to be quiet," he whisper-shouted, pressing his phone to his ear as he tried to call someone. "I can't fucking think straight."

Gravity flinched.

And there went the remainder of my goddamn self-control.

I pounced on Tucker like a panther, separating him from Gravity and pinning him to the ground with my thighs. His head crashed against the sodden concrete, his pupils dilating in the dark. Any measly self-control I still had left deserted me completely at the sight of his face.

My fists began to pound him without rhyme or rhythm, raining down on his jaw, his neck, his forehead, his cheeks, and his temples like a vicious storm. Blood splattered across the walls, on the ground, on my face, and still, I couldn't stop. The sound of bones breaking and blood sloshing filled my ears. I was too far gone to hear the voices begging me to stop. Gravity's cries. The sound of sirens and police officers and shrieks of horror. My sole focus was him. Tucker. The shitty dad who'd triggered me into facing my own reality.

That you could be an abusive parent without even being present in your child's life.

That, in fact, your very absence was the cruelest form of punishment.

Tucker may not be my father, but he represented everything I hated about humans who did not step up to their responsibilities.

Tucker's blood burned my eyes and itched my face by the time two burly policemen managed to peel me away from him. He'd been unresponsive for a while by then, so I was entirely unsure whether he was dead or alive. Frankly, I didn't care. I did feel a little sorry that Gravity had to witness it, though.

Reality *drip-drip-dripped* its way back into my conscience, and I felt guiltier.

I was held by two uniformed men, escorted outside the warehouse. Dylan was holding Gravity tightly to her chest, following them briskly. Her red dress—and Grav's pj's with the little lemons—were both stained with Tucker's blood.

"Please don't arrest him!" Dylan begged, and I realized she was referring to me. The woman never failed to amaze me. "He didn't do anything."

Okay, that was a blatant lie, but I certainly appreciated the notion.

"It's okay, Cosmos." I smirked. "I've always wanted to be handcuffed." I winked, trying to make light of it.

"My ex tried to kidnap my baby!" Dylan screeched, ignoring me. "Call your station or whatever!" She was running after them.

They burst open the door of the warehouse, and we all poured into the humid summer night. Red and blue swirls of police lights danced across the buildings and the pavement.

"Ma'am, no one is getting detained or arrested. We simply wanted to remove Mr. Coltridge from the situation before he further harmed himself and his future," one of the officers clipped out dryly.

They stopped in front of my McLaren, eyeing it appreciatively.

Dylan skidded to a halt next to us, burying Gravity's face in her neck and holding her daughter's head tightly. "Is he dead?" Dylan blurted out.

"Unfortunately, no," one of the police officers said, almost apologetically. It was easy to see everyone shared our revulsion for the man. "They're handcuffing him right now, and he'll be transferred to a hospital. He'll be supervised while he gets treated for his wounds, then moved into county jail. I suggest you lawyer up and find someone really good, because New York prisons are overflowing, and you want this man out of your life."

Dylan nodded. "I'm going to see to it tonight."

"You do that. Do you have anyone giving you a ride back home, or do you need one?"

"I'll take her home," I said.

As soon as they were out of our hair, I snatched Gravity out of Dylan's arms and crushed her into a hug. I needed to feel the sensation of the little stinker's heart beating against mine to calm myself down before I got behind the wheel. I couldn't explain it. It felt like she'd somehow become an extension of me and that any harm that met her was inflicted directly on me.

"Are you okay, little stinker?" I choked out.

Her small head bobbed against my shoulder. Endorphins

flooded my bloodstream. They were both fine. Whatever happened, they were safe.

"Good, baby. Were you scared?"

"Naw," Gravity mewed with false bravado. "I was brave. Tiger-bikers don't get scared. *Rawr*."

I loosened my grip on her, careful not to hurt her with the might of my love for her.

There was no point denying it now. I hadn't only fallen in love with Dylan Casablancas—I'd also fallen in love with her daughter, with her life, with her *universe*. I wanted Dylan to let me in, to make me a part of her world. To share with me the magnificence that was her cosmos.

"Of course you were." I kissed her cheek. "I had no doubt, buddy."

Gravity pulled back to look at me, her little arms still wrapped around my neck. "Uncle Rhyrand?"

Please call me daddy. I always thought I'd ask her mom to do that, but now I realized I wanted this from Gravity. To take over the space Tucker had left up for grabs.

"Yes, baby?"

"Mr. Mushroom is dead." Her lower lip curled, and those big, dark blue eyes shone with tears.

I thumbed the hair away from her face. It was matted by the drying blood of her good-for-nothing sperm donor.

"I had to leave him behind."

"I'm sorry. Did I ruin it for you?" It was only now, when my hand was in front of my face caressing her, that I realized my knuckles were busted and bloodied, my fingers swollen.

"It's okay." She caressed me back, her soft, plump hand running over my face. My heart flared in my chest. "You did it to save me, so I forgive you."

I tucked Gravity inside her seat in my car, fastening her buckle extra-tight.

On the way back home, I threaded my fingers through Dylan's, and she let me. I didn't know if it was because of the adrenaline, the way the night had unfolded, or because she forgave me.

"Did you make it to the song 'Wildest Dreams?'" I asked, bringing her perfect delicate knuckles to my lips and kissing them.

"I did."

"And how was it?"

"It was perfect."

CHAPTER FIFTY-ONE
DYLAN

Dylan: How is Dot doing?
Row: Better. Turned out to be a fracture. Me and Seraf are giving her some TLC.
Dylan: Good. Tell her I'm sorry she had to deal with Tucker. I am so embarrassed I brought him into our lives.
Row: Shh. We got Gravity out of it. Now let's focus on making sure he is forever out of our lives.
Dylan: I guess it's time to tell you that you were right about...well, let's see, EVERYTHING.
Row: I wasn't.
Dylan: No?
Row: I was wrong about Rhyland. He stepped up.
Dylan: Row?
Row: Yes, little sis?
Dylan: I love you.

I spent the entire night staring at my daughter asleep, monitoring her breathing, following the rise and fall of her chest.

I couldn't rip myself from her side. There were going to have to be talks with lawyers, restraining orders, he-said-she-said depositions, and maybe even a trial, but I couldn't think about any of those things. In fact, I couldn't get past the fact that before Tucker threw my entire life for a morbid, four-hour spin, it was Rhyland who had all the power over me.

Rhyland and his decisions.

Rhyland and his ruthless, punishing beauty.

Rhyland and that flirty photo with Claire Larsen.

I knew who he was. He'd never hidden nor denied it. He was a hedonistic, fun-loving slut who enjoyed a variety of women. I was the flavor of the week, and oh, how he loved the taste of me. But that didn't mean he could offer more.

And maybe this was all real. Maybe I was his one in a million. But putting my heart on the line had turned out to be a price too hefty to pay. Because the way he saved Gravity, the way I saw him in action, the unbearable grip he had on my heart, frightened me. He could do with it as he pleased. And Rhyland was notoriously reckless with things. Case in point: he'd lost his pants before Bruce Marshall swooped in to save the day.

I'd spent this evening, prior to Tucker, sinking into a miserable oblivion because I thought he'd stood me up. Because he flirted with a starlet. If it weren't for Cal, Gravity would have seen the damage he did to me. And then Tucker showed up and reminded me that men couldn't be trusted.

No matter how many times they gave you orgasms.

No matter how many times they called you beautiful.

No matter how many times they made sweet, charming promises.

At five in the morning, I uncurled myself from around my daughter's tiny figure and rose up from her toddler bed, my bare feet gliding over the engineered wooden floor toward the living room.

Rhyland was asleep on my couch. He insisted on staying over so we'd feel safe. Mittens and Fluffy were nestled at his feet, snoring the night away. My heart cracked like an egg. He was such a sucker for those dogs. He was never going to get rid of them.

I took a seat in the hollow gap between his flat abs and the couch. He hadn't changed his clothes or taken a shower since his initial journey in the morning, and he smelled accordingly. Coppery, sweaty, and sour, like dried blood and a long, punishing day. I placed a hand on his cheek. Instinct made his hand lock around my wrist, but then his eyes fluttered open, and he released me, his scowl melting into an indulgent smirk that always made my heart beat faster.

"Hi," I croaked.

"Cosmos," he rasped. "My favorite sight."

In that moment, I didn't feel like the universe at all. Maybe like a black hole that sucked the life out of everything.

Rhyland read my face like an open book—leafing through the pages, racing through the paragraphs. My feelings were in plain sight. He understood immediately. He sat up straight. The dogs yelped in protest at his shifting position and skated down to the floor to resume their nap.

"Look, there was a surprise tornado." He stuck his fingers into luscious locks of hair that were no longer there, immediately running his palm through his new cut. "It came out of left fucking field. I woke up to the storm. All the flights out of Dallas got canceled. I got here as fast as I could. Destroyed Bruce's Ram. I gave Tate twenty-five percent of my shares in my company to borrow his plane. I—"

"I know you did everything to get here." The words wrenched out of my mouth with great effort, my stomach roiling. I didn't want to do this, saying goodbye when every hello made my heart skip a beat. But I also didn't know how to give up control over my heart without losing my sanity. "And I'm not mad about it. Although…I do wish you didn't give that bastard Tate what he wanted." My face crumpled.

"Fuck the company, Dylan. He can have it. He could take the penthouse, the shirt on my back. I came all this way in a tornado, against all odds, against all reason, to tell you something very important."

"And what is that?"

"*I love you.*"

The words hit me so hard they made me keel over, like an iron fist straight to my stomach. Growing up, I'd fantasized about hearing those words. Tucker spoke them so rarely, and always when we were in bed.

But now?

Now I was shit-scared.

Unlike Tucker, Rhyland wouldn't just hurt me—he'd destroy whatever was left of me.

Worse still, he might destroy Gravity. Continue the cycle and make her distrust men too.

Just because he was the good guy in this specific scenario didn't mean he wouldn't be the bad guy in the next. I didn't mean physically or maliciously, like Tucker. I knew he'd never do that. But he was… *Rhyland.* He could get tired of us and go his merry way. Up and leave once he'd had a taste of the billionaire lifestyle. Tucker had left, and he had nothing waiting for him. Rhy was going to have temptation at his feet from now until forever. Who could promise me he'd stay?

Ours was never meant to be a love story, only a cautionary tale. And unlike Tucker, getting my heart broken by Rhyland wouldn't put me back at square one.

It would put me on suicide watch.

He was everything I'd ever wanted, which was precisely why I couldn't have him.

"Rhyland." I closed my eyes, pressing my hand to his broad pecs, which flexed instinctively under my fingertips. "I saw your picture with Claire Larsen."

He cursed softly. "Nothing happened between us. I swear. Bruce wanted me to play nice, so we took a few pictures. I didn't even kiss her on the cheek. You have to believe me."

"I do believe you."

"Then what's the problem?"

"The problem is I cannot get past my distrust of men, and this weekend was a reminder of it. You were late. That picture of you with her surfaced all over the internet. Tucker kidnapped my daughter—"

"I had nothing to do with the latter," he interjected fiercely, his eyes narrowing into slits. "And the two former issues were a misunderstanding. You can't tell me this isn't real." He motioned between us. "Because it is, and even though you're not ready to tell me you love me, *I* know you do. I'm here. I've been here all along. I see the way you look at me, the way you laugh with me, the way you fuck me. You don't have to say you love me. You speak it with your entire existence, Dylan."

Gulping a greedy, shaky breath, I put my thumb on his cheek, cataloging him to memory. He wasn't wrong. I had fallen. Nosedived. Sunk into the endless abyss that was him. There was no coming back for me; I was always going to be his. But only from afar. Loving him up close would be my ruin. If he betrayed me the way Tucker did, I wouldn't be able to survive.

"Listen to me. I'm not Tucker." He grabbed my arms, searching my eyes in a way that made me avert my gaze to the floor. "I'd never do that to you. I'm crazy about you. About Grav. When he kidnapped her, I thought…I thought…"

"You thought?" The air stood still; the world stopped spinning.

"I was happily willing to give up my life to save hers," he finished. "No questions asked. No hesitation. I'm not asking you to do the same for me. I'm not even asking for a fraction of that. All I want is a chance to prove I'm not like them."

"Them?"

"Tucker. Your dad. The people who let you down. I'll never do that."

You already did, I thought miserably.

My expectations were unreasonable. And sure, Rhyland might

try to meet them, but he was bound to fail. If not fail then to live miserably, unable to mingle with women, be delayed on a trip, or move freely. Truth was I was doing this for him as much as I was doing it for myself.

"I'm sorry, Rhy." I unscrewed the engagement ring from my finger and placed it on the coffee table. The exposed skin felt cold without it. "I'm going back to Maine. If there's one thing yesterday taught me, it's that I need my mom by my side."

"Wrong fucking lesson." He stood up swiftly, pacing the living room with his hands clutching the back of his skull. "Your take should've been that you need to be with *me*." He stubbed his thumb into his chest. "*I* solved the problem. *I* found Gravity. *I* confronted Tuc—"

"I don't want to be saved!" I stormed to my feet, tossing my hands in the air. "I want to be left alone, free of complications and drama. I want to not worry about gorgeous Hollywood starlets and canceled dates and broken hearts and kidnappings. I was fine before we got together—"

"Bluntly speaking, you were dead inside."

"Comfortably numb," I retorted.

He released a whoosh of air, staring me down as if his eyes were cocked guns, ready to fire. Heat rolled off his large, looming body as though he were dissipating into a cloud of rage. "What do you want, Dylan?" His nostrils flared. "Do you want me on my knees?"

The silence buzzed between us like a persistent bug.

"Well?" he barked. "Do you?"

Would you?

It was as though he unheard my spoken question, because he answered, "In a heartbeat. My ego stood no fucking chance. Neither did my heart. So what's it gonna be?"

"No," I admitted quietly. "It wouldn't help. I've made up my mind. I'm taking Gravity in the morning and driving up north to stay with Mama and Marty."

Max at the Alchemist was going to be a couple bartenders short, with Tucker down for the count and me running away, but he'd been filling up spots ever since Faye's health scare.

Rhy grabbed my cheeks, pulling me into him. My body gravitated toward his instantly, like a magnet. Foreheads meeting. Lips touching. My chest flush against his.

"You're walking out on this?"

"I have to, Rhy. It's become too risky. Too high-stakes. You made me fall, but you will not make me shatter. I have to do this. For me. For my daughter. I have to get away."

"I love you, and you're turning your back on me, just like them," he said quietly.

Them. His parents. Hurting him destroyed me, but I knew he'd move on if he understood.

"No, Rhyland. I'm turning my back on myself. You deserve more than I could give you. I won't let you settle for a woman who would never be willing to fully give you her heart."

"Even if I'll settle for less?" His eyes darkened.

"Especially if you do," I said quietly. "You are worthy of the kind of love you are willing to give."

He was about to argue, but I shut him up by crashing my lips against his. The kiss that followed put me somewhere between heaven and hell, stuck in a limbo of unbearable physical pleasure and an excruciating heartache. His mouth claimed mine hungrily, tongue finding my own, and before I knew it, he was on top of me on the floor, my hands fumbling with his belt as he hiked my red dress up, tugging my panties to one side. We didn't have time to get undressed. We both knew it was goodbye. It tasted as much, the bittersweetness of it exploding in our mouths and dripping down our chins.

And I loved him, in that moment, more than I'd loved anyone else in my entire life.

Because I knew that he was giving me a piece of him to keep before we parted ways.

CHAPTER FIFTY-TWO
RHYLAND

I was nursing my third bottle of whiskey since Dylan left when my door came down, followed by Row's chilling baritone reverberating, "Timber!"

Unflinching, I kept my glazed stare on the TV. I had no idea what the fuck I was watching—I just knew Dylan always watched it when she lived downstairs. A bunch of grossly underage and overfuckable doctors in a TV drama. I couldn't remember what season I was on, but I was eighty-three percent certain most of the cast members had already died in the most unlikely way possible, and whoever hadn't died had left. I was beginning to get to the root of Dylan's trust issues.

"Is this…puke next to you?" Row's repulsed voice hovered somewhere above my head, and I spotted the tip of his combat boot shuffling a Chinese takeout container around.

"Could be refried rice. Your guess is good as mine," I slurred into the rim of my whiskey bottle, taking another swig.

"Why are you watching *Grey's Anatomy*, man?"

"Waiting for a nip slip."

"Don't hold your breath."

"Tempted to. Finishing it all seems like a grand idea."

Row snorted, ignoring my theatrics. "Why not just watch porn?"

"As a former sex worker, I'm diligent about ethically sourced porn. You'd be surprised to know how hard it is to come by. All puns intended."

Row picked up the container in front of me, sniffing it and making a face. "Definitely day-old vomit. I'm staging an intervention."

"Great." I jumped off my couch nimbly. Or maybe I was more drunk than I realized, because I bumped against my coffee table and almost smashed it. My toe *did* feel like it was bleeding. "Tell your sister to come. She might convince me to go to rehab."

Row made what I guessed was his version of a sympathetic face, scratching at the stubble on his jawline. His wedding band gleamed. *Cocky asshole.* What did he care? He'd gotten his happily ever after. I should probably ask how Cal was doing, but I couldn't find it in myself to care about anyone who wasn't my own sorry ass.

"Look, man, I'm sorry. I always thought you'd be the one to break her heart, not the other way around." Row sucked his teeth.

"How come?"

"Figured you don't possess one."

I grunted in response. I hadn't thought I owned one either. Not until Dylan avalanched her way into my existence with that sassy mouth, which also happened to know how to suck my nuts using just the right amount of pressure. I stared off into the middle distance.

Row flicked the nape of my neck.

"*Ugh.* What was that for?"

"I could practically see across your pupils a porno of you and my sister. What the fuck?"

I pushed him off, staggering my way to the hallway and into the bathroom for a piss. I bumped into every wall, piece of furniture, and goddamn atom in the air on my way there. How shit-faced was I? The answer was probably thirteen.

Wait—what was the question?

"Why're you here?" I slurred as I flicked the toilet seat up (a habit I'd *never* possessed before Dylan), aimed my cock, and started pissing.

"Bruce is blowing up my phone asking where the fuck you are, and I was in town, so I thought I'd check on you." I heard my best friend weaving around the house, picking up dirty dishes, planting them in the sink. "Oh, and Tate mentioned something about how you might have offed yourself sometime this week. He said you were unhinged on his plane."

"I broke my own phone," I ground out. "Fucking hell, I witnessed the man nutting into someone's eyeball in the halftime of a high-stakes poker game just to take the edge off. He needs to seriously reexamine his life if he has the audacity to call *me* unhinged."

Row's head popped out from the hallway into my bathroom. "You need to haul your ass into the shower, down three gallons of water, and shovel the pizza I'm about to make you down your throat while I clean this pigsty—you hear me?"

"Why?" I grumbled.

"Because Marshall is on his way here, and you're not losing this fucking deal. Now, are you too drunk to take a shower?"

"What do you take me for?" I spluttered. "Of course not."

Lies.

I *was* too drunk to take a shower.

Turned out I was too drunk to recognize one too. At first, I strode into my walk-in closet and took a nap inside my hamper. Row eventually fished me out of there and tossed me into an ice-cold shower, clothes on, and that was what finally woke me the fuck up.

"Hey. What the shit?" I skidded up on my feet like a deranged baby gazelle, slapping the glass door with my open palm. "I could get pneumonia."

Row was standing on the other side, arms crossed, looking like he'd finally run out of every single fuck he'd ever possessed. "And?"

He arched an eyebrow. "You already have alcohol poisoning. You're headed to the hospital either way."

I ended up scrubbing myself back into something semicivilized, brushing my teeth three times, and chugging down water and Row's authentic thin-crust Italian pizza. The apartment looked spotless. I didn't know how, but he'd somehow gotten rid of the puke stench too. A good friend. Especially considering the fact that up until four days ago, my dick was so far in his sister's ass I knew the shape of her kidneys.

Row glanced at his watch. A Rolex. Funny, but I didn't miss mine. Somewhere in the past nine weeks, I'd realized I was obsessed with designer crap because I figured it would fill the void my parents left. But that never happened.

"Look, Bruce should be here any minute. I'm going to dash out. You'll be okay, Rhy."

I was sitting at my kitchen island, pouting like a little bitch, feeling very much the opposite of okay. "How do you know?" I asked, surly.

Row gave me an incredulous look. "I don't. It's just shit people say, you know." He shrugged. "But in all likelihood, you will survive."

"I don't think there's any surviving your sister."

"Speaking of her, I heard she's a wreck too. Maybe it's not over?"

"Wait, what?" My head jerked up.

The fucker was already pulling the door handle open, going his merry way. "Ciao, assface." He saluted. "See you later."

"Wait, wait." I shot up, stalking after him. He slipped out, and I smashed right into the body of Bruce Marshall.

Yay fucking me.

Even his sorry ass of a face, giant cowboy hat, and ridiculous buckle couldn't spoil my mood.

Dylan was miserable? That was great news. Maybe I still had a chance.

"Howdy, partner." He tipped his hat down.

Another bout of nausea washed over me. This time, I wasn't drunk, just grossed out by the conversation that was yet to come.

"I'm gonna go ahead and invite myself in and make myself some coffee while you explain to me the whole lil-miss debacle." He breezed past me, heading straight to my coffee machine. After flicking it on, he leaned against my counter, curling his hands over the edge and giving me a look.

I could pull a story out of my ass about how we were together and had broken up recently because of the Claire Larsen fiasco. Dylan would back me up on it, I knew. And still, something had become indifferent in me.

If I couldn't have her, nothing else was worth owning. Including a billion-dollar company.

I was done jerking this nutjob off. If he didn't want what I was offering, he was free to go.

After paying me seventy million dollars as part of a walk-out clause. Thank you, Tate Blackthorn.

"You want the truth?" I chuckled humorlessly.

"If it ain't too hard for you to utter." He took off his hat and placed it next to the sink. "You gave me ten different versions of a lie so far, and none of 'em did the trick."

"It was a ruse," I said flatly. "You were ancient and backward, and I figured if I played house with someone to convince you I was a decent human, you'd sign the contract. Dylan was here, familiar, and available. You caught us trying to rip each other's heads off, drew your own conclusion, and we went along with it."

"What'd she get out of the bargain?"

Her pussy licked at least twice a day. Period days included.

"Money."

"So you lied to me?"

"I lied to you," I confirmed.

"*Tricked* me," he continued.

"Look, you can use all the synonyms in the world. Answer's still yes."

"You sure all of it was an act?" He cocked a bushy white eyebrow. "'Cause y'all sure as heck looked chummy."

I fingered my jaw, rolling my tongue from one side to the other. "Lines got blurry after a while. She needed some help with her kid, so I babysat for her. We spent some time together. So yeah. It was business with benefits."

"Past tense?" He studied me intently. He'd completely forgotten about the coffee he was going to make for himself.

"Past tense. She moved back to Maine."

"You dumped her after I signed the contract?" he boomed, sending his palm crashing against the counter. Spit adorned the side of his mouth.

I flashed him a bitter smirk. "She ditched me after the Claire Larsen bull crap, after I missed the concert…and other stuff. I tried to make her stay. Tried to explain myself. I was willing to get down on my knees. But it tapped straight into her trust issues, and she couldn't get past that. So yeah, thanks for that."

"You're welcome." He ignored my sarcasm. "And the ring? You got her a pretty thing, didn't you?"

"She returned it," I said bitterly.

What I didn't mention was that I'd kept it. Taking it back to the jeweler meant accepting defeat and admitting to myself that we were done.

"She's on her way to Maine now. Her mom's place. Looking for premed college programs there."

Row had volunteered this information after I grilled him like a well-done steak.

"I see." He stroked his goatee. (Those should be illegal, by the way.) "What do you think I should do about the contract now?"

I shrugged. "Frankly, I don't give a shit. I'm not really invested in anything that doesn't include winning her back."

I was thinking to start things off by buying her a university or something. And a daycare for Gravity. I was new to grand gestures, but I wanted to go big.

"Well, Coltridge, if you're trying to win her back, you're doing a shit job of it, sittin' around sulking in your penthouse like a Jane Austen character."

Bruce Marshall had jokes. Too bad he managed to crack them only when my life was a hot, flaming dumpster fire.

"She's literally in her car on her way to her mom."

"In that piece of junk car I saw the other day?" he snorted. "You can beat her to it."

I mulled his words over. Trying to beat her to Maine was probably impossible, unless she was walking there by foot, but arriving soon after was probably a better idea than buying her an entire college.

"I'm going to keep the contract intact and maintain all working business with you, so don't you worry your pretty lil head 'bout that."

I raised an eyebrow.

"Well?" He smiled big. "Aren't I getting a thank you?"

"You put me in this position. It's your fault I pretended to be in love with her in the first place."

You tricked me into falling in love with a woman who warned me not to fall.

Even as I said these words, I knew they were bullshit. Falling for Dylan was as inevitable as falling asleep. A natural, feral instinct.

A beat of silence stretched between us before snapping like an elastic band when he said, "I knew it was all an act."

"Come again?" My head shot up. I remained calm, but inside, my blood was sizzling with rage.

He pushed off the counter, sauntering toward me. "I'd met you a few times by then. You were charming, dazzling, handsome, and sought-after. You had a great idea. But your eyes. They were... *subdued*. There was nothing behind them. They were empty. Pair that with your wild antics, general laziness, and the fact that people had been sayin' you got too many cobwebs in the attic, and I wasn't too sure about that deal.

"Then I walked into that meeting with you, and you were standing on the street, bickering with this pretty lil miss. And you looked irritated and furious and…well, *alive*. You looked alive. Your eyes were no longer dead. And in that moment, I realized I couldn't get into business with you if you had nothing to lose other than money. Money is a terrible motivator. You needed fire beneath your feet. Something to up your stakes. And she was so dazzling. As pretty as you are, if not better-lookin'. She was flustered and panicked, but she still stood her ground. And those sparks were flyin'. I could feel their heat. Thought it'd be a good idea to set you two up. What you needed was someone to take care of. And it worked."

"No, it didn't work!" I roared when he was close enough for me to grab and bash his head against the wall. I didn't, though. Solely because there was still a slight chance Dylan might decide to change her mind about us. "For the millionth time, she dumped me. Because of *you*."

He patted my shoulder fatherly. "You'll get back together."

"How do you know?"

"I've got good instincts."

"You knew we were lying to you?" I followed him with my eyes as he returned to the counter to grab his hat.

"Yes." He screwed said hat over his head. "And I saw you falling in love right in front of me. It was beautiful to watch. Best show in the world."

Bruce wobbled his way back to the door. He grabbed the handle and opened it but stayed on the threshold, throwing me a casual look from over his shoulder. "I expect you to be back at the office on Monday at six thirty in the god-dang morning, Coltridge. Until then, you're going to get your head outta your ass, go up to Maine, and beg Lil Miss to take you back."

CHAPTER FIFTY-THREE
DYLAN

I made a mistake.

That much was crystal clear to me even before I parked Jimmy in front of my mother's house.

It no longer felt like mine. Not that Row's New York apartment ever did. I understood, as I killed the engine of the car Rhyland had put together from scratch while we still hated each other, that home was not a place; it was a state of mind. And I'd managed to zone into it only when I was around the ridiculously hot, infuriating, charismatic man upstairs.

"Mommy." Gravity kicked the back of the passenger seat with the new kicks Rhyland had bought for her. A pair of ombre rainbow boots. It was ninety degrees outside, and she'd paired them with a yellow summer dress. "I need to go pee-pee. Let's go."

I wiped my cheeks quickly, realizing they were wet with tears. I'd spent the entire day driving here. It was deep into the evening, and now, when I put all these miles behind me and New York, I knew without a doubt that I'd run away because Tucker's actions had shaken me to the core.

My instincts were to run away.

Run away from danger, from the big city, from men.

Run away from happiness, all to protect me and my daughter.

But my daughter wasn't in danger with Rhyland. He'd go to war for her and win. He had.

"Yeah, baby. Let's get you all settled in."

I pushed my door open and unbuckled Grav. We were greeted by my very relieved Mama and Marty, who fawned over us after the Tucker disaster. Mama made Grav her favorite: chicken nuggets and ketchup pasta, even though, as an Italian from Naples, she found the combination as sacrilegious as vandalizing a church. When Marty asked if he should grab my suitcases from the car, I politely declined. I couldn't explain why, but I didn't want to admit to myself that I was back here for good.

We were quiet as Gravity ate, bathed, and was tucked into bed, getting her bedtime story and words of affirmation from both my mother and me. When I closed the door to her room—which didn't feel like her room anymore—Mama jerked her head silently toward the backyard. There, two glasses of red wine awaited us: the cheap stuff, along with *cuoppo* rolled around in yesterday's newspaper. There was an assortment of fried seafood with a slice of lemon tucked inside. Mama used to make us this treat in the summers, since my father was a fisherman and always came home with extras. It reminded her of her own childhood.

We fell into the recliners and listened to the gurgling sound of the wraparound pool.

"You must've been very scared." Mama's voice pierced the silence eventually.

I pressed the cool glass of wine to my cheek. "I was," I admitted. "I also had a feeling...I can't explain it. Like Rhyland was going to come and save the day."

It was ridiculous, but when Rhyland explained he'd installed a tracker on Mr. Mushroom (RIP), I was relieved but not surprised. Subconsciously, I always knew that if there was a man on this earth who could save me, it'd be him.

"He is a good egg, Rhyland. Always has been." Mama sipped her wine. "When your brother was younger, before he settled down with Calla, Rhyland took care of him. Moved around with him. I don't think he'd ever admit it, but it was because he knew Ambrose was messed up here over what happened with his father." She knocked her fist against her temple. "Row was angry at the world. Angry at what happened with your father. Short-fused. Rhyland was ready to save him from himself. He's a nurturer. I think he fights it because he doesn't want to be, but at his core, he knows how to take good care of people."

I felt like crying again. What was up with my waterworks? I'd made it years without shedding a tear. But I felt miserable for walking away on him. For repaying all Rhyland's good deeds by abandoning him. I chose to do the one thing that triggered him. Walk away. And I was finding it hard to forgive myself for being here.

"Mama, I think I'm in love with Rhyland," I said miserably.

"Oh, *cara*, I know. You've been in love with him since you were six."

"No, I haven't." I flashed her a scowl.

She gave me a private smile. "Okay."

Shit. I had, hadn't I?

"Then why did you let me go out with Tucker?" I demanded, feeling irrationally upset with her for a mistake I'd made myself.

"Would you have listened?" Mama gave me a "bitch please" look. Neither of us touched our food. She sighed, smoothing out an invisible wrinkle in her housedress. "Look, I knew what you thought of me. You saw me as this little woman who let her husband hit her. You were mad at me for not protecting Row properly from him. And you were right. I was mad at myself too. I didn't feel like I had the tools and logic to give you life advice when I made such poor decisions for myself." She pressed her fist to her mouth, tears clinging to her lower lashes. "And by refraining from interfering, I unknowingly sent you into the arms of a very bad man. A man just as bad as your father, as it turned out."

"No, Mama, I never disrespected you for staying with him." I pushed my chair closer to hers, putting my hand on hers to stop her from smoothing the wrinkle-less gown. "I was angry at Dad but never at you. You were in a foreign country, in a small, largely unwelcoming town, a mother of two young children. No job, no prospects, no help. I'm sorry if I made you feel...*less*."

Now she was crying, and so was I. Not because of Tucker—Tucker was going to prison, I knew. On my seven-hour drive up to Maine, Row had managed to catch me up on all the legwork his private investigator was doing even before the kidnapping scenario. He'd hired someone as soon as he realized Tucker wanted to see Grav. Apparently, my ex had a rap sheet longer than *Moby-Dick*. He'd accumulated a lot of arrests in several places, including Australia, South Korea, and Greece. From larceny to disorderly conduct and DUI, he pissed off a lot of people in a lot of continents. In fact, it appeared that he returned to the States because no other place would have him.

I was crying because I might have lost the love of my life, all because I was too scared to love him.

"It is Dad I'm still angry at," I explained. "It's his fault I can't trust men. That I want to think of them as disposable."

"But then look at Marty and me." Mama's face lit up. "He put my heart back together when I didn't even think I had anything left to give to people who weren't my children and grandchildren. Happily ever afters happen all the time. And they are especially satisfying if the road to them is bumpy."

"Mama, I screwed up," I moaned.

She gave me a stern look for my choice of words but let it slide. "Why do you think that?"

"I left him when I knew people leaving was his red line. His parents were very neglectful to him growing up. They blew his inheritance money and left him with their dogs to travel the world."

"Poor Rhyland. I always had an inkling." My mother made a face. "He'll forgive you."

"Do you think?" I winced. I hoped so. God, I did. But even

though Rhyland had been nothing but amazing to me, I knew he had his own limits. He was no pushover.

"Yes. You two will be just fine. *Il dolore aiuta a crescere.*"

"Hmm?"

"Sorrow helps one grow," she explained. "Those things you suffered through weren't in vain. They gave you perspective. They gave you strength. The thing I've come to learn about having a partner you love is this." Mom stroked my cheek compassionately. "It's not always going to be easy, but it's always going to be worth it."

"I need to call him." I stood up.

Mama's hand shot out to stop me. She shook her head. Her smile did the chiding for her.

I dropped my head back and groaned. "Ugh, really?"

"Really."

"But I just got back."

"You'll be fine."

"Gravity is asleep."

"Leave her here."

It's not that I was too lazy to make the journey back to New York. It was that I wanted to talk to him *immediately*. To grovel my ass off.

"I love you, Mama."

"I love you more, *cara*."

CHAPTER FIFTY-FOUR
RHYLAND

"You're shitting me," I sighed.

"Rhyland!" Zeta, Dylan's mother, reproached me from her doorstep, waving a kitchen towel threateningly at me. "Watch that language of yours. I said she is not here, and that is that."

"Where is she, then?" I asked impatiently.

It was two in the fucking morning, and I was running on no sleep, no food, and no fucks. I wanted to see Dylan. And since I didn't have a private jet at my disposal, I'd made my way here in the McLaren, breaking approximately every traffic rule known to man.

"She went back to New York to ask you to take her back." Zeta tugged her robe tighter around her chest.

"I'm not leaving until she—Wait, what?"

"She understood she made a mistake as soon as she started driving to Maine," Zeta explained with a smile.

"And she never heard of the word *U-turn*?" I was on the brink of dancing, crying, high-fiving myself, and hugging Zeta. Possibly all at the same time.

Dylan was coming back for me.

Hold your horses, Coltridge. You're not even there.

"I don't appreciate your tone, young man. She wanted to spend some time with her mama after what happened with Tucker."

"You're right. You're absolutely right," I said breathlessly. "I'll be out of your hair right now. Just let me see Gravity before I leave."

"She's asleep."

"I know. I need my daily fix of inhaling her hair, and I'll be on my way." I was such a fucking red flag I was surprised no bull had assassinated me yet. It sounded so creepy and cheesy. "I won't make a sound. I promise."

Zeta cursed in Italian, shaking her head and flattening her hand against the door to open it up for me.

"My daughter better marry you, or I will."

CHAPTER FIFTY-FIVE
DYLAN

When I made it home, Rhyland wasn't there.

I unlocked his door using the spare key he'd given me. The place was impeccably organized, clean and empty. The addictive scent of leather, wood, and man filled my nostrils, making me ache for him.

My knee-jerk reaction was panic. Where did he go? When was he coming back? Was he with someone else?

No. I knew for a fact the last option wasn't possible. Heat uncurled in the pit of my stomach—something that resembled an orgasm but was much more profound. The realization floored me.

I trusted him.

I trusted him not to be with someone else, even if we weren't together. And that was huge.

After my dread and sadness subsided, determination took over.

It was actually a good thing he wasn't here yet.

I had a plan.

CHAPTER FIFTY-SIX
RHYLAND

I pushed Dylan's apartment door open.

She wasn't there.

I tried to tamp down my worry.

I knew she'd gotten here before me because I'd been texting her mom throughout my drive.

Maybe she came straight to my penthouse.

Rather than take the elevator, I took the stairs up two at a time. I needed to see her. *Taste* her. When I pushed the door open, she wasn't there. I pulled my phone out, ready to concede in this wild-goose chase, call her and ask where the fuck she was, when I noticed a note stuck to my stainless-steel fridge. It hadn't been there before. I didn't even own any magnets. Squinting, I walked over to it.

Meet me at the Stonewell Mall ASAP.

—Cosmos.

(P.S. your dogs are with me)

(P.P.S. not in a ransom kind of way. They were whimpering and wanted to be taken out.)

(P.P.P.S. You do realize they're your dogs, right? You're never letting anyone adopt them. Just admit you're a big softie)

She used the nickname I gave her.

The one she apparently loathed.

I grabbed my keys and bolted out. I shook my head the entire walk to the local mall. It was ten in the goddamn morning. I didn't remember what day it was. Or what year, for that matter. I broke into a jog at some point, eager to get to her. I knocked down two delivery boys on bikes and nearly seriously injured an elderly lady. The mall was two blocks down from our building, and by the time I got there, I was sweating harder than Jeffrey Dahmer in a zombie movie. I hurried through the sliding automatic doors, realizing the mall was huge and she hadn't specified where she'd be.

She didn't have to.

She was standing right in front of me.

Dylan.

The generic mall fountain was her backdrop.

People were pushing strollers around her, walking around with their coffees and suits, taking business calls, fretting over menus in restaurants, and there she was. The woman of my wildest dreams.

The woman who's about to become my reality.

The dogs were next to her on a leash, napping on the floor.

As soon as she noticed me, her worried brow smoothed, and her lips broke into a childlike smile. I hurried toward her like a congressman reunited with his long-lost brain cells. She raised a hand before I could scoop her up in my arms.

"Wait," she said.

I stopped, doing my best not to grumble my protest. We both looked like we could use a meal, a shower, and a two-week vacation. We'd been driving back and forth across the East Coast like a traveling circus.

"Yes?"

"Open your hand," she commanded.

I did, even though I normally only responded well to orders when we were in bed.

She pressed a smooth silver coin into my palm. "A family heirloom," she explained. "From Italy."

I opened my mouth to say something, but she stopped me. "Make a wish, and throw it in the fountain."

I saw exactly what she was doing. Paying homage to the wishing well we'd visited at Bruce's.

I didn't have to think twice. I turned to the fountain, made a wish, and tossed the coin.

"What did you wish for?" she asked.

"*You.*" Swiveling my body to face her, I took her face in my hands, drawing her close. She was shaking, gripping my hands on her cheeks.

"I'm sorry I left. I never should've done that." Her voice was raw, drenched with grief. "We all deserve to have room to make mistakes. I know that better than anyone."

"You went through hell and back. It's understandable."

I was a sucker for this woman, and I'd have forgiven her for anything, including my own murder.

"No. There's no excu—"

But I didn't want her to grovel. I wanted her to remember why we were both here, running on zero sleep. I crashed my lips against hers, drowning out her protests, and when she whimpered and tried to push me away, I bit down on her lower lip, drawing it into my mouth and swirling my tongue to tease it. Finally, she melted into submission, locking her arms around my neck and extending her own tongue to dance with mine. This was entirely inappropriate for the time and place, but considering my desperation for this woman, bystanders should be grateful we were keeping our fucking clothes on.

When she ripped her mouth from mine, her lips were red and swollen, her eyes drowsy.

"It's not going to be easy," she warned.

"I'm used to hard things." I cocked one eyebrow smartly.

"I'm sassy and stubborn and can be completely insensible," she continued.

"Thank fuck for that. I'd get bored after a minute if you were anyone else."

"I come with a kid."

"I have enough space in my apartment." Pause. "*And* my heart."

"I also come with baggage."

"Never been a light traveler myself."

"I want to live on a farm."

"I can afford places both in the city and on the outskirts."

She was running out of warnings, and I was running out of patience. I wanted in her pants. I wanted to take her back to my place and worship at her body's altar.

"I'll drive you crazy," she hedged.

"I'm already mad about you."

"You don't want kids. I might change my mind," she pointed out.

"No, no. I changed my mind. I *love* kids. Want a ton of them. Like, maybe four or…six."

"What if I don't want another kid?"

"Then we'd travel the world and enjoy our independence."

"What if I want four more?"

"Then we'd travel the world after hiring a harem of trustworthy nannies and bring them with us."

She swatted my chest, which was rumbling with barely contained laughter.

Silence.

"Is that all?" I asked.

"No. There is one more thing."

"What is that?" I drawled.

"I love you back."

That confession resulted in another R-rated kiss.

"What I feel for you is far greater than love and eons more dangerous." I pressed my forehead to hers. "I want everything you have to give, Dylan, and I am an only child. Not good at sharing. You're going to have your hands full."

"My hands are capable." She gave me a peck on the lips. "My mouth too."

I bit my fist in response, going down on one knee and taking out the engagement ring she gave me back before she left for Maine. "Dylan, baby, this ring was meant for you. It was always yours, from the moment I saw it at the jewelry store. It was way out of my budget at the time, but I still knew it couldn't be anything else, because this screamed you."

"It was my dream ring." She let me slide the ring back onto her wedding finger.

"I know. I asked your mother for that board before I came back to New York. It's in my trunk. I'm going to embarrass you for a few hours by dissecting every single thing about it."

"Rhyland."

"Hey, I'm not finished Then I'm going to fulfill every single dream you've ever had."

"Even the Chris Hemsworth one?" she sassed.

"Fine. Ninety-nine-point-nine-nine percent of your dreams."

She laughed. "Thank you."

"For what, baby?" I stood up.

"For making me courageous. For teaching me how to chase my dreams again. With you by my side, I think I can actually become a doctor. I want the big wedding I dreamed about when I was a kid. The puffy, dessert-looking dress that is out of fashion but that I married my Barbie in. The ring you chose for me, which was perfect. The violins."

"We're having violins?" I grinned.

"We're having violins," she confirmed.

"Did Barbie marry Ken, baby?"

"Yes." She kissed me, clinging to me. "But Row's G.I. Joe was her side piece."

I snorted into our kiss, scooping her up. She wrapped her legs around me.

"Also with Spider-Man, Batman, Korg, Valkyrie, and the green PJ Masks figure," she mumbled into our kiss.

"Christ, Dylan."

"Hey, Ken emotionally checked out of that marriage as soon as they went to their beachside honeymoon in my kitchen sink. Kudos to her for moving on."

I kissed her again. "I love you."

"I love you too."

"I love Grav too, you know."

That last one earned me much more than a kiss.

EPILOGUE
RHYLAND

SIX MONTHS LATER

"She's screaming, kicking, and making a fuss." My phone was glued to my ear, and I stared at the pitiful mess at my feet. "I had no idea the first day of preschool was going to be this stressful for her, Row."

"My sister is only a hundred and twenty pounds. Get her off the floor, and take her back to your car," my best friend grumbled. "How hard can it fucking be?"

"Four times a night, and sometimes when I'm still inside her."

"I'm going to kill you."

"My jokes are my art, and I will die for my art."

"Okay, Pic-*ass*-o, pick her up before the paparazzi arrive," Row enunciated.

I was attracting all kinds of attention now that I was a semi-famous tech mogul.

"Fuck. She'll use her claws, but okay."

I hung up the phone and tucked it into my pocket. Dylan was still crying on the floor outside the preschool. Yeah, the same one she was supposed to give an answer to some months ago and never did. Luckily, I'd had the foresight to pay the application fees and fill out all the forms so Grav would have a spot there. I knew Dylan would end up going to college and would need to put Gravity in the three-day program. Cherrie was very accommodating of the fact that I'd signed a child who was not technically under my care to her school.

And the little stinker? She was a rock star about it. She was joining class during the second semester, so we skipped the fancy signs and photo shoots, but she showed up today with an apple to give to her teacher and the neon-green UGG boots I got her as a gift so she'd always remember her individuality, even if she needed to wear a uniform now.

She'd waved us goodbye without so much as a glance and run off to join her classmates and teachers. It was Dylan who was a hot mess.

"I'm going to miss her so much," my fiancée hiccupped on the floor.

I followed her brother's suggestion and hurled her up into my arms. A mental breakdown on the steps of the most prestigious preschool in Manhattan was not a great look.

"You're going to be fine," I muttered into her ear, carrying her honeymoon-style to the car while she burst out in another bout of weeping. Dylan was a tough cookie. Watching her crumble like that was jarring, to say the least. "May I remind you, you'll be busy reading through books and studying your hot ass off?" I tried to avert her thoughts from Gravity.

"It's February. I have six months before my semester starts," she moaned into my neck, lolling her head back and forth.

"Good thing you have the wedding of the century to plan, then," I grumbled. "That'll keep you busy."

Even though I was now richer than God, Dylan had turned out to be a thrifty bride. She was planning the wedding for August so she could focus on her studies later. She'd been accepted to Fordham's premed program and was over the goddamn moon. She'd also moved out of Row's apartment and up into my penthouse with Gravity the day I asked her to marry me for real, but she still took care of Row's apartment for free, because she was a better human than I was.

"The wedding's already planned. All we have to do is show up," Dylan protested as I tucked her into the passenger seat.

"That, I can do." I rounded the car and joined her in the driver's seat. "Can I take you out on a date?" I turned to wink at her.

She checked the time on her phone. "Aren't you supposed to be at the office?"

Ever since we soft-launched App-date three months ago and quite literally broke the App Store (and the internet, several times), I'd had my hands full and had been working fifteen-hour days. Fake dating had turned out to be lots of people's favorite trope, because we offered a hundred bucks' worth of dinner vouchers to any two users who sent us proof of marriage or engagement as a result of the app, and the couples just kept on coming, to the point that we'd had to start striking deals with restaurant chains.

"No. I'm supposed to be inside *you*," I corrected her.

"Let's skip to the food part then." She rubbed her palms together. "I'm ready."

"Nah. I wanna wine you and dine you and show you how much you mean to me."

"Rhyland." She sighed. "We're getting married in a few months. I'm living off boiled eggs, coffee, and Pinterest inspo at this point. What makes you think I want to be wined and dined?"

"This right here." I pulled out my phone and showed her a screenshot of a social media post I'd found of hers, dated back to when she was twenty. She was still with Tucker back then—yes, the same motherfucker who was serving four years in prison these days—and living in Maine.

Dylan squinted, reading the caption out loud. "'My actual dream is to eat my weight in *pasta alla ruota*.'"

I raised my eyebrows meaningfully.

She laughed. "Rhyland, I'm supposed to get into a wedding dress next week for measurements."

"And I'm supposed to pretend I don't want as much of you as possible inside it?"

"That is a very kind way to tell me you'd love me in all sizes."

"It's the truth," I said dryly. "And I want all your dreams to come true, so that's where we're going."

But what Dylan didn't know was that I was taking her to a restaurant downtown, where her brother would be waiting. Cal too. And Kieran. Her mom and Marty. Everyone.

She needed emotional support on this first day of Gravity going to school, so I'd set it up for her.

As it turned out, it was my shitty upbringing that drove me to want better for my own family. With us, things would be different. We would give our kids all the love and attention they needed and spare some for any friends who might have it tough at home too.

When Gravity came back from school, she'd have all her family celebrating this new milestone in her life.

"I can't believe you took some time off and we're not spending it having sex," Dylan sulked.

At least I'd gotten her to stop crying about Gravity.

"Can we at least have a quickie in the restaurant's restroom?"

"Not if you don't want me and your brother to kill each other," I muttered.

"Hmm?"

"Nothing." I grabbed Dylan's hand across the central console and brought her knuckles to my lips, kissing them softly. "Behave, Cosmos."

"Make me," she challenged, grinning.

I made a pit stop at our apartment, leaving everyone to wait for us, and I did.

DYLAN

THE WEDDING DAY...

Rhyland Coltridge posted a picture.

Dylan_loves_Rhyland4ever commented: Gorgeous suit xo

Rhyland Coltridge commented: It's chewable 😋

Dylan_loves_Rhyland4ever commented: One day our child is going to see all this and need intense therapy.

Rhyland Coltridge commented: Nah. We're raising the standard for her. That's our moral duty. Can't wait to marry you, Cosmos.

Dylan_loves_Rhyland4ever commented: Can't wait to marry you, hot stuff.

TheRealKieranCarmichael commented: Last chance to make a run for it and marry me, Dyl. Just sayin'.

Rhyland Coltridge commented: I'm going to snap both your legs and make chopsticks out of them.

TheRealKieranCarmichael commented: 🥷 was worth a shot.

"Holy shit, Dyl, this dress." Cal cupped her mouth, staggering backward in my bridal suite.

"Christ almighty." My mother made a cross sign with her fingers. "Goodness me."

"You look…" Cal started.

Hideous?

Awful?

Ridiculous?

There was no way to sugarcoat it. The dress was objectively atrocious. They'd had a good amount of time to get used to it, but they never had.

There was a lot of puffiness—enough to make the bottom part look like a never-ending mountain of whipped cream. I'm talking layer upon layer of nausea-inducing foam. When you got to the upper part, it didn't get any better. The strapless satin bust was fine, but I'd insisted on puffy lace sleeves, traditional tulle, and a huge pearl necklace. I looked completely over-the-top, but this was the wedding dress I'd wanted when I was a small child, and I'd decided to make all this girl's dreams come true.

That could also explain my dubious choice of having a donut wall, pink flowers only, a pastel color scheme, and a champagne fountain.

A refined wedding, it was not. But a fun one, it surely would be.

"I know, right?" I twirled around in my wedding dress, taking a sip of my champagne. "I look outlandish."

"I think you look like the most beautiful bride ever!" Gravity exclaimed loudly, sending Auntie Cal and my mother intense warning glares. "When I grow up, I want to get married in the same dress."

"No," Mama and Cal said in unison. We all laughed.

Gravity shook her head, leaning down to polish her cowgirl boots.

Oh yeah. I almost forgot. I decided it wasn't only my dream that would be fulfilled today. My daughter was given full and complete control over her outfit. She'd promptly decided she wanted to dress like Uncle Bruce.

Yup. The wedding was a hot mess. But hot messes were the best kind of fun.

"Do you need anything?" Cal squeezed my shoulder, and for the first time in a long time, I thought to myself, *No. I don't. Everything I need, I already have.*

"I'm okay, thanks." I squeezed her hand on my shoulder with a smile. "When am I due to come out?"

"Not for another half an hour," my mother assured me, fixing the top of her fancy hat. She too had gotten to fulfill her dreams today—Rhyland had restored her vintage car, the first she'd ever owned in America, and she and Marty had driven here in it. "You have time, *cara*. Do you want me to bring you anything to eat?"

I shook my head. "I'm not hungry."

There was a knock on the door.

"It's probably Row." Cal whirled and made her way to the door. She flung it open and then immediately slammed it in the person's face. "Blasphemy!" she cried out.

"What's happening?" My heart gave a dangerous leap.

Was it Tucker? Was he back? I knew logically he couldn't be. Unless he escaped from prison, which would result in even *more* prison time. I knew my ex was a dumbass, but I suspected even he had his limits.

"It's Rhyland." Cal clutched her necklace.

"I want to speak to my bride," I heard my fiancé say from the other side of the door and couldn't contain my grin. I knew why he was here—he was worried I'd get cold feet.

I also knew it was one hundred percent not going to fly with my mother.

As expected, a string of unholy Italian curses left Mama's mouth, punctuated by a clutch of her chest and her galloping toward the door. "You're not getting inside, Rhyland! How dare you think you can see the bride before the wedding? It's bad luck."

"Don't need luck. Got love."

Mama flashed her daughter-in-law a "can you believe this prick?" glare. I doubled over laughing.

"Whatever you have, it is not common sense. You are not seeing my daughter before she walks down the aisle, and that is that." My mother stomped.

"Rhy," I called out. "I'm okay—really. You don't have to check on me."

"I still need to speak to you." He sounded serious.

I looked between Cal, Mom, and Grav. "Give us a second."

"You cannot be serious!" my mother cried out. "Dylan, it's tradition that he doesn't see you."

"I know what she looks like," Rhyland pointed out from behind the door.

"Not in her wedding dress," my mother countered.

"To be honest, that's not a bad thing, considering the dress." I laughed.

"I actually *have* seen the wedding dress," Rhyland confessed. "Dyl showed me an article about it. It won an award for ugliest wedding dress of the century. Impressive."

Rhyland stepped inside, filling the small space with his presence. He looked like the best gift I could have been given.

He wore a flawless black tux and a bow tie. His hair had grown back almost fully and was now slicked back in a small bun. My heart swelled at the sight of him.

Mama sighed with exasperation. Cal hoisted Grav into her arms.

"Wait—no." Rhyland stopped Cal. He had one hand behind his back and an unholy cocky smirk on his face. "Little stinker?"

"Yes, Daddy?" she squeaked.

My heart melted. *Daddy.* Gravity finally had one. And it was the best one she could ever have hoped for.

"I got you a little wedding gift." He kissed her forehead. "Close your eyes."

"Okay!"

"No peeking," he warned.

She squeezed her eyes hard, and Rhyland moved his hand from his back, unveiling an identical replica of Mr. Mushroom.

He'd brought back the dick. I couldn't help it. I fell over myself laughing.

"Oh no, not again," my mother moaned.

"Again," Rhyland confirmed. "Open your eyes, sweetie."

When Gravity saw her new stuffie, she completely lost it.

Grabbed it and pressed it to her chest, running in circles in her cowboy boots. Like Mama, I wasn't exactly thrilled that my daughter would resume her attachment to a fluffy pink penis, but I wasn't exactly in a position to judge. Rhyland's penis had saved my life.

Mama, Cal, and Grav filed out of the room afterward, giving us a chance to talk—not before my mother cautioned she'd be outside listening in case there were any shenanigans.

Rhyland grinned, capturing my hands and bringing them to his lips.

"Hi," he said.

"Hello."

"I hope I didn't interrupt."

I shook my head, still smiling like a fool. "No, but I have to leave in about twenty minutes. I'm getting married."

"Lucky guy."

"What did you want?"

"To ensure I still have a bride, mostly." He gave me a sheepish smirk.

I loved how careful he was with me, how considerate. He hadn't let my bravado fool him into thinking I was braver than I was. We'd both sworn we'd never love, never marry. This was huge for both of us.

"You still have a bride," I confirmed, reaching up on my toes to kiss his lips. "Do I still have a groom?"

"That was never in question." He shook his head, his expression turning serious. "I have a confession to make."

"If you cheated on me, I am going to murder you," I said in a frighteningly even tone.

"I said I have a confession, not a death wish."

"Carry on." I nodded.

"I call you Cosmos, but not because of the sky." Rhy brushed his knuckles along my cheekbones, tucking a stray lock back in place. "I call you that because of the flower. It is beautiful and resilient, a fighter for its species. It braves all weather and often reseeds itself without help. I call you Cosmos because you're everything this seemingly gentle flower is—adaptable and tough while being graceful and mesmerizing at the same time. You are living proof anyone can blossom if they choose to, shitty circumstances be damned."

"This is what you came here to say?" I bit down a smile. "That you named me after a flower?"

"After the *best* flower," he corrected.

"Is it my turn to confess?" I asked.

There was a knock on the door. Apparently, we only had a few minutes left, not twenty like I'd thought.

"Yes." Rhy gave me a confused look. "Unless it's about fucking Kieran at some point in your life—in which case, I truly don't want to know. I'd hate to finish his soccer career. He only has a few more years left."

I snorted. If only he knew that Kieran wasn't interested in me romantically.

"No. I can confirm we've never hooked up," I assured him.

"Very good. What is it, then?"

"As I grow older and wiser, I realize people are made of memories and that my favorite memory is…well, you."

There was another knock on the door. I hurried up, gulping in air.

"And as I look back at our memories, I can't help but think we should create more of them together…" I was rambling, but I was grateful, a little drunk on alcohol, and a lot drunk on love.

"What are you saying?" he whispered, his voice rough with emotion.

"I'm saying I might—not right now, but sometime in the future—want to have children with you." My eyes clung to his. "And I'm also saying that a vasectomy is reversible and that you might, um, want to consider that."

He pressed his lips together, trying to contain his amusement.

"You want me to breed with you, Dylan? Is that what you're telling me?"

"No," I protested. "I'm not a cow. I want you to give me a baby, and I'm asking you if you'd be open to that."

Another knock on the door. *Jesus Christ.* People didn't get the hint.

"Name the time and place," he challenged.

"When I finish med school," I said tentatively.

"Fine." He kissed me. "You have a date, *wifey.*"

"Thank you for giving me everything I've ever wanted." Now it was my turn to sound like I was cracking under the weight of all my feelings.

"All your wildest dreams, baby."

READ ON FOR A SNEAK
PEEK AT THE NEXT
FORBIDDEN LOVE BOOK,
HANDSOME DEVIL

PROLOGUE
TATE

From: Dr. Arjun Patel, MD
(arjunpatel@stjohnsmedical.com)

To: Tate Blackthorn
(willnotanswerunsolicitedemails@GSproperties.com)

Tate,

While I understand your schedule is demanding, I urge you to pay me a visit in the next couple of weeks.

I instructed my secretary to prioritize this meeting. You are not well. I repeat, YOU ARE NOT WELL.

You suffer from multiple disorders that need to be mitigated immediately.

I understand you prefer to liaise directly, but if this is a time constraint issue, I'd be happy to schedule appointments through your PA.

I eagerly await your reply.
Dr. Arjun Patel.

CHAPTER ONE
TATE

It wasn't on my bingo card for this year to contaminate the water of a two-thousand-year-old ancient thermae, but life had a way of surprising me every now and again.

"Perhaps now would be a good time to stop flailing about, Mr. Boyle," I suggested stonily, my voice muffled by the plague doctor mask I was wearing.

Breathing through an upholstered leather beak was decisively inconvenient, but the Roman baths of Bath were littered with security cameras, and while severely allergic to humans, I had a feeling I was even more averse to prison food.

Plus, I had it on good authority that Boyle wasn't a fan of crows, so I thought it to be a Hitchcockian touch.

Nothing short of polite, Darrah Boyle stopped thrashing in the shallow water upon my request but not before hitting his head on the edge of the Roman bath's stair and splitting his forehead. The sound of bone cracking rang and echoed through the empty arena. My nostrils flared.

I despised clumsiness.

Crimson crawled across the green-hued water, visible even in the pitch-black of the night. Clenching my teeth, I tapped on the side of my right leg twice, then six times, then twice again.

I was not a fan of going off script. This was definitely a diversion from my plan. He was not supposed to bleed. I wanted his corpse unsoiled and bruise free.

It's not in your plans.
It's not in your plans.
It's not in your plans.

"Plans change," I said loudly, authoritatively, to myself.

Uncurling my fingers from his blood-soaked hair, I pushed up on my heels and watched as his ashen, naked frame drifted along the rectangular body of water, face down. A minute passed, then three. Barring him being Aquaman, he was obviously dead.

I briefly considered leaving him inside the columned bath to be found. It would look like an accident. An inebriated ex-felon, freshly released from an American prison, who came for a late-night dunk where swimming was prohibited. Knocked his head and drowned.

But I couldn't. Wouldn't.

There were rituals to follow. A ceremony to be made.

Two, six, two.
Two, six, two.

With an exasperated, long-suffering sigh, I strode into the thermae to retrieve my prey. Water enfolded my Tom Ford Chelsea boots, soaking my tailored pants. The fog of the spring water swallowed his body in thick mist, and I had to fish my phone out of my peacoat and turn on the flashlight.

I checked for messages, but there weren't any. Not even from my personal assistant, Gia, whom I'd called a half hour ago about a missing document I needed for work.

I would deal with her later.

The quiet swishing of the water as I treaded through it drowned out my slow and steady heartbeat.

Boyle's body floated toward a corner of the stairway. I gripped his hair in my gloved hand, dragging him up to the limestone pavement. I used the toe of my boot to roll him over so that he faced me. A sloppy, sodden sound rang in my ears. His blue face was splotchy, his skull distorted and slightly caved-in from the injury. His lips were liver hued.

You couldn't even have a clean kill, Andrin's voice mocked in my head. *You just had to make a mess of it, didn't you, Boy?*

I shook my head, ridding myself of his voice. It was my first kill. Practice made perfect, and I had at least two more people to help hone my craft.

See, five years ago, Darrah Boyle, along with two other inmates, murdered my father in prison for a bet. A game of cards. A reckless, meaningless moment.

My father was a powerful man. The type not to land himself in prison for anything short of murder.

As it happened, he did kill someone. *Accidentally.*

Nothing unintentional about what Boyle did to him, though. So paying with his life was the only logical outcome. An eye for an eye, a tooth for a tooth, et cetera.

I had always straddled the murky line between businessman and criminal.

Tonight, I stepped over that line. Hell, I fucking sprinted through it, all the way to another continent.

To track down Boyle and his partners in crime, I'd had to get in bed with New York's notorious Camorra family. The Ferrantes were a lot of things. None of them outstanding members of society.

"I suppose you could say you popped my cherry." I reached for the inner pocket of my double-breasted coat, producing a black thorn still attached to the twig. I pressed it to Boyle's cold, purple mouth. It was an unordinary, telling detail. Black thorn.

Blackthorn.

Whoever needed to know I was coming for them next was about to find out once daylight flooded the baths.

"It's been a pleasure. Thank you for participating." I stood to my full height. A thin trail of blood began leaking out of Boyle's mouth. His eyes were wide and full of horror.

Soon, this place would be swarming with police and journalists and curious spectators.

Soon, articles would be written, TV anchors would weep, and national panic wound ensue.

Soon, but not yet.

The night was an old friend, always ready to conceal me as I tended to my nefarious business.

I slipped out of the baths and into the winter night, sliding into an untraceable Alfa Romeo I'd paid cash for. Checked my pocket watch, a family heirloom dating back three hundred years.

Twenty minutes ahead of the timeline I'd set for myself. I smirked. Punctuality soothed my soul.

I drove back to London, whistling a cheerful tune.

Once at King's Cross Station, I tossed the Alfa Romeo's keys into a trash bin midstride and sauntered into a waiting vehicle, reuniting with my London-based driver, Thierry.

"Where is Miss Bennett?" I settled in the back seat of the SV Carmel Range Rover, plucking my leather gloves off one finger at a time. I'd discarded the mask earlier, in an open wheat field.

Thierry frowned at his watch, his eyes swinging to the rearview mirror, where our gazes clashed.

"It's one in the morning, sir," he pointed out in a French accent.

"Did I ask for the time?" My brow quirked in mocking amusement.

"No." He cleared his throat, shrinking into his leather seat. "Miss Bennett, I believe, is in Chelsea. It's her birthday today."

Was it, now?

"The first night she's had off since the Taylor Swift concert in September," he rambled on, his voice drenched in pleading.

"Where in Chelsea?"

"The Swan and the Wine."

"Off we go, then."

Thierry pressed his lips together, the word no threatening to tear from between them. I eyeballed him through the mirror, challenging him to defy me. Some people avoided confrontation. I actively sought it.

"I think," he began, his soft tenor ridiculous for a sixty-year-old, six-three man in a tailored suit. "You should allow her the night off, if I may suggest so, sir."

"You may not," I informed him flatly. "Now floor it."

Thirty minutes later, Thierry parked outside the Swan and the Wine, killing the engine. He drew in a breath, burying his face in his hands. He was fond of Miss Bennett. Most people were, for an unfathomable reason.

I dragged my gaze dragged to the back window of the car, where it settled on the trendy pub. The Georgian building was painted burgundy, the pub's name in bold, golden lettering over a black background. Pots overflowing with colorful flowers adorned the windowsills and arches of the wooden doors.

Through the wide, wood-paned window, I found the subject of my irritation occupying a table in the corner of the tavern, wearing a pink *Birthday Girl* sash over her sensible, pale-blue tweed dress. By her side was a man I presumed was her boyfriend, Ashley; along with football sensation Kieran Carmichael; one of my business partners, Ambrose aka Row; and his utterly hot mess wife, Cal. Minus the hot, really. She was a seven on a good day.

I knew Cal and Gia were close. Kieran was friends with Row, so he had likely been invited by proxy.

Theoretically, I *should* have been offended at not being invited. After all, Gia had met Cal, Row, and Kieran through me. However, I couldn't muster anything other than mild relief. I'd take drowning Irish mobsters in historical pools any day of the week over pretending my assistant's birthday was something worth celebrating.

Alongside them sat three women I presumed were Gia's London friends. I stared at my English PA as she tipped her head back and laughed at something her boyfriend said. Asshole did not look that fucking funny. Clearly, her standards were low.

She shook her head, giving his chest a playful shove, then scooped up her silly neon cocktail, taking a demure sip.

I pulled out my phone—my sleeves and ankles still damp—and texted her.

> Tate: Miss Bennett, I asked you a question. Answer me.

Her phone lit up on the table, illuminating her face. She scowled at it, rolling her eyes and flipping it screen down.

Rage singed my veins. She was ignoring me.

Her boyfriend stood and offered her his hand, which she took. They slipped into their coats and emerged from the double doors, carrying their drinks. Outside, they leaned against a beer garden bench. Ashley lit them both cigarettes, passing one to her.

I didn't know she smoked and the revelation unsettled me. Not because I cared. If she wanted to expedite her demise, I was happy to buy her four packs a day. The world was overpopulated as it was. I did not, however, like surprises. And this was outside the confines of her personality.

My assistant was prim and proper. A smart-mouthed ice queen who managed to be both sassy and kind. Not easily defined and yet entirely predictable.

She wore sensible clothes, with sensible makeup, and ate sensible lunches. Her curly, ebony hair was always pulled back tightly in either a high bun or a sleek ponytail. She spoke softly but sternly, like a governess. Always carried useful things in her bag no one below the age of eighty should carry—paracetamol, Q-tips, pens, miniature nut packs, lip balms, tissues, baby wipes, and an extra pair of socks.

Actually, I could use that extra pair right about now.

My fingers drummed on the side of my leg again.

Two, six, two.

Two, six, two.

"Sir, please," Thierry choked out, undoubtedly guessing my next move. I ignored him, pushing open the back door and striding out. I plastered an indulgent smirk on my face.

The moment Gia noticed me, she stiffened, her smile melting into a frown. The cigarette tumbled between her fingers onto the pebbled ground. Ashley—was that even his name?—wrapped a protective arm over her shoulder. Thinking he could shield her from me was pitiful. Optimism was such a senseless trait.

Though trite and largely dull, Gia Bennett was, regrettably, a stunner.

She was Jamaican and white Cuban, second-generation English after her parents met in Cambridge, and had smooth, tan skin, a long, elegant neck, and two prominent dimples. Her naturally thick and curly eyelashes covered sensual amber eyes, almost honey-like in color and consistency. Her soft, luscious mouth had the most distinctive Cupid's bow, and a pert nose and two graceful arches to call cheekbones adorned her delicate face. My friends Rhy and Row claimed Gia resembled Nara Smith, but the truth was, she defied category. I didn't think there was another human attractive enough to compare her to. If God existed, which I seriously doubted as a secular modernist, he must've spent extra time on the smallest detail in creating her because every inch of her was pure perfection.

Her years as a competitive tennis player were present in every arc and bend of her body. She was lean but muscular and firm. With narrow calves, toned arms, and bitable collarbones. She moved with purpose, in a gait that was both graceful and unintentionally seductive.

She was, sadly, a remarkable beauty.

And that remarkable beauty was staring back at me looking like she wanted to do very ugly things to me.

"Why are you wet?" she asked, the first to break the stunned silence. No alarm betrayed her voice, merely irritation. She was the only human alive who wasn't terrified of me.

Up close, her boyfriend was tall, dark skinned, and striking. He wore a Thom Sweeney jacket and an adequate watch, so I gathered he wasn't a complete loser.

"You are not in a position to ask any questions," I informed her, smoothing a hand over my coat. "In fact, you should feel so lucky to keep your job after ghosting me. Come." I hooked my index finger in her direction, swiveling on my heel and striding back to the Rover. "You're needed at the office."

"Now?"

"No time like the present."

"I could think of a better time, and that time is not two in the bloody morning," she countered in that defiant manner of hers, which reminded me that no matter how hard or far I pushed her, how unbearable or unreasonable I was, I still couldn't, for some reason, break her.

And I tried.

Oh, I tried.

I was trying this very second, in fact.

She bent and she pretzeled—she even cracked sometimes—but she never fucking broke.

ACKNOWLEDGMENTS

This book couldn't have happened if it weren't for a handful of talented, patient, saintly people. And my children aren't among them.

Raising kids is *hard*, y'all. I don't know how single moms do it, but spending my days writing courageous, fiercely independent, beautiful Dylan taught me a lot about the human spirit.

This book materialized thanks to my editors Tamara Mataya, Bryony Leah, and Sarah Plocher. Thank you, ladies, for your time, your talent, your craft, and your devotion.

To my Bloom editors—Christa, thank you for all you are. And to Gretchen, Shaina, Letty, Kylie, and Sabrina. I appreciate all you do for me and for my books.

To my cover designers at Books & Moods—Julie, Mary, and Val—for the three different stunning covers. I love you big.

To Stacey Ryan Blake for the gorgeous ebook formatting. You always nail it.

To my PA/momager, Tijuana Turner, without whom I wouldn't be able to function properly. What is there left to say other than I adore you?

To my beta readers and ride-or-die friends: Parker S. Huntington, Ava Harrison, Vanessa Villegas, Ivy Wild, Nikki Ash, Lena, Ratula, Sarah (yes, again), April, Issa, and Liah. Thank you for keeping me sane (until the next book).

To Kimberly Brower, my agent, who suggested Dylan should end up with Rhyland and not Kieran, because "where's the tension in that?" You were, of course and as usual, right.

To Madison and Siena of Bloom's marketing team for working their magic and Sarah, Lori, and Kasey at Literally Yours PR for all the love and attention. You mean a lot to me. To Shauna and Becca from The Author Agency, and Issa, April, and Kassie from the Bookish Girls. A million thank-yous for all the love and dedication.

Big thanks to Hodder & Stroughton for putting these books in stores all over the UK and Commonwealth countries and to Bloom for putting them in U.S./Canada stores. Because of you, I am able to awkwardly explain to booksellers all over the world that actually, I'm the author, and it's really okay that I'm signing these books, because I wrote them.

To the bloggers, influencers, and readers who read, share, and review my books: thank you for making my dreams come true. This will never be taken for granted.

Finally, to my husband, children, and entire family, who often need to share me with the characters I write.

You are and always will be the most magical world I want to live in.

L.J. Shen xoxo

To every girl who was ever made to feel less-than for her choices.
You are magic.
Burn the patriarchy.